Catherine Cookson was born in Tyne Dock and the place of her birth provides the background she so vividly creates in many of her novels. Although acclaimed as a regional writer – her novel THE ROUND TOWER won the Winifred Holtby Award for the best regional novel of 1968 – her readership spreads throughout the world. Her work has been translated into more than a dozen languages and Corgi alone has sold almost 40,000,000 copies of her novels, including those written under the name of Catherine Marchant.

Mrs Cookson was born the illegitimate daughter of a poverty-stricken woman, Kate, whom she believed to be her older sister. Catherine began work in service but eventually moved south to Hastings where she met and married a local grammar school master. At the age of forty she began writing with great success about the lives of the working class people of the North-East with whom she had grown up, including her intriguing autobiography, OUR KATE. Her many bestselling novels have established her as one of the most popular of contemporary women novelists.

Mrs Cookson now lives in Northumberland.

OTHER BOOKS BY
CATHERINE COOKSON

NOVELS

Slinky Jane   Hamilton
Hannah Massey   The Black Velvet Gown
The Mallen Streak   Goodbye Hamilton
The Mallen Girl   A Dinner of Herbs
The Mallen Litter   Harold
The Gambling Man   The Moth
The Slow Awakening   Bill Bailey
The Iron Facade   The Parson's Daughter
The Girl   Bill Bailey's Lot
The Cinder Path   The Cultured Handmaiden
The Man Who Cried   Bill Bailey's Daughter
Tilly Trotter   The Harrogate Secret
Tilly Trotter Wed   The Black Candle
Tilly Trotter Widowed   The Wingless Bird
The Whip   The Gillyvors

AUTOBIOGRAPHY

Our Kate   Catherine Cookson Country
Let Me Make Myself Plain

Catherine Cookson

The Garment

CORGI BOOKS

THE GARMENT
A CORGI BOOK 0 552 13716 2

Originally published in Great Britain by
Macdonald & Co (Publishers) Ltd.

PRINTING HISTORY
Macdonald edition published 1967
Corgi edition published 1990
Corgi edition reissued 1991
Corgi Canada edition published 1992

This book is set in 10pt Plantin by
Chippendale Type., Otley, West Yorkshire.

Corgi Books are published by Transworld Publishers Ltd., 61–63
Uxbridge Road, Ealing, London W5 5SA, in Australia by Transworld
Publishers (Australia) Pty. Ltd., 15–23 Helles Avenue, Moorebank,
NSW 2170, and in New Zealand by Transworld Publishers (N.Z.)
Ltd., Cnr. Moselle and Waipareira Avenues, Henderson, Auckland.

Printed and bound in Canada

PART ONE

As she stared at the black, frost-patterned panes of glass the voice that had been whispering at her became loud in her head. 'Put it out,' it demanded. 'Go on, put it out.' And her eyes flashed to the light above the dressing-table to the left of her, then to the switch at the side of the window, and she imagined that her whole body, arms, legs, head, and even her bowels, rushed forward to the central point that was the little brass knob when all she did was lift her arm slowly and, after hesitating for a fraction of a second, switch out the light. As it snapped the clear outlines of the room from her gaze she closed her eyes, waiting for the panic to rise in her, but it only fluttered, a stationary flutter, for through her lids she could feel the soft-toned radiance of the four wall lights.

The fluttering took wings. 'Now these,' commanded the voice.

But that would mean walking the whole length of the room from the window to the door where the wall switches were. She couldn't do it . . . it would be all right going, but it would be the coming back . . . in the dark.

Before the thought had dissolved in her mind she was walking towards the bedroom door, and as she put her finger on the first of the two switches she fixed her eyes on the floor. After the click her eyes did a swift hopping movement around the room, and then she felt slightly dizzy. All was merged now in a soft green glow. It was like looking through water. The white bedroom suite was no longer white but a delicate shade of blue; the bed, with its quilted coverlet, floated like a pale gold oblong box gently back and forth over a sea bottom, for the mustard carpet had taken on the appearance of moving sand; the rose curtains on the long window at the far side of the dressing-table looked almost blue, even black where they touched the carpet. But those on the french window facing her seemed to retain their own hue and were the only things in the room recognisable in this unfamiliar light. Her body began to play tricks with her again. It was dry now and hard, knobbly hard and aggressive. Each particle of her was thrusting out, pushing, grabbing at the air to pull her towards the window. With a slight movement of her finger the last two wall lights disappeared and for a brain-screeching moment she stood in total darkness.

Although every artery in her body was clawing its way to deliverance and the window, she herself moved slowly, and when she reached it she put her two hands flat against the shivering glass, then, with only a slight intake of breath, she opened the glass doors and moved one step out on to the balcony.

She was out in the night, standing without light in the night. How long was it since she had looked at the night like this? She couldn't remember, she didn't want to remember. Her breathing became deeper, slower, steadier, it was as if she was emerging into the world, coming out of the womb, being born again, and all that had gone before was the experience of a past existence. As the air went deeper into her lungs she wanted to shout with the joy of relief, but she stifled it by clamping her lips with her fist. No more shouting of any kind, no more yells corkscrewing through her head, it was all over and done with. She had been born again. The

8

only difference was, she would not have to wait for years before becoming aware of her surroundings, she already knew where she was. Of course she had always known where she was. No matter how bad she had been, she had always known where she was. At least in the daylight. But this was night, blackness around her, below and above her, but strangely no longer in her. She was facing the night and defying it.

There were no stars. It was a black night, she could not have picked a blacker with which to test her quivering courage, and she was suspended high up in the night and was no longer afraid . . . well, only a little.

Sit down and look around, she said to herself, then answered, It's too cold. But again she was obeying her courage and her hand was already on the wrought-iron chair that took up a third of the balcony.

When she sat down she put her hands between her knees and pressed them close. It was a childish action and she couldn't remember having done it for years, not since she was a girl and had first come to this house, as a bride. . . .

The darkness of the sky seemed to thin itself out as she sat, and she saw against it a deeper darkness made by the pattern of the trees, some of which bordered the drive to the main road. The drive was to the left of her. Slightly to the right of her there was a break in the pattern, which had been made only recently when she had had the old beech cut down. There had been trouble about that. They couldn't understand it. Nor could she have expected them to, only she knew why she had had the beech cut down. Yet she mustn't be too sure of that. This thought brought a tinge of fear again.

In the day-time she could see, through the gap made by the beech, the fells, each rise, mould, hill and crag all known to her so well that even now she could see their shapes through the darkness. Apart from the cottage that stood out there, in the far distance, to the right, there was nothing at all, nothing for miles but the fells.

But to the left of her, beyond the drive and down the hill, lay the village. Five minutes' walk from the gate lay the village . . . lay the world. All the physical substance of the world was in the village. All the types in the world were in the village. There was James Buckmaster, butcher and greengrocer, small and thin, very thin for a butcher, not hearty and brawny. But why should butchers be hearty and brawny? They, like everyone else, lived double lives. Perhaps he felt hearty and brawny inside. Then Mr Brooke, who dealt in groceries and drapery and had part of his shop for chemist accessories and photography. Mr Brooke had a head for business. He delivered his groceries as far as ten miles away, and he was a sidesman of the church, and his wife didn't speak to the women who went into the towns to supplement their larder, yet what was a wife for but to support her husband? Ironic laughter began to rise in her on this thought and she suppressed it hurriedly and turned her mind to the residents of the village again.

Although there were no street lamps in the village it would not be dark, for Mr Barker of the Stag always saw to it that there were two lights at least burning outside the bar. Mr Barker was a nice man, a kind man. They said he wouldn't last very long, for he was drowning himself in his own beer. He had a very large stomach, but also he had a very large smile, so perhaps the smile would keep him afloat even when the beer threatened to drown him. . . . Again there was laughter rising in her, but it had a touch of merriness about it this time.

Then Miss Shawcross, Kate Shawcross as she was called, the postmistress. Why was it that there was always a postmistress in a village, seldom a postmaster.

10

She hadn't thought of it before, but she didn't want to think of Kate Shawcross, and her thoughts swung away to Peggy Mather, which wasn't really very far, for Peggy lived with Miss Shawcross – she was her niece. She was also cook-general at Willow Lea, and at this moment was down below in the kitchen preparing dinner, a Christmas Eve dinner, a family dinner. She pushed her mind deliberately away from Peggy Mather, for there had returned to her body a slight trembling. She began comforting herself. This time tomorrow she would be able to think of Peggy Mather and lots of things that she hadn't dared allow herself to dwell on, for this time tomorrow she would know whether she was to be free or not. Don't look at it in that way. She chided herself for her thinking. And, now in spite of her efforts, her mind wandered back to Kate Shawcross and the post office and the matter of lighting. Kate Shawcross had never kept a light outside her shop to help the travellers through the village. Even the light inside the shop was a dim one and she put that out at closing time. Yet she was supposed to be a good woman. Going on the interpretation that she taught Sunday school and dressed the altar and had for years subscribed handsomely to this and that church fund, she was a good woman all right. Yet some people were not fooled by the interpretation, they knew why Kate Shawcross had been so liberal. Mr Blenkinsop, the verger, had put it very neatly one day when he said that her goodness wasn't so much because she loved God as God made man. That had been very neatly put, very neat. After his wife died Mr Blenkinsop had wanted to marry Kate Shawcross; they said it was because she was a warm woman, having come into a considerable sum from an uncle in Canada, a man she had never clapped eyes on. They also said that Kate was indignant at the proposal. So Mr Blenkinsop had his reasons for being

11

nasty and they were to do with . . . God made man.

Again there was a quirk of laughter in her, but this time it was not relieving laughter, for it was weighted and held in place by bitterness. The laughter subsiding, the bitterness rose. It came up through her body like a square weight and when it had reached her throat and lodged there she admonished it harshly, saying, Enough, enough. No more of that, either.

She raised her head and looked towards the village again. In the far distance, right at yon side, there was a faint glow straining up into the darkness. That, she knew, would be the reflection of Dr Cooper's lights. He had a light hanging over his front gate and another always burning in the surgery, and the surgery curtains were never drawn. When all the other lights in the village were out, even those at the Stag, Dr Cooper's front light remained on. He was a light in a dark world, was David Cooper. Everybody didn't think so; his ways were too advanced for the diehards. But to her he was alike a mother and father confessor.

The word confessor caused her mind to shy again, and she lifted her gaze in the darkness over the village, and immediately her eye was caught by what looked like a falling star, so high was it in the blackness. But she knew it was no star, it was the headlights of a car and they had thrust themselves into the blackness through the gate of Toole's farm which clung to the side of Roeback Fell. James Toole would be coming down to the Stag. They said he came to the Stag every evening to get away from his wife, who was also his cousin, for Adelaide Toole was a bitter woman. Well, small wonder with what she had lost.

Now her head sank down on her chest, for her conscience always talked loudly to her when she thought of Adelaide Toole. For Adelaide Toole's bitterness lay at her door. She said as always, I couldn't help it, I didn't start it. And this time she added, Did I? Did I?

She was looking towards the gap where the beech had once stood and through it towards the fells, and it was as if she was speaking to someone out there, for she whispered aloud now beseechingly, 'It wasn't my fault, was it?' She lifted her hands from between her knees and, leaning forward, placed them on the rimed iron of the balcony. It was as she did this that she heard her family return and an unusual commotion below her on the drive. Immediately she straightened up and sat still. And she told herself not to move, let them find her here. It would not prove to them, how could it, that she was on the threshold of a new life, but it would show them that she had at last ousted fear, and therefore there was no longer any necessity for worrying, or whispered family councils concerning her. . . .

In a few minutes the room was plunged into light, and she turned around to face them. After staring wide-eyed at her across the distance of the large bedroom, they rushed to her, they poured over her, exclaiming, touching, patting, dearing and darling-ing, oh-ing and ah-ing.

Beatrice, plump, solid, already maternal as if the mother of twelve instead of a scarcely two-year-old was crying 'Oh, what's happened? Come in out of the cold. Oh! You're frozen, just feel your hands.'

And Stephen, already the gangling, lanky parson in embryo, exclaimed, 'Are you all right? What possessed you?'

Then Jane, a week off seventeen and not yet old enough to be diplomatic, really spoke for them all when she said, 'Oh, Mammy, you did give us a scare. Why did you put the lights out?'

With a movement of her head Grace Rouse spread her smile across them and said gently, 'I wanted to.'

In their amazement they could not resist looking at each other, and she turned from them in time to stop herself saying, 'Don't worry, your Christmas is not going to be spoilt; there are not going to be any scenes. Don't worry, my dears.'

'I'll get you a hot drink and I'll also have a word with Peggy.' Beatrice's voice was very matronly now. 'The light wasn't on outside either. The whole front of the house in darkness. I can't remember ever seeing it like that before . . . well, not for years. As Jane said, it scared the wits out of us. Sit down there, dear.' She put her hands on her mother's shoulders to press her into a chair, and repeated, 'I'll bring you a hot drink.'

Grace smiled rather sorrowfully to herself. Beatrice was very solicitous; she had been solicitous since she arrived yesterday. She wanted something – not for herself, of course, but for Gerald. Gerald would be wanting a loan, another loan. She had felt it coming for some time. Well, she was sorry but he was going to be disappointed. She hoped he didn't ask tonight, for her refusal would blur the festive atmosphere, and she didn't want that. No, she hoped he would leave it until Boxing Day, just before they returned home. Gently she disengaged herself from her eldest daughter's hand, saying, 'Don't fuss me, Beatrice. I'm perfectly all right, dear, and I'm going downstairs.' She walked away from them towards the door, and there she turned and surveyed them, and as if they were children once again and she was explaining something to them that was a little out of their depth, she said, 'You can't stand still. Your grandfather used to say, "If you don't push on forward, you'll be kicked back." I think I'll push on.' Then she laughed, a reflection of the joy-tinted laughter that had at one time characterised her. And on this she opened

14

the door quickly and went out on to the landing, for she knew she was embarrassing them.

She had taken three soundless steps when she stopped again, her narrowed eyes drawn across the wide space that was furnished more like a room than a landing, to the head of the stairs where hung the picture of her late husband. The heavy, gold-enamelled openwork frame stood out from the white wall, with the painting of the man in his dark clerical attire appearing to be painted on the wall itself, the whole giving the impression of three dimensions. She was used to the picture, she passed it countless times each day, but she never looked at it, at least not with her eyes, yet her mind was nearly always on it. Even now she did not look at the figure but the frame. The top was entwined in flowers, live flowers that would surely die tomorrow, and at the bottom, clipped into the frame, were two vases, and these were filled with anemones.

Jane was at her side now, her voice soothingly soft, almost a whisper. 'I put them there, I've been think-ing about him all day. It's over a year now . . . and . . . well . . . '

Grace moved forward away from her youngest daughter towards the head of the stairs and when there she did not stop, but as she passed the picture the eyes of her mind looked up at it and a voice from the dark depths of her which would not be repressed cried, 'Blast you!'

Before her feet touched the second step the fear was back and she was attacking yet beseeching it at the same time: 'No! No! Don't start again, don't think like that. That kind of talk must stop too. There must be no more vileness. Let it end. For God's sake, let it end. I'm afraid no more.' The voice in her head took this up and yelled with a semblance of the old panic. No more. Do you hear? I'm not afraid any more.

15

By the time she stepped into the hall there was only the echo of the voice with her, and she paused a moment and drew in a shuddering breath before looking round at her family walking in single file down the stairs, their expressions perturbed, each in its own way. Swiftly she put out her hand and caught that of Jane and drew her close. This action deepened their perplexity, but on Jane's face there was also a look of surprised pleasure as hand in hand they crossed the hall towards the drawing-room.

Beatrice and Stephen did not follow them. After an exchange of glances they moved down the stairs into the hall and turned towards a narrow passage and to a door at the far end, and just as Beatrice was about to go into the room the sound of her husband's voice coming from the direction of the kitchen, where he was having a jocular exchange with Rosie Davidson, Peggy Mather's occasional help, made her pause and wait until he came into sight. Across the distance she beckoned to him, and when he joined them the grin slid from his face and he asked in an undertone, 'What's up?'

Beatrice made no reply but went into the study, the two men following her, and not until the door was closed and she had seated herself in a great leather chair by the side of the fire did she answer her husband. She said briefly, 'It's mother.'

'Oh!' It was expressive, and Gerald paused before he went on, 'What's wrong now?'

'Nothing's wrong; apparently everything seems to be all right. You'll never believe it but we found her in her room with all the lights out, standing on the balcony. Didn't we, Stephen?'

Stephen had taken up his position with his back to the fire. He liked standing this way . . . his father had always stood like it. Winter or summer, his father had taken up

16

this position, with his back to the fireplace . . . he could always feel his father's presence strongly in this room.

He realised that the eyes of his sister and brother-in-law were hard on him and that he hadn't answered Beatrice's question. He stretched himself, neck upwards, again in the manner of his father, giving the impression that he had been debating his reply, then he said, 'She seems no longer afraid of the dark. In fact, I would say she's no longer afraid of anything.'

'Well, it's long overdue.' Gerald twitched his tweed trousers well up his legs before sitting down opposite his wife. 'It's a pity she couldn't have got over her nerves earlier, it would have saved us all a lot of worry.'

'And Daddy.' Beatrice looked towards the desk that stood between the two windows which were replicas of those in the room directly above. The desk was long and solid and took up quite a large space between the windows. The only articles on it now were an ink-stand, a tray, a blotting pad and a framed photograph. It was at the photograph that Beatrice was looking, and her eyes showed a film of moisture as she murmured, 'Poor Daddy.' The door of her conscience was tightly closed as she thought this.

Gerald uncrossed his legs, then, pulling a pipe from his pocket, he proceeded to fill it while he repeated to himself, 'Poor Daddy.' Well, there was no doubt he had had a time of it, but to be honest with himself, it was a phrase Gerald frequently used, to be honest with himself he had felt no real sadness at his father-in-law's departure, even though the old fellow had always, except on one notable occasion, been decent to him. To his mind he was a type you couldn't get to the bottom of. Hearty and all that, jocular, always ready to help you, with advice at any rate, but still there was a something . . . he had never felt easy in his presence. Yet of the two,

17

give him the old man every time, for his mother-in-law, he had to admit, gave him the willies. If the old man had never made him feel entirely at ease, she always made him feel darned uncomfortable. She looked at you as if you were something the cat had brought in, with that air about her as if she were royalty. And after all, what was she? A coal merchant's daughter, that's all she was. Of course . . . he gave a little hicking laugh to himself . . . he wouldn't have minded being that particular coal merchant's son and having a share of the dibs he had left. She must be rotten with money. Yet with all of it she was as mean as muck. A clarty thousand to Beatty for a wedding present. He would like to bet she could have given her five and never missed it. True, she had settled another thousand on Yvonne when she was born, but she had tied that up so it couldn't be touched until the child was twenty-one. She might have been near barmy these past few years, but her business faculties hadn't been impaired, that was a certainty. Now there lay before him the job of tapping her.

His tongue came out and rubbed the fringe of his short, fair moustache. What if for some reason she didn't catch on to the idea and Livsey sold his share of the garage elsewhere . . . ? She couldn't do it. What was seven thousand to her, anyway? Pin money. Just look at this house, like a luxury hotel, with the stuff that was in it. But the snag was, she didn't like him. He knew she didn't like him, so what if she didn't rise to the offer? The thought was unbearable and brought him almost with a spring to his feet. This action had to be explained to the startled and enquiring glances of his wife and brother-in-law, and, never at a loss, he asked quickly, 'Where's Yvonne? I've just thought, I've never heard her. Is she asleep?'

18

'Asleep! No, don't be silly. She's at Miss Shawcross's. She begged me to let her stay for half an hour or so. Stephen and I had just slipped down to the church, and she was finishing the altar. She would have us go back with her to the house. She talked all the time about the new man. She can't stand him, she still considers it Daddy's church, she always will.'

Gerald made no comment on this, but he thought, Daft old bitch. Another one rotten with money. Why was it women who were always left money? Buttoning up his coat, he looked at Beatrice and said abruptly, 'We'd better go down and fetch her, she'll be sick with excitement and you know what that means. And then we've got the tree and the parcels to see to.'

At the reminder of the Christmas chores Beatrice sighed, letting out a hissing breath that spoke of boredom.

When she had left the room, followed by her husband, Stephen, his back still to the fire, started a swaying movement. From his toes to his heels, his eyes half closed, his hands, his back, his buttocks and calves soothingly warm, he rocked himself gently into a reverie. . . . He liked this room, he loved it. He looked upon it as his; in fact the whole house was his. Well, as good as, he was the only son. Beatrice had a place of her own, and the way things were going Jane wouldn't be long before she left too. That would be determined tomorrow, he supposed, when the man turned up. He wondered for a moment what he might be like. That he was a lecturer at one of the colleges in Durham was something, anyway; she wasn't letting herself down like Beatrice had done in marrying Gerald Spencer. Beatrice had hurt him over Spencer more than he would care to admit. Spencer was a type, and that had been proved conclusively when the marriage had to be rushed. Funny about that. The business had upset his father terribly yet

19

he remembered his mother hadn't turned a hair. He knew exactly how his father had felt about it, for he had felt the same, nauseated, repulsed in some way – the whole thing was beastly.

The swaying which had lulled began again, and almost with a challenge his thinking made a statement. 'You'll never marry,' it said, and he took it up. No, he'd never marry because priests should never marry; you couldn't serve two masters, and as far as he could make out a wife was a master. And then there was the other side of it, the physical side. He actually shuddered on this thought. The Catholic Church had an advantage over the Church of England in the fact that they forbade their priests to marry. He sometimes wished, but just faintly, that he was in the Church of Rome. There the pattern was all cut out. There you were really a priest and your actions decided for you, but could you be a priest with a wife and children hanging around you? No, the title reverend or vicar was more suitable. He suddenly stopped his rocking and chided himself for his cynicism. But immediately he reverted to it. It was no good hoodwinking himself, he wanted to be known as a priest, not a vicar or a parson or a reverend. A thought coming directly on top of this minor explosion caused his lids to blink rapidly over his near-sighted hazel eyes: Would his mother marry again? The thought settled itself and continued. That's if she became really . . . quite all right. She had money and was still youngish and was what could be called good-looking. He had heard it said that she had been beautiful when she was young. He couldn't see it himself. Although she was his mother, her face didn't appeal to him. The eyes were too large for the face, and wide-eyed women, he understood, weren't supposed to be intelligent. He liked intelligent women, women who could talk of other things besides furniture and cooking. Of course there was her music, but on the whole she was just a domesticated woman. . . . But what if she should marry again? It would mean another man in the place that was his father's . . . living or dead, would remain his father's. This house could never be another man's house, that was except his, and he would rent it but never sell it, and one day he would come back and live here, perhaps sooner than he expected. Having a bishop for a great-uncle, and having been called after him, might be of some use after all. . . . Yet suppose his mother really did decide to marry again and go on living here?

As with Gerald, the thought was not to be borne, and he quickly went out into the hall and through a side door which led directly into the garage where the holly was stacked in a corner, and he began sorting with careful precision small pieces that would hang from the china bracket that surrounded the drawing-room. In his selection he was careful to pick nothing that would scratch the delicate grey walls . . .

Grace was now sitting on the drawing-room couch, relaxed as she had not been for months, even years. She was listening to Jane telling her, and in some detail, how she had met the most wonderful man in the world. Why was it, she thought, all girls of seventeen talked the same when this thing hit them? It was sad, even terrible, that the illusion should be an integral part of life; there was no way of jumping over it or side-stepping it, it had to be gone through. The only comfort was, that at that age you weren't aware of how naked you were to others, nor how tiring or boring or really painfully lovable. At that age you talked young, and why not? Why not indeed.

'Yes, darling, I'm listening.'

And she went on listening to how Jane had met the man of her dreams. His name was George Aster, and despite his being fifteen years her senior she knew it was the real thing. Grace hoped so, from the bottom of her heart she hoped so.

'I feel awful, Mammy, about having fibbed to him over my age, but, anyway, I look eighteen, I know I do; and I'm not telling him until after the holidays and things are settled in some way; and he means to have them settled, he's determined.' She gave a nervous giggle then added, 'You'll love him, Mammy.'

'Well' – Grace smiled dryly now – 'I may not do that exactly. Mothers-in-law are not supposed to, you know, but already I feel that I like him.' As she said this she edged herself out of the depths of the couch and to her feet and went towards the fireplace, thinking, Who wouldn't have affection for the man who is promising you freedom. . . . It was dreadful to think like this, as if she wanted to be rid of Jane. But that wasn't true, oh no . . . no. She hadn't expected her to talk of marriage for a year or two yet, perhaps even longer, and she had faced up to the fact that not until the future of her younger daughter was secure in one way or another could she say to herself, 'Now . . . now I will live.'

But what if Jane should repeat the pattern that had been her own life? This George Aster was even older than Donald had been when they married. She mustn't let this happen, not even to save herself. She saw her reprieve sinking into the years ahead, and the panic began to rise in her again. But she quelled it. Age had not been the sword that hung between her and Donald. It would have made no difference if they had been exactly the same age, none whatever.

'Since I have felt like this I have understood about you and Daddy.' Jane looked towards her mother's back, slim as a girl's but stiffer. The shoulders had for the moment lost their droop and appeared unusually straight, and it seemed to be to them that Jane appealed, 'Mammy, I feel I must talk about Daddy. You mustn't mind any more. Not being able to mention him has shut him out somehow, and today, especially today, I have felt him near, as if he was sort of . . . well, I can't explain rightly, but sort of demanding to be let in. That's why I put the flowers on his picture . . . '

'Stop it, Jane!'

Grace's sharp cry seemed to slice off Jane's voice, and after staring at her mother's back for a moment she bowed her head and bit hard on her lip.

There followed a lull full of unease, then to break the tension came the sound of carols from the driveway and at the same time the drawing-room door opened and Stephen entered, his arms full of holly.

Grace turned to him, as if in relief, and asked, 'Are there just the children?' Her voice was quite calm now, and Stephen nodded to her, saying, 'Yes, about a dozen of them I would say.' His voice had a stiff, stilted sound.

'Will you see to them?'

He did not immediately reply, but laid the holly down by the fireplace and then said, 'Andrew's at the front door.'

'Andrew?' Grace repeated the name as if it was unknown to her. 'Oh, I thought he wasn't coming back until Boxing Day, or thereabouts.'

'Well, he's here at the door.' Stephen straightened up and his voice reached a high level as he asked, 'Why can't he use the back door?'

'Don't be silly.' It was Jane answering as she rose from the couch. 'You know Peggy would hit him on the head with the frying-pan if he dared put his nose in her kitchen. . . . "Hell hath no fury . . . " But why should he, anyway?'

'Well, it isn't his place to come to the front door.'

'Stephen!' For the second time in minutes Grace's voice appeared to come out of the top of her head. The name was ejected so sharply that both Stephen and Jane held their positions as if competing in a game of statues. 'Don't speak like that, Andrew's not just a . . . a . . . he's a friend, who's always given us his spare time; he only took on the odd jobs and the garden to . . . to oblige your father. I've told you that before. Jane . . . Jane, go and let Andrew in.'

'Yes, yes, all right, Mammy.'

Stephen turned from his mother's stare and busied himself with the holly. He was consumed now by a disturbing anger. If he had his own way he knew what he'd say to Andrew MacIntyre, 'Go! And don't come back any more, inside or outside of this house!' He had never liked Andrew. And his father hadn't liked Andrew either, although he had never said anything against him; in fact he had never heard his father speak his name, but he still knew that he hadn't liked the man.

There were a number of things he himself held against Andrew MacIntyre. Not least of them that he had never addressed him as 'Mr Stephen' or 'Young Master Stephen' as the other villagers did. And then there was the fact that he did not call his mother by the title of 'Madam' or 'Ma'am'. It was odd when he came to think about it but he couldn't remember hearing him call her anything at all, no name whatever. It was as if he considered himself her equal, the equal of them all for that matter. That was why he kept himself apart from the villagers. He was too big for his boots, was Andrew MacIntyre, always had been. He did not chide himself that this was no Christian way to think. His feelings towards Andrew MacIntyre had long ago become a condition which had no claim to charitable thought.

The carol singers were now attempting 'Away in a Manger' in a variety of keys. The carolling became distinctly louder when the drawing-room door was opened, which was explained by Jane laughingly saying as she entered, 'Beatrice is back and Yvonne insists on joining in; half of them are in the hall . . . Here's Andrew, Mammy.'

The man who came forward into the room could have literally filled Stephen's description and not only with regard to his feet, for he stood six feet two inches tall, yet there didn't seem enough flesh on his body to do justice to his frame; it looked like the body of a young man that needed filling out. But the delusion was dispelled when you looked at the face, for there was hardly a trace of youth in it, not that it was lined or aged; the impression came rather from the eyes, deep-set brown eyes. And the impression was added to by the white tuft of hair that sprang away from the right temple. The rest of his hair was not black, merely dark, but it took on a hue of almost Spanish blackness in contrast to the white tuft.

'Hallo, there, Andrew; do come in.' Grace did not move from her place near the fire, but she lifted her hand and the gesture seemed to draw the man into the room. When he reached the head of the couch he stopped and she said, 'You're back sooner than you expected. We didn't think to see you until Boxing Day.'

'I left my aunt much better. She insisted that I come home for Christmas and I was nothing loath.' His voice was thick and deep and had not a Northumbrian but a Scottish burr. And his manner of speech was stilted and formal as if he had rehearsed what he had to say.

'Is she alone?'

'No, she's got a friend with her, so I felt justified in leaving.'

'Do sit down, Andrew.' She pointed to a chair and then went and sat on the couch, and as Jane sat down again beside her she did not look at her but groped out and clasped her hand.

'Why can't you get your aunt to come and live nearer, Andrew?' Jane was leaning forward asking the question. 'Living such a long way off.'

'She likes Devon.'

'You know what, Mammy?' Jane's legs were tucked under her on the couch now, and her face took on a mischievous twist as she said, 'I bet it isn't any aunt that Andrew goes to see. I'd like to bet it's a girl friend . . . what do you say?'

The sound of Stephen dropping the hammer on the floor, whether intentionally or unintentionally, brought all their eyes to him. He was looking at Jane, but Jane, having no fear of her brother, ignored his look and repeated, 'What do you say, Mammy?'

'I would say it is Andrew's own business.' Grace was looking at Andrew and he at her, then, moving his deep gaze on to Jane, he said softly, 'I came back because my girl lives here.'

Jane threw back her head and let out a gurgle of a laugh. Ever since she was eight and had proposed to him openly one day, saying, 'When I grow up will you marry me, Andrew?' and had realised that he was in some way shocked, she had taken a delight in calling him her lad.

'Jane has a friend coming tomorrow, Andrew,' Grace was smiling at her daughter.

'Yes?' Andrew's eyebrows moved up enquiringly.

'He's a special friend, Andrew.'

'Yes?' He looked at Jane and she exclaimed with a deep nod, 'Uh-huh.'

A piercing scream coming from the hall checked the monosyllabic exchange, and Grace screwed up her face against the sound as it was repeated again and again. There came now cries of 'Goodbye, goodbye. Thank you, goodbye. Merry Christmas . . . same to you. Goodbye,' followed by the front door banging, then into the drawing-room was borne Yvonne, kicking and struggling in her father's grasp, and yelling at the limit of her lungs, 'Want to. Want to. Down, Daddy. Want to.'

Gerald, stalking to the hearth, dropped the child none too gently on to the rug by the fire, and immediately his hands released her she stopped her screeching.

Yvonne looked round the company – there was hardly a tear stain on her face – then suddenly she laughed and, turning over on the rug lay on her stomach and kicked her toes into the soft pile.

'Something's got to be done in that quarter,' Beatrice nodded downwards. 'She's becoming a perfect little devil.'

'If you want to have harmony have a child in the house. What do you say?' Gerald addressed Andrew in a condescending, man-to-man style, and Andrew, getting to his feet, answered quietly, 'That's one thing I can't give my opinion on.'

'No, no, of course not. Well, you don't know what you've missed.'

Grace too rose to her feet and, looking at Andrew, she said quietly, 'You'll be on your own tomorrow, Andrew?' And without waiting for an answer she continued, 'Will you come and have dinner with us?'

Andrew was looking at the woman before him. Then his gaze moved from her to the members of her family, to Beatrice, the son-in-law, Jane and, lastly, Stephen. They were all staring at him, waiting he knew for his answer. He looked back at Grace again and it was a moment before he spoke. 'Thanks, I'd like that,' he said briefly. 'Good night now.' The good night was for her. Then, giving a nod that included the rest of them, he said again, 'Good night.' As he went towards the door he paused for a moment and, turning and looking back towards Grace, he said, 'A Happy Christmas to you.'

'And to you, Andrew.'

Their voices were low and level.

No-one saw him out, and when the door had closed on him the silence still held, giving him time to cross the hall.

Beatrice was the first to speak. 'But, Mammy,' she said, 'there'll be company, Jane's friend . . . ' She paused to cast a glance towards Jane. 'George.'

'George will be all the better for meeting Andrew, Beatrice.'

'But Andrew will be awkward, Mammy; he'll be out of place, it's never happened before.'

'Andrew won't be out of place, Beatrice . . . I knew Andrew before I knew any of you.' Grace flicked her gaze quickly around them. 'I've never known him to be awkward in any company. Andrew is one of the family; I've always considered him so.'

And now she looked towards Stephen and she saw that his face was working. At this moment he was without his façade, and when she said, 'Well, Stephen, what have you to say about it?' she watched him wet his lips and wait a moment before speaking, and she knew he was going to great lengths to control his temper.

'Well, since you ask, and since you appear to be so much better, I feel that I should speak frankly.' He paused and she inclined her head towards him. 'It wouldn't have happened if Father had been alive, would it? And I can't see that the excuse is that he's alone tomorrow. He was alone on Christmas Day two years ago when Father was here and there was no talk then of inviting him to dinner, and I feel I know why.' Again he paused. 'Father didn't like the man, he never liked him. Why he kept him on I don't know, but there's one thing I know for a certainty: he would never have received an invitation to Christmas dinner from Father.'

Whatever effect Stephen's words had on his mother was not evident – except for a slight pressure on the lips her expression remained the same – but the effect certainly showed on the rest of them, for they all looked startled at his audacity. Then just as Grace was about to reply Jane broke in, her words tumbling over themselves, 'You . . . oh, Stephen, I don't know how you can say such things. Father did like Andrew, he did. As for George' – she glared at Beatrice now – 'if I wanted him to meet anyone it would be Andrew, and if he felt he was above meeting Andrew he wouldn't be the one for me . . . so there. You are nothing but a lot of silly . . . silly snobs. And snob isn't the right word either. . . . Oh, I don't know. . . .'

'Be quiet, Jane, it's all right.' Grace's hand was on her arm. Then she turned and looked at Stephen and her voice was very low, even gentle, as she said, 'What you seem to forget, what everybody seems to forget, is that I am still mistress of this house, and if I want Andrew to dinner I'll have him to dinner. Andrew is . . . ' Her voice was trembling now. Her lids began to blink rapidly as she looked from one to the other, and when no-one spoke she turned away and made for the door. Having passed into the hall and closed the door behind her, she held on to the knob for some seconds, for her legs were shaking so that she felt she would drop, and to her dismay the sickly feeling of dread and anxiety was blocking her chest once more.

As she made her way to the foot of the staircase her walk became slightly erratic and she looked down at her legs. As she did so the expression on her face changed;

the look of deep pain and anxiety seeping from her eyes was replaced by one of desperate urgency, and after supporting herself for a moment with a hand on the balustrade she did not mount the stairs to her room but crossed the hall towards the dining-room. It was imperative that she followed up the stand she had made in the drawing-room with a test. She would open the hatch to the kitchen and say to Peggy, 'Is everything going well, Peggy?' That alone would be a strengthener of courage.

When she opened the dining-room door Peggy Mather was bending over the table moving a cruet to a new position. Grace had spent most of the afternoon setting the table and now the voice of courage said, 'Tell her to put that back where it was,' but she wasn't brave enough to comply. And she walked into the room as if she hadn't noticed what Peggy was doing. Then she went and stood some way behind her, for it was easier to address her from behind.

The woman at the table was broad hipped, and as she bent forward her buttocks pressed themselves out of her print skirt bringing it up into a peak showing a pair of hard, fleshy calves. Even her bulk was intimidating. She had always stood a little in awe of this woman right from the very start, yet it was nothing compared with the feeling Peggy Mather had aroused in her these past few weeks.

She tried to speak now as mistress to maid, as if there was nothing more between them than that, but her voice failed her as she said, 'Is everything going all right, Peggy?'

'Why shouldn't it be? It isn't the first time we've had a dinner at seven instead of one . . . it's all the same thing.'

Grace watched the broad back straighten up. She watched her walk with her heavy step towards the service door, and when it had swung to behind her she sat down. Then, joining her hands together, she did a very unusual thing: she began to pray.

Less than half an hour later Stephen and Beatrice came to her room. Stephen came first. He looked slightly crestfallen and more youthful than she had seen him for some time, and when he apologised for his behaviour, saying, 'I'm sorry, nothing like that will ever happen again', she wanted not only to put out her hands to him but to take him in her arms. Yet all she did was to look at him kindly and say, 'It's all right, I understand,' and she did understand. She understood a little how he was feeling at this moment of contrition, for was he not her son.

When a few minutes later Beatrice came into the room and exclaimed, 'Oh, Mammy, I do like you in that grey, it looks super, I haven't seen you in it for ages,' she felt a little sick, a little sad, for she guessed that they had put their heads together, determined that the Christmas festivities should not be marred, at least through them. The incident that had happened downstairs was unfortunate, and the outcome of it they were waiving until tomorrow, she could almost hear her husband's voice endorsing their decision . . . 'sufficient unto the day is the evil thereof'.

For the first time in three years Grace went to sleep in the dark, and when she woke in the dark and found that she had been to sleep she was hardly afraid. There was a soft stillness about the room and the whole house, and she guessed that it was snowing. She told herself to get up and see, and then she remembered no more until it was morning, and she awoke again to a quiet stir about the house broken by excited cries from a room across the landing.

It was Christmas morning and Yvonne was opening her stocking. She had no desire to go and witness this event. When her own children had been small it had thrilled her to watch them unpacking their stockings, but Yvonne did not seem to belong to her, not even as a grandchild. She was a spoilt child.

As she lay she hoped that no-one would come and disturb her for a long while, for she wanted to savour this feeling that she had woken with, this feeling of newness, of courage, of having at least been able to conquer the dark. She stretched her long legs down the bed, then, twisting round, she lay on her stomach, her face buried in the pillow. She would make everybody happy today, everybody. And she would go to church . . . yes, she would go to church. That would please Stephen. . . . Yes she would go to church. And this evening she would play to them. . . .

It was ten o'clock before the breakfast things and all the debris from the presents were cleared away. She couldn't say that any of her Christmas presents had brought her delight. They were mostly things for use in the house; these no doubt they thought would please her, and she was sure she had conveyed that impression. Her gifts to them had been in the form of cheques, small ones, but they all, even Gerald, had received them with expressions of surprised delight.

She had a strong feeling that Gerald was trying to corner her. He had never left her for a moment last night. It had almost become embarrassing. He was too solicitous by far.

And now when she had come upstairs to get ready for church and he made the excuse to follow her by bringing some wood for her fire, she knew he had succeeded in his efforts and she must face up to it and get it over.

32

He stood outside her door calling, 'Fuel up, Mother', and when she said, 'Come in, Gerald', he entered, boisterous and gay, his arms laden with logs.

'That's kind of you, Gerald. I always feel guilty about my fire, but I can't stand electric fires and I have tried.'

'Why should you; you usually see to it yourself, anyway. . . . If you can't have what you want in your own house it's come to something.' He pushed a log on the centre of the fire and pressing it home firmly with his boot added, 'And I don't see why you should have to mess about with fires either. Peggy's got nothing to do most of the time, only you to see to, and she's got help to do it at that.'

'Oh, she's kept pretty busy and there's nothing like fires for making work.'

Gerald straightened up and dusted his hands, then, turning and taking up a position not unlike that of Stephen he looked at her and said in a voice that could only be described as tender, 'You know, Mother, I haven't had the chance to speak to you alone, but I just want to say from the bottom of my heart that I'm glad to see you so much better.'

She turned from the dressing-table with a ring in her hand, and she looked at it as she slowly pushed it on to her finger. She even paused to admire its effect before saying, 'Thank you, Gerald; that's very kind of you.'

'Y'know, Mother' – Gerald let his head fall back on to his shoulders, then drop forward again before proceeding – 'if it wasn't that you are so much better' – he stressed the 'are' – 'I wouldn't, not for the world, say what I'm going to say now, and as time's short and they'll all be yelling for you in a minute, I'll come straight to the point. . . . You know . . . or of course you don't know that Livsey is selling out, and he's willing to let his holding go as a sacrifice. . . . Now' – he held his hand up as if he were directing traffic at the stop sign – 'I know that that word is suspect but nobody's going to put one over on me, not in my own line of business, so you can take my word for it that it just means what it says. Well, Mother, you know how I stand. I haven't got seven thousand pounds. I wish I had, and this is what I want to ask you. . . . Mind, I'm not asking for a loan . . . ' Again his hand was at the stop sign. 'I'm asking you to do a business deal. And this is it: will you buy Livsey out? You'll have profits, part control, the lot . . . Now it's like this . . . '

'Sit down, Gerald.' Grace's quiet tone checked him and she pointed to a chair. Then she drew the dressing-table stool near to her, and when she was sitting opposite him he put in hastily but in a less strident tone, 'Well, just hear me out, Mother, before you say anything.'

'It's no use, Gerald.'

He made no reply to this but he smiled at her and nodded. He was used to this kind of beginning; he was also used to pressing home the point. One acquired the technique in the car business. 'All right, all right. Now just listen, just for a minute. . . .'

Grace looked downwards to where her hands were joined tightly together and she bit on her lip before saying in a voice that was no longer quiet, 'It's no use, Gerald, you're only making it worse for yourself. I mean what I say, I can't help you' – she raised her eyes and looked straight into his round and to her unpleasant face as she ended – 'for the simple reason that I haven't any money.'

'What!'

His disbelief was scornful and it brought her head up and gave an edge to her voice. 'You can say "What!" in that manner, but I'm telling you the truth. I haven't any money, at least not your kind of money. It will come as news to you, I know, but I haven't had . . . what you call money for some time now.'

'What about the business?'

'It's mine in name only.'

'You were bought out?'

'No, I wasn't bought out in the way you mean. To put it briefly, Uncle Ralph speculated some years ago. As you know, he owned half of everything; something went wrong . . . many things went wrong and he was facing bankruptcy. The firm was taken over but still run under our name. I was left with enough to put Stephen through college and see Jane settled.'

'But this place?' Gerald spread his arms wide, embracing the house. 'You can't run this on tuppence a week.' He refrained from adding, 'Cooks, gardeners, the lot.'

His tone jarred on her and she wanted to cry, 'What business is it of yours?' but she knew his hopes had been dealt a very hard blow, so she replied quietly, 'It doesn't cost so much to run as you might think, and in a very short time the house and everything in it will be sold.'

'Good God!' He was on his feet. 'And the others know nothing about it?'

'No, they know nothing about it. It won't concern them very much, anyhow. Stephen will have no use for a house like this, his home will be in a vicarage in some part of the country. And Beatrice is in your hands . . . ' Grace paused here before adding, 'And Jane's future will be settled over the holidays – at least I hope so.'

'God Almighty!' Gerald was being entirely himself now. 'And you think they're not going to mind?'

'Oh yes, I know they'll mind and be disappointed.'

'Disappointed. Huh . . . ! Well . . . ' He looked down at her. 'We . . . ll' – the word was drawn out this time – 'all I can say is that it's a damn fine kettle of fish.'

'I'm sorry you should feel so bitter about it, but after all, Gerald, it may surprise you to learn that I have dealt with you very generously. You've had two thousand pounds and more in the last three years. It was a very difficult thing to do to decide on giving Beatrice and the child that money when my affairs were in such a chaotic state, and no doubt in the future I may be glad of two thousand pounds. No, Gerald, under the circumstances your family has been treated very fairly.'

Gerald stared at her. There was a black rage welling up in him; her seeming indifference to his plight infuriated him. Not only had she killed his hopes of eventually owning his company but his future was dead also. He hadn't realised up till now just how much he had depended on her generosity to her grandchild and eventual legacy to her daughter. This woman had been a source of security for him, an insurance policy. If things didn't go right, well, there was always Beat's mother. Not a little of his present success was due, he knew, to his connection through marriage with Cartner and Cartner.

So bitter were his feelings that when Grace spoke again he did not hear her. But after a moment he turned on her and said, 'What did you say?'

'I was asking you, Gerald, not to tell Beatrice or the others about it just yet. Of course, they will have to know. You can tell Beatrice if you wish when you return home, but I'll explain to Jane and Stephen before the holidays are over.'

Gerald made no answer to this, but he thrust his lips out before bringing them in to form a tight line across his face. Then, turning abruptly on his heels, he left her.

It was some moments before Grace moved from the seat, and then she went slowly to the wardrobe and took out her mink coat, and when she had put it on she looked at herself in the mirror. She could up to a point understand Gerald's feelings. In a coat such as this, in a house such as this, it was hard to credit she was a woman without substantial means.

Apart from the child, Gerald had the house to himself; they had all gone to church, and even if Yvonne had not been sick he knew that he couldn't have sat through an hour of waffling feeling as he did. He was ready to explode. He looked to where his small daughter lay asleep now, curled up in the depths of the couch. She had a clarty thousand and no more to look forward to. That was eating him as much as the fact that unless he had a windfall of some kind or another he would remain a working partner in Livsey's for the rest of his days. And for that stuck-up cow to keep it to herself and she supposed to be ill, in the middle of a breakdown. She couldn't possibly have been as bad as she made out otherwise she would have blurted out the whole business among some of the other stuff she had spewed up. Enough to put you to shame, some of the things she had said, and it took something to make him blush, by God it did. She was a deep one, was his mother-in-law . . . But he just couldn't get over it . . . her broke. He swung round and looked at the room. Keeping up all this bloody pomp and her broke, it didn't make sense. And then the Christmas boxes. Twenty-five pound cheques to each of them, even the children. It didn't seem much when you reckoned it up, a hundred and twenty-five pounds, but a hundred and twenty-five pounds was a hundred and twenty-five pounds when you were broke . . . ! Broke, be damned . . . ! her broke likely meant she had a bare three thousand a year to survive on.

He must have a drink. Softly he walked past the couch and out of the room, and when he entered the dining-room he made straight for the cabinet standing in the corner. Opening its doors wide, he ran his finger along the line of bottles on the top shelf before selecting the brandy. And all this liquor. What did she keep this stuff for? Supposedly for her uncle and relations. That was my eye. She likely tippled on the quiet; there was no-one to check on her most of the time. Would you buy this amount of stuff if you were near penniless? He threw off a good measure of brandy, then as he stood savouring its warming effect he looked down at the empty glass and said aloud, 'She's lying.' His hand went out to the bottle again, and he was in the act of pouring himself out another brandy when the front-door bell rang.

Who the hell could this be? Not MacIntyre already? He hoped not. He didn't want to be stuck with him until the others came back.

When he opened the front door he saw standing there a man of medium height, dressed in a greatcoat and holding a hat in one hand and a small case in the other.

'Yes?' His enquiry was not convivial.

'I'm Aster.'

'Aster . . . Oh, good lord . . . come in, come in.' He closed the door behind the man. 'You weren't expected until one o'clock. Come by special train or something?'

The man was looking slowly around the hall, and he said with a laugh, 'No, hardly that, but a friend of mine was driving this way and offered me a lift . . . I took a taxi from yon side of the village.'

'A taxi? You were lucky. It's a wonder they came up this way with the snow lying. . . . Here, let me have your things. I'm the only one in, everybody's at church. I'm Spencer, Beatrice's husband. You might have found an empty house, only my little girl was sick – excitement, you know. Up half the night waiting for her stocking . . . I bet you could do with a drink.'

For the moment Gerald had pushed aside his own concerns. He was playing the host in a way he would never have done had Grace been in the house.

He led the way across the hall. 'In here . . . now, what'll you have . . . ? Let's see.' He stood in front of the cabinet, again a door in each hand. 'We run to whisky, gin, rum, cherry brandy, brandy plain. Advocat. . . .'

'Oh, a whisky please, neat.'

'A whisky neat. A whisky it'll be.'

'What a remarkable place.'

'Eh? Oh this . . . the house . . . yes. And you've seen nothing yet.'

'Jane didn't tell me. I expected a vicarage . . . you know, the usual kind.'

'Well, this is the vicarage, or was when the Reverend was alive. Anyway, it was used as such, but the real vicarage is at the other side of the village, near the garage . . . Oh, it's a long story. Jane will tell you some time, I suppose. Well, drink up. . . . Cheers!'

'Cheers.'

'Sit yourself down.'

'Thanks.'

Gerald took up his stand on the hearthrug, and from his advantageous position he summed up the visitor. Well, all he could say was: he certainly wasn't much to look at. To hear Jane ramping on he had expected a six-footer at least and all that went with it. The fellow was no more than five foot five, tubby in fact, and looked his age. He might have the advantage on top . . . well, he needed it some place. But now it was up to him, he supposed, to keep the ball rolling until the others came in.

During this process and the next half-hour the man learned a great deal about Gerald, and, becoming a little tired of the theme, he skilfully turned the conversation to the house and garden again.

'You have some very fine trees here.' He stood up and went to the window. 'The willows are magnificent. . . . Ah-h! That's a lovely sight, isn't it?' He pointed to where a large willow, its lower branches borne down with snow, stood in the middle of the wide stretch of white sun-gleaming lawn.

'Oh, that's nothing.' Gerald came to his side. 'Wait until you see those at the back.'

'It's a wonderful place . . . wonderful.'

Gerald made no answer to this, for the remark dragged his mind back to his own affairs. Aye, it was wonderful, he'd say it was wonderful, and according to her it was for the market. He wished they were back; he must tell Beatrice about the way things had gone and damn all promises to the contrary. This fellow, he was finding, was heavy going. Had nothing to say except enthuse about the place. He was turning from the window when his companion's exclamation of 'Good gracious!' brought him round again and he looked to where he was pointing to the path circling the lawn. 'That man . . . why, I know him . . . don't tell me he lives here.'

'MacIntyre . . . ? No . . . well, not in this house. He lives over on the fells. He does the odd jobs, part time, mostly at nights and week-ends. He's a farm-worker really.'

'Really . . . ! Well, how strange.'

'Why, is he a friend of yours?' Gerald's eyes narrowed.

'No, no, I wouldn't say that. We've only met twice and then just for a few minutes each time. But he's the kind of man whom you couldn't forget in a hurry . . . he's got a white tuft of hair here, hasn't he?' He pointed high up on his temple.

'Yes . . . yes, he has.'

'That's him.'

They both watched Andrew follow the path that led towards the side of the house and the front door.

'Where'd you meet him . . . he hardly ever leaves these parts, except occasionally to visit an aunt in Devon.'

'It was there we met . . . Devon.'

'This last week?'

'No, some months ago – around Easter, to be correct. That was the second time. The first time was about two years ago. I lost my way when I was on a walking tour and came across him. I was making for Buckfast Abbey and got lost in a wood. You can, you know,' he smiled. 'I was thinking I was there for ever when I came on a clearing and a cottage. There was a field beyond. It was in the field I first saw him . . . It was most arresting, he was coming down the slope with his wife. It was rather a steep gradient and I think she must have slipped, for he pulled her up into his arms and swung round and ran with her down the remainder of the hill to the gate. I remember envying him his colossal strength . . . it was rather a beautiful sight, if you know what I mean, a man running down a hill with a woman in his arms. You don't often come across it in real life, you've got to go to the films to see anything like that these days, and then it's usually done by a stand-in Hercules.'

'He was with his wife?' Gerald's voice was low and his eyes were wide and he nodded his head slowly as he spoke.

'Yes. I didn't make my presence known for a moment or so, I didn't want to break in on the scene and . . . well . . . embarrass them, but even when I did show myself, and with quite a bit of preliminary noise, I remember I nearly scared the wits out of them, at least her, for she dashed into the house. It left me a bit mystified until he explained. She had seemingly been very ill and was still convalescent, and as they rarely saw anyone in that isolated part my presence had evidently startled her.'

'Yes . . . yes, it would, I can see that.' Gerald was still nodding his head. Well, could you beat it? MacIntyre with a wife — a woman would be more correct, and tucked away in a nice secluded spot right in the heart of a wood. Well again, what d'you know? His mother-in-law's family retainer, who would be lonely on Christmas Day so must join the family circle, and while he was eating his Christmas pudding no doubt his mind would be in the woods . . . with the little woman. There was a loud snigger inside him. He couldn't wait to see Andrew's face when he was confronted with this fellow. It was a small world, wasn't it? Coincidences were funny things, upsetting things. He was going to enjoy himself today, mainly, he realised, not because Andrew's face was going to be red, but because of the disillusionment that was awaiting his mother-in-law when she learnt of the double life of her perfect odd-job man.

'I found him a most interesting man. He had a wide knowledge of trees. He walked with me and put me on the road to the Abbey. I remember wishing it had been longer. Then this Easter I went that way again and there they were as before. She's very shy, isn't she? Has she quite recovered?'

Gerald was saved from making a reply to this question by the sound of laughing voices entering the hall. The church-goers were back and Andrew would come in with them — oh he couldn't wait for this — so for answer he said, 'Here they come, come on and show yourself.' He put his arm round the other man's shoulders and pressed him forward, and so it was almost side by side they entered the hall.

There before them was gathered the family. Beatrice was in the act of peeping into the drawing-room, Stephen was pulling off his muffler and coat, Jane had her back to them. She was in the fore-lobby gathering some late mail from the wire cage, but standing together like the central figures in a picture were Grace and Andrew. They had been joined in gentle laughter a moment before they looked towards Gerald and the man at his side. When the man came swiftly forward with outstretched hand Grace, with mouth agape as if she were being confronted by the Devil, shrank closer to Andrew. And then with a desperate movement she turned her face and body towards him as if seeking shelter from the advancing guest.

The man was shaking Andrew's stiff hand, and his now hesitant and perplexed tone pounded through Grace's head as he said, 'Well, isn't this the most unusual thing, I never thought we . . . we should meet again, not in this part of the country, anyway.'

There was a pause in the pounding, and when the voice came at her averted face saying quietly, 'I hope I find you better,' she knew with a great surge of relief that she was to be freed of this excruciating moment and that she was about to faint. As she clutched at Andrew and felt his arms supporting her, she heard Jane's voice crying, 'George! George! Oh, Mammy!'

PART TWO

PART TWO

1

Whenever Grace looked back to the incidents that occurred in the early years of her marriage her mind always picked on the first night Donald and she spent together. She could see herself sitting bolt upright in the bed waiting for him, her heart pounding so hard that she felt its jerking ever behind her eyes. They were spending the night in an hotel in Dover before crossing by car ferry the following day to make their way through France to Rome, where they would stay for the next two weeks.

The bulbs in the bedroom were shaded to the extent of making the lighting appear dim, and she had sat peering through it towards the dressing-room door. The dressing-room had come as a pleasant surprise to her. When Donald had spoken of the booking he had referred to it as the room, not rooms, but it was so like him to be considerate of her feelings on this night.

When the intervening door opened and he entered the room in his dressing-gown, she was torn for the moment between two ways of greeting him, one with lowered head and the other with arms eagerly outstretched. She chose the latter, and when he was sitting on the bedside close beside her he took her face between his large hands, his fingers pressing her temples, and he stared into her misted eyes for some time before gently kissing her. And then he began to talk. With his voice soft and sometimes hesitant, he asked her: Did she know that love was God conceived . . . God distributed . . . given by Him to His creatures for the sole purpose of creating souls? Did she know that? Did she know that it was a most precious thing, a thing to be cherished, never to be squandered, as precious as the chalice holding the holy wine, to be sipped at, never to be gulped . . . did she know that? Consciously she knew none of these things, she was only aware of being lulled, almost hypnotised, by the magic of his voice. She only knew that he was wonderful, so kind, so understanding.

It was some months before she realised that the substance of his talk on their wedding night was the foundation on which their marriage was laid.

When finally he stretched his long length down beside her, there was a change in her feelings for which she could not account, for his tenderness proved to be enough for her. She did not miss the consummation of the marriage until, waking the next morning, she thought with a guilty start, Oh, I must have fallen asleep, and when she saw him lying looking at her, seeming even to be drinking her into himself, she wondered why she, of all people in the world, should have been selected for such happiness, and how could there be anyone so blind as not to see the wonder and goodness of her Donald. This thought took her mind to her Aunt Aggie. Aunt Aggie didn't like Donald, never had from the day he came to commiserate with her on the tragic death of her parents in the car crash. He was too smooth, too good-looking, too much of a la-de-da, Aunt Aggie had stated openly. Her Aunt Susan and Uncle Ralph liked Donald, and both said that he was the kind of man her mother would have liked her to marry. For had not her parents moved into the best part of Newcastle so as to be able to give her a background that would in no way be incongruous to the boarding-school education they insisted on her having, and which was to prepare her to meet, and mate, with someone like Donald. Yes, they said, poor dear Linda would have been over the moon at her daughter's choice, for was not Donald Rouse, besides looking and talking like a gentleman, the nephew of a bishop.

Yet no approbation of her Aunt Susan and Uncle Ralph could make up for her Aunt Aggie's open hostility, for she liked her Aunt Aggie – loved her; she had always had a guilty feeling about her affection for her Aunt Aggie because she knew it was stronger than that which she had for her parents. But now she was finished with her Aunt Aggie; she couldn't be anything else after the things she had said about Donald, kept on saying about him even to the very night before the wedding.

'That fellow's after your money, that's all he wants,' that's what she had dared to say about Donald, who was a parson. On that last night Aggie had shouted so that she had rushed and closed the drawing-room door and begged, 'Oh, be quiet, Aunt Aggie. Donald will be calling any minute. Oh, how can you say such things?'

'I can and will. Somebody's got to say them; the others can't 'cos they're mesmerised – like you. Look, Grace.' Aggie's voice had dropped and there came a note of urgent pleading into it. 'Listen to me. He's a good-looking fellow granted, although he's old enough to be your father, but from my experience that kind of man doesn't look for a good-looking wife – not your type, anyway.' Her voice sank even lower now as she went on, 'Don't you realise it, Grace, you're not only good-looking, you're a beautiful girl. You could have anybody you had a mind to point at. I could name half a dozen men in this town who would jump if you raised your finger. The only reason they are keeping their distance at present is because you are so young and your folks haven't been dead six months yet. But that doesn't seem to trouble your parson friend. And another thing, if that fellow had wanted anything but

49

money he'd have been married afore the day at his age, going on thirty-eight.'

Grace was crying now and had protested, 'Oh, Aunt Aggie, how can you?'

'I can and I will,' she had repeated over again, 'and I'm going to tell you this, Grace. It will be the sorriest day's work you'll do in your life if you marry that man the morrow. I tell you I know the type. They're like some of the great big whopping turnips you see, fine on the outside but boast inside. It's all the same with these big beauties, and you'll find you'll want more than a good-looking face on the pillow to get you happily through marriage. Aye, you will. And what about your music, eh? What about that? D'you think he'll let you go on with that . . . ? You wait and see.'

And now as Grace lay looking into the beautiful face she knew Aunt Aggie was wrong, so terribly wrong, and she felt sorry for Aunt Aggie, because for years she had been looked upon as the oracle of the family. Her father used to say nobody could hoodwink Aggie. She had a head on her, had Aggie. How many women after losing their husbands would, or could, carry on his job, and the tricky one at that, of buying and selling property? But Aggie had done it. Yes, Aggie was astute, and cute.

As Donald rose from the bed, his hand trailing slowly from hers, she forgot her Aunt Aggie, for who could think of a domineering, middle-aged, fat little woman when they were murmuring, 'Oh, darling, darling, I do love you.' Yet somewhere in her mind, she was vowing, I'll make Aunt Aggie eat her words. I will, I will. No-one, no-one in the world must dislike Donald . . . anyway, how could they?

By the end of the honeymoon she was a little tired of looking at architecture, Byzantine, Gothic, and the rest, and she was secretly looking forward to taking up her life at the vicarage, and, as she said to herself – doing things with it. She knew exactly what alterations she was going to make to that big, draughty house, but she knew that she would have to move cautiously, for Donald had emphasised, and strongly, that she must be prepared to live within his means. And to think that Aunt Aggie . . .

Donald had himself been only three months in the village of Deckford, and, as he said, was still feeling his feet. He was also, she knew, still smarting under the reason for his banishment from St Bernard's. He had made light of it when it happened, saying to her, 'You want to know the reason why I've got to go. Well, can you give me your undivided attention for the next few days to listen to the history of the Church – I'll have to start with the Reformation.' His voice had become sad as he ended. 'I am, as you know, innately what you might call High Church, and St Bernard's is innately what you might term Low Church. My job, when I was sent there, was to bring the two to a moderate meeting point, but I'm afraid my zeal has carried me over that point and annoyed a number of people, so I am being banished to a little village, but where, oddly enough' – he laughed here – 'they are rather partial to trappings.' It was on the day he told her this that she knew she loved him and couldn't live without him, and on the day he actually moved to Deckford he asked her to marry him and she fell into his arms . . .

But it was decreed that Grace was not to live in the vicarage at Deckford. The weather took a hand in her destiny, for during a gale, and only three days before they returned from Italy, one of the two large chimneys crashed through the roof and caused a great amount of damage. Uncle Ralph, taking things in hand, made it his business to find them temporary accommodation against their return. This accommodation was the home of the late Miss Tupping and called Willow Lea. The house and its contents were up for sale, and the business was in the hands of Bertrand Farley, Junior, who had been Miss Tupping's solicitor. Bertrand Farley saw no reason why the house should not be rented for a few weeks, for privately he could not see it being sold at any price. There was a slump hitting the country, and it was improbable he would get an early sale for a place such as Willow Lea . . .

So it was that Grace returned to a home which delighted her heart with its air of graciousness, and she determined right away that she was going to do all in her power to remain there, for her Donald, she saw at once, loved the house. Although he said not a word in its favour until a month later when they were about to leave it. It was this moment that Grace had been waiting for and she put into words what had been in her mind since she had first entered the door. Why shouldn't they live here permanently? Why couldn't they buy it?

What? Donald was up in arms. The suggestion met with a complete refusal. No, she knew the arrangement they had agreed on, they must live within his means. Of course he liked the house, but that did not mean, etc., etc. Grace was not deterred: she sent for her Uncle Ralph and Aunt Susie, and there was a meeting in the drawing-room during which Donald gradually, but only gradually, became amenable. Once his consent was gained, the rest was a mere formality.

Willow Lea was bought as it stood, furniture included, at the bargain price of £4,000. There was only one snag that promised to be an irritant, a codicil concerning Benjamin Fairfoot, the gardener.

Benjamin had started with Miss Tupping's family when he was a boy, and when Miss Tupping had had a new house built for herself she and Benjamin Fairfoot between them had designed and created the gardens, and the codicil provided against Benjamin's dismissal. Whoever purchased the house must sign to the effect that he would be kept on as gardener, as long as he so desired.

Grace saw nothing in this to worry about, it did not even call for consideration . . . of course Benjamin would be kept on, he was part of the garden. She liked Ben, he talked Geordie and reminded her of old Jack Cummings, except that up to date she hadn't heard him swear. Jack Cummings had been one of her father's men when they lived next to the coal depot. She knew that it was because she liked to play around Jack and had acquired a little of his vocabulary that her mother had insisted on her being sent away to school in the first place.

Uncle Ralph's opinion of the codicil was much the same as Grace's own. 'Oh, that's nowt,' he said, 'I'd say you're lucky to have such a fellow as that thrown in. You're lucky altogether, me lass.'

Donald alone questioned the matter of Ben's compulsory employment, the reason he voiced being that they couldn't afford a gardener. Grace had laughed over this. 'We can afford three gardeners,' she had said, 'and a full staff inside too. And, what's more, we're going to have them.' It was a silly thing to say, taking things far too quickly, and it brought upon her head a lecture.

'No, Grace, that'll never do. The gardener . . . all right, because our hand is forced . . . and a little help in the house, that'll be all right too. But you must remember, Grace, that I'm just an ordinary parson, and only by continuing as such can I hope to hold my parish together. Any show of undue affluence would be bound to estrange at least one part of the community.'

She knew that he was referring to the folk versus the others, and she sighed. She knew he was right. Her Donald was always right, he was so wise. He had explained all this to her before, the difference between the folk, as he called the villagers, and the others. Among which were the Farleys, the hunting Tooles, the doctor, and the schoolmaster in that order. Oh yes, Donald was right.

From when did she first start telling herself several times a day that she was happy? Before she had been married three months? Yes, a while before that. Her days at the beginning left her very little time for private thoughts. Running an eight-roomed house with the part-time help of Mrs Blenkinsop, and getting initiated into the duties of a parson's wife, which, besides visiting, included taking an active part in the Women's Guild, the Sewing Meeting and the Literary Evening, the latter a new innovation instigated by the vicar, left her a little tired by nightfall. Sometimes she would sit on the rug before the fire, her head resting against Donald's knees, her hand on top of his hand where it covered her hair, and she would almost fall asleep listening to his endearments.

'My energetic little girl is overdoing it.'

'No . . . no, I'm not.' Her voice would often sound as if it was coming through sleep.

'I'm going to take you to bed and tuck you up.'

Whenever he spoke in this way she would be roused and say, with a sort of childish petulance which in no way suited her, 'Oh, aren't you coming, Donnie?'

'No, I'm not coming. Come along, up you get.'

She would be in his arms now and he would be putting on an act of mock sternness. 'How am I going to get any work out of you tomorrow if you don't get your sleep?'

'But, Donald . . . '

'No but Donald, it's bed for you.'

'Yes, and for you.' Her finger would be tracing the outline of his mouth.

'After I get my sermon finished.'

'But you did that last night.'

'No, I didn't get at it. I had to do the address I am giving on Saturday in Newcastle.'

'Oh, Donald.' Her head would fall wearily against him and he would carry her upstairs and into their room and drop her with a playful plonk on the bed. He never stayed while she undressed. When some time later she would be in bed he would come in again and stroke her hair and kiss her lips, and lastly her eyes, and tuck her up before putting out the light. Sometimes she would sigh happily, then drop off to sleep, but at other times, and more frequently as time went on, when this little scene was enacted, she would kick her legs down the bed or turn on her stomach and push her face into the pillow. . . . She had not cried yet. . . .

About this time her mind was lifted from herself by the fact, the stupendous fact, that Aunt Aggie was coming to visit them. It was Donald who had really brought about this minor miracle, for, from shortly after their return, he had voiced his opinion that it was a great pity her Aunt Aggie was estranged from them, and Grace must try to bring about a reconciliation. She had, on this occasion, received a little private sermon on the poison of malice and the health-giving properties of forgiveness, and as she listened she thought, Oh, if only Aunt Aggie could see him as he really is.

If at that moment Grace herself could have seen him as he really was she still would not have believed that her wonderful Donald could not suffer the thought that anyone could know him and find him not to their liking.

So Grace went to see Aggie, and again she went, and yet again, and at last Aggie said yes. Yes, she would come to see the grand new house . . . but just because she was interested in property, mind – that was the only reason.

The morning Aggie was due to arrive Grace sidled out of bed around six o'clock, very careful not to wake Donald, and began an onslaught of rearranging and preparation for the visitor. Mrs Blenkinsop, when she arrived at eight o'clock, did not take kindly to the bustle that was already in progress, and Donald, when he came down to breakfast, exclaimed, 'My! My! All this for the dragon. You never make so much fuss about me.'

'Oh, Donald, I do. You know I do. And besides, Aunt Aggie isn't a dragon. She's a darling really, once you get to know her.'

'She scares me stiff.' Donald was in a playful mood.

'Oh, that's funny.' She was laughing at him. 'I can't imagine anyone scaring you stiff.' She dashed at him now and, flinging her arms around his neck, kissed him.

'You're the one that scares people. D'you know what you do? You scare the pants off them.' She accompanied this latter with small jerks of her head, then giggled as she watched Donald's eyebrows move up.

'And where, may I ask, did you hear that edifying piece of news?'

'Ben.'

'Ben. . . . Oh . . . when?'

'Yesterday, after you had failed to persuade him to move those hydrangeas.'

'Well?'

'I was coming up the drive, walking on the verge. I heard part of the persuasion, and then I heard him leading off to himself.' She fell into an imitation of Ben's voice. ' "Scare the pants off 'em down there" – he was meaning the village – "but he's not going to scare 'em off me. No, by damn!" '

'Tut! tut! You mustn't repeat words like that. . . . But he said that, did he?' Donald disengaged himself, and she looked at him in some surprise as he added, 'Well, we'll see.'

If he hadn't made the last statement she would have imagined that he was only amused, but now she could see that he was slightly annoyed. But as for him scaring any of his parishioners, it was, when she came to think of it, ridiculous, for his attitude towards them, she considered, was over-conciliatory, except when he was in the pulpit. When there, there was nothing conciliatory about him. At times, if she had dared criticise his sermons, she would have said in the idiom of her father, 'That was hot and heavy this morning.' But not for the world would she dream of criticising anything he might do with regards to his work. His business was putting over God, and all his energies were spent in that direction. Unbidden there came to her mind the picture of herself kicking her legs down the bed before turning on to her stomach.

The picture was not new, and because in some way it was a reflection on Donald she chided herself vigorously once again on its appearance. She was the wife of a vicar, she mustn't forget, and parsons were different, there were many things as the wife of a vicar she would have to make herself not only get used to but like. The latest was praying together, privately at night at the bedside.

It was around about the time of Aggie's visit that she began to look towards the nights with a slight dread, to see them as a time of conflict, and there was no-one she told herself to blame for this but herself. Certainly not Donald, Donald was wonderful. It was she who was at fault. The truth of the matter was that at rock bottom she wasn't good, there was a baseness in her. A

57

burning, craving, unsatisfied, restless baseness. Oh, she knew herself and she must try, try hard to conquer this unworthy feeling.

There were times also when she wished she had someone to talk to . . . her mother or someone. She did not bring Aunt Aggie into the category of someone, she could never now talk to Aunt Aggie about herself – at least not when it related to her marriage. Aunt Aggie must be made to realise how happy she was with Donald and come to like him. . . . Yet she wished there was someone. . . . But had there been, could she ever have put into words what was troubling her? No. No. Never. . . .

Everything was ready except flowers for the table, and she knew that these would have to be coaxed out of Ben. But that wouldn't be difficult, she had a way with Ben. She liked him and, strangely, she felt more at home with him than with anyone else in the village, but she was wise enough to keep this fact to herself. She ran now through the hall, out into the garden, and round the side of the house and just remembered to pull herself to a walk before she reached the greenhouse. This running everywhere was something that Donald had checked her for. But she never seemed to be able to get to places quickly enough, she had to run.

'Hello, Ben.'

'Mornin', ma'am.'

'I'm on the scrounge, Ben, for something for the table.'

And her vocabulary would, definitely, she knew, have brought a protest from Donald had he heard her. One was careful how one spoke both to the folks . . . and the others. Jokes were for the privacy of one's family, as also was slang . . . if it must be used. But this manner of speaking was an attitude that Ben knew and understood. She had learned from the little he had said about his

58

previous mistress, and the great deal Mrs Blenkinsop had told her, that there had been no starchiness of man and employer between them. Looking at this wonderful garden she could understand that it could never have come into creation without sympathetic co-operation. Her attitude might not be similar to that used by Miss Tupping, but it was one that Ben in his surly way appreciated, and she was aware of this.

'Well now, what have we got?' He considered a moment. 'A couple of roses suit you?'

'Roses? Oh, Ben, marvellous.'

There was not more than half a dozen late roses left, and when lovingly he cut four of them, trimmed the stalks, and handed them to her she said with genuine feeling, 'Oh, that's kind of you, Ben.' It was as if the garden was his and he was bestowing a gift upon her.

'That's all right, ma'am.'

'Thanks, Ben.' She turned from him, forgetting not to run, and she took the path round the vegetable garden towards the back door. She was still running when she burst into the kitchen crying, 'Look, Mrs B., what I've scrounged. . . .' Her voice trailed away and the hand holding out the roses moved slowly downwards as she looked at the young man standing near the dresser. He was in rough working clothes and had his cap in his hand, and after looking at her for a moment he said, 'Good morning.'

'This is Andrew MacIntyre, ma'am; he's come with a message for the vicar. I've just told him he's out.'

She laid the roses on the table, then asked, 'Is there anything I can do?'

'It's from Mr Toole. He says to tell the vicar that there's a mount for him for Thursday's meet if he cares for it.'

'Oh.' She sounded a little surprised. 'He usually phones.'

'He tried twice this morning but the line was engaged, and as I was passing this way . . .'

She was looking at him, waiting for him to finish, and when he didn't go on she said, 'Thanks.' Then again, 'Thanks, I'll tell him.'

He nodded his head once towards her, then, turning and looking at Mrs Blenkinsop, he said briefly, 'Good morning.'

From the kitchen window Grace watched the tall, rather gangling figure cross the courtyard before she asked, 'Is he in our parish, Mrs B?'

'Lord alive, I should say so. But I saw by your face, ma'am, that you hadn't come across him afore. And that's nothing unusual, he scarcely comes down to the street unless he has to. He's from Peak Fell, in the cottage up there.'

'As far away as that. That's likely why I've never seen him in church.'

'Huh! You're not likely to see any of the MacIntyres in church, ma'am. If they're anything they're at the opposite pole from the Church of England. They're Scots and a close family. . . . All Scots are dour, don't you think, ma'am?'

'I haven't met many, Mrs B.'

'Well, from my experience I'd say they are. The MacIntyres have been in the village around fifteen years – quite a while it is, fifteen years – but nobody knows much more about them than on the day they came except that she was a teacher of sorts and he was crippled with arthritis . . . laziness I would say, for he can get around on his sticks when he likes. He hasn't done a bat to my knowledge in all the years he's been here except carve little animals and such which he sells now and then. It's yon Andrew they live by, and if you ask me—' Mrs Blenkinsop's voice stopped abruptly, then she added, 'The vicar, ma'am, I've just caught sight of his tails flying.'

'Oh, is it?' Grace stopped herself from bounding towards the door, and, picking up the roses from the table, she said, 'I'll do these in the cloakroom, they'll be out of your way there.'

But the green baize door of the kitchen had hardly swung to behind her when she ran across the hall and into the study.

'Hello, darling.' She flung her arms around his neck, the roses still in her hand, and as they waved about the crown of his head she cried excitedly, 'See what I got out of Ben, four of his best; I've got him eating out of my hand.'

He closed his eyes and refused to look at her as he said with mock severity, 'Conceit and pride ill becomes a vicar's wife.'

'Oh, Donald.' She dropped her head on to his shoulder and began to giggle, then after a moment she raised it quickly, when, with more than a touch of censure, he commented, 'It's a pity they've been cut. I think they would have looked better and remained alive longer if they had been left in their natural setting. There are so few now and it was so nice to see them in the garden at this time of the year.'

She loosened her hands from behind his head, then, after looking at him for a moment, her gaze dropped and she said softly, 'Yes, yes, I suppose you're right, Donald, it was very silly of me to ask him for them. I rather pestered him. I'm sorry.'

That the roses had been cut had vexed Donald, but his vexation would only be aggravated if he knew that Ben had done the cutting without any pressure. She had been stupid to brag about him eating out of her hand. So again she repeated, 'I'm sorry.'

'Well, they're cut now.'

'Don't be vexed.'

'I'm not.'

'Kiss me.'

He kissed her and then turned away, and she exclaimed with nervous, false jocularity, 'I've got a present for a good boy.' She paused before delivering it. 'There's an invitation from Mr Toole; he says there's a mount for you at the meet on Thursday.'

His head came round and his eyes brightened with pleasure. 'He called?'

'No, he had phoned twice this morning and couldn't get through so he sent one of his men with the message, an Andrew MacIntyre. Have you met any of the MacIntyres? I never knew they existed, and I thought I had met everybody from miles around.'

'Oh, the MacIntyres.' Donald's neck stretched out of his collar and the smile left his eyes. 'Yes, I've met the MacIntyres. Dyed in the wool bigots.'

'You've visited them then?'

'Yes, shortly after I came here.' He paused, and when he continued his voice had a rasping sound. 'When you get an ignorant bigoted Scot there's nothing much more can be added to the description.'

'But the young man seemed quite nice.' Her comment sounded tentative.

'Oh yes, I should say he's all right, at least on the surface, for he's bound to have his father in him somewhere. But I suppose there must be a deal of good in him, for I understand that Toole has taken a great interest in him since he was a boy, and he's no fool where men are concerned. At one time he wanted to send him to an agricultural college, but the father would have none of it. Of course his point of view is understandable: the boy is their only means of support.'

'Is the father really ill?'

'Not so ill that he couldn't be better if he tried, and that's Doctor Cooper's version too.'

'What a pity – I mean that the boy couldn't have gone to college.'

'Yes, it was. But then if Mr Toole hasn't been allowed to help him, the daughter is going to do her best.' This last was accompanied by a pursing of the lips and Grace cried delightedly, 'You mean Adelaide . . . she's . . . '

'Yes, head over heels I should say, and if her father allows it, and it's probable, for he likes the young fellow, yon Andrew MacIntyre will fall very firmly on his two big feet.'

'Oh, I hope it comes off. I like Adelaide . . . she seems full of life.'

'It is whispered that she has a temper.'

'And what is wrong with that, Mr Donald Rouse?' Donald had recovered from his slight irritation over Ben and she could tease him.

'Everything.'

'Are you serious?' Grace dropped her head to one side.

'Yes, I am serious, Mrs Rouse. I think a woman with a temper is something to be abhorred. Just think what it leads to, temper of any kind, but in a woman . . . a bad-tempered woman. . . .'

'Oh, Donald,' she broke in on him, 'I must see to the table, and these flowers, but do come along, darling, and tell me all you know about bad-tempered women.' She made a grab at his hand and turned to pull him after her, but found herself jerked back to him.

'You're not taking me seriously.'

'No, Donald dear, I am not.'

'Do I suspect you're laughing at me?'

'I wouldn't dare laugh at you, sir.' Her face was straight but her eyes were shining, and she was striving not to giggle. She was happy inside, she loved Donald in these playful exchanges. The nights were forgotten. She could tell herself she adored him.

'You must not laugh at me, I am a very nervous man at the moment. In a short time I am to eat before your aunt.'

Her head went back and her laugh rang out, 'Eat before your aunt. Oh, that does sound funny, Donald. . . . This is the house of my aunt . . . *ce ci est la maison de ma tante.*'

As her laugh soared again his hand went up quickly to silence her on the sound of the front-door bell ringing, then he punched the air and hissed, 'Miss Shawcross. You see what you've done, almost made me forget. Look, come this way.' He drew her quickly across the room and through the french windows, along the terrace and through a similar window into the drawing-room, and there hastily closing the window behind him, he chided her with raised finger. 'I meant to get this explained before she came. It's about the play.'

'The play?'

'Yes; you see, what I hadn't fully understood before was that she had always played the piano for the children, not just last Christmas, and when . . .'

'But it was all arranged that I should play, I chose the music and—'

'Yes, yes, I know, my dear, and her playing is atrocious, we all know that, but it would hurt her so much if this little duty were to be taken away from her. I've felt for days that there was something wrong, and when she approached me this morning I discovered . . . well, that was it . . . the play. I told her that of course you hadn't understood,

64

and if she would call up during her dinner hour you would let her have the music, she's quite willing to work to your choice. . . . Oh, my dear, don't look so disappointed.'

'But I wanted to play for the children, Donald, I've been looking forward to it.'

A flatness had come upon her day. Playing for the children at the Christmas concert and Nativity play was to constitute her first real social engagement as the vicar's wife and she had given to it quite a lot of thought. It was actually Donald himself who had suggested she should do this. There were not more than fifteen children from the scattered community who attended Sunday school and they offered material that had no artistic claim, but this had in no way deterred her – in fact it had set her a challenge. The Christmas concert and Nativity play was going to be the best ever heard or seen in the village. She would show them that although she was very young to be the parson's wife she was capable, very capable.

Donald was patting her cheek and saying quietly, 'I've got an idea to show off your talents on a much larger scale . . . an evening concert, you could let yourself rip at that. What do you say?'

At this moment she was too disappointed to be other than herself, so the only reply she made to this solace was with her eyebrows. She gave them an upward lift.

'Oh, my dear, come along.' There was the slightest edge to his voice now. 'What is there in playing for children; much better to make your début at a proper concert. One of the Miss Farleys plays the 'cello, and Blenkinsop, although you mightn't credit it, is no mean hand with the violin.'

'All right.'

'Come on then, smile. If your Aunt Aggie sees you like this she'll swear I'm starting to beat you and she'll say, "I knew it. I was right." '

She gave him a playful push and he squeezed her hand before going out on to the terrace towards his study and Miss Shawcross.

Blast Miss Shawcross. Grace gave no girlish sign of guilt on this thought. She was getting a little fed up with Miss Shawcross. This wasn't the first time during her short sojourn in the village that her opinion had had to be waived in favour of that of Miss Shawcross. There had been the business of the new literary group and its procedure. Miss Shawcross's suggestions had been followed because Miss Shawcross did such an amount of work for the church and it was only fair to give her a little say in this new venture. There had also been the dressing of the altar. The brass vases Grace considered looked too heavy when filled with flowers and she had substituted two silver ones, but the week after their arrival they had been relegated to the dim corners of the altar, and the brass ones were back dominating the scene.

'Let the matter be,' Donald had said, 'it's not worth a fracas. She has done the altar for years, in fact since she was a young girl; until now she has almost come to think that it belongs to her.' And then he had added, 'The church means so much to her, you'll have to remember that, my dear.'

And now the play – Miss Shawcross had won again.

This latter thought came to Grace in the form of a shock. She was made aware that she was in the midst of a contest, a contest which required the use of guile, and she could see quite plainly that if she was even to hold her own she would have to avail herself of this guile. The picture presented looked rather nasty, and she turned from the window and shook her head as if trying to throw the whole business off. Miss Shawcross was an old maid, a stuffy, prim old maid. She would tell Aunt Aggie on the quiet about Miss Shawcross and they would have a laugh. Yes, that was the best way to deal with Miss Shawcross, laugh at her.

Grace was bursting with pride and happiness. Aunt Aggie liked the house, she had thoroughly enjoyed her lunch, and, what was more – oh more important than anything else – she seemed to be getting to like Donald. Donald had gone out of his way to be charming to her and in Grace's opinion he was irresistible. Aunt Aggie would have had to be made of stone if she hadn't melted under this treatment.

There was one incident that Grace feared might throw a spanner into Aunt Aggie's capitulation. This was when Donald, taking the key from his waistcoat pocket, went to the sideboard and, unlocking the cupboard door, drew out the lead-lined wine box. In the box were four bottles and a number of glasses and then he turned and looked at Aggie, saying, 'What will you have? Sherry sweet, sherry dry?' He pointed to the bottles in turn, 'Sauternes . . . ? Or whiskey . . . Irish?' He laughed, and Aggie replied, 'I think I'll have the Sauternes, thank you.'

Grace could see that Aunt Aggie was slightly puzzled. The only glasses on the table were those for water, and when Donald placed the glass of wine before Aggie and another by the side of her plate, she felt that some explanation was due, and just as she was about to give it Donald raised his hand in his customary fashion and said brightly, 'Leave the explanation to me, my dear. I am the culprit and I must answer for my sins.' Before continuing he went and pushed the wine tray back into the cupboard, locked the door, then took his seat again, and, leaning across the table towards his guest, he said,

'The truth is, I'm a secret tippler, Aunt Aggie.'

There was a peculiar gleam in Aggie's small bright eyes as she said flatly, 'Well, that wouldn't surprise me in the least.'

'Oh, Aunt Aggie . . . ! and you, Donald.' Grace turned on him. 'You'll have her believing that. . . . It's because of Mrs Blenkinsop, Aunt Aggie.' Grace's voice was a whisper now as she leaned towards her aunt. 'Parsons and their wives are not supposed to have wine with their meals, it would be all over the village. . . .'

'Let us stick to the truth, Grace,' Donald put in quietly. 'It is not that parsons are not supposed to have wine with their meals, parsons are not supposed to be able to afford wine with their meals. There's a fine point there. But I'm a crafty man, Aunt Aggie. I married a woman with money who could afford to pander to my secret craving.' Donald did not look at Aggie as he said this but lifted the glass to eye level and twiddled the stem between his fingers. And he kept his eyes on the glass as he ended, 'But there is nothing I enjoy more than a glass of wine.'

From across the table Aggie nodded slowly at him, before saying, 'Well, at least I'm with you there, for if there's anything I like better than a glass of wine meself, it's two glasses of wine.'

The vicar let himself laugh at this triteness, and Grace thought how odd it was that these two should agree on the one point which she had dreaded might be the means of widening the gulf between them. Donald's system concerning the wine came under the heading of duplicity, and she hadn't expected her aunt to condone it. No, she had expected her to attack it, with a 'well, what did I tell you?' She was very relieved.

Lunch over, the atmosphere all she could desire, she lost no time when she was alone with Aggie in bringing before her notice the virtues of her husband. That which she felt would impress her aunt most was the fact that he would not allow her to use the car for visiting, nor would he use it himself for such a purpose. Moreover, there was the fact that he insisted they could only afford Mrs Blenkinsop for half days. And finally, he only had three pairs of shoes and he wouldn't buy any more until at least one pair was worn out.

'Well, he can't manage to wear more than one pair at a time, can he?' Aggie's dry remark was delivered without a smile and brought Grace to fluster. 'Yes, Aunt Aggie, but you understand what I—'

'Yes, yes, I understand all right.' Aggie patted Grace on the knee. 'Don't frash yourself, child. We'll get along all right, I suppose, when we get to know each other a bit better, but don't you work too hard at it or you'll wear yourself down to your hunkers. . . . I'll accept the fact that you've married a saint.'

'Oh, Aunt Aggie.' Grace had her head half lowered as if she had been caught at some misdemeanour, but when Aggie burst out laughing she joined in and threw her arms about her aunt and hugged her, crying, 'Oh, now I want nothing more.'

'Sit down and don't rumple me.' Aggie pushed her into a chair, then asked, 'What are the folks like around here, nice?'

'Yes. I'll take you through the village in a little while and you'll see some of them for yourself. I said they were nice and they are, all except one, a Miss Shawcross.'

'Miss Shawcross? Who is she?'

'The postmistress.'

'Ah, the postmistress, middle-aged, a church worker and . . . after the parson.'

Grace's eyes were wide as she exclaimed, 'You're a witch, Aunt Aggie – that's Miss Shawcross.'

'Is it, by gum?' Aunt Aggie bristled in mock anger. 'Come on then, let's have a dekko at her.'

Grace's laugh was high and free. Oh, it was good to be with Aunt Aggie again. She wanted nothing more now – nothing . . . ?

Some time later in the afternoon, after Aggie had visited the church and met Mr Blenkinsop, had been introduced to Dr Cooper as he came out of Brooke's the grocer's, had met Sep Stanley the baker and, like Grace on her first visit, had been given a hot buttered roll, they made their way to the post office and Miss Shawcross, and they were careful not to exchange glances as they entered.

Aggie Turner's shrewd eyes immediately saw that Miss Shawcross was quite different from her own jocular description; she was younger than she had expected, she was bigger than she had expected, and immediately she found that the woman claimed her sympathy, and this she hadn't expected either. As she looked into the large, plain face, she thought, 'It's a pity. By, it is that, for if he had come here before he had seen Grace that time of the accident, here's the one who would have been Mrs Rouse. At least she would have had a damn good try, and I would have said good luck to her.' This woman, she thought, would have made a far better parson's wife than her niece ever would, no matter how hard she kept on trying, and she was trying so hard at present that it was painful to watch her, and all because she was clean barmy about the man. Yet it looked as if she herself had misjudged the fellow, for, going by his present behaviour, he wasn't squandering Grace's money. But, of course, Aggie's business acumen prompted the thought, he had got quite a bit out of it already and in a way that brought no pointing finger at him. He had a fine house and furniture, and he was living much more comfortably

70

than he could ever have hoped to do on his own income. Still, she must be fair. Apparently he had his principles and was living up to them. Moreover, she was glad to know he had his own frailties. She had liked the touch of the wine business at lunch.

'What do you think?' asked Grace, when they had left the shop and were walking circumspectly through the village.

'I'm a bit sorry for her. Now! Now! Wait till I finish.' Aggie discreetly raised a finger. 'I also think I'd go very carefully. Don't pull her to shreds in front of him, of – of Donald. Your best plan, you know, would be to try to get to like her.'

'Oh, Aunt Aggie.'

'All right. It's only a suggestion, but remember you'll have to live with her for a long time.'

On this Grace let the matter drop – she was very puzzled at her aunt's reactions to Miss Shawcross, and not at all pleased.

The afternoon was sunny and even warm, and so they made their way on to the fells, Grace's primary idea being to show Aunt Aggie the village from the top of Roebeck Fell. An hour later, after much talking and laughing, they found themselves on top of Peak Fell from where you could see nothing for miles but the rolling hills, and Grace said, 'What does it matter, we'll go halfway down the valley and take a cut up to Roebeck Fell.'

'That you won't, not today,' said Aggie. 'I've got the feeling my feet are worn down to my knees already. We'll take the shortest cut for home and soon.'

'Oh, sit here for a while longer, Aunt Aggie. Isn't it beautiful!' She stretched out her arms to embrace the scene. 'You know something: this is the first time I've been on this fell. It's more beautiful than any of the others.'

71

'Yes, it's very beautiful.' Aggie nodded as she looked round. 'That's if you like it wild. There's not a habitation to be seen. I can't say my fancy bends this way. I'm more comfortable in Northumberland Street in Newcastle.'

'You've got no poetry in you. This does something to you.'

'Aye it might' – Aggie's voice had dropped, as it did when she was aiming to be funny, into the north country idiom – 'but aal Aa knaa at the minute is that A'm froze . . . Look' – she sought for a handkerchief – 'me nose is runnin'.'

'Oh, Aunt Aggie!' Grace's laugh rang out over the hills as she pulled Aggie up towards her, saying, 'Come on, then, let's be moving. There must be a shorter cut down than the one we came up by.'

Aggie's statement that there were no habitations on the fells was proved wrong when after walking not more than ten minutes they came upon a cottage. It was two-storied and made of rough quarry stone. It looked stark and ugly and had none of the warm mellowness attached to the houses in and around the village, many of which were built of the same material. The front door of the house led straight on to the steep road which had levelled itself out for a short distance at this point.

They were some yards from the house when they heard the shouting. The raised voices spoke quite plainly of a row in progress. Grace looked at Aggie and Aggie pursed her lips and nodded as she commented under her breath, 'Skull and hair flying.' The voices ceased before they reached the house, but just as they passed the door it opened and a woman and a young man stepped into the road, then came to an abrupt halt as they stared at the two women opposite them.

The young man Grace recognised as Andrew Mac-Intyre and the woman she took to be his mother. It was odd, she thought, that during all the months she had been in the village she hadn't seen him, yet here she was meeting him twice in the same day. 'Good afternoon,' she said.

The woman moved her head just the slightest as she murmured, 'Good afternoon.'

'This is my mother. This is the vicar's wife, Mother.' The young man was looking at Grace as he spoke.

The woman inclined her head slowly and Grace said, 'How do you do, Mrs MacIntyre?'

'Very well . . . ma'am.' She seemed to have some difficulty in adding the ma'am.

'You have a beautiful view.' Grace half turned from them.

'Yes, it's a grand view,' said the woman.

'And a grand walk up to it,' came wearily from Aggie. 'I'll be glad when I get off my feet.'

Whether or not this was a hint to be asked in to take a seat for a time the woman did not rise to it, instead she suggested a short cut for their return journey. 'You can halve the distance,' she said, 'and come out behind Miss Tupping's . . . I mean your house, ma'am,' she added apologetically. Then, turning to her son, she said, 'You're going down. Will you show the ladies the way, Andrew?'

The expression on the young man's face did not alter, so there was no means of knowing whether he was vexed or pleased, and when he spoke he looked neither at Aggie nor at Grace.

'If you'll come round this way,' he said.

After saying goodbye to Mrs MacIntyre they both followed him round the side of the house. Grace, going first, looked at his back. It was very slim, especially around the hips, and his walk was slow as if he had all the time in the world at his disposal . . . yet he had come through the door of the house quickly enough. He must have been rowing with his father; it couldn't possibly have been his mother, her glance was too soft on him. He was very like his mother; he had the same eyes, round and brown, almost black, but his hair wasn't as dark as hers.

'Are you all right, Aunt Aggie?' She turned now to where Aggie was picking her way carefully down the steep, rock-strewn path, and Aggie replied, 'Yes, I'm all right, as long as it doesn't get any worse.'

'Your mother said this path leads to the back of our house. Does it go down through the wood?' She was speaking to his back.

'Aye . . . yes.'

As she slithered over the rough ground she remarked, 'I wouldn't want to take this short cut often,' and she laughed to soften any suggestion of criticism.

'It isn't usually as bad as this. The rain's loosened the rocks. My mother didn't think when she suggested it. I'm sorry.' He had stopped and was now looking beyond her towards Aggie.

'Oh, I don't mind.' Aggie's voice was reassuring. 'As long as it shortens the journey I'll put up with it.'

'Well, it does that.'

As they went on again Grace thought, He's got a nice voice. Unlike his face and disposition there was nothing surly about it. It was a warm sort of voice, with the Scottish 'burr' thick on it. He might have lived in Northumberland for years but he hadn't lost the Scottish twang. She felt she wanted to listen to it, but his economical use of words offered little opportunity.

At one part the path crossed directly over a stretch of stone road, and she remarked, 'This looks a good road, where does it lead to?'

'The quarry.'

74

'Oh, I didn't know there was a quarry about here.' She looked at his averted face.

'It's not worked now.' His tone did not seem to invite further enquiry and she did not press the matter further.

A few minutes later they entered the wood and when they came to where three paths met in a small clearing he spoke without turning, saying, 'We fork left.'

Ten minutes later they emerged quite abruptly from a narrow path between the brambles into a field not more than twenty feet wide, and there, bordering its other side, was the hedge of Willow Lea.

'Well I never!' With this mundane exclamation Grace looked around her.

'So we've arrived,' commented Aggie dryly a moment later. 'And thank you very much.' She nodded at their escort. But after gazing towards the high hedge she looked up at him again and demanded, 'But can you tell us how we're going to get over that?' She pointed across the field.

'Oh, there's a gate farther up, at the far end, Aunt Aggie,' Grace put in. 'It's locked, but if I shout I'll make Ben hear – the greenhouses are just to the right of it.' She turned now and looked at the straight countenance of the young farm-worker, and, smiling, she said, 'Thank you very much for bringing us and for showing me the path. I often go into the wood, but I've always had to get in by the main road.'

He nodded as he looked at her but made no comment. Then, touching his cap, he said briefly, 'Good-day.'

It was meant for both of them, and Aggie said, 'Goodbye and thanks,' but Grace found herself answering him with his own words. 'Good-day,' she said.

As they moved along the field towards the gate, arm in arm, Aggie commented with a chuckle, 'By, he was pleasant, wasn't he? I've laughed me head off.' And Grace, quoting Mrs Blenkinsop, stated authoritatively, 'Oh, it's likely just his way, all Scots are dour.'

That Aunt Aggie's visit had been a great success was borne out as she stood in the bedroom adjusting her smart toque hat in the mirror. As she did this she looked to where Grace was standing behind her, then with lowered eyes she said, 'I'm glad to see you happy, child . . . and I suppose this is the time I should admit to being wrong, eh?'

'Oh, Aunt Aggie!' Grace pulled her round from the mirror and Aggie protested, 'Now look what you're doing, mind my hat . . . this bit of nonsense cost me a pretty penny, let me tell you.'

'Oh, Aunt Aggie!'

'Don't keep saying "Oh, Aunt Aggie!" and don't think that I'm going to join Susie and Ralph and start dribbling over him, that I'll never do.'

'That'll come, there's plenty of time yet.'

Aggie gave her a sharp push and sent her laughing on to the landing, crying, 'Donald! Donald! She's braying me!' and Donald, from where he was waiting in the hall, shouted back, 'Well, it's about time somebody did, for I've got to confess I'm not up to it.'

The atmosphere was homely and happy, and surrounded by it they waved Aggie and her car off down the drive, then turned and went into the house arm-in-arm.

This, Grace felt, had been the happiest day of her life, even happier than her wedding day. If she remembered the incident concerning Miss Shawcross she looked upon it now as one of the pin-pricks that parsons' wives are called upon to endure. There was always at least one Miss Shawcross in every parish.

Even when at ten o'clock Donald said he couldn't come upstairs just yet as he had some writing to do, which would take about an hour, her happiness still remained at an even keel. She spent rather longer than usual getting prepared for bed, then sat propped up reading.

She stopped reading before eleven, and when at half-past there was still no sound of movement from the room below, her legs jerked themselves down the bed and she turned on to her stomach.

At twelve o'clock she was tossing and turning from side to side in an effort to stop herself from going down to the study. He did not like that, she knew he did not like that.

When later, after what seemed like an eternity but was not more than twenty minutes, she heard him coming up the stairs and creeping quietly into the room, she was lying on her side, her face buried half in the pillow and half under the bedclothes. And when she felt him standing at the bedside looking down at her she made no movement. He had hoped to find her asleep; he was finding her asleep.

She pulled in the muscles of her stomach, screwed her eyes tight and bit her tongue . . . she still hadn't cried.

2

The musical evening took place at the end of January. Miss Shawcross started it off with a song. It was as well, Grace thought, that she was accompanying herself, for certainly nobody else could have followed her rendering of 'The Barcarolle'. Yet she was clapped roundly when she finished. She was followed by Miss Farley playing the 'cello. Miss Farley looked bored. Next Mr Blenkinsop was widely acclaimed with his violin solo; the comic sketches of Mr Thompson, the schoolmaster, brought forth laughter and a great deal of guffawing, but Grace did not consider he was funny at all, for he exaggerated the Geordie dialect beyond all recognition. Her own proposal to do a Tyneside sketch had been quickly squashed by Donald, and she had been given to understand once again that one did that kind of thing in private, not in public, and especially did this apply if you were the vicar's wife. He had chosen the pieces that she should play, they were 'Mazurka in A Minor' by Chopin and 'Serenade' by Schubert.

Her playing was received well but not enthusiastically. But later, when the concert was over, being brought to an end by yet another song from Miss Shawcross, she was congratulated by young Dr Cooper and his wife. 'Look in some night,' he said, 'and give us a treat.' And his wife had added, 'Yes, do come. I've been wanting to ask you for ages, but you're so busy I didn't like to bother you.'

Grace knew that this was a gentle dig at their, or at least Donald's, connection with the Farleys and the hunting

Tooles, but she liked the doctor, and his wife too, and she promised to make a date on which to visit them.

Of the others only Bertrand Farley told her that he had enjoyed her playing, and as he stood at the school-room door he held her hand just a fraction too long and his eyes seemed to boggle more than usual as he looked at her. 'You know, I think you should have made the piano your profession . . . but you got married instead, eh?'

There was a look in his eyes that caused her to turn away with a mumbled 'Excuse me' under the pretence that someone was claiming her attention. She didn't like Bertrand Farley. She didn't like any of the Farleys, for that matter. She had the idea, and correctly, that they imagined they were the lords of creation, at least in this part of the world, and acted accordingly. Being solicitors who represented most of the inhabitants of the village and surrounding country helped the illusion.

She found Donald in the vestry with Miss Shawcross. Donald had his back to her and Kate was standing in front of him. It was impossible not to notice the expression on her face – the only description Grace could give to herself was that it looked alight – her lips were parted, her eyes were shining, and in this moment she did not appear as Grace usually saw her, a plain, heavy-faced woman. She looked even beautiful.

At her entry Donald stopped talking and turned towards her, saying, 'Well, that's over. And what a success. I was just congratulating Miss Shawcross on her wonderful performance.'

Kate Shawcross had neither moved nor taken her eyes from the vicar, but now her head drooped in a girlish fashion that brought her, at least in Grace's eyes, back into focus, for the coy action made her look silly. She still did not look at Grace as she flustered, saying, 'Now I must see to the clearing of the room.' It could have been that Grace had never entered the vestry, at least for her.

It was on the point of Grace's tongue to make some cutting remark, some slighting, scathing remark on the foolishness of the woman, but, remembering Aggie's warning, she forced herself to remain silent.

Donald seemed in high good humour, and as they were walking up the hill towards home, her arm tucked into his, he suddenly remarked, 'And it was a success without the aid of the bagpipes.'

She turned and looked at him in the dark. Andrew MacIntyre had refused his invitation to play the bagpipes at the concert. She did not know what had transpired between them, but she knew that the refusal had annoyed Donald. Yet this had happened weeks ago, and now Donald was speaking of it as if it had occurred only today. She knew that his mind at this moment was filled, to the exclusion of everything else, with the fact that someone had refused an appeal of his. The tone of his voice when he spoke of Andrew MacIntyre was the same as he used when speaking of Ben.

She was silent for the rest of the way home because she was sad. She had been sad since the concert ended, for not once had he mentioned her playing. And now the sadness was intensified because it was being fed by a disturbing thought: Donald was being vindictive. Lesser men could be vindictive, but he wasn't in the category of lesser men; and, moreover, he was a vicar, and even ordinary men of the Church should be above vindictiveness.

Strangely, it was on this night that she first cried, not because Donald had once again evaded loving her and was now gently snoring, but because she had a feeling that she couldn't sort out. It was as if she had lost something.

It was in the spring of 1937, when Grace had been married ten months, that Uncle Ralph spoke to Aunt Susie, and Aunt Susie thought they had better consult Aunt Aggie and see what she had to say about the matter. So they got together and talked about the subject nearest to their hearts. The matter was so serious that they did not start on their high tea before they took it up. Uncle Ralph came straight to the point as he stuck his thumb down into the broad bowl of his pipe, saying, 'Well, Aggie, let's have your opinion of her.'

'What do you want me to say?'

Both Ralph and Susie looked at her and Ralph said, 'We want to know what you think'; and Susie put in, 'Is she pregnant, Aggie?'

'Not that I know of.' Aggie turned her gaze on them both.

'She talks to you, Aggie,' said Susie, her lips a little prim now. 'She's always talked to you more than to me, or even to her own mother. Linda used to say that.'

'She may talk to me,' said Aggie, 'but she tells me nothing that she doesn't tell everybody she meets, and that is that she has the most wonderful husband in the world.'

'Well, I just don't know what to make of her.' Ralph lit his pipe for the third time. 'She's jittery, Aggie; she's not the girl she was last this time, and she's as thin as a rake.'

'Have you thought of speaking to him?' asked Susie.

'What!' Aggie rounded on her sister-in-law. 'You mean me to talk to him and ask him what's wrong with his wife?'

Susie had risen to her feet, and her head was up and her chest was up and her chin out as she said in a tone that could only be termed huffy, 'Well, you needn't bawl at me, Aggie; it was only a suggestion. Why' – she looked at her husband – 'you would think I had asked her to commit a crime.'

She turned her back on Aggie, and Aggie said, 'Oh, don't take it like that, Susie; it was never meant like that. But it was the suggestion that I should talk to him. Why, I could no more do that than I could fly across the Tyne. You might as well know that I don't like him any more than I did afore she married him. I thought I might, but no. I put on a front for her now, and on the surface everything looks all right, but I've never liked the fellow, and I never will and that's the truth of it. But I don't want to be prejudiced. He seems to think the world of her and she of him. Nevertheless, now that we are on the subject, I can tell you that I feel, and I've felt it for months . . . there's something wrong somewhere.'

Both Susie and Ralph stared at Aggie. That she had admitted to feeling there was something wrong was to them paramount to stating the actual cause, which from their expression could have been some dread disease.

The outcome of the meeting was that Ralph must speak to Donald. But Ralph did not like this idea at all. Donald was a nice chap, none better. He paid little heed to Aggie's opinion of him; women had prejudices against men, it meant nothing. Vaguely he thought Aggie's opinion of Donald was mixed up in some way with him being a strapping handsome fellow while her own man had been a little titch of a bloke. A live wire doubtless, but he hadn't been a figure of a man that would attract a woman. Yet he had attracted Aggie, or had she just taken him because she was getting on and chances were few and far between for her at the time? It was a deep question this; the further you got into it the more muddled you became. He was back to where he started: Aggie was prejudiced.

During the following week Ralph dropped in to Willow Lea and he had a chat with Donald on the quiet, the result of which left him with the impression that Donald, too, was worried about his wife. His manner at first had been stiff and evasive and suggested to Ralph that this was his house and what happened in it was his concern alone. Yet before very long he was admitting that yes, he had been a trifle worried over Grace losing weight and energy during the last few months. But no, he could not give any reason for it. He had added that her happiness was his one concern and he spent his private life solely with that concern.

Ralph's report took the line that Donald was a grand chap, and if there was anything wrong it didn't stem from him. Donald, he said, had suggested a number of times that she see the doctor, but Grace had pooh-poohed the idea. However, now he meant to insist.

Later, when Susie and Aggie were alone together, Susie commented knowledgeably, 'It's the first year. Things are often difficult, you know, in the first year.' She made this remark as though Aggie had never been married, but Aggie let it pass. . . .

Donald, true to his word, arranged that Grace saw the doctor; in fact he forestalled any opposition on her part by telling her that Dr Cooper was coming that very afternoon to look her over. He made this statement with studied casualness across the dinner table and showed no reaction to Grace's defiant rejoinder, 'Well, he can go away again; I won't see him.'

'Don't be childish, Grace . . . please don't be so childish.'

Grace lowered her eyes towards her plate. She had an almost uncontrollable desire to jump up and beat her fist on the table and yell at him, 'I don't want a doctor, you know I don't need a doctor, you know what's wrong with me.' The thought when it reached this point acted as a shock and steadied her, and her mind gabbled hastily, 'Oh dear, dear God, don't let me think such things.' She raised her eyes and looked at the crown of his bent head, the hair falling away in shining waves, without a streak of grey anywhere. It looked strong and virile, he looked all strength and virility, and yet . . . The heat enveloped her neck, it spread upwards to her face and downwards to her waist and again it brought a feeling of shame to her. In contrition she wanted to spring up and fling herself on him and say, 'Kiss me. Oh kiss me, darling.' She knew that he would kiss her, he never kept her short of kisses, but they were kisses without fire, bloodless kisses, passionless kisses. . . . Yes, that was the word: passionless kisses.

For over three hundred nights she had slept with Donald and his kisses were withering something in her, that something that had been wonderful, beautiful. Its going was stripping the flesh from her bones; she had lost eighteen pounds in weight in the last few months. This thing that was dying in her had the symptoms of a disease, and she felt, and not hysterically or morbidly but knowledgeably, that she could die of it; if she didn't do something soon she could die of it. Yet the cure did not lie in her hands, it lay in his.

She watched him now as he excused himself and rose from the table, and he turned his back to her as he said, 'You'll remember that I go into Durham this afternoon for the meeting. I don't know what time I'll be back, maybe about seven. It's a glorious day, perhaps you'll feel like a walk after seeing the doctor.'

She heard her own voice saying quite calmly, 'Yes, I think I'll take a walk over the fells.'

He was winding his wrist-watch as he said, 'But you'll wait until he comes, won't you, Grace?' It was an order put over in the form of a request, and she answered flatly, 'Yes, I'll wait until he comes.'

It didn't matter whether she saw Dr Cooper or not, he couldn't do anything for her. . . .

David Cooper walked into the house unannounced about three o'clock. He had, over the past few months, been a number of times to Willow Lea to play bridge, and the vicar and Grace had visited his home a few times. These were social visits, return courtesy visits, when everyone was on his best behaviour, when it would have been practically impossible for a doctor or even a psychiatrist to get underneath the façade, yet he knew things weren't right with the vicar's wife. To him she was a high-spirited girl who was being clamped down. She wanted an outlet; a family would be the solution. That was likely the whole root of her present trouble. He had wanted to ask the vicar about this when he had suggested looking her over, but he found it difficult to talk to him. There was a reserve that emanated from him, together with his manner of always taking charge of a situation that was very . . . off-putting. The vicar, the doctor thought wryly to himself, was the man who was always the interviewer and never the interviewed.

'Hello there!' He stood in the centre of the hall calling, his eyes moving between the elegant drawing-room and the stairs, and when Grace appeared at the stair head he said again, 'Hello there!'

'Hello,' she said, and as she came down the stairs she wagged her finger playfully at him, 'Renee is always telling me how busy you are, and this is a sheer waste of time.'

'Yes, I think it is myself.'

'There you are then, so why bother?'

'Simply because I'm being paid for it. I've got to eat, and a wife to support, and with quads due in two

85

months' time I just can't afford to turn down offers like this, easy money. . . . Where are you going, upstairs or downstairs?'

'Quads.' She had to laugh. Then she turned from him, adding, 'Upstairs, in my lady's chamber I suppose.'

Not more than ten minutes later he was putting his stethoscope back into his case and Grace was asking from the dressing-room, 'Well, am I going to die and you're afraid to tell me?'

Some seconds passed before he answered and then he said, 'There's nothing wrong with your body that I can see . . . what's on your mind?'

There was no answer to this, and a few more minutes elapsed before Grace came into the bedroom. She was fastening the belt of her dress and she asked, 'What do you mean?'

David Cooper puckered his face up, and, giving an impatient shake of his head, said, 'Don't let us stall, Grace. You're worrying about something. Come on, let's have it.'

'Worrying?' Her eyebrows moved up in surprise as she stared him full in the face. 'What would I have to worry about?'

'You tell me.' He was returning her stare. 'Do you want a family?' He watched her blink, then lower her gaze from him as she said, 'Of course I want a family; every woman does – at least most do. Is there anything wrong in that?'

'No, that's definitely the right outlook . . . Does Donald want a family?'

'Well . . . ' She turned away. 'Yes . . . yes, I suppose so.'

He looked at her as she walked towards the window, and said quietly, 'Do you mean to say you've never discussed this?'

'There's been no need, it's understood.' In the silence that followed her remark she thought, 'Of course it's understood. Love and marriage were for the sole purpose of creating souls, hadn't Donald said that?' . . . Oh – she closed her eyes and chided herself – she must stop this way of thinking about Donald.

Dr Cooper left the matter where it was and came to her side as she stood looking down into the garden, and after a moment he remarked, 'There's old Ben still at it. He's aged since he lost Miss Tupping.'

'Has he?' Grace turned to him. 'Of course, I wouldn't know; he looks the same to me as when I first saw him. I like Ben.'

'I'm glad you do. He's a funny old fellow but as straight as a die. He had one interest in life and that was his mistress. They were more like father and daughter.'

'Father and daughter? I've always been under the impression that Miss Tupping was old.'

'Not old as people go, she was only about forty-five.'

'Really?'

'Yes. She was under sentence of death when she had this house built, you know, and she started on the garden expecting to give it the last year of her life. The earth repaid her and gave her nine more years. She was my first patient, and I had to pass sentence on her. . . . And the day she died I found Ben lying on the ground behind the greenhouse crying into the earth.'

Grace made no comment. The picture the doctor conjured up before her was too deep and sad for comment. She looked down on the stooped back of the old man and asked what seemed an irrelevant question. 'Why have you stayed here all these years?'

'Because it's a healthy place.'

'Healthy?' She turned her head towards him again, her eyes narrowed. The way she had repeated the word healthy conveyed a question which might have been interpreted as having said, 'What have doctors to do with healthy places? It was in the unhealthy places, surely, that they were needed.'

He lifted his gaze to the beech that bordered the lawn and replied, 'Renee's had T.B. She went down with it the first year we were married.'

Again she could find no comment. She had never guessed that Renee had been ill, she looked strong and robust and so boisterously happy now that she was having her first child after ten years of marriage.

Renee had infected her with all the excitement about the coming baby. That was until the last few weeks, when she had come to think of her new friend with something that could only be called envy. But now she was filled with contrition and not a little shame. Renee with T.B. and Ben lying on the ground crying. Why had David told her these things – to take her mind off herself? Well, whatever his reason it had certainly achieved something, for she felt better, not so deflated. She had a sudden longing to be alone, to make new resolutions to herself, resolutions concerning patience and understanding, resolutions to think less about herself and her own feelings and more about . . . Donald and his needs. . . . But what were his needs? This last was flung at her from a section of her mind that had become surprisingly analytical in the last month. This section would tear things apart and present them to her and say, 'Stop hoodwinking yourself.' Once it had said, 'Tell Aunt Aggie,' and she cried at it, 'What! Do you think I'm mad?' This section was becoming rather frightening, for it was taking on a permanency and almost creating another personality, so much so that she referred to it as a separate person, at times saying to herself, 'Take no notice.' Once it had frightened her by saying, 'Aunt Aggie was right, you know. He didn't want the actual money, just the things the money could buy. Look at what he's had lately, that rigging out of the choir boys, the new hassocks, chairs for the church hall, and now he's touting for the five hundred to close the subscriptions for the screen. Well, I'll see him in—'

'Shss! Shss!' she admonished the voice that was an echo of her father's.

'What are you going to do with yourself this afternoon?' said the doctor.

'I thought of having a walk on the fells.'

'Good idea. The higher you get, the better the air. Walk until you're tired. How are you sleeping?'

'Not too well.'

'I'll send up some tablets for you, just enough for two or three nights. It's a habit you know, this sleeping business.'

'Everything's a habit.'

He was at the door now and he turned and looked at her for a moment, then nodded and said with a smile, 'Yes, you're right there; even living is just a series of habits.'

The doctor gone, Grace went upstairs again and changed her shoes and picked up a coat. Then she crossed the landing to the storeroom. A door from this room led to an outside staircase which had two purposes: that of a fire escape and an easy means of carrying the fruit into the house. This side of the house, which was the back, was accessible to the orchard. Last year, under Ben's direction, she had packed the fruits away.

As she passed the greenhouses she hailed Ben, and he came to the door and, looking from her light coat to the sky, he said, 'You makin' for the fells, ma'am?'

'Yes, Ben.'

'Ah well then, I wouldn't go far.'

'No?' She looked at him in surprise. 'And it such a beautiful day?'

'Aye, yes now. Be different in an hour or so's time. Look over there.' He pointed over the top of the trees to a small group of harmless-looking clouds, and he added, 'That's a sure sign. Bet you what you like we have rain afore we have tea.'

'Oh, don't say that, Ben.'

'I do, ma'am, so be careful.'

'I will, Ben, but I'll be back before tea.'

'Do that, ma'am, do that.' He nodded and gave her what was to him a smile.

She let herself out through the gate, and within a few minutes was in the wood taking the path that she had first come to know when she had walked behind Andrew MacIntyre.

It was strange, she sometimes thought, that she had seen Andrew MacIntyre twice on that one day and only twice since. The first time was on the road above the village. He was in a field which was somewhat higher than the road and his head was on the level with Adelaide Toole's as she sat on her horse. They were both laughing and she remembered that they looked young and happy. She remembered also that after seeing them she was left with a feeling of loneliness, not because they looked and sounded happy but, strangely, because they were young. Adelaide was her own age, yet she had felt old enough on that day to be her mother, for it was a day following a night when she had cried herself to sleep. Adelaide had greeted her cheerily on that occasion, but Andrew MacIntyre had not spoken, he had merely inclined his head towards her and his face had taken on a sober look, but only until she had passed on. She knew this because she had not gone far along the road before their joined laughter came to her again.

The next time she had seen him was one day not more than a fortnight ago. She had passed the cottage on the fells at least a dozen times since the autumn and had seen no-one at all, but this day they were all outside looking at something on the road, Mr and Mrs MacIntyre and Andrew MacIntyre, and when she came up to them she saw that it was a small terrier bitch with puppies. A different scene from that which she had come upon the first day she had passed the house, for now the mother and son were laughing at the antics of the pups and the father was looking on. Mr MacIntyre she saw should have been a tall man, but he was very bent and stood with the aid of a stick. His body looked like that of an old man but his face was that of a man in his fifties. Neither Mrs MacIntyre nor Andrew had introduced him to her, and after passing the time of day with them, and remarking on the sweetness of the puppies, she had continued on her way feeling as if she had trespassed on their property. They were using the road as if it was their garden, and she was left with the impression that she had walked through it without asking permission.

She now climbed up through the wood until she reached the flint road, and here she hesitated as she had done once or twice before when she had the desire to explore the quarry, really explore it. She had been as far as the end of the road and looked over the barbed wire into the vast crater that the workings had left. The water in it, the accumulation of the rainfall of years, was blackish and forbidding, and it had always checked her adventurous desire to walk round the perimeter of the quarry or to find out if there was even a way around it, for from the end of the road there was no sign of a path. Yet from her first visit she knew that someone went into the quarry, for in one place the barbed wire had been pressed down to make easier access.

So today when she looked at the wire she thought, 'Where one can go another can' and she was under the wire and in the enclosure of the quarry before the thought had finished in her mind.

Once over the wire fence she stopped. It was strange, but she had the feeling that everything was different on this side of the wire; it was as if the quarry had no connection with the wood. The atmosphere in the wood was soothing; here only a few steps within the wire, she felt a surge of unrest, even fear. When she found herself half turning towards the wire again, she murmured aloud, saying, 'Don't be silly' and then, surprised at the sound of her own voice, she closed her eyes and smiled.

There was no possible way of her getting to the edge of the crater from where she stood, for bracken, bush and bramble had entwined to make an impregnable barrier at least thirty feet wide, and only because this sloped downwards could she see the water. And from this distance she guessed she must be looking almost into the middle of the quarry.

The only way clear enough for walking was by the wire fencing, and this did not lead to the quarry but away from it. Yet she had only followed it for some yards when she saw to the left of her the narrow cutting in the wall of bracken. It was just wide enough for one person to walk through, and as she stood looking at it there came to her again the feeling of fear, but this time it was intensified and she had the urge to turn like a frightened child and dash out of the enclosure.

Was the land boggy and this feeling a warning? Tentatively she put her foot among the grasses, but the ground felt rock-like. Hesitating no more, she entered the path. Although it was open to the sky, it seemed dark inside. She walked quietly and slowly, wondering with a quickening of her heart beats what she would find round the next corner, for the path twisted and turned continuously until it came abruptly to an end.

She was now looking on to what appeared to be a small lake. The water was still. There was no life to be seen on its surface and no indication of any underneath. Between her and the water's edge lay about ten feet of baked mud and this stretched away for some distance, looking for all the world like a deserted beach. At the far end there rose, almost vertical, a wall of rock jutting out towards the water. It was as clean and bare as if it had just recently been sliced. There were boulders of rock mounting one on top of the other to the right of her, and her only path now seemed to be the mud beach. Fascinated, she walked along it towards where it skirted the wall of rock.

There was not more than two feet between the water and the point of the rock and she had her eyes cast down on the water as she rounded the point. And then her hand came up across her mouth to stifle her exclamation of surprise. There, not a couple of yards from her, lay Andrew MacIntyre. His hands behind his head, his eyes were closed as if he was asleep. But she hadn't time to wonder or make her retreat, for the next instant he was on his feet and staring at her. . . . They remained gaping at each other until she gabbled, 'I . . . I'm sorry. I . . . I didn't know. . . .' As she had felt she was trespassing through his garden when she had walked down the road past his house, now she had almost the feeling that she had barged into his bedroom. He and his family seemed to create a privacy about them that was most disconcerting.

'I was out for a walk.' She was still trying to explain.

His blank silence was unnerving, and she was on the point of turning with what dignity she could muster and making her escape when he spoke, and the tone of his voice brought an immediate show of relief to her face, for he said, 'Don't go, please don't go. You see, I thought you were a sort of . . . of apparition.' His voice was so quiet, his expression so gentle, his manner so easy, that for a moment she didn't think she was looking at the dour Andrew MacIntyre.

'You see, very few people find their way around here.'

'Yes, yes' – her laugh was nervous and high – 'I can understand that . . . it's a weird kind of place.' She looked up to the wall of rock that towered above them. Then, turning her gaze to the water, she said, 'It's a wonder people don't come here to swim.'

'It smells too much when it's stirred up.'

'Really?' She was looking at him again. 'It's a pity. Well' – she smiled up at him – 'I must go and leave you to your reading.' She glanced at the book lying on the ground. 'I'm sorry I disturbed you.'

'You didn't disturb me.' His voice had changed, it was as if he was contradicting her now. And then he added, 'I was just about to make my way homewards, anyway.'

She watched him bend over and pick up the book, and as he straightened up she turned away and went round the point of the rock again.

They walked along the mud beach, and when they came to the narrow, bramble-walled passage, he led the way, and it was very like the day he had shown her and Aunt Aggie the short cut down to the back gate, for she was looking at his back and he was silent now as he had been then. It wasn't until he lifted the wire up to allow her easier passage through into the wood that she made herself speak, and then she asked, 'Are you going to the farm now?'

He shook his head. 'No; this is my day off, I wouldn't be here else. The quarry is only for high days and holidays . . . or when you want to escape and be by yourself.'

'Oh, I'm sorry.'

'I didn't mean that.' His face was dead straight.

'It's all right. I understand.'

'Look. Look here.' He was bending slightly towards her. 'You don't understand.'

'Yes. Yes, I do.'

'No you don't.' His brows were drawn together, his voice was harsh, and now his face looked not only dour but grim. 'There are times when you want to get away from people – not all people – just . . . just some people . . . and I wouldn't have said that if . . . '

As he hesitated she put in quickly, 'Well, that's what I mean, that's what I understand, the desire to get away from some particular . . . people.' She had nearly said particular person. She understood how he felt all right . . . oh, she understood perfectly, and her knowledge made her fearful.

She was looking intently at him, and becoming aware of a number of things at once: that his expression had changed yet again and his whole face now looked gentle; that he had a nice mouth; that he never addressed her as Mrs Rouse or ma'am; that he was young, and strangely was making her feel young, even younger than him; and, lastly, that here was someone who would kow-tow, or bow, to no-one, and that was why Donald didn't like him. It was this last thought that dragged her wandering mind and feelings abruptly into line again.

She had a strong desire now to get away from him, even to run. She conquered this by assuming an air of sedateness, and as she pulled her eyes from his face and moved away she said, 'Ben says it will rain before tea.'

He was behind her now, but keeping at a distance, as his voice told her when he answered after a pause, 'He's right.'

When they came to where the stone road ended she turned to him and said with stiff politeness, 'Well, goodbye.'

He was standing some yards from her, his deep brown eyes looking almost black. 'Goodbye,' he said.

They both seemed to turn away simultaneously, he going up the steep incline that led towards his home, and she cutting across the hillside towards the main road.

When she reached the road she did not go down to the village but skirted it and came out near the little cemetery that backed the church.

There was no-one in the cemetery and the vestry door was closed, but the main door was open and she went in and walked between the six stone pillars of the chancel, then turned towards the alcove where the little side altar was, the children's altar. And here, on the single wooden kneeler, she knelt and with her hands tightly clasped and her head down she prayed, prayed earnestly. And as she prayed, Ben's promised rain began to beat on the roof.

Andrew MacIntyre had not taken more than a dozen long strides when he stopped and, turning abruptly, watched, from his vantage point, the vicar's wife scurrying along the path between the trees towards the main road.

He'd never had such a surprise in his life . . . never. To be thinking of her, then to open his eyes and see her standing dead in front of him. It had shaken him. Why had she come into the quarry? It must have been her first visit, and he could take it for an omen. He had gone in there to decide for good and all what he must do. He had come to the point where he had made up his mind that the madness that was growing in him must be cut out; for it could lead nowhere. There was a 'gift horse' waiting for him to saddle. He had known for two years now what was in Adelaide's mind, but had made no move in that direction, not only because of her father, and the hell he might kick up, but because Adelaide herself aroused nothing more in him than sincere liking. Even now, when he sensed that old Toole had had it out with Adelaide and she had brought him round to her way of thinking and he might even welcome him in the uplifting capacity of son-in-law, even this could not make him see Adelaide in the light of a wife.

Although he had worked for Toole for years he had never felt inferior to him – and that was another thing that made life and the future difficult, for he considered his own mother a better woman in all ways than his master's wife. His mother had been educated, whereas Mrs Toole had at one time gone to the village school. Of course everybody tried to forget this, but would they forget he was a farm labourer if he aspired to Adelaide Toole. As for his father – on this thought Andrew's lip curled back from his teeth – if it wasn't for him they wouldn't be in the position they were today. For himself it didn't much matter . . . he could fend . . . but his mother, tied up there for life. Why did women do it? Why? Was some part of them mentally blind? Her, too. He could now only pick out the colour of Grace's dress as she jumped the ditch to the main road, but her face was vividly before him. She was different from anyone he had ever come across, sweet and kind, and intelligent. You only had to listen to her to know that. Yet she had picked a fellow like Rouse. . . . Parson! Psss! Big-headed nowt! With that air of authority as from God himself. His stomach had turned the first time they had met. He had wanted to start an argument with him, to tie him up with the flaws in his own doctrine . . . and he could have done just that. Hadn't he been brought up on the Bible? So much so that he had, as a child, thought that his father had written the book. But this was getting him nowhere. Recriminations were useless, he had learnt that too. The main thing was that she was unhappy . . . he knew she was unhappy. What was he to do? What could he do? Would she be like his mother and go on all her life suffering because it was her duty . . . ? God, no!

3

Miss Shawcross had come to tea. She was sitting in the drawing-room to the side of Grace and opposite Donald, and Donald was playfully chaffing her. Donald was always playful with Miss Shawcross; it could be said he treated her like a beloved sister. It certainly couldn't be anything else. This thought brought Grace's cup to shake gently in its saucer, but not with laughter.

'Can you see us all running over the fells taking pot-shots at the German parachutists?'

Miss Shawcross made a sound that was a cross between a laugh and a giggle; it was a sound that irritated Grace.

'But there' – Donald's voice was serious now – 'I mustn't joke about this matter, war's no joking matter at all, and if the worst comes to the worst we will undoubtedly all do our bit. . . . Now about the rota, Kate.' He leant forward. Then his jocularity returning, he said, 'But have a piece of this sandwich cake, it will give you strength for the battle.'

Kate Shawcross's laugh filled the room. She laughed, with her eyes closed and her head down. She stopped laughing as abruptly as she had started, then, taking from her bag a sheet of foolscap paper, she began to explain the rota.

Grace sat looking at them as they earnestly made their arrangements for their part in the coming war. It was early in September, 1938. War was in the air. Any minute now it seemed that England would be at war: they had already been issued with gas-masks, and there was talk of digging holes in the ground and sleeping in them. The thought of war did not frighten her except when her mind settled on children. Grown-ups could fend for themselves, but children, especially the little children, like those in the Infants in the village school. . . . She did not question that her concern for the children was because her mind was thinking of nothing else these days. Children, children . . . a child. What if she had a child and it was killed by a bomb. She shuddered from head to foot, then became strangely still as a voice said from within her, 'I'd chance it.'

She looked at Donald again. His face was serious now, beautiful and serious. No wonder Kate Shawcross could not take her eyes from him. She was being talked about in the village for running after the vicar, but that did not seem to trouble her, she seemed oblivious of everything in life but this man.

The feeling of annoyance, scorn, and even jealousy that Grace had felt at different times over the past two years towards this woman had vanished as if they had never been. Now she had for her another feeling. It was pity. For Miss Shawcross was in love with a shell . . . a shell filled with God. There was no room for a woman inside that shell, except as a mother or a doll. . . . Donald was a man with a doll. She herself was the doll, sometimes to be kissed, fondled . . . and forever frustrated.

This time last year she had come to look upon God as her rival for Donald. This feeling had gone on for some months and had been a terrifying experience. One could not pit oneself against God and yet she had attempted to do just that. Thankfully it was brought to a sudden end one day when Donald took her on a visit to a friend of his in Harrogate. This man was also a parson. He was a good man, it showed in his face, and he had seven children . . . men could be men of God and still men.

She had been married to Donald seven hundred and eighty-four nights. This way of thinking worried her. She didn't think she had been married just over two years, she counted the time in nights. And each night now seemed to bring fresh terror to her, for she would lie awake seeing one more new aspect of the man by her side. She had faced the fact many months ago that Donald was a man who should never have married. One fear-filled night she had almost turned on him and shaken him out of his sleep to cry at him, 'You have committed a sin, you who are always preaching against sin; you have committed the worst sin against human nature. Do you hear me?' She had got up that night and crept from the room and went, of all places, into the storeroom because there she could open the door and look out into the night without fear of anyone seeing her. Although each night she dissected him and looked at his lack and weaknesses, she was still in love with him. She knew that he had a vindictive streak in him, submerged but nevertheless there. She knew that he had a cunning knack of getting his own way. She knew also that he used the pulpit to strike, and not only in the defence of God. No-one could answer you back when you were in the pulpit. Yet she felt that in part he was a good man, never ceasing to go out of his way to help someone. Perhaps it was more correct to say, he got others to do that. Anyway, she supposed organisation was part of his job.

'And where are you going to put this big brawny piece?' Donald put out his large white hand and touched Grace's face.

Miss Shawcross turned her eyes from the vicar and, looking at Grace, said, 'Oh, I haven't put you down anywhere because of you not feeling too well.'

'But we can't have this, she's got to do her bit.' Donald was looking tenderly towards Grace, patting her hand the while. 'We'll have to put her on the diplomatic staff, eh?'

Miss Shawcross laughed at this and Grace said, 'Can I fill your cups?'

Fifteen minutes later Donald left the house with Miss Shawcross. He was going to visit the Tooles, as Mrs Toole was in bed with phlebitis.

Long after they had gone Grace sat in the drawing-room, staring out through the french windows into the garden. She knew she had reached a point where something must be done. She could not go on like this any longer, she must speak to Donald, come out into the open. Aunt Aggie had said to her only last week, 'Isn't it time you started a family?' And she had made no answer to this. A few months previously she would have come up with some excuse such as, 'Oh, there's plenty of time for that.' And then there was Dr Cooper saying, 'You know you can't live on tonics. Nature is a tonic and you've got to use her.' He had paused before he added, 'You understand what I'm saying?' She had nodded. Yes, she had understood perfectly what he was saying and tonight she was not going to be baulked. It wasn't that she hadn't tried to bring the matter into the open a number of times, but whenever Donald felt that the subject was broaching he kissed, patted and teased and put the situation on ground from which it was impossible to say, 'I want a baby'. But tonight she would close her ears to his prattle. She turned her head slightly to the side on this thought. It made her sad to realise that she could think along these lines, terming Donald's beautifully modulated words as prattle.

*

At seven o'clock Donald had not returned and she went out into the garden in search of Ben. Ben had no set hours, and Grace found that when in the old man's company she forgot herself and her worries. Perhaps it was because that in character he was closest to the men amongst whom she had been brought up, those on the Tyne. From Ben she saw reflected traces of her father and Uncle Ralph, and old Jack Cummings.

She found Ben clipping the top of a lonicera hedge. Without any formal greeting he addressed her immediately, saying, 'He said take two feet off this.' He never gave Donald any other title but 'he'. 'If I was to take two feet off un you would see the top of the tool-shed from the front drive. 'Twouldn't do, an' I told him.' He turned his small bright eyes on her. 'See what I mean, ma'am?'

'Yes, Ben. Yes, I do.' Then she asked enquiringly, 'The vicar said he wanted two feet off?'

'Aye, this afternoon just gone, he came out here and said it should be taken down altogether. Too dark green he said it was . . . did you ever hear the like, too dark green? Why, I never did. And I pointed out to him that it's the darkness of this here hedge that acts as a background for the lavender and such.' He pointed to the side, and Grace, looking towards the bushes, said, 'Yes, yes, I see.'

'Miss Tuppin' planted this hedge, ma'am, because it was quick growin'. "We don't want to see the roof of that black shed from the drive, do we, Ben?" she said. And I said, "No, ma'am, we don't want that." "Lonicera is the thing," she said, "it's quick," and there she put it.'

Ben was talking easily about his late mistress these days and Grace knew it brought some solace to him to be able to do so. She also felt that she was the only one to whom he talked in this way and she gave him the opportunity whenever she could.

103

'Ma'am.'

'Yes, Ben?'

'Only yesterday I came across a recipe of me mother's, it was for reviving an appetite. It's a mixture of herbs and I brought it along for you.' Ben did not look at Grace as he spoke but went on cutting slowly and expertly at the hedge. 'I remember me mother sayin' it would make a man eat like a horse.'

He stopped now and, laying down the shears, drew from his pocket a square of yellowed paper. Opening it slowly, he handed it to Grace.

In the swift glance she gave the paper she made out the words dandelion and rosemary. Then she looked at him and said softly, 'Thank you, Ben, it's very kind of you.'

'Well, what I say is' – Ben was at the hedge again – 'these new-fangled medicines . . . well, you might as well drink dish-wattar. The old recipes are lost or forgotten an' so people die.' His voice sank on the last words and Grace knew he was thinking of his beloved mistress, and she wanted to say, 'But you kept her alive for nine years, Ben . . . you and the garden,' but all she said was, 'Thank you, Ben'; then added, 'I'll have it made up, I promise you.'

He did not turn towards her, not even to nod, and she walked slowly away reading the prescription that was to make her eat like a horse. Oh, Ben, dear Ben, it wasn't herbs that she needed to put on flesh.

She stopped and looked around the garden, then looked towards the back of the house. She should be as happy as a princess in a fairy tale; in this atmosphere she should be relaxed and at ease, her body should be afloat and in harmony, whereas it was a mass of jangling nerves, and only needed a sharp word to set the tear ducts quivering. With a sudden spurt she ran towards the house, through the hall, and up the stairs into her room, and, throwing herself face down on the bed, she cried into her hands. Why had this to happen to her? She wasn't bad, she wasn't wicked, she only wanted . . . she only wanted . . . wanted . . . wanted. Her brain was yelling the word, 'wanted . . . wanted . . . wanted.' Then as her fists clutched up handfuls of the eiderdown, it added on a voiceless scream, 'To be loved . . . to be loved. . . .'

Donald did not get back until just on dusk. From her bedroom window she watched him coming up the drive. When he did not come in the front door but skirted the house, she knew without bothering to ascertain that he had gone to look at the hedge to see if Ben had carried out his orders. Tomorrow there would be words and a battle of wills between them. There had been words before when Ben had usually emerged the victor, and doubtless he would do so again, and in her heart she was with him. Not because he was right in this case as he had been in most of the others, but because it hurt her somehow to see him ordered about in what was, spiritually at least, his garden, and, moreover, he was an old man. It was odd, she thought, at this moment, that Donald never brought his Christian attitude to bear with Ben, and he should have done so, if only to try to get him to attend the services.

She reached the hall just as Donald entered it. She did not fly to him now as she had once done and fling her arms about his neck. She saw immediately that he was annoyed, very likely with Ben, but when they got into the drawing-room it was not of Ben he spoke but of the Tooles. Mrs Toole wasn't well at all and she was worried about Adelaide. Apparently things weren't going as they should with Adelaide. It was all to do with that MacIntyre fellow. They had been like second parents to that boy. Mr Toole had gone so far as to indicate to him that he would be welcome as a son-in-law, but the fool had done nothing about it. It was hurting both Mr and Mrs Toole, not to say anything about Adelaide.

She went and stood in front of him, and, catching hold of his hands, brought his attention to her. 'Donald . . . Donald, I . . . ' Here she stopped and her heart gave a number of thumping beats before she finished, 'I would like to talk to you.'

Did she see a shadow come over his eyes, or was it that he was still feeling annoyed with Ben? It was his way when annoyed about one thing to talk about something entirely different . . . this was another trait that she had reluctantly been forced to recognise.

He released one of his hands from hers and, putting it to his brow, said, 'Yes, yes, of course,' then added, 'you don't have to ask like that . . . like . . . like a parishioner. If you can't talk to me, who can you talk to?' He followed this in the very next breath by saying, 'Is there any coffee on hand? My head is thumping – it's the heat, I think.'

Slowly she released his hand and without a word turned from him and went into the kitchen. Taking the percolator from the stove she placed it on the tray that was standing ready and carried it back into the drawing-room, and there she poured him out a cup of coffee before sitting down.

The coffee finished, he lay back in the chair, stretched out his legs, and sighed. Then with eyes closed he said, 'Now, my dear, what is it you want to say?'

Her body felt cold and rigid. Could one look at a man sitting in a chair with his eyes closed and his legs stretched out and say, 'I want a baby . . . come up to bed and love me, I want a baby,' or words to that effect?

Her silence brought his eyes open but he did not move. 'Is it important?'

'Yes.'

He closed his eyes again and remained motionless, and she continued to look at him. His body seemed to have spread over the chair; she did not see it as a beautiful body any more. It was soft and flabby, even fat in parts. It was only when he was standing stiffly upright or striding along, his tails flying, that he gave the impression of an athlete. But she knew his body was no athlete's. She looked at his black-clothed legs and the thought came to her that she had never seen them without a covering of some sort, and only twice had her hands felt their bare flesh. . . . Were all marriages like this? No, no – she gave this answer emphatically to herself – all marriages could not be like this, or else the madhouses would be more full than they were now. This thought lifted her swiftly to her feet, and the movement brought his eyes open again and he stretched himself and said, 'Oh, I wish I hadn't anything more to do tonight. Well, my dear, come along, what is this important business you want to discuss?'

'I'll talk about it upstairs. Will you be long?'

'Only about half an hour.' He rose and came towards her. And now he put his arm about her shoulder and said, 'You go on up, I won't be long.'

Did the look on his face say he understood? Did it promise something? She stared intently at him for a moment before lowering her eyes. Then slowly disengaging herself from him, she picked up the tray and went out of the room. . . .

In spite of the balcony window being wide open the bedroom was hot and the air heavy. Her undressing was slow, for her mind was not on it. That is, not until she was on the point of picking up her nightdress from the bed, when her hand became still and she looked at the bundle of drooping voile. She looked at it for quite a

107

long while before releasing it from her hand and turning round. And now she began to walk about the room as she had never done before. It was a strange feeling to walk about like this, unclothed. Back and forward, up and down she walked. And as she walked she listened, and just after the half hour was up she heard movements in the room below, followed by the sound of the front door being locked.

As she heard his steps mounting the stairs a tremor passed over her and she became still. She would time his steps across the landing, and when he opened the bedroom door she would be in the act of walking across the room. But when he opened the door she was sitting at the dressing-table, her naked back to him, and the entire front of her body gleaming at him through the mirror.

There are moments in a lifetime when all the five senses of the body are in agony at once. It is torture that dare not be repeated often. It is a torture that breaks the mind before the body. At such times you can smell your own humiliation, you can taste your own despair. You can feel the actual recoil of the other's revulsion. You can see the disgust squaring a mouth to leave the teeth bare. You can hear the hateful crying of self-denouncement.

Grace experienced this agony when through the mirror she met his look, for not only his expression but his whole body showed his reactions to her nakedness. It shrivelled her up. She couldn't endure it. It was as if he was being forced to look at some debauched creature. He looked like a trapped priest. As she clapped her hand over her mouth she cried through her fingers, 'Don't look at me like that!'

'I'd put your nightdress on; it ill becomes you to act in this way, Grace.'

Even before the deadly cold words were finished he had turned and closed the door, not quietly as was his wont but with a bang. With her hand still tightly pressed across her mouth she stared wildly into the mirror and she saw there, not her own flesh but a verse of Genesis:

'AND SHE CAUGHT HIM BY HIS GARMENT, SAYING, LIE WITH ME: AND HE LEFT HIS GARMENT IN HER HAND, AND FLED, AND GOT HIM OUT.'

He had looked at her as Joseph must have done on the wife of his Egyptian master . . . but she was no-one else's wife, she was his wife . . . but he didn't want a wife, not to lie with. She had clutched at his garment with her naked body and what had happened? He had got him out.

Oh God! Oh God! Her body dragged itself round away from the mirror, but although she stared about the room she could see nothing, for her vision was blurred. Yet she was not crying. She bent over and covered her face with her hands, 'Oh God! Oh God!'

She was still muttering 'Oh God! Oh God!' when she made a sudden rush towards her clothes and, tearing at them, began frantically to dress herself again.

When she had zipped the side of her dress up her movements stopped. Her two hands underneath her arm-pits, she looked down at the carpet and asked, 'Where will I go? Aunt Aggie's. . . . No, no.' But her Aunt Aggie would understand, she knew she would understand. Yet how could she put into words what she had done to bring about this situation? And would anyone understand this unbearable feeling of rejection . . . ? She couldn't go on, she couldn't. She was unclean. He had stamped her forever as something unclean.

She went through the storeroom without switching the light on, and when she ran down the iron steps to the garden the night appeared light in comparison. Hardly pausing in her running, she snatched the key to the garden gate from the nail just within the door of the greenhouse, and when she had unlocked the gate she did not stop to close it, or to remove the key, but ran across the narrow belt of grass and into the wood.

She had never been in the wood at night before, not even in the twilight, and if she had been in her right mind the darkness would have terrified her. But there was no room for terror in her at this moment, there was no room for anything but shame and a desire to be rid of it as soon as possible. She ran with her arms outstretched, warding off obstacles, and when she stumbled for the third time she went flat on the ground. As she lay breathless and dazed she imagined in the stillness all round her that she could hear the sound of footsteps. Still she was not frightened, only determined that the footsteps should never catch up with her.

She was running again and her feet told her when she had reached the stone road. She flew along it with a surety, as if she could see her way ahead, and she was at the wire fencing before she realised it, for its impact nearly knocked her on to her back. It was as she bent under the wire that she saw the light of a torch spreading into the trees, but she was in the enclosure and she knew that he would never find her here, not until she had done what she had come to do.

She had never told him about her visits to the quarry, she did not think he even knew of its existence. Once through the narrow lane of brambles she did not make for the mud beach but began to scramble over the shoulders up towards the top of the shelf of rock. At the far end there was a sixty-foot drop, and at the foot of the cliff there was no mud, just huge lumps of quarrying stone overgrown with bracken.

When the sharp stinging drops of rain hit her face, they pierced through the unbalanced state of her mind and brought her climbing to a gasping halt, and she thought for a moment with normal surprise, 'It's raining.' Then once again she was scrambling frantically upwards. She could hear quite clearly now the sound of Donald running, and she knew that her own footsteps were leading him to her, and she cried to herself, 'If he touches me I'll kill him, I'll kill him – kill him.'

When her feet reached the comparatively level ground on the top of the quarry the blackness, intensified by the rain, took all sense of her bearings from her and she ran this way and that not knowing in what direction the edge lay. When the torch flashed over her, she blinked into it before turning and rushing blindly away. A second later she was struggling like a wildcat. It was only when she realised that the arms that were holding her were hard, not soft and flabby, that she became still.

'There, there, you're all right. Go easy, don't be frightened.' The voice enfolded her, soothing her. She remained still against the man, her head resting on his shoulder until she began to shake as if with ague. A torrent of tears seemed to have solidified and blocked her throat, stopping her breath and causing her to heave as if she was being suffocated. When his voice came again, saying with deep gentleness, 'Don't be frightened, nothing can harm you', it was too much. She made a sound that could have come from an agonised animal before the tears spurted from her eyes, nose and mouth at the same time.

'There now, there now, don't, don't cry so. Look you're getting wet. Put this round you.' She felt him putting his coat over her shoulders, she felt herself being led back down over the boulders, and she was only vaguely aware that they had passed the rock point and the place where she had first seen him lying.

'Sit down here a minute, it's dry and out of the rain.' He lowered her to the ground, and when his hands left her she turned and lay on the earth and buried her face in her arms.

After some long time his voice forced its way to her, saying, 'No more now, no more. You'll make yourself ill. Come on, sit up.'

But she could not sit up. Her body was being rent apart with her weeping, and he said no more, only patted her gently until slowly, gradually, the turmoil subsided and she lay quiet and exhausted.

As she stared into the black inkiness of the earth, her mind began to settle and find its balance once more, and it came to her that she was lying up here in the quarry beside Andrew MacIntyre and that he must think her insane. Slowly she eased herself up into a sitting position and, her words checked by her jerking breath, she said softly, 'I . . . I don't know what . . . what to say. I don't know what you must think of me.'

'I think you're very unhappy.'

She felt herself jerk as if she had been prodded. She could not see him but she knew that his eyes were on her.

'You've been unhappy for a long time, haven't you?'

She felt her face stretching with amazement. Nobody had known how she felt, nobody had known that she was unhappy. She had seen to it that she had talked and laughed as usual, and Donald had seen to it that he was very sweet to her, even lovable, in public.

112

She heard her voice, hardly audible and still uneven with her sobbing breath, asking, 'How – how did you know that?'

'I've watched you.'

'Watched me?' She turned her face full in his direction, and now she could just make out the dark outline of him. She had not met him more than a dozen times since she had seen him lying on the beach here. That encounter would always remain in her memory, for it had driven her to church. She remembered praying that day that Donald would love her and that she would never stop loving him. She had never come across Andrew MacIntyre in the quarry since that day. She had only come here when, like him, she felt she would be alone. Her encounters with him had been on the road or at the Tooles' when she had seen him working on the farm.

'You're not happy with him, are you?'

As she had flown only a few minutes ago from the house she now wanted to fly away from this man.

'Why did you marry him?'

She heard herself saying softly, 'I loved him.'

'You thought you did.'

'You mustn't say such things.'

'Why? Because you're the parson's wife or because you won't face up to the truth?'

She felt his hand groping towards her, and when it covered hers she made no resistance.

'I don't know your name, your Christian name, they always call you Mrs Rouse up there. I've given you all kinds of names . . . what is it?'

Her mind was starting to whirl again but in a different atmosphere, and her voice was just a whisper as she said, 'Grace.'

'Grace.'

113

She shuddered and blinked in the dark, terrified now of something she couldn't name. She made an effort to get away from it by saying, 'I . . . I must get back,' but she made no move to rise. And then she asked, 'Why were you in the wood?'

'I was coming from work.' He paused, then said hastily and below his breath, 'No, that isn't true. I was standing on the edge of the wood – I often go down there – and I heard you running through the garden. I thought you were having a game with someone. You passed me not more than an arm's length away, and I waited to see who was after you, and when nobody came I knew you were in trouble. I think I knew it from the minute I heard you running.'

Her head was bowed low now as she asked, 'Why were you down there?'

There was another considerable pause before he gave her an answer, and then it was not to her question. 'That day you appeared round the bend there, I'd been thinking of you; I was thinking of you that very minute and I opened my eyes and there you stood. I'll never be able to explain what I felt then, but I can tell you now. I knew then what I had guessed from the first time I saw you: I knew you were for me, the only one for me, parson's wife or no.'

She knew a moment's horror and made to scramble to her feet, but his hand, without moving, held her to the ground. 'Don't be frightened – you have nothing to fear from me. Sooner or later you'd have to know. Things happen like this, no matter what people say, and it happened to me that day in your kitchen when I first set eyes on you.'

She turned her face towards him again and her expression was full of wonder now. This was Andrew MacIntyre, the dour Scot. He was talking with the ease which she attributed only to men like Donald, and he was telling her. . . . What was he telling her? That he was in love with her? Again she recalled the day she had run from the quarry through the woods to the church, and there came to her now the real reason for her praying. She, too, had known it then, but would not face it; she was the parson's wife and she loved her husband. But she was confronted with it now and some part of her still protested loudly: 'This mustn't happen. It is wrong, this mustn't go on. There must be nothing between me and Andrew MacIntyre. It would be a situation that would be unbearable. Andrew MacIntyre, Mr Toole's man . . . Andrew MacIntyre, a farm-worker . . . Andrew MacIntyre who lives in the little stone cottage on the fells . . . Andrew MacIntyre, who was dour, unsociable, taciturn and who wouldn't play the bagpipes at the musical evening.' On this last thought something faintly resembling a laugh passed through her, and she found herself turning her body towards him and allowing a breath of a whisper to say his name, 'Oh, Andrew.' The next minute she was enveloped in a storm of weeping again. When his arms went about her and she felt herself pressed close against him she did not protest in any way, and when a short while later she felt his mouth moving against her temple she said again, 'Oh, Andrew.' Of her own will she moved her mouth up to meet his. And when with a sudden jerk his body pressed hard against her and bore her sideways to the earth she did not shrink away.

The passionate abandon with which she gave herself to him both startled and elated her, and the knowledge that she was being loved brought compensation for her husband's rejection and gave her a shield to hold up against the look that the sight of her nakedness had brought to his face. She had, as it were, had a painful abscess lanced, and the relief was indescribable.

Somewhere at the height of the ecstatic, swirling pinnacle of released joy she thought that those lines in Genesis were being justifiably reversed. It was the Egyptian who would not lie with her, but Joseph had, and his cloak was over her and she knew he would never lift it from her.

4

'Oh, girl, what have you done? And I'm not referring to that MacIntyre fellow either, although I think he's a swine of the first water.'

'He's not, Aunt Aggie.' Grace brought her head up from its dropped position, 'He's not.'

'Well, I have me own opinion and I'm going to stick to it. But it's your life I'm referring to; you've made a mess of it, and I'm going to say right now I told you so. But there, it's done, and now there's no way out for you that I can see, for if I know Mr Donald there'll be no mention of divorce. He should never have married in the first place. I knew it, I had a feeling about it, but now that it's done he'll bring God on to his side and fasten you to him for life.'

'I don't care. I've made up my mind, I'm going to leave him.'

'And take up with this MacIntyre fellow?'

'Yes.' She was looking straight ahead.

'Is it all cut and dried?'

'No.' She turned and looked full at Aggie and her voice shook as she pleaded, 'Don't condemn me, Aunt Aggie; you don't know what it's been like.'

'Condemn you?' Aggie came swiftly forward and put her arms about her. 'Oh, lass, I'm not condemning you, I'm only sorry from the bottom of me heart that it needed to happen. The only criticism I've got to make is that I could wish you had gone off the rails with somebody nearer your own class. To take up with . . . with that

117

kind of fellow, and after the education you've had.'

Grace sighed. 'Don't forget, Aunt Aggie, after all Dad was a coalman.'

'He was nothing of the sort,' put in Aggie indignantly, 'not in that way. He managed his own business and was on a footing with men like old Arthur Wentworth, councillors and such. And there's Charlie Wentworth. There's not a time that I meet him but he asks after you.'

'You don't know Andrew MacIntyre, Aunt Aggie. He's . . . he's . . . ' she could not find the words with which to describe Andrew and his effect on her. She only knew now that the feeling she had for him had been breeding in her for some time and that it was different from anything she had felt for Donald. She could now look on the love she had borne Donald as a girlish infatuation; she could even term it a 'pash' on a parson. She leant against Aggie's high breast and released the breath from her lungs as she said, 'You've got no idea of the relief, Aunt Aggie, now that I've talked to you.'

'You should have done it earlier – I knew there was something wrong. There should be some way of stopping men like him marrying at all.'

Grace moved her head against Aggie, shutting out the light as she said, 'It was the look on his face; I don't think I'll ever forget it to my dying day.'

'Nonsense.' Aggie's body gave a quick wiggle of impatience. 'You can get that out of your head as soon as you like. He's no man, never was. I knew that from the minute I clapped eyes on him. Why, my Arthur never wore a thread of anything from the day we married, and I might as well tell you now I didn't either.'

Grace's eyes were closed but she could not conjure up a picture of her Aunt Aggie running around naked before her husband, but she could still see the look on Donald's face.

'That man's as full of pride and conceit as an egg's full of meat, and that's all he's full of, for the rest he's boast. I told you that right at the beginning: he's as empty as a watery turnip. . . . What did you tell him afore you left?'

'I just said I was coming to you. But I'm not going back, Aunt Aggie, I'm not. I can't, I just can't.'

'All right, all right, there's nobody forcing you. I'll phone and tell him that you're not feeling too good and you're staying the night, that'll give you a breathing space.' She stroked Grace's hair back from her temples and then added softly, 'Don't worry, child, things will straighten out. Rest yourself there till I put the car away.' She patted Grace's head, then added, 'There's one thing I'm thankful for and that is, Susie and Ralph are away. You won't be having any committee meeting on the matter and that's something.'

She smiled, but Grace could not return it. The committee meetings would eventually take place, they were merely being postponed. She sank deeper into the chair. Strangely now she found she was relaxed as she had not been since the day she became Grace Rouse. She no longer felt herself to be Grace Rouse, a parson's wife, and she could never again be Grace Cartner, the gullible, romantic-minded girl. Was she already Grace MacIntyre? Perhaps. Andrew had said last night that this kind of thing happened. Most people, nice people, would say that it didn't, not in a snap of the fingers like that. Yet it hadn't been a snap of the fingers, it had been maturing quietly for two years, justifying itself by some inward call that each had heard. Her call to him must have been loud and clear, for he recognised it and accepted it at once. He was much wiser than she. His wisdom was a natural part of himself and had nothing to do with learning. Last night, just before he had let her go, he had said, 'Tomorrow morning you will loathe yourself, but when you do, remember this: I love you, and no matter what happens I'll go on doing just that.' He had added with just a trace of humour, 'I'm not dour for nowt.'

How right he had been. She had loathed herself, but thankfully this feeling had not lasted.

When she had returned through the garden last night she had been surprised to hear the church clock striking twelve. In just two hours her world had completed a somersault. The light was still on in the bedroom, there were also lights on in both the drawing-room and the hall, and she saw from the head of the stairs that the front door was wide open. Had he gone to the village to raise the alarm? She doubted it. To admit that his wife had run away would cause a loss of face. She couldn't see him risking that until he was absolutely sure that she wouldn't come back when her tantrum was over. That was the name he would give to the episode.

She was crossing the landing going towards the spare room with some of her clothes when he came up the stairs, and just for a moment she felt sorry for him, for he had a frightened look about him. But her sorrow was short-lived, for immediately on sight of her his whole countenance darkened and subdued anger bubbled from his lips as he demanded, 'Where have you been?'

When she turned from him without answering and pushed open the door of the spare room he strode quickly after her, and from the doorway he reprimanded her, saying in the same tense, subdued tone, 'It's about time you grew up, Grace; this is no way for a woman to act. Don't you realise you are no longer a girl being petted and cajoled by your . . . family?' The stress he put on the word family brought her eyes flashing round on him.

His private opinion of her family had come over in the intonation he had given the word.

As she looked at him standing there filling the doorway with his bulk, she realised with surprise that she no longer stood in awe of him. An hour ago she had given herself to another man; she had sinned, a grievous sin, and yet because she had sinned she had the courage to look fearlessly at this man who had been to her as a god. If her journey into the darkness had resulted in nothing more than running wild through the woods and the quarry until she had come to her senses and returned penitent to this house, she knew that her abasement would have been complete, but on her wings of flight she had stopped to sin and in doing so had gathered courage into her body, together with a new and extraordinary feeling of easement. She had been unfaithful and in this moment she was exulting in it.

'Don't you realise that you've had me worried sick?'

It was on the point of her tongue to say, 'Yes, so much so that you got a search party out to look for me,' but instead she said flatly, 'I'm very tired, I want to go to bed.'

She watched him draw himself up even straighter. 'You're not sleeping in this room.'

'Well, if I don't I won't sleep anywhere else.' As she said this she made the movement of turning round a casual act. Then going towards the chest-of-drawers she added, 'I'd like to be left alone.'

'Grace . . . Grace, do you know what you're saying?'

'Yes, I said I'd like to be left alone, to sleep alone.' She looked at him over her shoulder. 'You shouldn't find that wish difficult to grant.'

She saw the blood slowly leave his face until it looked a pasty smudge of flesh and became one with the colour of his eyes. Even his lips looked grey.

'We'll have this out in the morning.' His voice, his whole body, emanated bluster.

When the door closed on him she felt a momentary feeling of triumph that settled into scorn. Her remark at least had struck home. His façade of working late, sermons to write, talks to rehearse, of being very, very tired, had at last been penetrated. No more would he be able to hide behind such lies. But Donald never lied, he simply evaded . . . skilfully evaded.

She did not go to bed but sat by the window looking out on to the back garden and she wondered just why she had put up with the situation all this time. There were two answers. Ignorance of the sexual side of marriage, and a natural diffidence to speak of this side to anyone. When she had entered into her marriage she felt she was equipped with all the necessary knowledge. You loved a man, you slept with him, the outcome was a baby. You became aware of this when your periods stopped and you felt sick. It took nine months to have a baby and during this time your husband worshipped you. And had not millions of women got by on no more knowledge than that? But how had the others made out? The ones that had been led up the garden path and then had the door quietly shut in their faces – had they gone to their mothers, or their doctors, or their priests and poured out their pain? Perhaps. But there would be others like her who had been able to do none of these things. Then had they gone mad, had a nervous breakdown, or been gladly seduced?

She, she knew, had been on the verge of a nervous breakdown, but now she was saved. She had been gladly seduced.

She sat on until the night began to lift and the dawn appeared. She had been sitting with the eiderdown hugged around her and now she pushed it off and made her way quietly out of the room and downstairs to the kitchen. There she made herself a cup of strong tea. She had no fear of being joined by Donald. The sound of his snoring as she crossed the landing had told her that, however much his mind was troubled, it was not preventing him from having his sleep out.

Back in her room she once more pulled the eiderdown about her, and as she gazed out into the swift rising light she tried to see into the day ahead and to what action she should take.

At what point in her thinking she fell asleep she did not know, but she was woken with startling suddenness by the sound of Ben's voice yelling from the garden. She sat up, blinking her eyes rapidly, not sure for a moment where she was, and then as she rose painfully from the cramped position in which she had been sleeping Ben's voice came to her again. When she put her face close to the window-pane she could see him near the greenhouse. He was standing waving his arms about and still yelling. What was happening? What was the matter? She could see no-one else in the garden. Then, as she watched and saw him coming towards her window, she knew he was making for the side of the house and the kitchen door. Hurriedly she smoothed down her hair and her dress. She still felt dazed with sleep, and her eyes seemed full of sand. On crossing the landing she saw that Donald was already about, for the bedroom door was wide open and there was no sign of him.

As she entered the kitchen she saw Ben through the far open door; his fist was clenched and shaking in front of Donald's face, and he was crying at the top of his voice, 'Sawed down her hedge, did you? Sawed it down, you cruel bugger! That's what you are, you're no man. Well, this is the finish for me. I'll not work for you another minute, no, not if I was starvin'. Do you hear?'

'I told you I wanted that hedge cutting well down; I told you quite plainly yesterday and all you did was to take an inch or so off the top.'

'You go to hell's flames. I know why that hedge was put there in the first place an' I told you.' He thrust his hand outwards in the direction of the drive. 'There's no green hedge there now, is there? No, all you can see is a tarred roof. Nice, isn't it? But if it hadn't been that it would've been somethin' else. You were just waitin', weren't you? Giving your orders right, left and centre about things you know nowt about. Playing God Almighty inside and outside the church. Well, let me tell, mister, you're not comin' God Almighty on me. I'm on to you and your ways. I saw through you from the start. It's folk like you that cause murder, aye it is that. Well, now I'm finished. You get me cards and me pay ready and I'm downin' me tools. And I'll say to you me last word . . . ' Ben's old face quivered upwards. 'You're a two-faced, mealy-mouthed nowt, and a cruel bugger into the bargain, and there you have it.'

The old man turned away, and after a moment Grace stepped slowly out of the kitchen and into the yard and looked at Donald. She saw that he was going to great lengths to control himself. And when she spoke to him it was not so much a question as a statement. Coldly she said, 'You cut down that hedge? You must have got up early this morning and purposely gone out to cut down that hedge, Ben's hedge.'

'It is not Ben's hedge.'

'Then it is my hedge.'

His face became scarlet and his jaw-bones seemed to lift from their sockets before he said, 'Very well, Grace, since you emphasise your ownership, I shall make arrangements for us to return to the vicarage – it is still available.'

124

As she turned from him, his voice rapped at her, 'Where are you going? I forbid you to go near that man.'

She stopped and, turning round, looked at him. And there rose to her tongue Ben's words, 'You cruel bugger', and it was as much as she could do not to repeat them. But had she said them they would not have surprised him any more than when she said, 'You can forbid me to do nothing that I want to do.'

She left him with his eyes wide open and his lips apart, and as she hurried round the house towards Ben she kept saying to herself, 'It's impossible, it's impossible', for she knew in this moment that she had not only ceased to love him but that she almost hated him. He must have risen early this morning, not to come to her and try to sort out the events of last night, but deliberately to cut down a hedge that he must have known would be a wanton thing to do. Ben had disobeyed his orders, so Ben must suffer. Ben, although he did not know it, was also suffering because she had disobeyed her master's orders.

When she came upon Ben he was standing at what last night had been a thick trim hedge. The main stems of the lonicera had been sawn through and pulled away. They lay in a heap at the side of the path; all that remained of the hedge now was a straggly torn mat of bush about two feet high.

'I'm sorry, Ben, oh I am.' She stood by his side, but he did not reply; only his head drooped lower and he shook it slowly from side to side before turning away towards the greenhouse. When she followed him and he still wouldn't say anything to her she realised that the old man was crying. It was as she watched the tears sliding from one wrinkle to another that she knew she must go away, she must leave this house. She said to Ben's stooped shoulders, 'I'll come and see you, Ben, I'll get you a garden of your own, I will, I promise you.'

Ben's cottage on the other side of the village had nothing more than a pocket handkerchief of a garden, and she knew how the old man would miss his work, so she was not just using soothing words but meant what she said when she made him the promise. He still gave her no answer and she turned about and went quickly towards the house. . . .

When half an hour later she came down the stairs wearing a light costume and hat and carrying a case she was confronted not only by Donald but by Mrs Blenkinsop, and this situation could not have made things easier for her, for, ignoring Donald and looking straight towards the older woman, she said, 'I'm going to my aunt's, Mrs Blenkinsop, she isn't very well.'

'Oh, I'm sorry to hear that, ma'am.'

Grace knew that at the moment Mrs Blenkinsop believed her, and Donald did nothing that would tend to make the situation other than a natural one, for he followed his wife out and along the side of the house to the garage. But once in its shelter his wrath burst over her, but in a controlled quiet way that would not carry beyond her ears.

'What are you playing at, Grace? Don't be silly. You can't go running off to your aunt's because we have a little misunderstanding. Go for a drive and then come back, but don't go near your Aunt Aggie's. I . . . '

'You forbid me?'

'I'm asking you not to.'

'I'm going to Aunt Aggie's and I'm going to talk to her. I should have done this a long time ago. If I had I wouldn't have served my time to become a nervous wreck.' She opened the door and got into the car, and from there she looked up at him. 'In a very short time I would have had a breakdown and everybody would have been sorry . . . not for me, oh no, but for you. That the poor vicar should have a wife with nerves.'

They were staring at each other, and she saw his eyes change colour. She had noticed this before. It was as if he drew over them a thick veil of protection. She watched him gulp before speaking.

'Of course you're suffering from nerves, and it's because you've been acting like an hysterical girl for months.' His voice became lower still. 'There are more things in marriage than silly romance, and one of them is duty. You seem to forget that you have a duty to me.'

'Ask Miss Shawcross to take it over.'

'Grace, how dare you! You are both uncouth and coarse.'

'Yes, yes, I suppose I am. I come from that kind of stock. You have never thought much of them, I know. You don't really think much of anyone below the standard of the Tooles and Farleys, do you? The folks and the others – remember? The cheque-book buyers versus those with cash.'

She pressed the self-starter, and when her foot came off the accelerator and the noise in the garage subsided she heard him say, 'It's unbelievable, I can't believe it. What's changed you like this?'

'Oh, Donald!' She was talking through her teeth now. 'For God's sake don't be such a hypocrite.' She leant towards him until her face was not more than a few inches from his, and actually hissed at him, 'You're trying your damnedest to get confession going in the church, aren't you? Then I'd advise you to set an example and go and be your own first penitent. That should give you the answer. . . . What's changed me. . . . Huh!'

'Grace, wait; I beseech you, wait.'

The car moved out of the garage; they were in the open now and there was Mrs Blenkinsop at the kitchen door. She smiled a farewell and Grace returned the smile, even lifted her hand in a wave, and then she was off along the drive, out of the gate and on the main road. Away, away, and she was never going to come back.

Aggie did not go out immediately to park the car but went into her office and hastily wrote a letter. Then, after she had installed the car beside her own in the converted stables at the end of the cul-de-sac, she hurried down the main road and to the pillar-box and there posted the letter. As she returned to the house she thought, 'He should get that first post in the morning. Today's Wednesday; I should have word back by Friday and something should be settled at the week-end. That's if the light of day hasn't brought him cold feet . . . the young swine. . . .'

The following morning at half past eleven no-one could have been more surprised than Aggie when, answering a ring at the front door, she was confronted by . . . the young swine himself.

Andrew MacIntyre had his hat in his hand, he was wearing a brown suit and thick-soled, highly polished boots. 'I got your letter.' His attitude was characteristic and to the point, as was Aggie's reply, 'Have you flown?'

'No I came on me bike, it's me day off.'

Aggie glanced behind her. There was no sign of Grace, and she said quickly, 'Come in. Go into that room.' She pointed to the left. Then, closing the front door, she glanced towards the stairs before following him.

As Aggie took her seat at her desk she said curtly, 'Sit down.' And when he was seated she looked at him squarely and said, 'Well!' then added, 'This is a nice kettle of fish. You know what you are, don't you?' She jerked her head towards him, and when he made no reply she added, 'Well, what have you got to say? Nothing, I suppose.'

'I've got plenty to say but I'll wait until you're finished.'

Well! She said the word this time to herself as she sat up straight and scrutinised him. He certainly was no weak-kneed youth, but still he wasn't going to get it all his own way, she was going to give it to him hot and heavy, by gad she was. 'All right then. I'll have my say. What do you mean by . . . by . . . ?' Now she was stuck for the right words. She could hardly say 'raping my niece?' nor could she say 'taking down a married woman?' Grace, by her own account, had been more than willing. But she had to say something, so she finished, 'by ruining my niece's life?'

'I haven't ruined her life; that was done the day you let her marry him.'

She didn't say, 'I didn't want her to marry him, I would have stopped it if I could,' but snapped back at him, 'Nobody could have stopped her, she was in love with him. She was potty about him.'

'What did she know about it? She had been tucked away in school.'

'How old are you?'

'I'm twenty-four.'

She was surprised, he didn't look that old. 'Oh, and I suppose you know all about it, and would have done better than him?'

'Aye, I would that. And I would now, but it isn't always possible to do what you want.' For the first time Andrew looked away from Aggie and his voice took on a softer note as he ended, 'I'm sorry about what happened.'

'Oh?' Aggie raised her brows. 'Are you telling me that you want to back out?'

His eyes came up swiftly to her again. 'No, I don't want to back out as you call it, but there are circumstances. . . .' He wetted his lips. 'I've no money; at the end of the week I won't have a job – I've given me notice in – and I have to support my parents.'

Aggie nodded her small head. 'Oh. Your prospects are very bright, aren't they? And what do you expect us to do about it . . . ?' Her words were cut off by Andrew getting swiftly to his feet.

'I don't want . . . us . . . to do anything about it. The matter lies between her and me.'

'Well, there's one thing: she's got enough money to keep you both.' Her eyes, narrowed now, were tight on him.

'Well, she won't be called upon to use it, not on me.' His words and tone now caused Aggie's head to droop slightly. Then it came up with startling suddenness as she said, 'You're not going to take her away then?'

'I'm not going to take her away.'

Aggie was now on her feet, her head tilted to look up into his face. 'Then may I ask what you are going to do?' she demanded angrily.

'I'm going to stay where I am.'

'You mean to stand there and tell me that you're going to stay . . . ?' Aggie stopped. 'Well, she won't go back. What do you say to that?'

Aggie watched the skin around his mouth pale before he said, 'That will be up to her.' Then, drawing in a sharp breath, he added, 'Now can I see her?'

Aggie continued to look at him for a moment longer. She couldn't make him out. Things had not gone according to her plans. After the preliminaries were over and the shouting had died down she had seen him installed on a farm, a farm of his own – Grace's money could run to it easily. But here he was telling her he wasn't going to leave Deckford. She did not say another word as she left him, but when she got upstairs into Grace's room the words tumbled out of her.

'He's downstairs – no, not Donald, Andrew MacIntyre.' She took Grace by the arm and shook her none too gently. 'I know what you've got in your mind, but let me prepare you for a disappointment: he won't leave Deckford. He's left his job, by the way – why, I don't know – but he won't leave the place. Again why, I don't know, but that's for you to find out.'

'How did he know I was here?' Grace's voice was scarcely audible.

'I wrote last night and told him. I expected a reply some time tomorrow, but there he is, as large as life, downstairs in the office. Go on now. But mind, things are not going to go your way, I'm warning you.'

Slowly Grace descended the stairs. She was nervous, a little afraid, a little bashful, more than a little ashamed to face this man. Andrew in the dark had been a boy matching his youth with hers, but in the daylight she knew he would be Andrew MacIntyre and another being. But all these feelings disappeared when she entered the room and, after closing the door, stood with her back to it looking across the small space towards him.

He made no move towards her but just stood, his eyes bright and dark, returning her deeply troubled stare. It was the hunger in them that reached out once more to the loneliness in herself and within a second she was in his arms, her head on his shoulder, her mouth pressed into his coat, muttering over and over again as she had done the night before last, 'Oh, Andrew; oh, Andrew.'

He did not attempt to kiss her, but after a moment he pressed her from him and put her into a chair beside the desk, and, drawing another one up close, he asked, 'Has your aunt told you anything I've said?'

131

'She said you were leaving the Tooles.' She did not now ask why – she knew. And then she ended, with her face screwing up in some complexity, 'But she said you won't leave the village. Is this true, Andrew?'

'Yes, I can't leave there.'

'But why?'

'My people.'

'But, Andrew, listen to me.' She leant forward and gripped his hands. 'I'm not going back there. I never want to see it again, or anyone in it. You told me the other night that these things can happen. Well, I believe you, for now I know it. I want to go away with you, Andrew, and I have enough money to set us up in any kind of business, farming or anything. And if Donald won't divorce me it won't matter. If it came to the point . . . ' Now she stopped and looked away from him towards the lace-curtained windows and she repeated, 'If it came to the point I could have it annulled.'

'Oh, Grace, what have I done?' He was looking at her hands. 'I should never have let that happen the other night. I know now I shouldn't. I knew it at the time, yet I've been livin' these past months just to hold you.'

'You're sorry?'

'No, no, I'm not. No, be damned, no never that. You know I'm not sorry – not for myself, that is. But for you. You would, I suppose, have gone on; like my mother you would have gone on.'

'I wouldn't, Andrew. I couldn't have gone on, I was heading for a breakdown. I never slept properly for months. I was ill. I know I was ill, and no matter what happens I'll never regret the other night, Andrew. . . . ' She looked up into his face. 'You mightn't know it, but you not only saved my life, you saved my sanity. If I had gone down through the wood the way I came up something would have snapped in me.'

'Oh, Grace.' He gently touched her face. Then his eyes dropped from hers and he shook his head slowly from one side to the other. 'What I want to do now is take you up and run with you to where nobody will ever find us. But I can't; I can't, Grace. I can't leave her.'

'Her?'

'My mother.'

'Your mother?' The surprise and disappointment in her voice brought him to his feet and he turned his back on her as he said, 'For twenty years she has worked and slaved after my father. Her life has been sheer hell. He is crippled with arthritis, as you know. Besides that, his mind is crippled an' all. He hates people, everybody, even me. Most of all me, I think. She won't leave him and I can't leave her. If she knew of this she would tell me to go. It is because I feel for her as I do that I am capable of loving you as I do. I can love you and let you go. I can love you without even touching your hand again. I have done, and would have gone on doing it.' He swung round to her now. 'That might be hard to believe but it's true.'

'But . . . but, Andrew, what's to be done? I can't go back there. At least' – she lowered her head as she murmured – 'I hadn't thought I'd be called upon to.'

'Don't come back because of me. Whatever you do, don't do that. I can see you at times . . . if you still want me to. I'll have to find fresh work, anyway, but that won't be difficult now – they are crying out for farm-workers.'

'Andrew.' She reached up her arms to his shoulders and said, 'Let me give you a farm.'

With one step he had moved from her reach and the small space between them seemed to widen. Then with a motion of his hand as if he was flinging something away, he said, 'No, not that. Never that. Don't you offer me that. I am one who must make his own way, and as far as I can see that'll never be very high, but nevertheless I must make and pay me own way. Don't ask me to be another soft-seated parson.'

'Oh, Andrew!' The hurt in her voice brought him to her and he pulled her up into his arms and held her close as he said, 'I didn't mean it like that. I just wanted you to know I want nothing from you but – but yourself.'

He was silent now, holding her hard against him, and as she felt the trembling of his body it came to her quite quietly, and therefore clearly, that whatever Andrew MacIntyre said his word would be her law. Mentally they might be poles apart, for she did not know the trend of his mind as yet, but physically they were as one, and because of this, if nothing else, she would be capable of enduring anything to remain near him.

And so it was.

'Do you mean to say you are going back to that house to live with him all because that pigheaded Scot won't move from the village?'

'I've told you, Aunt Aggie, why he can't.'

'Nonsense! His people could come and live near you, for that matter . . . something could be arranged.'

'His father is a bitter man, he won't leave the cottage. He hates the sight of people and he rarely sees anyone up there.'

Aggie made a complete circle of her drawing-room before she spoke again. 'Well, it beats me. What if Donald starts changing his tactics and making demands on you, futile or otherwise?'

'Don't worry, he won't do that – that's one thing I'm sure of. If I wasn't I don't think I could go back.'

'And how long do you expect to live under that strain? You'll only be able to see Andrew MacIntyre when you sneak into that quarry. Don't be silly, girl, it would break you.'

'Yes, yes, I agree with you it might, but nevertheless I must give it a try. Even if I don't speak to him, I know he'll be near and at hand if I want him. And it'll be a different kind of strain. I'll not break under this strain.' She shook her head slowly from side to side.

'Oh, to think your life has come to this. And they made game of Charlie Wentworth and thought he wasn't good enough for you because he was only second clerk in Raynors' office.' Aggie looked at her in dismay. . . . 'Well, when do you propose to go?'

'I'll go back this afternoon.'

'My God!'

There was no-one in the house when Grace arrived. Mrs Blenkinsop had gone home. The trolley was set for tea as was usual. The house was the same as when she had left it yesterday morning, yet not the same, and she knew it would never be the same again.

She was standing by the window of the drawing-room when Donald came up the drive. He stopped in his tracks when he caught sight of her, yet he did not enter the house through the french windows but went in through the front door and came into the drawing-room from the hall.

When she felt him standing behind her she gave a slight shudder, and when his hands came on her shoulders and turned her towards him she did not resist.

'Grace.' His voice was low, soft and full of forgiveness. 'Are you feeling better?'

'I'm feeling all right.'

'I'm glad to see you again. I've missed you; the house has been so empty.'

135

She looked up into his face. His expression was gentle and beguiling, but no longer did she see any beauty in it. Had she ever loved this man? Had she ever been mad about him? Yes, yes. There was no use in denying that. And he could have turned the girlish love into a passion that would have burned fiercely down through the years. The thought, down through the years, brought another shudder to her body. Would she have to live in the same house with him until they were old, or one or other died? No, no, she couldn't. Something would have to be done, something would have to happen. But in the meantime she would stay. She felt no sense of guilt at the thought of deceiving him. He had deceived her as no man should deceive a woman. His deception had amounted to torture, and he was all the more guilty because he set himself up as an example to other men. He who wasn't and could never be a man.

'Come and have some tea.' He went to put his arm through hers, but she forestalled this by walking ahead of him towards the trolley. As she busied herself pouring out the tea, he went and stood with his back towards the empty grate, his hands linked behind him, and he talked, talked as if nothing had happened between them to shatter the harmony of his days. He talked about the shadow of war that hung over the country and the preparations the village was making to meet it, and as she listened she knew that the incident of yesterday morning and Ben would not be referred to again. As for what happened in their bedroom the other night, that was already something he had buried so deep that it could never be uncovered.

'Mr Baker from the Stag has been very good. He has a small cellar attached to the main one. He's offered it for a shelter until we get things under way, that's if it becomes necessary, and we'll soon know that. Brookes says that food will be very scarce. He suggests we stock up; or, to be more correct' – he gave a little laugh at this point – 'it was Mrs Brookes who suggested this. I was talking to the doctor. He seemed to think he might be called up and seems worried over it, because of Renee, I suppose. Yet I should have thought at his age he would have been eager to go. He's just turned thirty.'

She would have liked to have asked point blank, 'Will you go?' He was thirty-nine. Men of that age could go. Oh, she wished. . . . She turned her head sideways away from the thought that sprang into her mind. She mustn't desire that – that was bad, vile, much more so than betraying him with another man.

When he came and sat beside her on the couch and took hold of her hand she drew it quietly away from him and, joining her fingers together, she pressed them for a moment between her knees before saying, 'If I am to stay here, Donald, I want a room to myself.'

She was staring ahead and did not see the reactions of her words on him, and it was some little time before he answered her, and then neither the tone of his voice nor his words surprised her, for he said evenly, 'Very well, it will be as you wish.'

He was relieved. She knew he was relieved, and for a moment she felt a fierce anger rise against him. He was a cheat, a hypocrite, he was also a coward. It might seem incongruous knowing her feelings towards him at the moment, but she would have felt less bitter against him had he made some protest against her request. And then he did, but in a way that deepened her scorn.

'There is only one favour I would ask of you, it will only be for a couple of days.' He refrained, she noticed, from saying nights. 'I heard from my uncle – you know, Uncle Stephen; he would like to see me and proposes staying over the week-end. He is due in Edinburgh on

Monday next and proposes coming here on the Saturday.'
He rose now and went to the fireplace and took up his old
position but with his back towards her, and from there he
said, 'He would think it unusual . . . you understand?'

Her anger almost burst from her now. It bubbled
inside of her, and it was as much as she could do
to remain still. Face must not be lost, his face; the
proprieties must be kept up for the bishop. She wanted
to turn on him and yell 'You hypocrite!' and not only
'You hypocrite!' but to give it an adjective, an adjective
brought from the memory of the years in the little house
at the head of the coalyard, and in spite of her anger its
appearance in her mind shocked her slightly.

5

It was now the middle of October and Grace knew for a certainty that she was pregnant and she was both elated and slightly distraught. She knew that the child was Andrew's, and yet. . . . The yet would loom quite large at times, for there would come back to her again and again the incident that occurred during the bishop's stay. She thought of it as an incident, an isolated, repulsive, even dirty incident. She also thought: Aunt Aggie was right again. Donald had made love to her. Whether his intention had been to convince himself of his potency or to appease her she did not know; she only knew that she had been sickened and repulsed and she had been left wondering why she had longed with a burning longing for almost two years for this to happen. Added to this was the frightening knowledge of the complete change in her feelings towards him. She would not have thought it possible for any human being to change so completely. If, two years ago, someone had confided in her, saying, 'My husband is not capable of loving me', she knew she would have said, 'Poor soul', and she would have been thinking, not of the woman, but of the man. She would have been sorry to the heart for the man, for, after all, she would have reasoned that sex was only part of marriage. You read that that was so. . . . Moreover, hadn't Donald said so. But now she could curl her lip at that statement. Sex was marriage – at the beginning, anyway. For the marriage to go right, that one thing had to be right. All things stemmed from it – harmony, peace, peace of mind and body, and, the most important thing of all, learning to like your man. And there was small chance of liking in the daylight a man whom you didn't like in the dark. There were extenuating circumstances, she knew, such as when a man was crippled, and a woman sublimated herself in a selfless love for him. But Donald wasn't crippled . . . and yet, in a way, he was – he had been born crippled. Realising this, she asked herself why she wasn't sorry for him, why she wasn't kind to him in her heart, and the answer came to her that it was because she knew him to be a cheat. He must have known his own make-up before he married her. He had felt the need of a mother to pet him, a doll to play with, and a woman to run his house and assist in his church, preferably one with a nice bit of money, but he had never wanted a wife.

There was one thing at least that the incident had achieved: it had given her an alibi. But at the present moment she didn't care if she had one or not, things were bound to come out.

She went into the kitchen now to see about dinner, and Mrs Blenkinsop looked at her closely and exclaimed, 'By, ma'am, you look peeky.' And then she added with motherly concern, 'You're not yourself these days at all, ma'am. Why don't you lie up for a while and have a good rest? It's the aftermath, all that excitement about the war that never was. Everybody's feeling it one way or another, the village is as flat as a pancake. It's funny, ma'am, but I could bet me bottom dollar that half of them's disappointed.'

'Oh, I wouldn't say that, Mrs B.'

'They are, ma'am. It would have given them the opportunity to carry on dizzy-lizzying all over the place, throwing their weight about.'

Mrs Blenkinsop mentioned no names but Grace knew

she was referring to Kate Shawcross. Mrs B. didn't like Kate Shawcross.

'About lunch, Mrs B.'

'Well, ma'am . . . yes now, there's the rabbit Mr Toole dropped in, or I can mince that chicken, whatever you like.'

'I think we'll have the chicken.'

'Just as you say, ma'am. Speaking of the Tooles' – Mrs Blenkinsop moved towards the sink, lifting in a stack·of dishes as she spoke – 'that Adelaide is getting her name up, I'm afraid.'

'Yes?' Grace did not turn away from the prattle of her cook, it was only through Mrs Blenkinsop that she knew of the real happenings in the village. People did not speak their minds to the parson's wife, and her nothing but a young girl after all.

'Well, since Andrew MacIntyre started at Tarrant's farm she's gone out of her way to be on the road nights when he's coming back. You would think she would take a hint, wouldn't you? Mr Blenkinsop said it made his ears red when he heard her.'

'Mr Blenkinsop heard her?' Grace was looking at Mrs Blenkinsop's profile, and the older woman went on washing the dishes, nodding down to the water as she said, 'Yes. He was in the field just above the road, beyond the cemetery you know, ma'am, at the back there. He was going to drop down to the road when he heard them. She was accusing him of egging her on and he was denying it. And then you know what he said, ma'am?' She turned her eyes towards Grace. 'He said, "Have I ever as much as kissed you?" That's what Mr Blenkinsop said he said. . . . I ask you. Then she snapped back at him, "No, but you've wanted to." Can you imagine it, ma'am? Her saying a thing like that to Andrew MacIntyre. Lowering, isn't it, for, after all, although they treated him a cut above the rest, he was only a farm-worker. Then he said, "It's all your imagination," and stamped off. But mind, as I said to Mr Blenkinsop, he's a fool. She's the only child and it's a fine farm, one of the best around here, and it could be his just for the lift of his finger. "Yes," I said to Mr Blenkinsop, "that lad must be daft." '

'Perhaps he doesn't love her, Mrs B.'

Grace was turning away when Mrs Blenkinsop laughed aloud. 'Oh, what's love to do with it? If he doesn't love her afore he'll love her after, and a good farm and plenty of dibs would help things along. Aye, it would that . . . Love? Huh! And the chance to get into the county fringe. Not that the Farleys would take kindly to him, and some of the others likely wouldn't recognise him at first, but things are changing fast and time wears people down, and if there should come a war – well, you know what changes wars make, ma'am.'

Grace left the kitchen. Had she stopped Andrew from having a good farm and plenty of dibs and getting into the county set? No, she wouldn't hold herself responsible for that. He could have plenty of dibs now, her dibs, if it was dibs he wanted, and as for the county fringe! She couldn't see Andrew in that set. Unlike Mrs Blenkinsop, she didn't look upon the Tooles as being of the county fringe. But nevertheless she felt sorry for Adelaide Toole. She liked Adelaide, the little she had seen of her.

What would Andrew say when she told him about the baby? It was a week since she had seen him, a week since she had been held in his arms. Why hadn't she told him then? What would Donald say when she told him about the baby? She felt sick on this thought, and her mind felt dizzy and muddled, yet even so one thought remained clear. They would both have to be told.

As she crossed the hall there came a ring at the door

bell, and when she opened it there stood Dr Cooper, and on the first sight of him she knew a sense of relief. Here was someone she could tell.

'Well, how are you this morning?'

She smiled at him, and as she closed the door she said enigmatically, 'Different.'

'Different?' His thick eyebrows moved upwards. 'Now what do you mean by that?'

'Come in here, into the morning-room – I've lit a fire. It's a bit chilly this morning, isn't it?'

'Yes, there's a nip coming. But never mind about fires or nips, tell me what is this mysterious difference?'

She turned and faced him, her face looked sad, 'I'm going to have a baby.'

'You are?' His voice was level. 'That's good news, very good news. Are you sure?'

'Positive.'

'Oh well, that's done me out of a job. What does Donald say to this stupendous news? Is he overwhelmed?'

'I haven't told him . . . not yet.'

His eyebrows moved upwards again and he nodded his head. 'And when may we expect the arrival?'

'I'm about five weeks.' She did not say six. What was a week, anyway? But she asked herself: was she already using the alibi?

David Cooper looked at her. Here was a young girl going to have her first baby and talking flatly and unemotionally about it, as if it was her fifth or even her seventh. The doctor went back on his thoughts as he said to himself: young girl? She was no longer a girl, and whatever had happened to her – and he didn't lay the change down to her pregnancy – it had changed her into a woman, and not a very happy one either. Something was wrong here and he couldn't get to the bottom of it. It had been all over the village a few weeks ago that she had dashed off in a car early one morning and left the vicar. It was over the business of Ben and the garden. If it hadn't been that the whole place was agog waiting for a war to start that incident would have raised much more gossip than it did. And so she was going to have a baby? If this had happened in the first year it would doubtless have smoothed things over, but now he wasn't sure. He wished she would talk.

'Can I tell Renee?'

'I'd rather you didn't, not yet.'

'Just as you say . . . I suppose I'll have to look you over. What about tomorrow afternoon? And stay and have a cup of tea, Renee's always delighted to see you . . . I won't tell her, she'll think it's just a check up.'

'Thanks, I'll come down.'

'Well, I must be off.'

'Won't you stay and have a coffee?'

'No, no thanks, I'm off to the Farleys. Papa Farley's got rheumatism – we used to call it gout. Do you know that Bertrand Farley has joined up . . . the army? I saw him in his uniform yesterday; it does something for him. I won't say he doesn't need it.' He gave Grace a dig with his thumb, and she laughed. They laughed together, and as they crossed the hall her laughter rose much louder than the joke had warranted.

She was still laughing when she returned to the breakfast-room, but when she stood before the fire with her foot on the fender and her hand on the mantelpiece her laughter stopped abruptly and with her teeth clamping down on her lip she began to cry – painfully slow tears.

It was Andrew, after all, whom she told first. Not from within the security of his arms under the shelter of the rock wall in the quarry, but on the open road outside an empty cottage at Culbert's Cut. She had come once again to look at this place, wondering whether she would buy it, and having done so would it then be easier to persuade Ben to accept it? It was going for three hundred pounds. That was quite a bit for this type of property, but what was three hundred pounds compared with Ben's idle hands? The cottage stood alone, about a quarter of a mile from the village, and the land around it was flat and open.

When she stepped from the garden gate on to the road and saw the lorry coming towards her she did not look at it twice, until its stopping drew her attention. And then she saw Andrew. He got out of the cab and stood beside the door, and she stood by the bonnet of the lorry. There was four or more feet between them, and this space held the village and any covert stroller like Mr Blenkinsop.

'Hello, darlin'.' The soft low burr of his voice gave the words a deepened caress, and her heart was warmed and eased by the endearment.

'You look whitish; are you all right?'

She did not answer for a long moment as she hesitated in her mind whether to tell him or not. She had imagined giving him her news with her face resting against his, but it might be a week, even two, before they would get the chance to meet again, and so she said, 'I'm going to have a baby, Andrew.'

No muscle of his face moved, but his eyes darkened. And then he asked softly, 'Are you glad?'

'Yes, yes, Andrew, I'm glad . . . are you?'

'Yes, yes. But it's you, if you're happy about it, that's all that matters.'

'Oh, Andrew.'

Their bodies were taut and still and their glances were held fast links of a chain.

'The only thing I'm worried about is later on.' Her

voice was trembling. 'I won't be able to go up to . . . to the quarry.'

'Don't worry about that, we'll work something out. . . .'

They were still staring at each other. The danger was imminent; she knew that in a moment she would fall against him. She said quickly, 'I must go.'

'Yes . . . Grace.' His hand was lifting towards her when swiftly he changed its direction and swung himself up into the cab. As the door banged she stepped away from the bonnet and now she was below him. He had his hand on the wheel but did not start the engine; he looked down into her eyes and said, 'I love you, lass. You're . . . you're the most beautiful thing on earth. . . . An' . . . an' I worship you.'

The gears were rammed in and he left his deep glance on her as the lorry moved away.

He said things at odd times like that, things that brought fire to her heart. His verbal love-making was jerky yet in a way profound and beautifying . . . If only . . . if only . . . She turned round and walked down the road towards the village and Ben's cottage. If only they could be together, live together, mellow together. It was strange but in this moment she did not think of him as he was now, but her mind was filled with the desire that they should be old together.

Andrew had his eyes on the road as he drove the lorry but he was not seeing it. He avoided the potholes by instinct, for between him and the road were his thoughts which seemed to be written large on the windscreen, and nowhere among them was one of elation at the news Grace had given him. One thought stood out from the rest: it said, 'Leave the damn place. Take her far away. You can't expect her to put up with it.' There was no answer to this on the windscreen, for deep within his bones was the pull of the woman in the windswept stone house on the fell. He had felt this pull and her need of him even from the age of three. They were so close that it seemed at times as if the cord had never been cut between them. She had said to him the other day, 'I'm not asking why you left Toole, you'll tell me in your own time, but I had to tell your father something so I said you had a row about your wage – he would understand that.' He had looked at her drawn face and said, 'Stop worrying, I'll tell you some time.' But as close as they were, could he tell her, tell her he was fathering a child to the parson's wife? If he did he knew it would bring his release – but he couldn't do it – not even for Grace. . . .

Not even for Grace.

Almost two more weeks elapsed before Grace could bring herself to tell Donald. She had done a great deal of thinking during this particular time, and it revolved mainly around whether she should go away or stay here. There were two things against her going away. First, she would see less of Andrew than she did now; second, and this was the point that was having more bearing with her as each day of her pregnancy advanced, if she went away the child would be born illegitimate, whereas if she stayed it would be sheltered by Donald's name, for she knew him well enough to be sure that he would do anything rather than suffer the public indignity of her lapse. These two things became bands as strong as steel, hawsers holding her in place. Yet the more she now saw of Donald, the stronger became the desire to get away from him.

During the past few weeks Donald had developed a sullenness. He might be relieved that he was sleeping alone, but the fact that he was not the instigator of this arrangement was apparently having a delayed action. He no longer made any pretence of playing the lover; there was no kissing and petting and dear-little-girling now. Often there was not even a good night between them. He also had an added irritation to bear . . . the garden. It was the time of year for cutting, and clearing, and there were great patches of browning Michaelmas daisies, phlox and other perennials giving striking evidence of neglect. Peter Golding, the man who had followed Ben, had left over a week ago, the job, as he said, being too much for any one man. And he had added, he wasn't serving his time to be a Ben Fairfoot.

Grace knew that Donald had been furious over this, and she had heard him say to Mrs Blenkinsop, 'Lazy blighter. I'll do it myself in my spare time. A couple of hours a day will keep it well under.' But apparently he hadn't had any spare time, for the garden had not been touched. As Ben had said, Donald knew nowt about gardening. Moreover, she knew that he didn't like work – not that kind of work, anyway.

And now came the day when they got the spare time gardener, the day when a new era of her life began. It happened that she had been sick. She was slightly sick in the mornings, but on this day there had been fish for lunch, cod, and the oil must have upset her stomach, for in the middle of the afternoon she felt ill, and she had no ease until she vomited. She lay down for a while until the desire for a cup of tea took her downstairs. It was as she stepped into the hall that Donald let himself in through the front door, and on the sight of her he came towards her, asking quietly, 'What is the matter? Are you ill?'

She shook her head and turned in the direction of the kitchen, and when he followed her and repeated his question she placed her hands flat on the kitchen table, her weight on them, and, looking downwards, she said quietly, 'I'm pregnant.'

He was silent so long that she was forced to turn and

look at him, and when she saw his face some understanding of his inner plight came to her and pity welled in her for him. His expression was a mixture of disbelief and blank amazement, but over all there was a look of wonder.

'You mean . . . ?' He wet one lip against the other, then, moving his head slowly from side to side, he brought out, 'Oh, Grace!' Then on a higher note, 'Oh, Grace!' She could imagine him going up the scale chanting her name until he burst into song. It was pitiable. Then like a great benevolent figure he flung his arms out wide. He was forgiving her for being a silly hysterical girl. He was forgiving her for being a demanding wife. He was forgiving her for her unpredictable conduct on the particular night some weeks ago when she had struggled like a wildcat, and necessity demanded he put his hand over her mouth in case his uncle should hear her protests. Definitely he was forgiving her this last, for look what he imagined it had achieved.

'No, no, don't touch me, leave me alone.' She sprang back from the enfolding arms and he stopped nonplussed for a moment. Then, smiling gently, he said, 'All right, all right.' And after a great intake of breath he asked, 'But tell me, are you happy about this?'

She could look at him and say quite truthfully, 'Yes, yes, I am very happy.'

'You'll feel differently now, Grace. Things will be different.' He was standing close to her, looking down on her bent head. 'I told you, didn't I, that things shouldn't be rushed. There comes a time—'

'Stop it! Stop that talk.' She moved away but turned her eyes full on him. 'I've listened to too much of that kind of talk. I want to hear no more of it.'

His face had taken on a pinkish tinge, and he remained quiet for a moment but still looking at her. Then he said,

'Very well. All right, don't let us argue.' His manner was placating and his voice was like warm oil; he was soothing the mother-to-be. 'Go and sit down and I'll bring you a cup of tea.'

Slowly, almost mechanically, she walked into the drawing-room, saying to herself over and over again, 'I can't bear it, I can't. I won't be able to stand it, I won't. I must tell him, and now, today, this minute, now.'

When he brought in the tray of tea his step was almost tripping, and if there had been a laugh anywhere in her she would have laughed, he looked so comic. She was momentarily relieved when he did not sit on the couch beside her but walked with his cup slowly to the window and stood there looking out into the garden. It would be easier to tell him over the distance. On this thought there returned to her the spasm of pity, for she could almost see him thinking. She could almost feel his pride, his sense of achievement. He imagined he had accomplished what he never expected to accomplish: he had proved himself to be a man. His back was straight and his shoulders spread wide with the glory of it. And then he turned to her and, as was his wont when deeply concerned with one thing, he talked about another, and so she did not tell him that he was suffering from self-delusion, for his words set the pattern of her future.

'I've engaged someone for part-time in the garden. It's that Andrew MacIntyre. He's only on four days over at Tarrant's so he'll do at least two days for me, and likely get through as much in that time as the others did in a week. I won't say I would have taken him if there had been choice of . . . Why, Grace . . . !'

As the cup fell out of her hand to the floor with a clatter and she fell over sideways she heard his voice echoing as if through a gigantic empty hall, 'Why Grace! Why Grace! WHY GRACE!'

6

In June 1939 Grace gave birth to a son; he had blue eyes and features that could be traced to neither Andrew nor Donald nor herself. If at this early stage there was a resemblance to anyone it was to her own father. The birth left Grace quieter inside and changed her still more. It intensified her feelings for Andrew, it created a passionate love for the child, and strangely enough created in her a tolerance towards Donald. She called him Stephen.

She had the baby at home for reasons best known to herself, and she did not stay long in bed after the birth but was up and actually had taken a walk in the garden by the ninth day. It was a Thursday and the nurse had put the baby in the pram under the porch, and Andrew MacIntyre, who was mowing the front lawn, came and looked at the child. He looked at it for a long time, and then he smiled at its mother. . . .

On 3 September war was declared, and Grace hardly noticed it except that it brought to her a fear for the safety of her child. But for that and the fact that Andrew had now to take a full-time job at Tarrant's which after all was a blessing in disguise for it deferred his call-up she might have ignored it altogether. Her life was wrapped around the child to the exclusion of apparently everything else. That the vicar's wife took no active part in the village's stand against this war passed unnoticed. The vicar's wife wasn't strong and having a baby had taken it out of her more than somewhat.

As far as the duties of a parson's wife pertaining to the

parish were concerned Kate Shawcross filled that bill. And this, too, passed without comment. Kate Shawcross was a wonderful organiser. Everybody knew that and in this time of crisis was glad of it. Kate went to the extent of seeing to the arrangements in the cellar below Willow Lea. Andrew MacIntyre had constructed some wooden bunks in the cellar, also a cupboard for holding stores. Miss Shawcross saw to a carpet being laid, bedding being brought down, first-aid equipment put ready to hand, candles and matches in case of emergency . . . two boxes of matches, for the vicar was naughty, he was always walking off with matches . . . she even soaked dozens and dozens of newspapers into a horrible pulp with which to seal the cracks in the boards that had been nailed over the ground level window of the cellar. . . . 'In case of gas, you know.'

When the first air-raid warning sounded over the village Grace did not have to be told to remember her drill. She did not know whether it was a practice or a real warning, but she grabbed up the child and flew with him down into the cellar. She did this almost nightly for the first fortnight of the war and nothing happened. From this time onwards she had ceased to fly, but on the sound of the air-raid warning she would gather up her belongings and the child in an unhurried fashion and make her way downstairs.

Donald was the centre hub of the village administration, and during these first few days of fevered tension he acted more like a general than a parson. Each evening found him at the ARP post in the school-room, where he was second in command to Colonel Farley. If the colonel was on duty from six to ten, Donald took over from ten to four. From time to time the air-raid warnings sounded and excitement ran high.

But in the weeks that followed, things, not only in

the village but apparently in the whole country, settled down like a monotonous routine, and for everyone, with the exception of Kate Shawcross, life in the school-room became slightly boring.

It was the first Christmas of the war and Aunt Aggie was coming to stay. Aggie rarely came to the house, and Grace was more than a little surprised that she had accepted the invitation to stay over Christmas. Besides the reason that she wanted to see Aggie and talk to her there was another reason that made her visit doubly welcome. She knew her Aunt Aggie would look after the child and enable her to see Andrew for a while. There was no-one in the village she could call upon to stay in the house while she went out – where could she say she was going in a blacked-out village? It was weeks now – no, months – since she and Andrew had even touched hands. They had glimpses of each other, they spoke at times, but the world of the village was looking on. If it hadn't been for the child, life would have been unbearable.

That night when she had first heard that Andrew was coming as part-time gardener and had fainted, Dr Cooper had kept her in bed for two days, and during that time she had been tormented by a number of different feelings, not least among them that the situation would take on something of indecency if Andrew came here to work. And the question kept coming to her: why had he done it? Why had he placed them both in such a position? She didn't get the answer to this until she had stood in the greenhouse looking at him. It was quite in order for the vicar's wife to go down and speak to the gardener, quite in order, and no-one could hear what she said to him in the greenhouse. Besides which, the all-round view would have shown anyone's approach. The only thing she had to be careful of was her expression, she had to veil her desire.

She had learned to do this when speaking to Andrew, but on that day she had looked at him with her heart in her eyes as she asked, 'Why have you done this, Andrew – it will be unbearable?'

'Not more than not being able to see you for days on end . . . perhaps weeks on end later on.'

'But, Andrew, we'll give ourselves away.'

'I won't.' He kept looking down on the box of soil, his hands moving slowly over it. 'I told you that I could love you without seeing you or touching you, and that's true, but when he asked me to take this on it seemed like a gift. It was too good to pass over.'

'But I'm afraid . . .'

'Don't be afraid.' He lifted the box up and as he placed it on top of a number of similar ones he said, 'I'll stay on as long as you do. When you're ready to leave just tell me.'

Andrew knew her feelings with regard to the child bearing a name. He, like her, knew that Donald would never divorce her. He would have given a great deal to see her away from this house; not that he was jealous of Donald, there was nothing to be jealous of – to him Donald was like a huge drum with a pea rattling inside, he despised him. It was Grace herself he was thinking of, and in this particular his conscience would trouble him, for was he not the real reason why she stayed put.

They worked out a simple means of signalling when they were to meet in the quarry. If the loop wire was removed from the staves that leant against the oak near the gate, then he would be waiting for her. Very often in the early days of her pregnancy the loop would be off but she couldn't get away. Donald would be in or someone would have called, so therefore the vicar's wife would not take her stroll out through the bottom gate and quietly along the field and up through the wood. One moonlight night as she entered the wood on her way to the quarry she bumped into someone in the shadow of a tree, and she only stopped herself from collapsing in fright on the sound of the well-known voice. It was Ben Fairfoot; he had held her arm as he repeated, 'Why, ma'am, I'm sorry, I'm sorry. I wouldn't have scared you for the world. I'm sorry, ma'am, I'm sorry.'

She was so shaken by the encounter that she could not go on. 'I was just taking a stroll, Ben.'

Poor Ben. On no account had she been able to persuade him to take the cottage at Culbert's Cut. There could only ever be one garden for him, and he had been walking round it . . . on the outside. He had not asked her where she was going, anyone else might have done so.

Then there was the night that she had slipped out feeling safe because Donald was taking a meeting in the village hall, only on her return to find David Cooper in the house.

'You've given me a scare,' he said. 'Where have you been, out in the dark?' And then he had looked at her shoes, at the mud around the rims. He had been puzzled, for it hadn't rained for days.

When you played a game like this you had to be careful; there were so many things you had to be careful about. Parson's wife or no parson's wife, people had the way of putting two and two together. Yet there still remained the fact that the name 'parson's wife' was like a banner held up to advertise morality. She wouldn't have believed it had she not experienced it. She could stop and talk to different men in the village and no wrong thought of it, but had any other woman been seen indulging in this way, then the heads would have got together and the tongues would have wagged. But as the parson's wife she was merely helping her husband to bring men to God.

It was laughable really, but she never allowed herself to laugh over it.

Now that Andrew, with every minute of his time taken up at Tarrant's, no longer came to do the garden and odd jobs, the quarry was their only means of contact, and their meetings were arranged by a few casual and enigmatic words while running into each other in the village or thereabouts. One such meeting had been arranged for the night after Boxing Night and Grace prayed it wouldn't snow, for apart from it being almost impossible to do that climb in the snow there would be the matter of footprints.

But on the night after Boxing Night Donald unexpectedly stayed at home. He had a slight cold and he made this the excuse for evading the duty attending the men's meeting in the schoolhouse, and as it wasn't his night to be on duty in the ARP section his conscience apparently wasn't troubled. Grace, in a turmoil of disappointment and agitation, knew that the cold was but an excuse to remain in the house and give him further opportunity of showing off his parenthood to Aunt Aggie.

All through Aggie's visit he had carried, played with, and talked incessantly to the child. He had even insisted on bathing him, which ceremony Aggie did not give herself the pleasure of watching. It was as if he was yelling at her, 'Well, isn't this proof? No matter what she told you, you can't get over this.' He played the father in such an outsize way that Aggie's teeth became continually on edge. His voice at this moment was floating down the staircase, and when Grace, on her way to the kitchen to get the baby's bottle, passed her in the hall, Aggie's eyes turned upwards in their sockets as she exclaimed, 'I don't know how you stand it. Does this go on all the time?'

Grace smiled. 'Not so much, not at such a high pitch. It's for your benefit.'

'Yes, I thought so.'

There came a ring at the kitchen-door bell and Grace turned from the stove, the child's bottle in her hand, to answer it, and when she saw Andrew's tall figure framed in the dark, her hand with the bottle went involuntarily to her mouth. She glanced quickly round before saying, 'Come in.'

'I have a message for . . . for him.'

She closed her eyes for a moment, then said, 'Oh. Oh, I see.' She walked to the other side of the table, it was safer at this distance. He was still looking at her as he said, 'Mrs Rolland, the shepherd's wife, she's dying. I was passing along the road and he was waiting for me. He asked me if I would take a message to the parson and the doctor. His wife had taken a turn for the worse.'

'Poor thing. She's been ill for some time, hasn't she? And away up there all alone. Yes, yes, I'll tell him.' She talked of the sick woman but she wasn't thinking of her, and as she was going from the table she looked round at him and murmured under her breath, 'Wait.'

Andrew waited. He stood stiff and straight with his cap in his hands, and when in a few minutes Donald swung into the kitchen he answered the vicar's, 'Oh, hello, Andrew' with a plain 'Good evening'. He never addressed him as 'sir'.

'You have brought a message from Mr Rolland. Do you think she is dying?'

'He seems to think so.'

'Dear, dear. Well, I must go . . . yes, I must go right away.' He turned round as if looking for his things, and as Grace entered the kitchen Andrew said, 'I took the same message to Dr Cooper. I told him I was coming on here. He said he would wait for you.'

'Good. Good. I don't fancy a bicycle ride over the fells tonight. Good . . . good. Get on the phone, Grace, and tell him I'll be there in a few minutes. And by the way' – he turned to Andrew – 'you can't have had any tea.'

'No, but that's all right.'

'Oh, you must have a cup of tea or something after coming all this distance out of your way. Now it's no problem, just wait a minute.'

On this Donald disappeared beyond the green baize door, and Andrew did as he had been bidden for the second time – he waited.

In a few minutes Donald reappeared, he was tucking a scarf into his overcoat. 'She won't be a minute, just giving the nipper his bottle . . . or handing the job over to her aunt.' He jerked his head and laughed. He was treating the gardener to his line of jocular equality which he found had a two-fold use: it put ordinary folk at their ease, but at the same time kept the picture of the upper stratum from which he addressed them in the forefront of their minds. This he accomplished with his voice: his words were ordinary, yet the tone in which he delivered them was anything but.

Andrew said nothing, not even when Donald gave him a hearty 'Goodbye, then' before going into the hall again. He merely inclined his head. But when he heard Donald's voice calling upstairs from the hall he shut his eyes for a moment and repeated to himself, 'Goodbye, my dear.'

There came the sound of the front door banging, and a few minutes later the kitchen door opened. But it was Aggie who entered.

'Well. Hello there,' she said.

'Hello.'

Oddly enough Aggie had not seen Andrew since the morning in her office fifteen months ago, and she was surprised at the difference in him. Although he seemed as thin as ever he looked bigger, taller and definitely much older. From the change in him it could have been five or six years since that morning.

'Go on up and see the child.'

'But . . . ' he hesitated, his eyes widening.

'She wants you to . . . she's waiting. Do you know your way?'

'No.'

'Up the stairs, second door on the right.'

As he went to pass her he stopped and smiled at her, and as she saw what the smile did in almost transfiguring his face she could understand in some part how this dour Scot had come to captivate her niece.

Grace had told her only this morning that he had never yet held the baby in his arms, and Aggie had already made up her mind to rectify this unnatural position by arranging for him to come to her house when Grace and the child would be there. But now there would be no need for her to be a partner in this form of deception. Yet for all that she said, 'If you should be in Newcastle any time you can look me up if you like, I'm in most nights after five. The phone number is Temple 3567 . . . it's easy to remember, 3567.'

He looked at her, his face grave now as he savoured all that her brusque, off-hand invitation implied.

'Thank you.'

He did not move away and she pushed him now with her voice, saying, 'Go on then, get yourself up, and make it snappy.'

Andrew had never been beyond the kitchen nor yet had he seen much of the interior of the house from the outside . . . he had always kept his eyes trained away from the windows when working in the garden . . . and so now the luxurious comfort of the hall, and drawing-room glimpsed through the open door, attacked his natural

159

pride and temporarily brought his native arrogance low. She was used to all this yet she had picked him, and she had loved him . . . did love him. After a moment's pausing, he bounded up the stairs. What were chairs and carpets, anyway? They hadn't brought her happiness, only he had been able to do that. Only he could go on doing that.

The second door on the right was open and Grace was standing in the middle of the room with the child in her arms. Slowly he walked forward, and when he stood in front of her she held out the baby to him. He looked down on it lying in its snowy-white drapery and hesitating, he motioned to his working overcoat.

'Take him.'

He took him. . . . This was his son . . . his son. As he held him and looked for some sign of himself in the laughing eyes and the gurgling, dribbling mouth, his thighs began to tremble, then his knees and finally his arms, and Grace, watching him, laughed gently before saying softly, 'He's beautiful, isn't he?'

'He's like his mother. . . . Take him. . . . I – I'm—'

Grace laughed again, and, taking the child from his arms, placed him in his cot.

They stood side by side now looking down on the baby, until Grace, placing a woolly duck in his hands and touching his cheek, gently whispered, 'Good night, darling, good night.'

Andrew said nothing, the sight of the child in the cot dragged at his eyes, and when Grace, having lowered the light, said, 'Andrew,' he seemed to have difficulty in turning round to her.

They were facing each other in the dim light of the room. The door was closed. It was an opportunity to fall into each other's arms, but neither of them made a move in this direction. Although the desire to throw herself on him was almost overpowering, Grace could not bring herself to love Andrew within the walls of this house, and strangely she sensed the same reluctance in him. She smiled tenderly at him, her heart in her eyes, and as she had touched the child's cheek so now her hand went out and touched his. In a moment it was caught and pressed across his mouth.. She gave a sharp gasp of breath as if the kiss had been on her lips and had checked her breathing. Unable to rely on the strength of her good intentions for a moment longer, she turned about, pulling her hand from him, and made for the door. Slowly he followed her.

Aunt Aggie was not to be seen when they got downstairs and, in the kitchen once more, Grace said, 'I'll make you some tea.'

'No, no, don't bother; my mother will be waiting with it ready.'

'How is she?'

'Oh, she's all right – she's altering my kilt.' He gave a wry smile now and drew his hand down the side of his face. 'Did you know I'm playing the pipes on New Year's Eve?'

'No. Oh, Andrew, where?'

'Here, at the do in the school.'

'No . . . ! When was all this arranged?'

'Oh, the do's been talked about for weeks, but I only said I'd play the other day. I . . . I thought perhaps it being for the Civil Defence and New Year's Eve . . . you . . . you might be there.'

'I would love to go; oh, Andrew, I would . . . and see you in your kilt.' She laughed. 'Will you play-in the New Year?'

'That seems to be the idea.'

'I must come. Aunt Aggie will stay a little longer if I ask her. And, Andrew—' She paused and her voice sank to the merest whisper. 'I'll do my best to get up tomorrow night, I can't tonight.'

His hand came out and gripped hers. 'I'll be there.' His eyes dropped from her gaze for a moment and he turned her hand over in his and looked at it, and then, pressing it close between his two palms, he said, 'Just in case you don't manage it and I don't get a chance to speak to you on New Year's Eve I'd better tell you . . . I've got to register.'

'Andrew!' She sounded aghast. 'But I thought, being a full-time farm-worker, you were deferred.'

'Yes, so did I. But there it is. They're putting women on so I suppose that's the answer.'

'Oh, Andrew . . . Andrew.' She could think of nothing else to say, for she was enveloped in anxiety. Anxiety for his safety, anxiety at the prospect of her loneliness when he would no longer be up on the fells, a mile away, but nevertheless near.

'Does your mother know?'

'No, I haven't told her yet.'

'Do you want to go?'

'Want to go . . . to the war?' He screwed up his face. 'No, I certainly don't. Want to stick bayonets into fellas and blow their brains out? Want to go to the war?' His voice was vehement now and he shook his head. 'The pipes rouse no clan spirit in me. I'm no fighting Scot, although I'm proud of coming from across the border. But war. . . .' Again he shook his head.

'Oh, Andrew.'

She realised from his outburst that he had strong opinions about this war. So far they had never been able to discuss anything other than themselves because their moments together were short and precious but she could see now that he must have done some thinking about the war because he, like all the other young men,

162

would be called upon to fight it, not like Donald and Colonel Farley playing at soldiers in the village. Oh – she shook her head at herself – she supposed she wasn't fair to them, because if there was such a thing as an invasion they would certainly fight. But invasion was a long, long-off chance, and in the meantime she knew that they and most of the older men enjoyed this game of war. It was like an outsize toy with which they could safely play without being held up to ridicule.

'I must talk to you somehow.' His voice was earnest.

'When will it be? I mean when do you register?'

'The third of January, but I may not be called up for weeks.'

Again she said, 'Oh, Andrew,' and the next moment she was in his arms and they were kissing – a short, hard, intense, hungry kiss. It seemed to be over before it had actually begun and he had gone through the door pulling it after him quickly in case the light should show, and she leant against the back of it, her arm crooked and her face hidden in it. What if he were killed and she were left alone? Without Andrew she would be alone. Even the child, somehow, wouldn't count without Andrew.

Aggie stayed and Grace went to the New Year's Eve party. The partitions between the three school-rooms had been pushed back and every seat that lined the walls was occupied, even while the centre of the floor was taken up by those indulging in the Lancers, the barn dance or north-country reels. At one point in the evening when the laughter and dancing were at their height, Grace's conscience pricked her with the thought that Aggie would have enjoyed all this and it had really been a bit thick asking her to stay and look after the child, especially on New Year's Eve, but Aggie had assured her that all she wanted this particular night was bed and a book and perhaps a glass of hot whisky and sugar.

Although Grace could see Donald laughing and chaffing with one and another she had the feeling that he wasn't enjoying himself; the affair was a little too rowdy for him. What was more, no church function, dance or social, had gathered anything like this number into the school-rooms. It was the excitement of war, uniforms, and the uncertainty of seeing another Christmas perhaps that had brought the village out. She had not yet seen Andrew.

At five minutes to twelve the whole company joined hands and the building swelled to the thunder of 'Auld Lang Syne'. Then on the stroke of twelve Mr Blenkinsop raised his fiddle high in one hand and his bow in the other and cried 'Quiet! Quiet, I say . . . ! Listen! Here he comes!' And there, as if from far away across the fells, came the sound of the pipes. Andrew was coming down the main street. Grace's heart began to leap with a strange excitement. Nearer and nearer came the drone. The faces about her were gleaming expectantly, waiting for the mo-ment to burst into cheering when the piper came round the black-out curtain. They were all looking towards the doorway at the end of the hall. Her heart was pounding. It was a moment filled with sentimentalism, patriotism, custom and tradition, even if of another country; but for her was added the knowledge that the piper was hers, and that he was playing for her alone, bringing in the New Year for her alone. There came a great burst of cheering as a hand jerked the curtain aside and Andrew MacIntyre, his kilt swaying, the pipes held high, marched into the room.

Her heart swelled with possessive pride; he looked so gallant, taller than ever in the kilt, handsome, fierce, even war-like. But he wasn't war-like, he didn't want to go to the war, he hated war.

164

The piper did a round of the room, then came to a stop in the centre of the floor and dead opposite to her. But this was not noticeable, for she was one of dozens standing in front of him.

As he finished on a long wail he was blotted from her sight. Everybody was milling together, 'Happy New Year! Happy New Year! Many of them, damnation to Hitler! Oh, we'll Hang out the Washing on the Siegfried Line.'

It was some ten minutes before she saw Andrew again. He had made his way casually towards her. She saw that he was laughing and his eyes were bright, and she wondered if he had had a drink or two. Funny, but she didn't know whether he took anything.

'Have you really got a clan, Andrew?' This was from young Barker, the publican's son.

'A clan! I should say so.' Andrew threw out his chest. 'The Clan MacIntyre.'

Those around laughed. Andrew MacIntyre was a fine player and he was in fine form tonight. Nobody could remember seeing him like this before.

'Have you a war-cry?' the boy now asked.

'We have that . . . Cruachan! Cruachan!'

'What does it mean?'

'Aw, it's taken from the name of a mountain.'

'An' do you ever shout it?'

'Oh, aye, whenever I see a Campbell.'

'A Campbell. Why for?'

'Och! Because they pinched our land from us, the thieving rogues.' Andrew was now talking the thick Scots accent and everyone about was laughing. 'We made the mistake of giving them money instead of a snowball and a white calf.'

'Away! He's pulling your leg, boy.' They pushed at young Barker.

165

'I'm not, I'm not. It's the truth I'm telling you. Once a year the MacIntyres paid for their land with a white calf and a snowball and it's not so very long ago either. But once they started paying in money the rent went up.'

'Oh, he can tell a tale. By, he can! And what a player, eh? Never would have believed it.'

Pride rose in Grace. He was not just a farm-worker, he was Andrew MacIntyre with a clan. He had behind him something that the ordinary man didn't have – tradition, clannish tradition. But what was a clan? All Scots had clans, in fact they were one big clan. She laughed at herself now. With or without the prestige of a clan she loved Andrew MacIntyre. . . .

At half past twelve, as the vicar's wife was handing out refreshments, Andrew MacIntyre approached her and asked her for the pleasure of the Lancers. There was nothing wrong in this – parson or peasant, publican and lawyer were equal on this New Year's morning. So Grace danced with Andrew for the first time. They were both light on their feet, their steps fitted, and as they got into the dance they became dangerously near forgetting where they were, for after changing partners and coming together again their glances would become entwined. Their faces full of youth and love, they could see no-one else. Yet no-one seemed to notice them – this was New Year's Day – perhaps with one exception, Dr Cooper. He had slipped in for a few minutes to see the fun and his attention had been caught by Grace Rouse and young Andrew MacIntyre, arrayed in his kilt, dancing together. They were both young and somehow they matched.

The danger must have made itself apparent to Andrew, for, the dance ended, he left the hall, after saying to a number of people including Grace, 'I'll have to be making my way over the fells; my mother'll be waiting up for her first foot.'

Almost at the same time as Andrew went out Bertrand Farley came in. He was accompanied by two other officers, and if there had been a doubt in Grace's mind as to whether Andrew had had a drink, there was no such doubt on looking at Bertrand Farley, for he was very merry.

That the entry of the three officers put a slight dampener on the company and took away some of the spontaneous informality, bringing in its place a stiffness to the men and a false decorum to the women, was not all Grace's imagination. But this could not last, this was New Year's Day, and soon two of the three officers were dancing.

When Bertrand Farley asked Grace to dance she wanted very much to refuse. Andrew had gone, the night was over for her, she wanted to get back home, but Donald wasn't in sight and she could hardly make a move without him. Several pairs of eyes were on them wondering how the vicar's wife would deal with young Farley and him bottled, and she saw that the least embarrassing thing would be to accept his invitation. Should she refuse, he would likely start on a bout of maudlin persuasion.

The dance was a waltz and they had been circling erratically for only a short time before he gave an exaggerated sigh, and, bringing his face down to hers, he whispered, 'Know somethin'? I promised myself this the first time I saw you. "She'll be a spiffin' dancer," I said. "I'll dance with her one day," that's what I said. Know somethin'? . . . I think you're the best looker in Northumberland . . . honest.'

He stopped in his dancing, pulling Grace to a halt. She had made no comment, and so he said, 'You don't believe me?' His bulbous eyes looked as if they were going to drop out of their sockets.

'Do you want to go on with the dance?'

The floor was so packed that the incident passed unnoticed.

'Look . . . ' His arm drew her more tightly to him. 'I know girls . . . I know women . . . all types, all classes. Oh yes, little Bertrand's been around.'

He was coming to a stop when she said, 'We'd better sit down.'

'No, no.' He waltzed her more swiftly now. 'I'm not drunk, don't think I'm drunk. I've had a few. It's New Year's Eve . . . no . . . New Year's Day. We're at war, d'you know that? And little Bertrand here might go and be killed. Any moment little Bertrand might go and be killed and then you'll be sorry you weren't nice to him.'

'Will you stop being silly, or do I have to sit down?'

For answer he waltzed her even more quickly. But when he stumbled and nearly brought them both to the floor she forced him to stop and said coldly, 'I think we'd better sit down.'

'All right, all right, anything you say. You order, I obey. And how! Let's sit on the balcony, eh? In the moonlight on the balcony. That's what the villain does. When the villain's going after the parson's wife he takes her on the moonlight in the balcony.'

At this verbal mix-up Grace laughed. She had to be annoyed or she had to laugh . . . she decided to laugh.

'What you want is a pot of strong coffee.'

'Anything you say. Lead on. Coffee it is. Coffee it must be. There's nothing stronger in this joint, I suppose. Old Barker's sold out. We called in there; he was as dry as a haddock. Not even any droppings. That's what war does. Expects you to be a brave little boy and no fire water. . . .'

Daft.' He talked as he rocked gently behind Grace along the passage towards the school kitchen.

There was only Mrs Twait and Kate Shawcross in the kitchen, and Grace, looking at Mrs Twait, asked, 'Is there any coffee left, Mrs Twait?'

'Yes, plenty.' Mrs Twait lifted up the jug from the stove.

'Happy New Year, Miss Shawcross,' Bertrand Farley was bowing low to the postmistress; and with a look that held no touch of Christian spirit or yet the spirit of a new-born year, Kate passed him without a word and left the kitchen.

'There, she thinks I'm drunk. I'm – I'm not drunk, am I?' He now appealed to Mrs Twait. And Mrs Twait's small compact body began to wobble with her laughter and she said, 'Well, I wouldn't say you were drunk, Mr Farley, but at the same time I wouldn't say you were a kick in the backside of it.' On this and a high laugh she also left the kitchen.

'Here, drink this.' Grace handed him a cup of black coffee. She had never liked Bertrand Farley, but at this moment, strangely, she saw nothing to dislike in him. He was silly, empty-headed, he was drunk and, who knew, as he said, he might be dead this time next year.

'Thanks. Thank you, my fair lady, my fair goddess of the pukka parsonage.' He took a drink of the coffee and then made a horrible grimace. 'Ooh . . . ! Oooh, my God! What stuff! Nevertheless thanks . . . Grace. . . . Nice name, Grace. I made up a poem about you once. Ah . . . that surprises you, doesn't it, that I can write poetry? Oh, I'm a deep one. You must get to know me. What about it, Grace – what about getting to know me?'

'Don't be silly.'

'I'm not being silly, honest to God. Serious, thought about it a lot. What you say, eh? What about it? I'll write

169

another poem about you . . . about Grace . . . Darling. Ha ha! That's funny, Grace Darling!'

She had turned from him to put the jug on the stove when his arm came round her shoulders. 'Grace Darling.'

Now she ceased to be amused and was on the point of shrugging herself away when a voice spoke from the doorway. It said 'Grace,' and they both turned to see Donald standing there.

'Are you ready for home?'

'Yes. Oh yes.' She moved hastily forward.

'I . . . I was just telling your . . . your wife . . . ' Bertrand Farley walked unsteadily towards Donald. Then, shaking his head, he said, 'What was I telling her? Oh yes.' He now thrust his finger towards Donald's chest saying, 'You've got a very beautiful woman, Mr Vicar, do you know that? You're a lucky bloke, do you know that, eh? And there's something else I'd like to tell you. You know I've always wanted to tell you this. That girl, that beau . . . beautiful girl should have stuck to the pian . . . piano; an' another thing . . . '

'I'm afraid I haven't got time to listen.' Donald's voice was deadly cold. He stared with almost open hatred at the blinking eyelids and blurred pupils of young Farley before turning from him and walking hastily down the passage after Grace. . . .

Ten minutes later they were going up the hill towards home and for the third time since leaving the hall Donald said, 'You must really think me a fool, I heard what he said. He called you Grace, darling, and a man doesn't do that on the spur of the moment, drunk or not. You can't tell me that.'

Grace had already given him the true version of this episode . . . she had stated her defence . . . and now she remained quiet until they reached the drive to the house when Donald, still talking, said, 'You forget your

170

position. You're the vicar's wife; you frequently forget that, and . . . '

'And Grace Darling was the lighthouse-keeper's daughter,' Grace cried flippantly. 'I tell you, Donald, he was quoting Grace Darling, he wasn't calling me Grace . . . darling.'

They were in the drawing-room now. The fire was blazing merrily, Stephen's first Christmas tree was sparkling in the far corner of the room, the holly was lying in strips at the foot of the coloured plates that lined the rack high up round the walls. The setting looked like a picture you would see on a Christmas card, charming, warm and inviting, yet at this moment she hated it and the whole house . . . and its master. Its master most of all, for there he stood, determined to go on with his cross-examination until she admitted the truth. What truth? She had told him the truth. She turned her back on him and closed her eyes as he said, 'Well, supposing I wasn't hearing aright, were my eyes deceiving me when I saw him with his arm about you?'

She had had enough; she couldn't stand the sound of his voice a moment longer, she would have to combat it with something. Swinging round, she said, 'No, they didn't deceive you, no more than my eyes did when I saw you holding hands with Kate Shawcross in the vestry.' If she had levelled a tommy-gun at his chest he couldn't have shown more surprise, and she cried at him, 'Yes, yes, now I'm the accuser and you are on the defensive. Dear, dear Kate,' – she mimicked his attitude and his voice – 'what would I have done without you? Dear . . . dear Kate.'

'Be quiet! Be quiet!' His face was as red as a turkey cock's. 'It wasn't like that at all, you misunderstood.'

'Oh yes, I – I misunderstood.' Her head went back on a harsh laugh. 'All right then, I misunderstood, but nevertheless you were standing in the vestry, her hands tightly locked in yours, and she was gazing up at you in adoration.'

'Be quiet, will you! I know the time you are referring to. It was nothing like that at all. I was merely thanking her for all the work she had done.'

'Yes, yes, I understand, and consoling her because she was disappointed there wasn't going to be a war and she wouldn't be called upon to run the village besides running the church.'

'Grace, if you dare say another word!' He was standing near her, towering over her.

'Yes, what will you do?' She waited while they glared at each other. And then she added, 'Because a drunken man talks a lot of damn nonsense you accuse me of encouraging him. You say I did it in front of over a hundred people because I danced with him. Yet I see you with my own eyes making love to Kate Shawcross—'

'Don't say that! Don't say that!' His voice thundered at her in denial. 'I wasn't making love to Miss Shawcross.'

'No, you weren't Donald, and I believe you, for you're not capable of making love to anyone.' She thought for a moment he was going to strike her. There was a terrible look on his face. But this could not daunt her and she gabbled on now, 'But Kate Shawcross doesn't know that; she thinks you're in love with her, and if it wasn't for me she would be mistress here, and of the church. . . . Oh, don't let us forget, of the church.'

'You're out of your mind, woman; you're out of your mind altogether.'

'I'm not out of my mind and you know it, and I don't care about Kate Shawcross being in love with you. I'm sorry for her, for she's being deceived.' Her tongue was running away with her. She was on the point of adding, 'as you are being deceived', and the next moment she

172

would have flung at him the name of Andrew MacIntyre. But the drawing-room door swung open and Aggie stood there in her dressing-gown. She stood looking from one to the other in silence, then she said, 'I'd be a little quieter if I were you. Besides waking the child, people away on the road will hear you, and there'll be plenty going up and down on this morning, at any rate.'

'This happens to be—' Donald had reached his full stature and his face had taken on a purple tinge on sight of Aggie.

Aggie raised her hand. 'All right, all right, don't tell me. This is your house and you are the master in it and you can shout as much as you like. But it doesn't appear to me to be very seemly for the vicar and his wife to be going on like this on New Year's morning. Unless of course there's an excuse because you are drunk. . . . And of course that's not something that can be ruled out altogether, is it?' Aggie's tongue too had run away with her, and with that last crack she knew she had closed the door on future visits to the vicarage. . . . Well, that wouldn't worry her, she'd had more than a bellyful of the big sanctimonious 'I am' during these holidays. How that girl put up with it she didn't know. She returned Donald's furious glare with a disdainful glance, then went out. And Grace, after one last look at her husband, followed her.

Not until they were in Aggie's room and Grace had sunk on to the edge of the bed did they speak.

'He's found out?'

'No, no.' Grace moved her head from side to side. 'You'll never believe it but he thinks I'm having an affair with Bertrand Farley.'

'Bertrand Farley? That goggle-eyed fathead?'

'That goggle-eyed fathead.'

'In the name of God!'

173

'Yes, Aunt Aggie, in the name of God,' and then she added, 'That's the second time I've been on the point of telling him the truth and something's happened.'

'Are you sorry?'

'I don't know. I really don't know, Aunt Aggie.'

7

It was in October 1940 that Deckford had its first raid. It was on a Tuesday night and it started at half past seven.

The inhabitants complained that the war had changed the village out of all recognition. What they really referred to was the RAF camp that had risen in the valley only a mile to the west of the village. It was a fighter base and both night and day planes flew backwards and forwards over the fells until, as some hardy souls said, they couldn't get to sleep if they didn't hear them. And then there were the RAF men themselves. Every day the village street was like market day in Morpeth, and on Saturday afternoon there was as much chance of getting a bus into town as of chartering a private plane.

And the evacuees. There were not so many as yet, but enough to make competition rather keen to billet airmen who were living out with their wives, for such couples meant more money and less trouble than looking after somebody else's bairns.

But there was no doubt that the countryside around the village had changed completely. The moorlands were studded with pyramidal shapes of concrete, rolls of barbed wire met you at every turn, and men had started to work on the far side of the quarry again, cutting out great slabs of rock where the workmen had left off years previously.

This last had come as a great blow to Grace, for Andrew, now in the Highland Fusiliers, was stationed in Scotland, which was, after all, not very far away, and after the first two months of square-bashing he had managed to slip home every other week. Following one period, when they hadn't been able to meet for nearly six weeks, Grace began to visit her Aunt Aggie every Saturday. Most times she took the child with her, but when she didn't Mrs Blenkinsop stayed on until her return. If on her visit she did not see Andrew there would be letters awaiting her from him, and in Aggie's comfortable little secluded house she would sit in peace and peruse them, then write at length about what was in her heart. Such was the pattern of Grace's life during the first months of 1940.

Saturday, 1 June, 1940, was a fateful day – it saw the end of Dunkirk. Three men from the village and Bertrand Farley, all in the same regiment, were known to be in the retreat, and nothing had been heard of them until three o'clock in the afternoon when Colonel Farley came rushing down to the ARP centre, his bloated, lined face aglow. He had just had a call from Dover: Bertrand was all right, as also were Ted Bamford and Steve Brignall. The colonel was on his way now to the blacksmith's house to tell Mrs Bamford the good news concerning her son.

The following week Bertrand Farley came home and Grace ran into him in the village street. He had an aura about him – he had been in Dunkirk. But to Grace there seemed to be only one apparent change in him: he had lost some flesh. His manner was still perky, even more so than usual. In spite of the trouble he had caused her at Christmas she could not help laughing at him. It was odd but she found that she even liked him a little now. He was silly, he was harmless, he was what her Aunt Aggie had called him . . . a fathead.

Miss Shawcross, looking into the street through the side of the black-out blind which she kept permanently drawn, saw at that moment the vicar's wife laughing with Captain Farley. The vicar's wife laughed too loud, she thought; she did not seem to realise that she had a position to uphold. Miss Shawcross shook her head. Poor, poor vicar. Even in her most revealing moments Miss Shawcross never allowed herself to allude to the vicar as Donald.

It was that same afternoon that Miss Shawcross asked the vicar if he knew that Captain Farley was home. She had seen the Captain talking to Mrs Rouse in the High Street.

A few days later Colonel Farley gave a small party, a sort of thanksgiving for the safe return of his son, and to it were invited the vicar and his wife. Grace knew that Donald would have liked to refuse the invitation but had been unable to see his way clear to do so, and she was well aware that his weather eye was on her from the moment they entered the Farleys' house. She smiled wryly to herself when, after a game of bridge had been proposed and two tables had been made up, she and Bertrand Farley were left adrift. She had refused Bertrand's invitation to play the piano, saying she had not kept up her practice and would rather not. But when he suggested they should look round the garden she accepted. He was not drunk tonight, he would not be silly.

She felt no compunction that Donald's bridge would be affected, and although she did not think the scene of New Year's morning would be enacted again she was quite prepared to undergo the same silent and censorious displeasure as that to which he had treated her for the most of January, for she preferred this to his jocular, bouncing, daddy-boy act.

Yet, being fair, she knew that the daddy act was not all pretence, far from it. He had a deep affection for the child; in fact she could give it another name – a possessive love. On one occasion she had come across him holding the boy tightly to him with the child's head pressed closely into his shoulder. His own eyes were closed and on his face had been a look that had touched her and drew from her a surge of conscience, and for a moment she had wished that the child could have been his.

There were two results of her walk in the garden that night. The first: the disquieting knowledge that Bertrand Farley was really in love with her, yet he had not made love to her in any way. The odd thing was he hardly spoke to her once they had left the house, but while they sat on the garden seat he had looked at her in telling silence, then had abruptly got up and walked away.

The second: when Donald and she returned home, after a journey during which no word was exchanged. Donald went straight to his study and there must have exceeded his daily drop . . . for the following day she found that quite some inroad had been made into a fresh bottle of whisky.

Sometimes on a Sunday when she would listen to him expounding from the pulpit she would wonder how, in his own mind, he reconciled the fact that their well-stocked wine-cabinet was supplied by the black market. Not through Mr Barker at the Stag – oh, no, that would never have done – but through Uncle Ralph. Uncle Ralph had friends and could get most commodities that money could buy. Nor did Donald question that he always had butter on his bread and bacon every morning. No. No. Men weren't supposed to notice trifles like that, their minds were taken up with higher things, they just ate what was put in front of them. She often smiled sadly to herself.

The months of summer wore away and so October came. The Battle of Britain had been won, but night bombing was on in earnest. On the Monday night before the attempted raid on the aerodrome, Colonel Farley,

Farmer Toole, Dr Cooper, Mr Thompson and . . . Miss Shawcross came to the vicarage to hold a meeting regarding the coming influx of evacuees. They were to be mostly children from the shipping districts of the Tyne. Before the meeting was over Bertrand Farley called. He was in possession of a service car and had come to pick up his father.

The meeting in the study over, Donald, ahead of the others, opened the drawing-room door to see Bertrand Farley standing in front of Grace and to hear the tail-end of his words.

After an exchange of greetings, the committee broke up, and when they had all gone, Donald, without speaking or even looking at Grace, once again went to his study.

The next night the air-raid siren went at seven o'clock. They were sitting in the drawing-room at the time and the sound apparently startled Donald. From the look on his face he might never have heard an air-raid siren before. He had not left her for a moment since teatime and Grace had begun to puzzle over this. Usually, following tea, he went either down to the village or into his study. But this night he had sat with her, even followed her into the kitchen. And now when the sirens went he exclaimed aloud, 'No! Oh no.'

Before the wail had died away Grace had rushed upstairs and collected Stephen, and when she reached the kitchen Donald was waiting for her. He had already donned his top coat and gas-mask. After switching off the lights he opened the door and guided her out and around the side of the house.

The night was black, but he did not switch on the torch until they reached the shelter, then he shone it on the steps for her to enter. Once inside and the door closed, he switched on the light. Then, looking round, he said, 'You have everything. I'll have to go, you'll be all right?'

'Yes, yes, I'll be all right.'

He seemed to be on the point of speaking again; instead he jerked his head with a half-angry helpless gesture and, turning from her, went up the steps.

She had reached out her hand to pick up a book from the top of the cupboard to take to the bunk with her when she heard the click, and her glance darted towards the steps and the cellar door. The sound was like the key being turned. She must have imagined it. Her hand had descended on the book when she swung round and went swiftly up the steps to the door and turned the knob. She knew that her face was registering blank amazement. Why had he locked the door? He had locked her in. She felt a slight tremor of panic rising in her. What had he locked the door for! What if a bomb dropped and she couldn't get out? 'Donald . . . Donald!' She looked upwards, yelling at the ceiling which was the floor of the hall. 'Donald . . .! Donald . . .!' He couldn't have gone away, he couldn't. 'Donald . . .! Donald!' After a moment she tried the door again, shaking it viciously. Then slowly she walked down the steps.

'Mm . . . mm . . . Mumma.' The child began to winge.

'Go to sleep, darling; it's all right, it was only Mummy calling.'

'Mumma.'

'There, there, don't cry. It's all right, it was only Mammy. Go to sleep. Ssh!' She sat patting Stephen, her eyes looking upwards. What had made him lock the door? He had been acting funny all evening, at least he hadn't acted to his usual pattern. Why had he sat with her? He had never sat with her after tea, not even when they were first married. There had always been something he wanted to do about that time. . . . Then the answer came to her. It came in the picture of his face as she had seen it in the drawing-room doorway last night when he stood looking at Bertrand Farley. Bertrand Farley's leave was up. More for something to say than anything else she had asked him, 'When do you go back?' and he had replied, 'Tomorrow. Report Wednesday o-seven hundred.' His jocular front was well in play again. 'But they don't get anything out of me, I travel in the small hours, so I needn't make a move until eight tomorrow night.' . . . Eight tomorrow night. No. No. It was too funny. But she remembered Donald had gone straight into his study without a glance at her. . . . He thought she had intended seeing Bertrand Farley off, so he had locked the door, locked her in here, and anything could happen. Didn't he realise that she couldn't possibly leave the child even if she wanted to? She sat down in the basket chair near the little table and, putting her elbow on it, rested her head on her hand.

The more she thought about the situation the more she was filled with anger . . . and then fear. She hated being locked in. As a child if she went home and found her mother out she would not lock herself in for safety but would open both the back and front doors, so leaving herself a way of escape. She had never been able to sleep in a room when the door was locked. She had never even locked her door against Donald, not that she had any need to.

It was about ten seconds to half past seven when she heard the sound of the planes and instinctively she knew they weren't ours. Their drone was heavy and different somehow. And then the first bomb dropped. The sound of it crashing into the earth was like great teeth grinding down into cinder toffee, and as she flung herself from the chair on to the bunk over the child the light in the low ceiling flickered twice, then went out.

'Mumma . . . Mumma . . . Mumma.'

'It's . . . it's all right, darling. It's all right, Mammy's here.' Her voice was trembling, her whole body was trembling. Oh God! Oh God! What if one fell on the house and she couldn't get out of the cellar? There came now the distant sound of the pop-pop of anti-aircraft guns, followed by the low, thick murmur of a plane seemingly crossing straight over the house. In the inky darkness she looked upwards, too petrified for a moment to move. Then the earth shuddered again.

'Mumma . . . Mumma. Dadda . . . Dadda. Stevie . . . '

'It's . . . all right . . . darling. Mam . . . Mammy's here.' She could hardly get the words through her chattering teeth.

There came more thick, dull droning, then the great tremor that ran through the earth seemed to run straight through her, and it was followed by another and another. . . . They were bombing the village, the little village. Why the village? There was nothing in the village. . . . The aerodrome. They thought they were bombing the aerodrome. Jesus . . . Jesus . . . she should pray, but she couldn't pray. She couldn't pray. If only there was somebody with her, somebody to speak to. Oh, Andrew! She didn't want to die without seeing Andrew. . . . And the child. O, God! Don't let anything happen to my child. If only she had a light. . . . The candles – of course, the candles. 'There, darling, lie still, lie still. Mammy's going to light the candles, Mammy's going to make a light. There now.'

She moved backwards off the bunk and groped towards the top of the chest where the books were. There was a candle already in its holder next to the bookrack. With trembling fingers she lifted it up and groped round the broad saucer rim for matches. There were no matches on it. Her fingers, like a blind man's, spread over the books and over the top of the chest. When she had covered its entire surface the panic whirled through her body and corkscrewed through her head, and she only stopped herself from screaming aloud. He couldn't have taken the matches, he couldn't have taken the matches. She was on her hands and knees feeling around the legs of the chest, around the floor. He couldn't have taken the matches. He was always picking up boxes of matches, but he couldn't have taken these matches, he couldn't. . . . And he had gone off with the torch. She remembered seeing that in his hand as he went up the steps.

He had locked her in, he had deliberately locked her and the child in, and they were bombing the village. But he couldn't have taken the matches. 'Andrew . . . Andrew, he has taken the matches, I haven't got a light, I can't light the candle. . . .' She was scrambling about on her hands and knees near the table now and she gripped at its thin leg with both hands and whimpered. Steady, steady. Don't scream. Go and lie down, put your face into the pillow, it will be like night. Go to sleep. In this instant there came another thud, and as the foundations of the house trembled she flung herself forward in the direction of the bunk, dashing her forehead into the woodwork.

'Mumma!'

As she smothered the child to her there came a different sound still – it was that of a falling plane. As it screeched on its downward plunge it seemed so near that she drew her head right down between her shoulders as if avoiding contact with it. It was only a matter of seconds before she heard the crash but they appeared like long, long minutes to her. Had it fallen in the wood? It had fallen somewhere near. People would soon be milling about and then she would shout and they would break the door open.

There was no sound of any kind now, not the sound of bombs or planes, or human footsteps. Nothing. She turned her eyes from the pillow and looked upwards.

The blackness was thick. She had heard of pit blackness which was darker than pitch blackness. This was the pit blackness that the miners had to endure when they were in a fall and the lights went out. Oh God! If only somebody would come. They would all be in the village. Had anyone been killed? Had Donald been killed? She hoped he had. Yes, she did, she did. He had locked her in and taken the matches. Be quiet, don't say things like that, they're wicked. Well, wasn't he wicked? He was a walking hypocrite. She hoped . . . Be quiet! be quiet!

'Mumma! Mumma!'

'Don't cry, my love.'

The child began to cry loudly now, and above his wailing she imagined she heard the sound of a car. She rose from the bunk and groped her way up the steps to the door. After a moment of waiting and no further sound coming to her, she called, 'Hello! Hello! Is there anyone there?' Only silence answered her, as deep and thick as the blackness about her. Suddenly she was thumping on the door with her fists, yelling, 'Open the door! Open the door! Help! Help!' She thumped until her arms ached and she dropped on to her knees exhausted.

The child was quiet now as if he, too, was listening. But her fear must have threaded its way to him, for as she stumbled down the steps, panic swamping her, he let out an ear-splitting scream.

Feverishly she gathered him up in her arms. Somebody must come soon. Donald would realise how frightened she must be locked in here and come hurrying back. Any minute now he would come hurrying back. He must come soon, he must. This unnatural quietness, this darkness would drive her . . . She did not finish but hugged the child closer to her and began to rock him.

A short while later, when he had dropped off to sleep again and still there was no sound, she stood up peering into the blackness. Then groping towards the chair she carried it carefully to the side of the steps where the window was, and, standing on it, she began to pick and claw at the packing between the boards. But Miss Shawcross had done her work well. She might have mixed the paper with cement for all the impression Grace could make on it. She knew there was no possibility of getting out this way. All she was aiming at now was a little slit of lighter night to penetrate this inferno of blackness.

When she found that her efforts were fruitless she got slowly down from the chair and carried it back in the direction of the table. And the quietness that was about her settled in her. It was an awe-filled quietness in which she watched her mind throw off restraint and drag up from its deep chambers repressed recriminations of the last three and a half years. When it began, as it were, handing them to her, she took them and delivered them in low, staccato sentences. 'I hate him! I loathe him! He's cruel. Ben said he was a cruel bugger, and he is. A Christian, a man of God. Huh! A man of God. Bloody hypocrite! Bloody . . . bloody . . . bloody.' Her swearing was brought to a sharp stop by the familiar, but now muffled boom of the clock in the hall above striking eight. She looked up – only eight o'clock. She felt she had been in this darkness for hours. But why wasn't there any sound? What had happened in the village? Had any of the houses been hit? Oh, if only someone would come soon. She hoped it wasn't him. She prayed it wouldn't be him. For she might do something. She might even kill him. 'Young wife stabs minister. Mind turned through darkness . . . no matches . . . no matches.'

She was still sitting at the table when the clock chimed the half-hour and at the same time the all-clear went. The next sound that came to her was the strokes of nine o'clock. She still hadn't moved.

185

The swearing was now confined to her mind, like the sound of a gramophone being played in a distant room, unintelligible but still there. She had been in this thick blackness for one hour and a half. Everybody in the village must be dead. Donald must be dead. Some time, perhaps tomorrow morning, somebody would come. She turned her head away on the thought of not being found until tomorrow morning. She knew that after tonight she would never be the same again, never feel nice inside again, for in spite of her double life she felt herself to be . . . a nice person still. But when you swore in your mind, you couldn't be nice, and if she was left all night and the swearing got worse, if she was left here until tomorrow morning until the Air Force got round . . . she shuddered from head to foot. . . .

When she heard the sound of footsteps to the left of her she turned her eyes slowly upwards towards the door, and when the key turned in the lock she did not rise and rush towards the steps but closed her eyes against the painful brightness of the torch.

She could say nothing, not even when she heard his voice, slower than usual, different somehow, asking, 'Why are you in the dark?'

The torch was lying on the table now, between them, and she was on her feet, her hands gripping the edge of the table, and she leaned forward, crouched over it like some wild animal ready to spring. And the words that came from her lips were thick and guttural.

'You . . . you cruel b . . . beast . . . swine. You . . . you locked me in . . . you locked me in!'

'Grace!' His voice was low yet commanding. 'Grace, be quiet. Don't talk to me like that. Why didn't you light the candles?'

'You . . . you took the matches.'

'Oh my God!' She saw him put his hand to his head.
'You bloody—!'

'Grace! Listen to me. Grace!' He had her by the
shoulders. 'Be quiet! Don't dare say such words, do you
hear, don't dare! Listen to me. Something dreadful has
happened this night.'

'Yes . . . yes . . . ' she flung his hands off her and
stumbled backwards. 'I know that. You tried to send
me mad, didn't you?'

'Is she all right?' The voice came from the top of
the steps and Grace looked up to see the dim outline
of Kate Shawcross. There seemed something different
about her voice too, there was something different about
all their voices.

Kate Shawcross . . . Kate Shawcross. He wouldn't
lock her in, oh no. 'I was locked in,' she cried.

'Grace!'

With a wild movement she bent down and gathered
the child to her, and like someone drunk she went up
the steps and into the glorious star-filled night that in
comparison with the blackness she had lived in for several
eternities was like the brightness of the sun.

As she passed her, Kate Shawcross asked in that different voice, 'But why are you in the dark?' and Donald,
his voice laden with contrition, answered, 'It's me, I must
have picked up the matches.'

'Oh no, vicar, no!'

Kate Shawcross now ran on ahead into the kitchen,
and within a few seconds three candles were glowing.
In their light Grace turned her furious wild gaze on
them both, her mouth open to speak, and then her lips
closed. They were both filthy, their clothes were torn,
and underneath the dirt that hid their faces they had the
same kind of pallor. As she looked at Miss Shawcross the
postmistress suddenly put her hand out to a chair and,

187

turning it round, sat down, and Donald, going swiftly to her side, said, 'I'll get you something.'

'No, no, it's all right.' Miss Shawcross looked up at Grace. 'It was dreadful! I'll never be able to forget.'

Grace turned her eyes slowly towards Donald and he said quietly, 'They bombed the village. They were trying for the airfield . . . Mrs Blenkinsop. . . .'

'Mrs B. . . . ?' Grace's lips just formed the word. 'Dead?'

Donald nodded.

Grace hitched the child further to her and sat down.

'And Mrs Cooper. Poor Mrs Cooper.'

Grace turned her wide staring eyes on Miss Shawcross now. The postmistress's head was bent and moving from side to side and the tears were raining down her face.

Stupidly Grace said, 'Renee dead?' Then she looked up at Donald again. 'The child?'

'She's all right.'

'David?'

'His leg is hurt, they've taken him to hospital. Renee must have just left the child in the shelter and gone indoors for a moment.'

'And old Ben Fairfoot.' Miss Shawcross was crying unrestrainedly by now.

'Ben? Ben? Dead?'

Miss Shawcross nodded her head deeply. 'And the three Cummings children . . . my Sunday-school children, and Mrs Watson . . . '

Grace watched her head sinking lower now, the tears dropping on to the table from her chin, and all she could say to herself was, 'Ben? Oh! Ben.' It was odd but it was Ben she was most sorry for. Yet he was old and would have died soon, and Renee was young. Renee had fought T.B. and conquered it, now she was dead. And Mrs Blenkinsop, she would never come into this kitchen again. Never again would she say, 'Mornin', ma'am,' never again would she give her the gen on the village, the undercover news. Poor Mrs B. . . . But Ben . . . Ben. Before these dreadful happenings her own ordeal sank away into a pocket and rested temporarily.

'Don't cry, please don't cry.' Donald was standing at the side of Miss Shawcross. He did not touch her, not even to put his hand on her shoulder. Grace would not have minded if before her eyes he had taken her in his arms and comforted her, kissed her.

'You must have something to steady you, we must all have something.' He turned round and left the room, his step heavy and slow, and when he returned he brought three glasses and a bottle half full of whisky.

'Drink this.' He handed Miss Shawcross a glass three parts full, and when without glancing at it she shook her head, he said, 'Drink up.'

'I . . . I don't usually, Vic . . . ar.'

'There has been nothing usual about tonight; you must drink it.'

Grace watched Miss Shawcross coughing and spluttering as the whisky hit her throat. She watched Donald finish his full glass of raw spirit at one gulp and when almost immediately he replenished it she made no comment to herself, for, as he had said, this was an unusual night. . . . Picking up her glass and easing the child on to one arm, she rose from the table, and she said no word to either of them as she left the kitchen.

Fifteen minutes later she was sitting in bed, a candle burning to the side of her. She was sitting propped up, staring ahead. Renee Cooper, Mrs Blenkinsop and Ben. There were others, but these were the three she herself had known, and now they were no more. Had Ben met up with Miss Tupping? She hoped so – oh, she hoped so. Perhaps Miss Tupping had already started a garden. . . .

189

Stupid thought, all stupid thoughts, meeting and coming together. All balderdash. When you were dead, you were dead, blown into a thousand pieces. . . . No, no, she mustn't think like that. It was better, more comforting, to think that at this moment Miss Tupping was leading Ben along the grassy path of a beautiful garden, a pattern of the garden that she had left behind. And there would be a lonicera hedge, a high lonicera hedge. She could see Ben and Miss Tupping standing before it and Ben would say, 'Well, here's one he won't cut down.' She was thinking stupidly, spitefully. She mustn't think like that; it had been a dreadful night for him, for all of them.

She heard Donald returning from taking Miss Shawcross down to the village. She waited to hear him come upstairs and go into his room, but some little time elapsed before the sound of his footsteps came on the stairs. A few minutes after his door had closed on him it opened again, and then hers opened. He opened it as he knocked.

Slowly he crossed to the side of the bed, and when he was standing above her he muttered thickly, 'I'm sorry, Grace, very, very sorry. I did wrong. For–for–forgive me.'

She looked up at him. Like Miss Shawcross he was crying. Whether he would have cried without the aid of the whisky she did not know but she realised with a start that he was tipsy, quite tipsy, and he looked both pathetic and ludicrous. She said flatly, 'It's all right, it doesn't matter.'

'But – b-b-but Grace, I'm sorry.'

She moved restlessly against the pillow. 'It's all right, I've told you. Anyway, in comparison with what happened tonight, it's nothing.' Yet even as she spoke she knew that the terror she had experienced in the blackness would remain with her for a long time. She did not think it would take twenty years to conquer it.

'Grace. Grace.' He was bending over her now, his hands on the bed.

'It's all right, I've told you, Donald. Go to bed; you'll feel better in the morning.'

'I – I can't go to bed, not by myself. I keep seeing them. I want comfort, Grace. Let me lie . . . lie in your arms.'

'No, Donald, no. You won't get to sleep.' She moved away in the bed and put her hand out in a protesting movement as he bent further over her. 'Go to bed. Please. . . . Please, Donald.'

'Oh, Grace, Grace. I'm unhappy, Grace.'

She closed her eyes against the wave of revulsion that swept over her when she saw him slide to his knees, but when from that position his arms groped for her, her eyes stretched and she said firmly, 'No! Donald, no!'

'Grace . . . oh, Grace.' He had hold of her.

'No, Donald, no! I tell you no!' She was shouting now.

'Ssh! Ssh! You'll . . . you'll waken the nipper. Just let me . . . me lie . . . lie here with my head on your breast like this.'

'No. No, I've told you. Donald . . . Donald, do you hear me? Get away!' Oh God! God in heaven! An unusual night he had said. What an ending to an unusual night!

She closed her eyes tight and the clock in the hall struck ten.

8

Grace had a new cook. She was not only a cook but a general help too, and full time. Her name was Peggy Mather. She was twenty-eight, big and of a surly disposition, and she was Miss Shawcross's niece. Why she had chosen to evacuate herself to this out-of-the-way village Grace did not know. The reason she gave was that she was fed up with the raids on the Tyne. Yet she showed no fear when the air-raid warnings went, and no matter what anybody else did she went stolidly about her work. What had really brought her from Newcastle to live with her aunt whom up to date she had rarely visited, Grace did not know and did not care, she was only too relieved to have her in the house, for now added to the household were David Cooper and three-year-old Veronica.

Young Dr Cooper was no longer young Dr Cooper. His small, slim stature had always made him appear years younger than he was, but the night of the raid had banked the years on him with one blow, and now he looked a man of fifty, not thirty-eight. After only three weeks' stay in hospital he had returned to the village, and in spite of protests plunged straight away into his practice; and as there was only a heap of rubble where his house had stood he had accepted without protest the invitation from the vicar to make his home with them.

It was in the morning-room at Willow Lea that he held his surgery. The expensive Persian carpet that had covered the hall had been taken up, chairs lined the walls between the doors, and the table was laden with old magazines.

Grace cast her eyes on the untidy jumble on the table as she crossed the hall towards the morning-room with a small tray in her hand. It always irritated her to see books and magazines thrown down open, but when a patient's turn came he or she just threw the reading material on to the table, never thinking.

She knocked at what was now the surgery door and David Cooper's voice called, 'Come in.'

'Oh, it's you, Grace. No more out there?'

'No.'

'This snow doesn't seem to have frozen the 'flu. If you ask me it's snowing germs. The whole Barker family are down now, mother and five kids.'

Grace put the tray down on the end of his desk. David talked a lot of shop these days, in fact he talked nothing else. It was over five months since the raid, but he was still fighting off the memory with work and talk of work.

'Drink that up while it's hot, David.'

'Thanks, Grace. . . . Grace . . . ' He was writing something rapidly on a prescription block and did not look up at her as he went on, his voice a low mumble now, 'Don't you think we'd better have a talk?'

She had been on the point of turning away but she stopped and looked down on his bent head. His hair was thin on the top, the rest was pepper-and-salt and had a grizzled look. She sat slowly down in the patients' chair to the right of him.

'You're pregnant, aren't you?' He still continued writing.

'Yes.'

'I remember asking you this question once before . . . does Donald know?'

'No.'

193

'Why haven't you told him?'

There was a long pause, and then she said, 'Because it isn't his.'

His eyes darted to her. Her words were like a jab in the arm penetrating his inner apathy.

'What are you saying?'

Her eyes dropped from his and she joined her hands together and pressed them tightly in her lap.

'Just that. Donald isn't capable of giving any woman a child.'

David bent forward; his hands went out and took hers from her lap, and as he gripped them he asked, 'Stephen?'

'No . . . and yet.' She shook her head violently. 'Oh, I don't know.' Then again she said, 'No. No, he couldn't be.'

He stared at her blankly. So this was it. He had always known it really . . . nerves didn't go to pieces like hers had done for nothing. Yet when Stephen had come he had thought he must have been wrong. Poor girl. Poor Grace. 'Can you tell me who it is . . . ? Farley?'

Her head swung up. 'Bertrand Farley?' She smiled sadly. 'Oh, David, not you too.'

The doctor moved his head ruefully. 'Well, I can't think of anyone else and I knew he was gone on you. You only had to look at him when you were about.'

'It should be funny, but it isn't. . . . Bertrand Farley.' She closed her eyes for a moment, then, looking at him again, she said rapidly, 'Donald thought there was something between us and on the night of the raid he locked me in the cellar. He thought I'd made arrangements to meet Bertrand. When the lights went out I was in the dark, the black dark.' She said slowly now, 'He had gone off with the matches. . . . You know his habit. Oh, David, it was terrible. . . . Oh, I know, David, it

194

was nothing to what happened in the village. I know what I experienced was nothing compared with that, I know, I know' – she kept moving her head – 'but it had a funny effect on me, David. . . . David, I'm no longer nice inside. I no longer like myself, if you know what I mean.' She moved her hands within his. 'I find I'm swearing all the time inside, inside my head. I started to swear at Donald down there in the dark that night, and now sometimes for hours on end I'm swearing, and it frightens me, David.'

'Now, now.' He patted her hand. 'Don't worry. It's nothing to worry about, not really, especially now that you've talked of it. That's the main thing to do, talk about it, don't bury it. Look, I'll give you a tip. When the opportunity arises swear out loud – that's the best way to stop the underground stuff.' He squeezed her hand and smiled faintly as he said, 'I do quite a bit of swearing inside too. We must get together one night and have a swearing match, eh?'

He was comforting, so comforting. He was looking at her now quietly, waiting for her to go on, tell him who the child's father was. She started by saying, 'I suppose you think I'm dreadful. . . .'

'Now, my dear Grace, don't be silly. I'm only sorry, sorry to the heart for you. And, strangely enough, sorry for him, too . . . Donald, I mean. . . . Yes. Yes, I am.' He nodded his head. 'You know, I can confess to you now, I've never cared much for him, there's always been a something. I suppose my subconscious knew all the time about his trouble, and it is trouble, you know? It's an illness. He's not the only one, there are thousands like him, you'd be surprised. He should have gone and got advice.'

She actually laughed at this. 'Advice . . . ! You don't know Donald. He's so eaten up with pride he'd rather die than admit he's in the wrong about anything. So he tries never to do anything wrong.' She made a harsh sound in her throat. 'He's a vicar and he lives by the book . . . and . . . oh God. . . .' She shook her head, then ended abruptly, 'Andrew MacIntyre is the father of my children.'

His gaze was holding hers and she couldn't help but feel a little hurt when she saw the look of blank amazement take up his whole expression.

'Andrew MacIntyre? Grace!'

'Oh, David, don't be shocked. Andrew is a fine man.'

'Yes, yes, I have a high opinion of Andrew, but . . . '

'Yes, I know what you are thinking: he's a farm-worker. But he's not just a farm-worker, he's a very intelligent man, a good man.'

David blinked. He was bewildered. 'Does Donald know?'

'No, but he soon will. I managed to get over Stephen but not this one.'

'How far are you gone?'

'Four months.'

'Have you any idea how he'll take it?'

'Yes, he'll forgive me and make me promise to give up . . . sinning. He'll also suspect about Stephen.'

'It's cruel, you know, Grace.'

'Yes, I suppose it is.' She paused a moment and then continued, 'Yes, I suppose it is. Stephen's become his private world.'

'When are you going to tell him?'

'Not until I must.' Quickly now she covered her eyes with her hand and murmured, 'I want to go away. Oh, David, I want to go away. I want to take Stephen and go right away.'

'You can't do that. You mustn't do that.'

'You're just thinking of him now, aren't you?'

'Yes, and no. I'm sorry for him, Grace. A big, bouncing individual, so maimed . . . don't ever think of taking

196

the child from him, don't. Leave him his illusions.'

She got slowly and steadily to her feet. 'Your coffee's got cold, David.'

His hand went out towards the cup, and she said, 'Leave it, I'll get you some fresh.'

There were no more words between them and she went out of the surgery. . . .

It was that same night when the children had been put to bed and David had gone out to answer a call that Donald stood with his back to the blazing fire, and, after rocking backwards and forwards on his toes for a moment, looked down at his shoes and said quietly, 'Haven't you got something to tell me, Grace?'

Her body actually jerked upwards in the chair, and when she turned her face sidewards and looked at him she realised with a shock that he was smiling and her thoughts began to spiral in her mind, the words knocking against each other, pushing for place. No! No! God! It's impossible. He's not such a fool. A bloody fool! Don't swear. Only a stupid fool would . . . A stupid . . . Don't swear, I tell you . . . Be quiet and think. . . . He thinks . . . he thinks that night . . . the night of the raid.

For more reasons than one she hated to look back to the night of the raid. It was over five months since that night and she was only four months pregnant. Had it been the other way about there would have been no risk, but could she get away with being four, five, or more weeks overdue? She must talk to David.

In the meantime she bowed her head under Donald's fatuous glance and tried to stop the spate of swear words that were now skating about in her brain.

9

It was a bright day in April, 1943, when Aggie let herself in the front door of her house. She was cold and tired, and all she wanted was to get a hot drink and her feet up for a while, but she had hardly closed the door behind her when the telephone bell rang in the office.

That would be Susie to see if she was still alive. If a bomb dropped in Wallsend Susie expected a splinter to hover over Newcastle to pick her out. Susie never gave her number or said the usual 'Hello', she always started with, 'You all right, Aggie?' and seemed very surprised when she learned that Aggie was all right.

Aggie lifted the phone. 'Yes . . . yes, this is Temple 3567.'

'Hold the line.'

She waited, and then at the sound of a voice coming over the wire her eyes widened and she said, 'Oh, hello, Andrew.'

'Listen, Aunt Aggie, I haven't got a minute.' He called her Aunt Aggie now and she liked it. 'Tell Grace I'll be passing through any minute, perhaps tonight or tomorrow at the latest, and if luck holds we'll make a stop. Tell her that, will you?'

'Yes, Andrew. . . . Hello . . . ! Are you there? Andrew. . . . Andrew!'

He had rung off. Well, that was short and sweet, anyway. Perhaps that meant that he shouldn't have been on the phone at all. They were coming down from

Scotland and going some place, the south likely; there was something in the air, in the air of the whole country, a sort of waiting. Churchill had something up his sleeve. Well, she'd better get on to Grace. She didn't fancy having to be the bearer of this message – it was weeks now since Grace and Andrew had seen each other, he hadn't even been able to get a forty-eight-hour pass. She picked up the receiver and gave Grace's number, and when the thick voice of Peggy Mather came on the phone asking, 'Who is it?' she said brusquely, 'Tell Mrs Rouse it's her aunt.'

'She's bathing the baby, she's busy.'

'Well, be kind enough to tell her that I want to speak to her.'

That fat, sullen piece. Aggie didn't like Peggy Mather, and she knew that Peggy Mather returned these sentiments. She stood waiting, moving from one cold foot to the other. Poor Grace, having to put up with that surly creature all day! Her on the one hand and the Laughing Cavalier on the other. . . . Oh, that man got her goat completely. What with his smarmy ways and that smile of his, and always playing the big daddy-boy. . . . Eeh! It was fantastic when she thought of it. Those two children that he held up as his own private achievement. . . . He almost put placards on them . . . and neither of the bairns his. It was – it was fantastic. . . . She didn't know how Grace stuck him, stuck the whole set-up. Something would have to be done. When Andrew came out of the army there would have to be a showdown. She picked up a pencil and started doodling on a pad. Would he come in with her? Would he make an estate agent! Well, he would have to have a job of some sort, something different from farm-work too, something with money in it . . . and prospects, because he wouldn't live on Grace, that was a sure thing, and very much to his credit that was. She liked

Andrew, she did. She wished things had been different. There was a strength about him that was older than his years. He was like a . . . 'Oh, hello there, Grace.'

'Hello, Aunt Aggie. Are you all right?'

'Yes, I'm all right. You sound just like your Aunt Susie, that's how she starts.' She heard Grace laughing, and then she asked quietly, 'You alone?'

'Yes.'

'I had a phone message, somebody will be passing through at any time. With luck they'll stop in the village. Could be tonight or tomorrow, he doesn't know.'

There was silence, and Aggie said, 'Hello, are you there?'

'Yes, yes, I'm here, Aunt Aggie. When did you get to know?'

'A few minutes ago.'

'Thanks, Aunt Aggie, thanks.'

'Well, I'll be off now. I've just got in and I'm perished both inside and out; the wind's enough to cut you in two. How is it there?'

'Oh, it's a lovely day, sunny, even warm.'

'You're lucky. Goodbye, my dear.'

'Goodbye, Aunt Aggie, and thanks . . . thanks. . . .'

Grace put the receiver down and, going slowly into the drawing-room, stared out into the garden to where Donald was hoeing between slightly erratic rows of vegetables. There was no semblance of Willow Lea's beautiful garden left. All the beds now had been utilised for food, and Donald had learned with back-breaking patience the art of growing it. Even so, his labours would have shown very little result if it had not been for his power of organisation which roped in the help of all ages at the week-ends.

She walked nearer to the window, everything suddenly racing inside of her. She must get the children in and bathed. He might be here tonight, Andrew might be through tonight. But how would she know? Would he come here openly? Why not, why not? If he didn't find her at their new rendezvous he would come here. He would see her. Whatever happened he would see her. Oh, Andrew . . . Andrew. Her eyes were tired straining at the mental image of him. She often thought that if anything happened to him she would have no picture of him, only that which was in her mind. And yet that wasn't so. She just had to look at Beatrice to see him. Beatrice had his eyes and his straight, strong nose. The nose mightn't make for beauty in her later on but it would give her character. Beatrice would grow up like Andrew, but Stephen wouldn't. She looked to where Stephen was now working side by side with Donald and Veronica Cooper. He had something of Andrew's extreme thinness and sometimes she imagined she saw Andrew's profile when the child looked upwards, but there the resemblance ceased.

It was always painful for her to witness the child's adoration of Donald. Whatever Donald did was the pattern which the boy set himself out to copy. He had even managed to imitate the inflection of Donald's voice.

Over the last four years Grace had watched, often with boiling anger, Donald manoeuvring for first place in the child's affection. And the same process was being enacted with Beatrice. She should be glad about this, she sometimes thought, but she wasn't. Beatrice had been born about ten days before time, which made her over three weeks late in Donald's reckoning. At one period she could almost see him checking up in his mind, going back to a particular Saturday when he had seen her and Bertrand Farley getting off the Newcastle bus. They had been laughing, and when Bertrand went to help her off the step she had slipped and nearly fell. Donald had been coming out of the church gate at that moment.

But he must have reassured himself, for from the moment the child was born he claimed her as his own.

She called now from the window, 'Stephen! Veronica! Come along, time to have your bath. Come along now.'

'Oh, Mummy!' Stephen turned his eyes towards her. 'Just five minutes.' Not waiting for her answer he looked up at Donald and asked, 'Just five minutes, can't I, Daddy?'

Donald straightened his back and, placing a hand on his hip, he turned round and called, 'Just five minutes.'

'Goody. Goody, goody, goody.' The two children began digging furiously with their small spades, and Grace grated her teeth against each other for a second. This was the pattern. Wonderful Daddy, wonderful Uncle Donald, able to get them five minutes by just saying the word. And he could get them chocolates when nobody else could get them chocolates. He would read them stories when nobody else had time to read them stories. He could take all fear of the nasty aeroplanes away from them by simply saying, 'Kneel now and say "I am in God's hands. No nasty bombs will fall near me. The Good Shepherd is protecting me and no harm can come to me".' Wonderful psychology that turned a man into a god, a god that granted your every wish and had the power to make others do the same. . . . But Andrew was coming tonight or tomorrow. She would see Andrew. If it was only for five minutes she would see Andrew, and things would balance themselves for a time. It was only when she saw him that she seemed to be able to see straight; when she needed comfort she could not even go upstairs and read his letters, for they were all at Aggie's. His last letter had said, 'On my next leave I'm going to tell my mother, although I've an idea she knows something already. Before the war I thought that nothing could make me leave her to the mercy of my father, but you see I've just had to, and she will be the first to see that my duty lies elsewhere now. The war can't go on for ever, so we must face up to things together. The sacrifice will be on your part as always. I love you, you are never out of my mind, I worship you, and as long as I live that's how it will be, Grace.'

She asked herself for the countless time since receiving that letter what he actually meant by sacrifice. Did he mean leaving the children with Donald? No, he couldn't mean that, he wouldn't want her to do that. No, he meant the sacrifice of her good name, for there would be no such thing as divorce. Or would there? Views were changing even in the Church. High Church people were getting divorces. But if she was divorced Donald might lay claim to the children . . . he would be the offended party. Yet if she went into court and told the truth . . . Court. Go into court and say that Donald . . . No! No! She could not expose him like that. Her head began to whirl as it often did these days, the words racing round one after the other. She must keep calm . . . keep all her wits about her, that could wait, Andrew could be here at any minute.

The convoy stopped in the village at twelve o'clock the following day. It comprised twenty-five lorries laden high with irregular shapes over which tarpaulins were tightly drawn. Besides the twenty-five drivers there were nineteen other men, two corporals and two sergeants, of whom Andrew MacIntyre was one, a first lieutenant and a captain. The convoy had been on the move since six that morning. They were to have an hour's halt.

Andrew had taken the hill towards the vicarage at a gallop and only pulled himself to a stop when he entered the drive. When he knocked on the kitchen door and it was opened by Peggy Mather he gave a start of surprise and then stared at her for a moment. He had seen that face before, and he suddenly remembered where. But that was of no importance at the moment. He asked quickly, 'Is the vicar in?'

Peggy Mather looked at him, not only at his face but taking him all in, and it was evident that she liked what she saw, for she smiled and said, 'No. Can I do anything for you?'

'Is Mrs Rouse in?'

'Yes, she's somewhere about; she was in the garden a minute ago.' As she stepped out from the kitchen to look along the path, Grace came round the corner, and after only a slight hesitation in her step she came forward and held out her hand, and Andrew took it.

'How are you, Andrew?'

'Very well.' He turned round and nodded towards the maid before moving off on to the drive with the vicar's wife, and slowly they walked towards the main gate again.

They did not walk close and they talked generally, Andrew telling her where they were parked in the village and the length of time they were allowed to stay. And then at the gate, turning and facing her squarely, he murmured low and thickly, 'Oh, I want you in me arms. Oh, Grace.'

She was staring up at him, no veil on her feelings now. 'You really must be gone in an hour?'

'Yes, I'm going to dash up home. I won't be more than fifteen minutes. Can you be there?'

'Yes, I'll be there.'

'Oh, God! Grace!' He still stood. 'It seems years since I saw you . . . touched you.'

'Go now. Quick. Fifteen minutes, I'll be there.'

Before turning into the drive again, she watched him sprint up the road. Her head was quite clear, and she made it her business to go through the kitchen before crossing the hall and out into the garden by the drawing-room window. She also looked in at the sand-pit where the three children were busily constructing a castle. She did not speak to them or disturb them, but went hurriedly down the garden, past the greenhouses and out through the bottom door. She kept her pace steady until she entered the wood, and then she began to run. She crossed over the stone road and went on upwards in the direction of the cottage. Their new rendezvous was a clump of shrubbery some way from the path. It was a place that any couple might have used, but never before had they been there except in the dark, but this was no time for discretion. In little over half an hour he would be gone.

It was doubtful whether the presence of Donald himself could have kept them apart at this time. For it came to her as she stood waiting in the shelter of the thicket that there was an urgency about this convoy that portended long separation, not just weeks, but months, even years. Perhaps for ever. What if Andrew went away this time and never came back. . . . She heard his feet racing down the path. The next minute he was before her and they were holding each other as if attempting to exchange their bodies.

'Oh, my darlin'! Oh, Grace, Grace! Let me look at you.' He held her face between his hands. His eyes seemed to lift each feature separately into the storehouse of his mind. Then he shook his head slowly. 'They talk about their women. Oh my God, but it sickens you. They've got women, but I've got . . . you.'

'Oh, Andrew. Oh, Andrew.'

'Don't cry, darling. Don't cry. It won't be for long. It can't be, and then we'll be together, you understand – together.'

Before her lips could part to speak, his mouth was on hers again and they swayed drunkenly for a moment until, without breaking their hold, they lowered themselves to the ground. . . .

The bliss was still on them as they stood folded quietly together, and it was in their last kiss, soft and tender, that they were wrenched apart by a harsh, grating voice exclaiming with awful condemnation, 'God Almighty!'

Grace stared open-mouthed with shock and fear at Mr MacIntyre where he stood supporting himself by two sticks not more than three yards' distance from them.

'Why you dirty sod! To think that a son of mine . . . And the parson's wife. God Almighty!' He raised his stick. 'Get out! Get to hell away . . . out of it!'

Andrew had pushed Grace behind him and his voice was ominously low as he growled, 'Be careful what you're saying or else I'm liable to forget who you are.'

'Dashed in just to see your mother, did you?' The old man's eyes seemed to gleam red. 'Does she know about your fancy wife?'

'I've warned you, mind.'

'Warned me?' The old man was shouting now at the top of his voice. 'Well, let me warn you, you bloody upstart. . . . Show your face in my door again and I'll brain you. So help me God! As for her, the dirty faggot, and a parson's wife . . . Huh!'

Grace flung her arms upwards, straining at Andrew's uplifted hand. 'No! No! Andrew! No . . . ! Oh no!'

'Get out of me sight.'

'Out of your sight? Aye, I will that, I'll get out of your sight, me cock-o'-the-midden.' The old man was thrusting forward with one of his sticks now, emphasising his words. 'I'll get out of your sight and into that English ranter's afore I'm five minutes older. And it isn't the day or yesterday I'll tell him that this started;

I've had me suspicions. Her slinking about the road. Aye, I'll away.'

Still clinging to Andrew's arm, Grace watched the old man turn and hobble drunkenly through the trees with an erratic agility that belied the fact that he was utterly crippled with arthritis.

'Oh, Andrew, Andrew, he'll tell him.'

'Yes, he'll tell him.' Andrew's voice was flat. 'He's been wanting something on me for years, to hit at my mother with, and now he's got it, God blast him! But it's no use trying to stop him short of shooting him. He'll tell him.'

He turned his face slowly from his father's disappearing figure and looked at Grace, and after a moment he said, 'Perhaps it's for the best, for neither of us would have had the heart to bring it into the open. I've always known it, even when I wrote that letter. First it would have been the children, and then not wanting to hurt him. Perhaps, after all, this is the best way, a clean cut. One way or another you will be free now. But, oh God!' He bared his teeth and jerked his head, 'If only I had a day or two and hadn't got to leave you to face this alone.' He rubbed his hand swiftly around his face, and then asked, 'What will you do? Go to Aunt Aggie?'

Grace shook her head dazedly. 'Yes, yes. I suppose so. . . . Oh, Andrew, I don't know where I am. It's all happened so suddenly. Somehow I can't believe it . . . and at the last moment like this.'

'Look, Grace . . . Oh, dearest, don't look like that. . . . Oh God, if only I had another hour or so. As it is, I'll have to dash back and tell my mother.' He caught her to him and kissed her hard and quickly once more, then, taking her by the hand he ran with her through the wood upwards towards the cottage.

Mrs MacIntyre was standing on the road, it was as if she had been looking over the fells in the direction her son would shortly be moving along the main road. Her face was tear-stained, and it was evident that she had been crying bitterly, for her voice broke as she exclaimed, 'Oh, boy, what is it?'

'Dad . . . he found us together. He's gone down to the vicar.'

'In the name of God, no . . . ! Oh, why didn't you stop him?'

'Stop him? How could I? If he hadn't told him to-day he would have told him the morrow. You know yourself he's been waiting for something like this for years.'

Mrs MacIntyre was not looking at her son now, but at Grace, and now she exclaimed in a gabble, 'He mustn't, he mustn't tell him. . . . The children. Have you thought of the children, and Andrew not here to take your part? You cannot stand alone.'

Grace could find no words to answer this and Andrew cried, 'But how can you stop him, Mother? Anyway . . . look at the time, I've got to go. It's no use.'

'I'll stop him, I can stop him.'

'You? Don't be silly, Mother.'

'I can.' She was standing straight and tall facing him, yet already poised for flight. 'I have one hold over him. He's terrified at me leaving him.' Before she had finished speaking she was off round the corner of the house, flying down the path to the wood. . . .

All at once Grace became quite still inside. During the past shock-filled moments she had been strangely afraid of Donald knowing. Now she thought: it's as Andrew says, it'll be a clean cut. They never would have been able to do it. If Mr MacIntyre reached Donald before Mrs MacIntyre caught him, well, that would be that, she would face up to it and get it over and thank God. Yes, thank God.

It was as she thought thus that the air-raid siren sounded and she gave a startled gasp and exclaimed, 'The children!'

They were running down through the wood again. When they reached the quarry road they branched off, and in a few minutes he had lifted her over the ditch and they were out of the wood and tearing down the main road towards the curve that would bring them in view of the vicarage gates. But before they reached it the plane soared over them and they actually saw it drop its bomb.

Within a split second Grace found herself picked up bodily and thrown in the ditch, and when Andrew dropped on top of her, the earth heaved and trembled as it had not done in the village since the night of the big raid.

'Oh, Andrew! Andrew! The children! The house!' Her mouth was full of dirt.

'Wait . . . wait, he's coming back.' The plane soared over them again and then was gone. There was no more sound; it was as if it had been sent to deliver a message and had done so. Andrew rose and pulled her to her feet and they were running again, flying towards the curve in the road. When they rounded it they both stopped dead; side by side and close together they stood leaning forwards as if frozen in flight. There was a haze of dust pouring upwards from a big hole in the road opposite to where the vicarage gate had been and on the verge of the road some way on this side of the hole lay a huddled form which Grace knew to be Mrs MacIntyre.

Andrew had reached his mother before Grace had covered half the distance, and when she came up to them he had turned her over and was shouting, 'Mother!

Mother! Mother! Mother!' There was a deep cut across her brow and blood was pouring over her face.

Grace, with her hand across her mouth, murmured, 'Is she . . . ?'

'No. She's alive.' He wiped the blood swiftly and tenderly from her face, then cast his agitated gaze up at Grace as she gasped, 'The children, Andrew, the children.'

As she dragged herself away from his side she was aware of men in uniform racing up the hill towards them and then, like someone in a daze, she was stumbling round the crater. There at the other side and what had been the beginning of the drive were two men bending over the torn, twisted body of Mr MacIntyre, and about a dozen yards farther up the drive, lying on his back, his head near the root of a tree, was Donald. She made to run towards him, then stopped, her hand over her mouth again, this time because she knew she was going to vomit. The guilt that was filling her was turning her stomach – not the guilt of loving Andrew but the guilt bred of thoughts that had escaped in less time than it had taken for the bomb to explode. . . . She hoped he was dead. . . . Oh, no! No, no, no.

She must have paused for only a second, for she was bending above the white, blood-drained face as a voice to her side said, 'He's breathing. It doesn't look as if anything's hit him. The blast likely knocked him against the tree.' She watched the khaki-clad figure lifting Donald's head, and then the man said, 'Yes, it's as I thought. He's bleeding a bit there, but it doesn't look much.'

'Oh, ma'am, you all right?'

Grace straightened her back and turned dazed eyes on the wiry figure of Mr Blenkinsop, and as she did so she took in that the place was now swarming with people and two men were running towards them with a stretcher.

As they came up one of them said, 'Coo! It's the vicar, poor—' He did not add the epithet.

She watched them lift Donald on to the stretcher. She did not speak or make any move towards them; and then Mr Blenkinsop, taking her arm, said, 'Come on away out of it, ma'am, up to the house.'

The house? No, she must go to Andrew and his mother. Poor Mrs MacIntyre! Her poor face. . . . But there were the children. She startled Mr Blenkinsop by tearing away from him up the drive. But she had not gone far before she pulled herself to a stop. What was she thinking about? The bomb had dropped at the gate, and if the children had been with Donald there would be evidence of them.

As Mr Blenkinsop came panting up to her side, Peggy Mather appeared at the head of the drive and she called coolly, 'Who's got it this time? That was near enough. The house almost bounced.'

Peggy Mather had never used the prefix 'ma'am'; and although its lack was on occasion decidedly noticeable, Grace had never had the nerve to enforce it. When Donald had pointed out it was her place to do just that, she had said it wasn't worth the bother. Peggy Mather was only temporary . . . the war over, she would go. In this moment of shock, fear, and revulsion, she was further startled to hear herself exclaiming in a high voice, 'When you speak to me in the future, Peggy, will you kindly address me as ma'am or Mrs Rouse. Now, where are the children?'

Peggy Mather's features had contracted until they looked like a piece of dried leather. The fact that she was taken aback was evident, and after a moment, during which she glowered at her mistress, she said with telling flatness, 'Round the back where you left them . . . ma'am.'

The verger, taking hold of Grace's arm once more, said soothingly, 'We'll go and have a look, ma'am,' and he led her away towards the back of the house, and as they went he told himself that the poor thing was suffering from shock or she would never have stood up to that one like that. A good job, too, and not afore time. His Mary, God rest her, would never have talked to the young mistress without a ma'am, but that Peggy Mather! He didn't know why Miss Shawcross kept her in her house; if she knew half of her carry-on she wouldn't.

It was with something of wonder that Grace looked down on the three children. They had apparently not moved out of the sand-pit. Stephen looked up at her now and explained, 'There was a big bang, Mammy, and Veronica said it was a bomb and wanted to go into the shelter, but I told her it wasn't 'cause Daddy said God wouldn't let any bombs drop today because it was so nice and sunny. And, anyway, I told her if it was a bomb you would have been here, wouldn't you, Mammy?'

She did not answer, only stared down on them, thinking God would not let any bombs drop today.

'What are you making?' Mr Blenkinsop was now bending his creaking joints over the sand-pit and looking down on Beatrice, but it was Stephen who as usual answered for them all. 'Oh, she's just muddling, she's still trying to build a castle. But I'm building a dugout, and Veronica's building a God-house.'

'Huh! Huh!' It was in the nature of a deep chuckle from Mr Blenkinsop. 'A God-house, eh?'

'Yes, that's what she calls them. But Daddy says God hasn't got a house, just churches. Veronica's silly. . . . You are! You are!' He pushed her, but she showed no resentment, only laughed, and went on industriously poking holes in a square of sand. And as Grace now looked down on her the words began to revolve in her mind, A God-house . . . a God-house . . . a God-house, until they turned themselves into a mad-house . . . a mad-house . . . a mad-house.

'Oh, there you are.'

Miss Shawcross came hurrying towards them, and as Grace turned from the sand-pit there penetrated the whirling maze of her mind the thought that Kate Shawcross looked distraught. And it also came to her with a strong feeling of impatience that this woman had the power to imbibe the essence of any event, for she looked at this moment as if she had partaken of the actual experience of the bombing.

'They're taking him to hospital . . . the vicar?'

'Yes.' Grace nodded.

'He . . . he was wounded? And . . . and you let him go alone?'

Something slipped in Grace's mind, lifting the haze from it, and her voice was cuttingly cool as she said, 'He wasn't wounded, he had merely struck his head on a tree-trunk.'

'But . . . but you . . . ?' Miss Shawcross's voice was breaking, 'you let him go alone?' Her words faded on a note of recriminating judgement.

Grace found herself rearing upwards, her head going back and her small breasts thrusting out. This woman . . . this woman to criticise her, and in front of Mr Blenkinsop. She had stood enough . . . she had put up with enough all these years one way and another. Kate Shawcross had usurped her position right from the start – yes, right from the start. How dare she! She would show her that she had reached her limit. 'When you speak to me, Miss Shawcross, will you kindly remember that I'm the vicar's wife.'

Twice in less than five minutes she had done what she had never dreamed of doing during the seven years of her marriage . . . pointed out her position as the vicar's wife. She saw how ludicrous the situation was. Now, when she had ceased to be the vicar's wife, when Mr MacIntyre had made it unnecessary for any more posing or lying, she was laying claim to the supposed privilege.

As she walked past Kate Shawcross, whose whole face was twitching, Mr Blenkinsop said in a small placating voice, 'There, there, we're all upset, very upset. There, don't take on, Kate . . . there now, there now.'

His voice was soothing, and Grace had the impression that he was patting Miss Shawcross's arm. Patting her arm . . . she would like to slap her face. Yes, she would . . . Why hadn't she gone to the hospital with Donald? She was not only repeating Kate Shawcross's question but asking the question of herself now. Why hadn't she gone? They would have let her. But she'd had to see to the children, hadn't she? Had it been Andrew lying there what would she have done? There was no need to answer that question.

She did not make her way into the house through the kitchen because Peggy Mather was there, but went towards the front door, telling herself that she must sit down, if only for a minute, before going back to the gate. She felt sick and faint . . . oh, she did feel faint. As the earth came up suddenly to meet her she heard Mr Blenkinsop's voice crying, 'Steady . . . ! steady . . . !'

When she came round she was in the drawing-room and a voice was still saying, 'Steady . . . ! steady!' but this time it was David's voice. 'Now drink this up.'

She drank some bitter stuff from a glass, then he gently lowered her head on to the couch again.

After a moment of blinking she looked wearily up at him. 'David.'

'Don't talk.'

'I must. Mr MacIntyre . . . is he . . . is he dead?'

'Yes.'

Dazedly she watched him look away, rubbing at his chin, and when his eyes came back to her he said, 'He's never been down as far as this for years; in fact I've never known him come to the village. He must have come down to the road with his wife to see Andrew off.' He paused. 'You know, of course, that Andrew was passing through with a convoy?'

She stared at him, not saying a word. He knew all about her – that is, up to now. But she couldn't tell him the dreadful truth that she was responsible for Mr MacIntyre's death. It was she who had killed him, not the bomb. He never came down to the road, no, and he wouldn't have come today but for her. She saw him lying in a twisted heap. She saw Donald lying against the tree. Had he managed to tell Donald everything before the blast blew them apart? Mr MacIntyre would have wasted no time, he would have out with it. Yet if they had been standing together wouldn't Donald have received the full force of the blast too? Perhaps they hadn't met . . . perhaps Donald was just coming towards him down the drive . . . perhaps, perhaps. The thoughts were trailing around in her mind. She felt sleepy. That stuff in the glass . . . she made an effort to rise, saying, 'I must see . . . see.'

'Go to sleep.'

'No, David, I must see. . . .'

'There now, go to sleep. That's it.'

As David Cooper stood looking down on her he thought with analytical coolness that it was a pity the position of old MacIntyre and the vicar hadn't been reversed. Then Donald would have been saved a great deal of mental agony, which, when this was over and Andrew MacIntyre was home again, he would certainly be called upon to face. He could not see any evasive action, no matter how skilfully used – and he had come to recognise this vicar as an expert in this field – being proof against these two young people and their needs. As for Grace, the vicar's death would have given her a reprieve, a mental reprieve. When Andrew MacIntyre had given her the child it had saved her from a breakdown, yet now she was heading fast that way again. The cure was in a way turning out to be worse than the disease. He wondered why old MacIntyre had been down on the road with his wife; he hadn't for a moment believed the reason was the one he had suggested to Grace. If he had gathered anything from his visits to the cottage over the years it was that Douglas MacIntyre hated his son while the mother loved him too much. This latter, no doubt, could in the first place have accounted for the old man's spleen, added to which he was full of the pride and bigotry which self-education engenders in some Scots. No, Mr and Mrs MacIntyre had not come down to the road to see their son off. Of this he was certain.

He did not know what the outcome of all this would be, but he hoped he wouldn't be living in the house when the balloon went up. It was very awkward. Although all his sympathy lay with Grace, there were definitely two sides to be taken into account.

10

'The man's not all there, he can't be. Do you mean to
say he hasn't mentioned it in any way?'

Grace shook her head slowly. 'Not a word.'

'Not a word?'

'No, Aunt Aggie, not a word.'

Grace looked beyond Aggie's broad figure towards the
window and the garden, a gaily flowered window-box,
and she remarked to herself that there hadn't been a
thing out in the box the last time she had sat here. She
was finding like Donald, she could be talking of one
thing while thinking of another. She should be keeping
her mind on what she was telling Aunt Aggie; instead
she was thinking of the window-box.

She had not seen Aggie since three days before the
bomb dropped, and that was well over a month now. On
that fateful day Aggie had taken herself off to Devon to
have a week with her late husband's sister, but the week
had spread into four, for Aggie had got her nose into
some property – not selling it this time, but buying it.
She had, during her stay there, purchased three houses.
One of her purchases she was very enthusiastic about,
a dilapidated cottage in a wood near Buckfastleigh. She
had apparently picked it up for a song, and not with the
idea of letting when the war was over, as she intended
doing with the other two, but of making it a place
where Grace and the children could go in the summer
for the holidays. Grace's thoughts now hovered about
this cottage; it seemed to be the very answer to her

present need. If it could be made habitable she would take the children there and be away from everybody – Kate Shawcross and Peggy Mather, all the faces in the village – away from Aunt Susie and Uncle Ralph and their 'committee meetings'. Her thoughts touched on everyone but Donald.

But what about Mrs MacIntyre? The last words Andrew had said to her over the phone were, 'Will you see to my mother, Grace?' and she had promised with loving emphasis, 'Yes, oh yes, I'll see to her, darling. Don't worry, I'll see to her.' Perhaps Mrs MacIntyre would come with her when she came out of hospital . . . perhaps. But what if she were really blind? No, no, she mustn't be blind, she couldn't be blind. They could do such wonderful things now, she couldn't be blind. Oh no! The protest against Mrs MacIntyre's blindness became loud in her head. She couldn't be made to carry that weight on her conscience too, Mrs MacIntyre's blindness.

'But one way or another he could have mentioned it.'

'Yes, Aunt Aggie, one way or another he could.' She found she was repeating everything Aggie said.

'Is he aiming to push you round the bend?'

'Whether he's aiming or not, he's succeeding.'

'Well, be damned, it's up to you, girl, not to let him. If old MacIntyre did tell him, why doesn't he come out into the open with it like a man, and if he doesn't know everything why doesn't he speak of the bombing? He came off pretty lightly, anyway.'

'He's supposed to be suffering from shock.'

'Shock be damned!'

'Yes, that's what I've been saying to myself. About this cottage, Aunt Aggie, how many rooms did you say it has?'

'Six – but mind, they're just boxes.'

'And it is furnished?'

'Yes, if you can call it that. It was left as it stood at the beginning of the war and the stuff wasn't very great then.'

'Could it be made habitable?'

'Oh yes. My, yes, of course it could. I'm only saying it isn't another Willow Lea, but it will be a grand little place when it has a good clean-up and some attention. All it wants is a handyman on it for a few weeks. I'm going down there in the summer and I'll rake out somebody and get the place ship-shape.'

'It will be ship-shape before that, Aunt Aggie.'

'What do you mean, girl?'

'I've got to find some place, some place for the children, some place where he won't think of looking for us. I'm just going to pick them up and go. It wouldn't be any use asking him if I could, even for a few months, he wouldn't hear of it. He'd just shut me up. In one way or another he'd shut me up . . . and effectively. No, the only thing is to pick them up and go.'

Aggie was staring down at her niece. 'So you've made up your mind at last?' she said quietly. 'Well, I'm glad to hear that. Sometimes I've thought you must be barmy, for anyone else in your place would have made the break after Stephen – if not before; and you know, sometimes I've thought he's got some weird power over you, keeping you there. It's as if he's got you inside an elastic band, and he's just got to twang it and back you spring.'

'Well, Aunt Aggie, I won't spring back this time. My mind's been made up for me. . . . I . . . I'm pregnant again.'

Aggie's eyes and mouth, even her whole face, seemed to spread outwards before she exclaimed, 'God Almighty! Are you out of your mind altogether to go and do a thing like that? Oh! God above!' She waved her two hands as if in supplication and then said angrily, 'But why weren't you careful? I warned you, girl.'

'How could I be careful, Aunt Aggie, when I wasn't expecting to have to be. He only had an hour remember, and half of that was taken up with seeing his mother. I didn't think there would be any need for care. These things just happen and you can't say at such a time as that, "No . . . no, I'm not prepared for it". . . . It's no use, Aunt Aggie, it's done. And don't look so upset. I'm not. It had to be this, it had to be something like this to bring things into the open. Andrew said that day, "Let my father tell him, it needs something like this to bring matters to a head", but that didn't work out. Or if it did, Donald's holding on to it like a secret weapon. But he can't hold on to this one. He won't be able to turn his back on this rising fact, or make any claim to it.' With a crudeness foreign to her she patted her stomach, then rose to her feet. And as she got up Aunt Aggie sat down. Of the two, she was the more agitated.

Grace looked down at Aggie now and asked, 'Have you told Aunt Susie and Uncle Ralph about this cottage?'

'No, I only got in last night and I haven't been round there yet, although she was on the phone this morning to see if I was all right, all in one piece. I'm to go round there for tea.'

'Then don't tell them about the place, Aunt Aggie, because if Donald started working on Uncle Ralph he would soon give himself away. Uncle Ralph is a strong believer in the rights of husbands.'

'But you'll have to let me get something done to the place before going in, the roof's leaking at one side.'

'Could we go down and see it?'

'Yes, we could make the trip, say, next week-end – I couldn't do it this.'

'That'll do. I'll ask Aunt Susie to have Beatrice. Stephen will be all right at home. I'd like to be settled in it within three months.' She did not say, 'Before I start to show.'

Grace now went and stood near the window and looked down on the window-box. 'You know, Aunt Aggie,' she said, 'I've got a feeling I'm going to enjoy carrying this one. Donald would have to stretch his imagination some to lay claim to it. There will be nothing he can do about it, and you've no idea what a feeling of relief that is. Knowing that I won't have to witness any more daddy-boy acting. That in itself was a form of torture. Oh, Aunt Aggie, what an odd life I've had.' She turned round now and smiled at Aggie, but Aggie could not return the smile – she was crying quietly.

Four months later Grace was still at Willow Lea but poised, as it were, for take-off. One incident after another had managed to delay her flight, two of the most important of them being that handymen and materials with which to repair the cottage were difficult to come by, and not until just over three weeks ago had it become ready. Then Stephen went down with measles, followed in turn by Beatrice and Veronica. But now there were no more obstacles. She did not think of Donald as an obstacle, for he would know nothing until they were gone. She hadn't been idle during the past weeks. Everything was packed, and, to make things easier for her, she was no longer under the keen eye of David. Three days ago he had taken up his new home in rooms over Stanley's shop. He had taken on a housekeeper, a Mrs Maitland, a war widow with a child of three, and Grace felt, and hoped sincerely, she would soon change her name to Cooper.

She was already penning in her mind the letter which she would write to Donald later tonight telling him she was leaving him because she was going to have a baby, whose father was also the father of Beatrice and Stephen. She would tell him not to try to find her, for if he should and made to claim the custody of the children she would have to speak, and in court, about things which would be embarrassing and painful to both of them. So it was better, etc., etc.

Over the past few weeks she had been taking certain of their clothing and belongings to Aggie's, and she was going now to get a box from the top of the nursery cupboard in which to pack some toys. In her own room she had just taken off the loose three-quarter length overall she usually wore, presumably to keep her dress clean when dealing with the children. The ritual of the four-o'clock drawing-room tea had ended, partly from choice and partly because meals since the advent of David's coming into the house had been somewhat erratic, so her wearing an overall, it being an attractive one, had brought no comment from Donald.

She was reaching to the top of the cupboard and had the box actually in her hand when her attention was drawn towards the door . . . and Donald. He was staring at her. Her vocabulary had no words with which to describe his look. His eyes were not on her face but on the globe of her stomach, which was accentuated by her skirt and her extreme thinness.

He stepped slowly into the room, closing the door behind him. They had the nursery to themselves, for the children were at this minute racing across the drive, their yells rising up to the open window.

She did not try to cover herself up; there was nothing to do it with anyway, except her hands, and these she kept hanging idly at her sides as she looked at him, thinking that she would have given anything to avoid this. She had tried, she had done her best, he had treated her for months now with coldness, almost ignoring her for days on end, except when in the company of David or visitors, when his manner was so skilfully general that no-one could have picked out of it any particular attitude towards herself.

'You . . . you're. . . .'

' . . . Yes, I am.' Her voice was quiet and held no tremor. She did not feel any fear of him at this moment, nor any shame at the admission. At last, at last, the air was going to be cleared. The dreadful years of lying were finished, her life would be open and aired, and from this day forward she would keep it aired. If she was forced to live in sin, well and good, it would be all right with her.

That's how she was feeling one moment, the next she had her hands in front of her face shielding herself as she cried, 'Don't! Don't!' In a split second Donald had whipped up from the nursery table a large, heavy, cutglass water jug. It seemed impossible that it wouldn't crash down on her head. She cowered almost double, when from the crook of her arm she saw it fall against the nursery cupboard, still held in his grip. Not until it had slid some way down the door did he release it, to fall to the ground with a crash but not to break.

She staggered back now away from him towards the wall. His face looked blue as if he was going to have a heart attack. He looked enormous standing there, his eyes pouring out their hate of her. Then much like those of an old senile man, the muscles of his body began to twitch. His legs, his arms, his face, he looked all atwitch. With a swaying movement he turned and faced the cupboard door and, putting his arm on it, he leant his head against it.

Still against the wall Grace stood and watched him. She was trembling all over. She had always guessed that something like this would happen, that's why she had wanted to get away without having to bring the matter into the open. He had nearly hit her with the jug: the suave, polished, controlled minister had nearly hit her. The blow might have killed her, and the child. She had dealt a blow to his pride that all his veneer was no proof against.

He turned now but did not move away from the door, seeming afraid to leave its support, but he looked across the room to where she stood and after gulping twice in his throat he muttered, 'You – you've brought me to this, you've made me . . . ' He looked at the jug, then his head drooped suddenly forward and he swung it from side to side. 'You've done this to me, shamed, humiliated. . . .'

At this moment Beatrice's voice bordering on tears, came from directly below the open window, screaming, 'No! Stevie. No, don't, Stevie.' Stephen answered but his words were not distinct and there followed another high scream from Beatrice.

Grace, knowing that Stephen must be up to something, wanted to go to the window, but she couldn't take her eyes from Donald. At this moment her whole being was filled with pity for him. She watched him stagger like a drunken man towards the low nursery table and stand with his knees against it for support. His body was still twitching and it twitched forward across the table as he groaned out under his breath, 'You're debased . . . no better than a street woman . . . a whore.'

Her pity vanished. 'Who's to blame for that?' She did not allow him to get anything in but went on quickly, bitterly, 'Well, tomorrow I'm relieving you of my debased self, I'm going . . . and for good.'

224

He pulled himself upwards, and as Beatrice's screeching reached an ear-splitting crescendo he thrust out a shaking hand towards the window and demanded in awesome tones, 'The children, you'd leave the children?'

'No.' She shook her head. 'No, I'm not going to . . .'

As if he were jumping bodily into a breech to prevent some fatal catastrophe he now flung his arms wide and began to move in the narrow space between the table and the wall with the gestures of a rapidly animated clockwork being, and as he moved he shouted, 'You can't leave my children . . . my children. You would leave them motherless and with disgrace on them. Do you hear? Disgrace!' The jerking movements stopped for a second before he went on, again gabbling, now almost incoherently, about his children, his children. Grace looked at him. He was like a child putting up a defence mechanism. He would not listen to the words that he knew she was about to say, 'I'm taking the children with me.' He would not admit such a possibility. If he talked fast enough about his children, then she couldn't possibly say she was taking them. His attitude now was like that of some backward individual who had only the sound of its voice to prove its power.

Suddenly she shouted as she sometimes did at the children, 'Stop it! This minute! Stop it, I say!' And when he stopped and stood staring at her, the sweat running down his face, she said in slow definite tones, 'I'm leaving tomorrow and I'm taking the children with me. Do you hear? And . . . and I'll tell you now . . . they're not your children.' There, it was out.

He bent low and placed his hands on the table looking like some great orang-outang in this attitude. His voice even held some animal's guttural quality when he said, 'They are my children; you'll never get them from me

. . . never. Do you understand that? Never will those children leave my side, I swear on it.'

'Stevie! Stevie!' Beatrice's voice was still screaming from the drive, and Grace shivered now as her calmness seeped from her and fear took its place.

In his bent position, with his head up, they were on eye level and they stared at each other while Beatrice screamed. They stared at each other until slowly Donald straightened himself up and, groping for his handkerchief, wiped the sweat from his face. He stood looking downwards for a few minutes taking in great breaths of air, and then, in a voice more like his own now, he said without looking at her, 'I want to hear no more, and I will forgive you if you will promise before God that this will never happen again.'

'I don't want your so-called forgiveness, and I give no such promise.'

His head came up slowly and he stared at her again. 'Grace . . . I said I would forgive you. Don't you realise just what it has taken for me to say those words? I'm a priest of God, but I am a man and you have done me a most grievous wrong, the most grievous wrong—'

'Grievous wrong? Huh!' It was a laughing sound but the muscles of her face did not stretch. In her head was a rising spate of swear words, which some part of her was trying, unsuccessfully, to press down. She nodded quickly at him now as she said, 'Once again I'll say to you: don't be such a bloody hypocrite. . . . Grievous wrong. . . . Oh, my God!'

'Stop that swearing. I won't have it, do you hear? Call me hypocrite or whatever your trivial mind suggests, but I won't have you swearing in my presence. . . .'

'Mammy! Mammy! Mammy!' The words rose up in a paroxysm of screaming, and such was their intensity they forced Grace to the window, and as she went there threw bitterly over her shoulder, 'Grievous wrong.'

Even as she glanced out of the window she was only
giving a fragment of her attention to the child who was
kneeling on the gravel below beating her little fists as she
screamed, for her mind was still full of words, dreadful
words, wanting to hurl them at Donald. Then in another
second Beatrice had her whole attention, for, following
the child's petrified gaze, she saw to her horror what
had all this time been eliciting her screams. Stephen
was climbing the trellis work that led up to the nursery
window. It was used as a support for the delicate tendrils
of the clematis, and he was now more than halfway up it.
Instinctively Grace's hand went to her throat. She knew
she must not shout at him, but the fears and tensions
of the last few minutes came over in her voice as she
exclaimed, 'Stephen!' The boy looked up, startled. Then,
pleased to see that she was witnessing his daring feat, he
called, 'Look, Mammy, I can climb. . . .' Looking up
at her in his moment of triumph his head had gone too
far back. As he released his hand for the next pull, he
overbalanced, and to a scream that out-did Beatrice's he
fell on to the drive.

Grace was out of the room, down the stairs and on to
the drive in a matter of seconds. Beatrice's screams had
reached the point of hysteria now, but there was no sound
at all from Stephen. As her arms went round him to
gather him up she was thrust roughly aside. 'Don't touch
him!' Donald spoke as if her touch would defile the boy
and brought up in her an emotion that bordered on rage.
But she had to stand aside to see him lift the child and
carry him indoors. As she watched him disappear into the
drawing-room with the limp figure in his arms she forced
herself towards the telephone, and there rang up David,
and as she gave the number she was surprised to hear herself still muttering, 'Grievous wrong. Grievous wrong.'

At nine o'clock that night Grace phoned Aggie, and when she heard the brisk tones saying 'Hello' she said without any preamble, 'Stephen's had a fall, Aunt Aggie. They think he might have fractured his hip-bone. He's in the Cottage Hospital.'

'No!'

'Yes, Aunt Aggie.'

'And you were to come tomorrow.'

'Yes, Aunt Aggie.'

'It's fantastic.'

'That isn't all. He's found out about the other . . . and you'll be pleased to know I'm to be forgiven.'

'Aw! Girl.'

'He won't let me have the children. . . . The elastic band has pulled tight again, Aunt Aggie.'

'My God!'

11

Grace's third child was born on 1 January 1944, and she called it Jane. Donald was confined to bed with 'flu at the time, and so any lack of interest he might have shown was not observed.

Stephen did not like the advent of another sister, for it took some of the limelight away from his iron-bound leg. Beatrice did not care one way or the other; so Grace seemed to have her daughter to herself. And this state of affairs went on until the child was six months old. Donald, to Grace's knowledge, had never looked at the baby, and she was glad of that. At least this child would be hers, for Beatrice had long ago followed in Stephen's footsteps and was Daddy's little girl. But Jane was hers and would remain hers.

With the birth of the child Grace developed a philosophy, perhaps a negative one, but nevertheless it had the becalming effect of acceptance. It was no use, she told herself, she would struggle no more. She would take things as they came — what had to be would be. She had her child — it was as if she had only one — and Mrs MacIntyre.

It was strange the comfort that Andrew's mother had brought to her in the past months. It should have been the other way round — but no, it was Mrs MacIntyre, now almost blind but for a faint light in the left eye, who gave her comfort while at the same time killing any hope for future reprieve from the life she was at present leading, for, as Mrs MacIntyre said, her sight was now in the ends of her fingers and these had become familiar over the years with every article of furniture in her home. Moreover, when she stood outside her front door she did not need anyone to point out what lay in front of her. The air on her face, mist-laden, wet, warm or stinging with snow particles, told her how the fells would be looking at that moment. . . . Was there any hope, then, that Andrew would leave his mother alone in the cottage, 'and go and live his own life a little way off', as she would say to Grace? 'But not too far, so that he could look her up betimes?' No, the pattern was already set.

But her new philosophy said: 'Don't worry. Wait and see, take it in your stride.' That was until the morning of her twenty-sixth birthday, which Donald had not acknowledged. From that day she no longer told herself to take it in her stride: she told herself to fight.

The telephone had rung as Donald was crossing the hall and he picked it up, and as she went into the drawing-room she heard him say, 'Oh, hello, David', and then a long pause and, 'I'm very sorry'. A few seconds later he was standing in the drawing-room. She was gathering some papers up from the table, her back to him, when she realised he was looking at her. This hadn't happened for a long time, not since the night in the nursery. She turned and faced him.

'David has just phoned. He tells me—' He paused, 'They have heard that' – his voice sank – 'that Bertrand Farley's been killed in action.'

She allowed him to hold her gaze as she thought: Oh, poor Bertrand . . . poor fellow. But as she looked at him her mind told her why he was giving her the news of Bertrand Farley's death in this way. He thought, he actually thought, that Bertrand was the father of the children. No bubble of laughter rose in her at this revelation – only a faint sense of wonder at the knowledge that this could prove that he knew nothing about Andrew. And yet against this supposition was the fact that he had never once mentioned anything concerning the bomb being dropped. Nor had he ever spoken of its effect on Mrs MacIntyre.

She turned from him and sat down on the couch, and it took all her control, when he stood in front of her, his gaze directed down on her as he said, 'I'm sorry. You know that, don't you?' not to cry out, 'Don't be such a bloody fool!' This was the first time she had sworn inside her head for a number of weeks, and it brought the usual feeling of sick revulsion against herself and she cried out at it, 'No not again, don't start that again.' After a long, silent moment Donald left her and the spate of words died away.

But that very afternoon they returned in force. It was when Donald looked at the child for the first time. Not only looked at her but took her up in his arms.

She was standing at her bedroom window looking towards the sand-pit. The pram was near the edge of the pit and she saw Donald coming towards it to tell the children as always that he was at hand again, for never did he return to the house, even after an absence of only an hour, but he made his presence known to them. Stephen was not in the pit but sailing a boat on the small fish pond some distance away, and on the sight of Donald he sprang up with the hampered agility of the iron supporting his leg and made a dash towards him, and once again, perhaps for the fourth or fifth time that day, he was lifted up high. Then it was Beatrice's turn, for whatever Stephen had she must have too. Even if she hadn't demanded it Donald would have seen that she got it. It was with one on each side of him that he walked towards the pram and, standing in front of it, looked down on the gurgling, fat and anything but pretty face of Jane. He stood for a long time like this while the children jabbered and talked and prodded their sister in various ways. Then through the open window Grace heard his voice remonstrating with them gently, 'Now, now, Stephen, you mustn't be rough. No, Beatrice, no, not like that.' When she saw him bend slowly forward and pick the child up into his arms her stomach seemed to turn over. The sensation was similar to that created by an enema – sickly sweat-making. And what followed next did nothing to lessen this sensation. She saw her husband carry the child to the garden seat, where, placing her on his right knee and putting his arm about her, he took hold of her right hand, then with his left hand he drew towards him Stephen's right hand and placed Jane's podgy fist in it. Then, taking hold of Stephen's left hand, he joined it to Beatrice's left with his own. There was now formed a circle and the circle was almost encompassed by his two arms. The ritual had been accomplished without a word. Daddy was showing them a new game and the children's faces were alight. Words were not necessary.

The feeling in Grace's stomach had brought a weakness to her legs, and she leant against the stanchion of the deep window-sill and in the silence of the room she talked to him, spitting out the words, 'You won't do it! No, by God, not with her you won't! You shan't take her from me. No, Donald, I'll play you at your own game. . . . You . . . ! You . . . ! You . . . ! You're inhuman, you must be. Oh the cruelty. . . . You . . . ! You . . . ! You . . . ! . . . '

The new phase was given its seal on the Sunday following this ritual of possession, for Donald preached a sermon on 'Forgive us our trespasses'. She was sitting in their pew, Stephen on one side and Beatrice on the other, and Donald, standing above her in the pulpit, asked the congregation how could they expect to be forgiven for their shortcomings if they did not forgive others, and not just for small sins, but for grievous sins. The sin of unfaithfulness had been bred like a germ through this war, but sins, like germs, must be attacked and exterminated. Yet who would think of exterminating the man because he carried in his body the germs of, say, influenza. No, you could kill the germs and save the man. So it was with sin. And he told them they were incapable of forgiveness unless they became humble. . . .

Grace was rearing inside. Unless you were humble. My God! Humble! Donald humble! And these poor Air Force fellows in the congregation and those girls. They would all be thinking he was at them. She wanted to turn to them and say, 'Don't worry, it's not you he's getting at.' Forgiveness . . . unless ye become as little children . . . humility. . . .

She looked straight at him, but he did not once let his gaze rest on her. Humility. What about stealing? Practised, calculated stealing. Not the stealing in a passion-inflamed moment of another man's wife. That was a clean thing, almost a virtue, compared with the daily, hourly, sucking in to himself the lives . . . the whole lives and emotions, the loyalty and love of two children whom he was determined now made into three. . . . Humility!

She just had to see Aunt Aggie.

When later that same day she made a flying visit to Newcastle she flung her arms wide as she asked Aggie, 'What can I do? I feel helpless against such . . . such wiliness. Oh, I could go, but . . . but it's Stephen.'

In reply Aggie made a statement which was not an answer. 'The unnatural swine,' she said, 'blast him to hell's flames.'

12

their shortcomings if they did not forgive others, and
not just for small sins, but for grievous sins. The sin
of maladjustments had been bred like a germ through
this way, but sins, like a germ, must be attacked and
exterminated. No, who would think of exterminating the
man because he carried in his body the germs of, say,
influenza. No, you could kill the germs and save the man.

As one nerve-strained day melted into another Grace
fought Donald in every way she could to resist his
usurping of Jane. The conflict was all the more intense
because no mention of it was made by either of them.

The ill-effect of the situation on Grace was added to
when she had to face the fact that never would she be
able to take Stephen away from Donald. She might as
well drain off the boy's blood and expect him to live as
separate him from the man he called Daddy.

The whole pattern of her life was becoming unbearable; only the sight and touch of Andrew could have
brought her easement. But Andrew was in Italy. From
North Africa and Sicily he had gone to Italy. His letters from there awaited her at Aggie's every Saturday
morning, but they nearly always ended with, 'It won't
be long now, it's nearly over, it's near the end.'

When the end finally came, hope for a time brought
colour back into her face if not flesh on to her bones
and she thought continually, 'Maybe tomorrow. Maybe
tomorrow. Maybe tomorrow.' But it was many months
later, and peace an accepted thing, before she saw
Andrew.

One Friday night, at six o'clock, Peggy Mather, in
the act of putting on her coat and wrapping a scarf
around her head against the snow blizzard that was
raging, heard the telephone ring, and she was about to
pull the back door open to leave when she heard it ring
for the second time. She stopped. The vicar was making

so much bloomin' noise in the nursery with those bairns that he couldn't hear the bell. And where was she? she wondered. She stamped across the kitchen and through the baize door into the hall, and when the phone rang again she picked it up and said, 'Hello?' After a moment she put it down and went to the bottom of the stairs and yelled in her loudest voice, 'It's for you – ma'am!' Never once did she use the word ma'am without giving it a telling quality.

Grace was in the bathroom tidying up after having bathed the children, and she only just heard the call. When she got to the top of the stairs Peggy Mather, from the folds of her scarf which she was now pulling over her mouth, muttered, 'Phone.'

'Thank you, Peggy.' Grace screwed up her face and cast her eyes in the direction of the nursery, from which were issuing high-pitched, gleeful yells.

When she took up the phone Aggie's voice came immediately to her saying, 'Hello there, you been asleep?'

'No, Aunt Aggie, but there was so much noise going on upstairs I couldn't hear the bell.'

'How are you?'

'Oh . . . you know . . . as usual.'

'How are you off for beef for the week-end?'

'Beef, Aunt Aggie? Well . . . ' Grace shook her head as she repeated, 'Beef? Not at all, we've had mutton for the last four weeks. I'm sick of the sight of it. Can you get me a piece of beef?'

'Yes, a prime bit, real Scotch.' Aggie laughed at this point and added, 'And not from under the counter either.'

Grace was smiling into the phone. Aggie sounded happy, even excited; she was always digging up something on her rounds. She knew so many people. But a piece of beef!

'Grace.'

'Yes, Aunt Aggie?'

'Hold on to something, I've got a surprise for you. In fact it's the Scotch beef in person.'

Grace moved the phone from her ear and looked at it, and then it was tightly pressed against her flesh as a voice, a low, deep voice, came over the wire saying, 'Grace . . . Grace.'

She closed her eyes and gripped at the edge of the telephone table, for not for the life of her could she utter a sound.

'Grace . . . ' The voice was lower, deeper. 'Grace . . . darling, are you there . . . ? Grace.'

Her mouth was open, the words were swelling up in her ready to pour out, when she heard Aggie's astringent tone calling sharply, 'Grace . . . ! Grace, do you hear me? Are you there?'

'Yes. Oh, Aunt Aggie!'

'Is anybody about?'

Grace shook her head again and was on the point of saying 'No' when she heard the door of the nursery close overhead and Donald's footsteps coming towards the stairs, and she said hastily:

'Yes, Aunt Aggie, yes.'

'You'll be in tomorrow morning, then?'

'Yes, Aunt Aggie.' Donald was in the hall now and she forced herself to talk. 'I've got enough coupons to get Beatrice the outfit that we saw. Yes, I'll be over in the morning . . . and . . . and meet you. Good night, Aunt Aggie. Good night.'

She put the phone down as Donald went into the study and, running upstairs towards her own room, she paused on the landing for a moment and looked towards the nursery. She should dash in there now and gather them to her and cry, 'Children! Children! Your daddy's come home. Three years and you haven't seen your daddy. But he's home now, home for good, for ever and ever and ever. Just like the fairy tales. Yes, just like the fairy tales, for ever and ever.'

13

Grace paused for a second before inserting the key into the lock of Aggie's front door. In spite of the snow on the ground and the knife-edged air she was sweating and trembling with it. She had not slept all night waiting for this moment, and now that it had come she was filled with a mixture of shyness, elation, and dread – the dread centred round Andrew's reactions to her changed appearance, for she felt that she was no longer beautiful. It was impossible to feel as she did inside and still remain beautiful, and there was the evidence of her mirror to prove it. She was thin to the point of drabness, the bones of her face pressed forward through her skin, her eyes no longer sparkled, her blonde hair now appeared tow-coloured to her and hung limply, without life. Would Andrew see her as she saw herself? The key seemed to turn of its own accord and the door swung open to reveal Andrew, an outsize, bronzed Andrew, standing rigidly posed halfway up the stairs.

'Grace.'

He did not leap towards her but advanced slowly, taking one step at a time, his eyes riveted on her.

When he reached the foot of the stairs she hadn't moved from the open door. Not until his arms came out towards her and he spoke her name again in a tone so deep it was akin to a groan did she fling herself forward into his arms.

'Darling, darling! Oh, Andrew!'

His mouth was moving in her hair, over her brow, around her face, and all the while she kept repeating his name, 'Andrew, Andrew.' When her mouth was covered with his the tenseness seeped from her body, and she seemed to fall into him, right through his hard bony frame into the centre of his being.

Clinging together, they went into the sitting-room, and, still together, they sat on the couch; and together they lay back, not speaking now, and kissed their fill.

It was some time later when Grace whispered, 'Aunt Aggie . . . where is she?'

'She had important shopping.' Andrew smiled whimsically. 'She's very tactful, is Aunt Aggie.'

They both laughed softly. . . .

Half an hour later Grace lay gazing into Andrew's face. It looked healthy and attractive, made more so by the unusual white tuft of hair to the side of his brow. Her fingers moving over it lovingly, she said, 'It might have killed you.'

'It might, but it didn't . . . it didn't even give me a week in hospital . . . I was never lucky.'

'Oh, Andrew!'

'Only in finding you . . . there's no-one in the wide world like you.' He had her face cupped in his two brown hands.

'You still think that?' Her question had a plea in it, and he pulled her towards him and held her tightly as he said, 'I'll go on thinking it until the day I die.'

There was a silence between them now until he asked softly, 'Tell me, how are the children?'

There followed another silence before she answered him, and then her voice cracked as she said, 'Fine, they're fine.' In the silence she had pictured herself on the landing last night after she had received the news of his coming, when she had wanted to run into the nursery and say to them, 'Children, your daddy's home.'

A strange sadness was now enveloping her; it was seeping into the joy of the moment, depriving it of harmony, of its high pinnacle of easement, and all because it had been impossible to say to her children, 'Here is your daddy,' and also impossible to watch the light of ownership, the pride of the creator, as Andrew looked on his children after a long separation.

She had longed, ached, lived for this moment, and she told herself that this was heaven and she desired nothing more. She thrust at the sadness, pushing it away, denying herself incompleteness, denying that a vital section of herself was even now in the nursery at Willow Lea.

When Andrew, with a soft yearning in his voice, said, 'What does Stephen look like?' she refrained from saying, 'Like you,' as he had refrained from asking, 'Does he look like me?' but she compromised by saying, 'Tall, thin,' and then added, 'He could be dour at times.'

They laughed together at this, and he playfully punched her cheek before he asked, 'And Beatrice?'

She ran her finger down the bridge of his nose, saying, 'This is in evidence and I don't think it's going to add to her beauty.'

He touched his nose and the twinkle deepened in his eyes as he remarked, 'It's a decent enough neb . . . at least my mother always said so.'

'Mothers are prejudiced.'

'Are you prejudiced?' He was pressing her head into his neck now and she nodded it against him as she murmured, 'Yes, very much so.' Then she added softly, 'Wait until you see Jane. She's like her name, plain and podgy, but she's a darling.'

'Yes?' He went on stroking her hair, pressing her face into his neck, keeping it hidden so that she would not see his expression and she knew this. In yet another silence that followed she knew that they were both stalling, warding off the time when Donald's name must be mentioned.

The sound of a key turning in the lock relieved them for a moment, and when the drawing-room door opened they were leaning against the back of the couch, their faces wreathed in smiles, each with a hand outstretched towards Aggie.

'Will you have a drop of soda with it?'

'No, I'll take it neat, thanks, Aunt Aggie.'

Aggie handed the glass to Andrew where he sat at the side of the fireplace, then, sitting opposite to him and bending forward, she asked quietly, 'What is it, Andrew?'

Andrew swirled the drink around in the glass, looking at it the while, and then, leaning his head against the back of the chair, he cast his eyes ceilingwards before saying, 'The war was easier than this – at least I could handle my part of it.'

'Something gone wrong between you and Grace?' There was an anxious note in Aggie's voice, and Andrew brought his head quickly from the back of the chair as emphatically he said, 'No, no, not between her and me.'

'What is it then?'

'It's the children.'

'Oh.' Aggie nodded her head slowly.

He finished the whisky, and after putting the glass on the table at his hand he bent forward, and, placing his forearms on his knees, he looked at Aggie and said, 'You know I had visions of picking her up the minute I got home, her and the children, and my mother as well, and going off somewhere. I was even prepared to live on her money until I got a job . . . I knew it wouldn't

241

take me long to find work. I even played with the idea of accepting your offer' – he smiled a little here before adding – 'even when I knew it was the worst service I could do you. I'm not made for selling things. Anyway, I knew I wouldn't be out of work. Wherever there was soil and cattle I would find a job. It seemed easy, simple, when I was all those miles away. It even seemed simple a week ago today when Grace and I met in this room, but it's simple no longer.'

'Did you go to the house?'

'Yes, I went to the house.' Andrew now turned his eyes towards the fire. 'I wasn't looking forward to meeting him. I felt . . . well, a bit scurvy somehow. That was before I saw him and then all that feeling went. I can't explain it, but when I looked at him any remorse at my underhand dealings vanished. He didn't appear to me like a man at all. I hadn't the feeling I had betrayed a man. When he stood there with Jane in his arms and said to me, 'You haven't seen Jane, have you?' I could have taken it in different ways – that he was taunting me, for instance, telling me he knew all about everything, and yet I reasoned that if that was the case, then it would be impossible for him to act as he was doing at that moment, for he was jolly and laughing and his face looked open. I couldn't credit any man with the power of being so subtle, of being able to act such a part.'

'Where was Grace in all this?' Aggie put in.

'She went into the house. I don't think she could stand it.'

'I don't think so either.'

'You know, Aunt Aggie, I'd been a bit perplexed the first few days because Grace didn't talk about the children, but when I stood on that drive and saw him with the three of them I understood, for if ever I saw three bairns adoring a man it was those three . . . my three.'

His face was turned completely away from Aggie now, and she could only see his profile, with the ear and jaw-bone twitching. After watching him for a moment she said, 'I've been afraid of this, but it's something you've got to face up to. I, meself, have had to face it, Andrew. . . . Grace can't take those children away from that man. Jane perhaps yes, but not the other two, and never Stephen, and she won't leave them and come to you without them.'

'I wouldn't want her to.' His voice was brisk and the words clipped.

'Well then, you've got to look at this thing squarely. You give her up and go away, or you carry on as you are.'

He had turned on her first words and now he answered them by saying, 'Oh, Aunt Aggie, don't be silly,' and then, moving his head from side to side, he added hastily, 'I'm sorry, but you know what I mean. There's no separating Grace and me whatever happens – it's one of these things that's there for life.'

'Well then, you've got to face the consequences, and don't forget, there's your mother – she won't leave the house. You're as tied as Grace is.'

'I know that only too well, but the awful thing is, Aunt Aggie, that I want the children more than ever now because of yesterday.'

'Yesterday? What d'you mean?'

Aggie watched Andrew pull himself to his feet and walk to the window and back before saying, 'Stephen said he didn't like me.'

'What? Stephen said that?'

'Yes.'

'How did that come about?'

'It was when I was on the point of leaving. Grace came out again; she was standing by the boy, purposely

243

I think, and she said to him, "Say goodbye, shake hands with Andrew" . . . I went down on my hunkers and held out my hand, and . . . and he backed away from me and put his hands behind his back and said, "I don't want to, I'm not going to." Grace spoke to him sharply. I could see that she was vexed, so I made my goodbyes, and had just turned away when the boy said clearly, "I don't like him, I don't like that man" . . . It brought me round in my tracks like a bullet.'

Andrew's eyes were looking into Aggie's, and the pain in them struck at her so sharply that she put out her hand and gripped his, saying, 'Don't take any notice of that. Why you know what, I remember telling my own dad that I wished he was dead and I would like to bury him, and I was only eight.' She laughed at this point.

Andrew, ignoring the joke, said, 'Yes, yes. I've thought of all that about kids being funny and saying unpredictable things, but the unusual thing about it was that he . . . the vicar . . . never checked the boy. Grace was all het up, but not him; he didn't even react like a normal man in such a situation and threaten the lad with a skelped backside or something like that. He just stood there with a smile on his face. I felt dreadful, Aunt Aggie, I don't think anything will ever hurt me as much as hearing that child say "I don't like him". I felt in that minute that I couldn't risk going through anything like that again and I'd have to get away. I felt like that until I reached home and saw my mother sitting before the fire. She hadn't said much since I returned, but she must have sensed that there was something wrong and she started to talk. She told me she was all right and that she would manage, she had managed all the time I'd been away, and I was to make my own life . . . make my own life. And there she sat staring into nothing and all through me, and she was telling me to make my own life, and as I looked at her sitting there it came to me that I had no say in the matter, either about Grace, or the children, or her. If I left the fells that minute it would be alone, for neither Grace nor the children nor she would be with me. Nothing had seemingly altered; it was as if I had never been away . . . well, there it is, Aunt Aggie.'

Aggie said nothing; she was searching for words that would be of comfort to him. He had, she realised, already faced up to the situation before he came to her and he wasn't finding it pleasant. She rose and picked up his glass from the table and, going to the cabinet, she poured him out another whisky, and then she said an odd thing, 'Do you think Stephen's yours, Andrew?'

He did not take the glass from her but stared with narrowed eyes into her face before saying, 'What makes you say a thing like that, Aunt Aggie?'

'Here, take it.' She thrust the glass at him, then, sitting down again, she went on slowly, 'Well, a number of things. The lad's disposition, for one, for he's like neither you nor her in ways. Then his looks. There's not a feature of yours in him that I can see, Andrew. But the main thing that's set me thinking this is a bit of reading I did recently, it was by a doctor and he was on about . . . you know . . . well, about impotency. He said – the writer – he was a doctor – well . . . ' She hesitated, embarrassed in her attempt at this delicate explanation. 'Well, he said a man could be nearly impotent and yet be able enough to give a woman a child. Impotency didn't mean he . . . well, he wasn't fertile . . . These things have been in me mind a lot lately and I couldn't say anything to Grace. And if it was his you wouldn't feel so badly about the lad's rudeness, now would you?'

The whisky still remained untouched in Andrew's hand. He seemed to have forgotten it; he even seemed to have forgotten Aggie for the moment; and then, with a sudden lift of his arm, he threw off the drink in one go and put the glass down. 'I'd rather go on thinking he was mine even if he hated me guts, Aunt Aggie.'

'Aye, I suppose you would . . . it's only natural. There . . I was just trying to ease you.'

He touched her hand. 'I know, I know.'

14

So the pattern of life was resumed, dominated by the circumstances that their love had created. Andrew went to work once again on Tarrant's farm with the promise of promotion . . . 'Perhaps to manager, who knew?' Mr Tarrant's own words.

Grace, once the jigsaw had fallen back into place again, tried to accept the situation. She had Andrew and that was all that mattered, she told herself. For days her mind would stay at a level of acceptance, until some subtlety of Donald's would send it spiralling upwards into a spasm of aggressiveness and hatred. One such occasion was when she came across him holding Jane high above his head; he was wriggling her fat body between his big white hands as he chanted over and over again, 'Daddy's girl, Daddy's girl,' only to break off and ask the question of the laughing face, 'Whose girl are you?' and then to give the answer, 'You're Daddy's girl.' It was a form of indoctrination.

She found the scene sickening, even sinister. There was something almost unclean in his insistence to lay claim to the children, especially this last one. She asked herself time and again how, knowing that the child wasn't his, he could try to project himself into her mind as her father. The words hypocrite and mealy-mouthed had ceased to have any meaning with reference to him. His attitude, his entire approach to life, needed words and exclamations that she herself was not capable of giving. She only knew that more and more proximity with him repulsed her. She shrank inwardly from him as if from something unclean. His sexlessness was more repulsive in its way than the extremes of a lecherous old man, and the miming of a father-figure more frightening than mad fantasy, and she was experiencing mad fantasy at nights now. In spite of Andrew's return – or perhaps because of it, because he was so near and yet so far – her nights were filled with dreams, mad fantastic dreams, dreams that she was wallowing among reptiles, flying, armless, legless, slithering white bodies, eyeless, mouthless, that turned themselves into hands, great soft white hands belonging to neither man, woman, nor child.

Then there was added to the complexity of her life something that was both irritating, and in a way humiliating, for Peggy Mather started to set her cap at Andrew. Openly, blatantly, she waylaid him, and openly she was rebuffed. As Adelaide Toole – now married to her cousin – had waited for him on the road as he returned from Tarrant's, so now, on certain evenings, did Peggy Mather. And as time went on and she made no headway the atmosphere in the kitchen suffered.

When they were together at Aggie's, Andrew would laugh about the situation with regards to Peggy Mather, as also did Aggie in an endeavour to make Grace see the funny side of it. But this Grace could not do; although Andrew was still only a farm-worker and she felt no shame in loving him, the fact that she was in a way contesting with a woman like Peggy Mather hurt her pride.

And then there was the cottage. She had never hoodwinked herself as to the reason why she had bought the cottage from Aggie. When it had failed to serve the purpose of a refuge for her and the children, she could have forgotten about it, but no, she determined to buy it, to make it her own, and not with the intention of it being a holiday home for the children. It was to be a place where she could be with Andrew alone for days, but strangely, except on two occasions, it never worked out like that. Andrew first saw the cottage during the second week after he was demobilised, when, accompanied by Aggie, he took his mother there for a short holiday. From that time on it became known in the village that Mrs MacIntyre liked, every now and again, to visit her sister in Devon. If during this time the vicar's wife went away for a week-end or a day or so to Harrogate or Whitley Bay with her aunt, who in their wildest dreams would connect the two incidents? Donald? Only once did he phone the hotel in Harrogate, and then Aggie answered him. Grace had gone on a day's coach tour, she herself was a little off colour. Late that night Grace phoned the house . . . and from the hotel in Harrogate.

The strains that this particular way of life imposed on her began to show as the months mounted and fell into years, and the stolen hours with Andrew seemed to have less power as a soothing salve as time went on. As the children grew, the silent battle for their love between her and Donald grew more intense. There were days when they did not exchange a word, not even at mealtimes, but communicated with each other through the children. 'Go and tell Mammy so and so. Go and tell Daddy this or that.' This form of strategy hoodwinked practically everybody except David Cooper.

In the village the parson's wife was known as 'a nervy piece', which was odd, they said, when the vicar himself was such a jolly chap, and so fond of the bairns . . . by, he was fond of them bairns.

At one period David Cooper felt bound to warn her of where she was heading. 'The brain is like a boil, Grace,' he said. 'Give it enough anxiety poultices, and it will come to a head and burst.'

The boil in Grace's brain took ten years to reach this point, and when finally it did burst it was not through the application of a heavy poultice but through what could be termed a light dressing in the form of Donald repeating a statement he had made many years previously . . . he was going to engage a part-time gardener. . . .

It was on an August afternoon in 1957 that Donald made this statement, but it was preceded earlier in the day by an incident with Stephen.

The boy had locked his door, and when Grace went to go into his room and found the door shut against her she asked for an explanation. Stephen, a slim, tall youth, still looking like neither his father, nor his supposed father, nor yet herself, told her that Donald had suggested him locking his door because he was being pestered by his sisters and it prevented him from getting down to study.

'Very well,' she said, 'then leave the key where I can get it. Peggy must clean the room and I want to see to your school things.'

When with a coolness that could have been termed insolence he answered her with, 'I'm not leaving it about, Peggy can come and ask for it,' she suddenly screamed at him, 'Stephen!'

Stephen, his face paler even than usual, was standing looking at her with a frightened look in his eyes when Donald bounced up the stairs.

'What's the matter?' He glanced quickly from one to the other. Then, his gaze coming to rest on Grace and his voice dropping into a tone of reprimand, he said, 'Screaming like that! What is the matter?'

'It is about the key, Father. I locked the door.'

'Oh! Really!'

The vicar closed his eyes for a moment. Then, looking at Stephen, he said quietly, 'Leave it to me,' and indicated that the boy should go downstairs. And he waited a moment before looking at Grace again. Then, still in a subdued tone, he said, 'Have you no control, yelling like that? Aren't you aware that Beatrice has two friends in the garden? What will they think?'

Her tone was as low as his but of a different quality as she hissed back at him, 'I don't care what they think. Do you hear? I just don't care what they think.'

'Well, you've got to care, especially what . . . what ours think. They are young people growing up, full of impressions, they are—'

'Oh, my God! Be quiet before I . . . I . . . ' She choked, then gasped, 'Full of impressions! Yes, they are full of impressions. And what have you done with their impressions over the years?' She was thrusting her face up to him now. 'I've just seen the result of your impressions. My son dislikes me. . . . Impressions . . . impressions . . . my son dislikes me. Do you hear? He was coolly insolent to me. He was showing me one impression you have given him of me.'

Donald, his face stiff and white, looked back at her, and his words were still quiet as he went on, 'I am not going to argue with you, now or at any other time. That's what you want, isn't it, to brawl and argue. Splash your emotions all round the house for everybody to hear. I never have argued and I'm not going to start. The only thing I'm going to say is that, whatever your son thinks of you, I'm sure you deserve it.'

As she watched him walk away there came a strong animal desire in her to leap on his back and bear him to the ground. She rushed into her room and, gripping the bed-rail, stood looking down on to the bed. He had achieved what he had set out to do: made her son dislike her, and without saying a word against her, for he was too clever to malign her. He had done that: turned her son against her. She wanted to run to Andrew, just run to him and look at him and become calm. Andrew could make her feel calm. But Andrew was in Morpeth, at the market with the cattle.

It was nearly two hours later when she went downstairs and into the dining-room, and saw through the open french window that Peggy had set the tea near the willow tree. In the far distance behind the line of firs she could hear voices coming from the tennis court, a recent addition to the garden. She was about to step on to the paved terrace when she saw Donald coming across from the court accompanied by a young man. She recognised him as Gerald Spencer, the brother of Beatrice's school friend who lived in Morpeth. He was in some car business. She didn't like him, he was too brash, but his sister seemed a nice girl. The tennis players now came round the trees, Beatrice and her friend, Stephen and Jane, and Jane as usual was not walking but hopping and dancing from one foot to the other, waving her racket over her head. And now she threw it up in the air yelling, 'Mammy! Mammy! We beat them, Joyce and I beat them.' She raced across the lawn and did a war dance in front of Grace, and Grace, putting her hand out, said, 'Jane, stop a minute.' She was listening to what Donald was saying to the young man.

Donald's arms were stretched wide and he was saying, 'Not for love or money, they can make so much more in factories, you know. I've been without help now for nearly three weeks and it's beginning to look like it.' He gave his ha-ha of a laugh. 'I'm not much of a gardener. I did try my best during the war, but, truthfully speaking, I'm not a man of the soil.' Again there was the ha-ha. At this point he turned a chair round for the guest and looked towards Grace, yet as she stepped across the terrace he continued as if unaware of her presence, 'I'll get a part-time man as I did before the war, just a few hours a week, and things went very smoothly then.'

'If you are anything like we are, you'll find the part-time ones as difficult to come by as the full-time ones.' The young man buttoned up his coat, then unbuttoned it. It added an air of authority to his words.

Donald was handing the guest a sandwich as he replied, 'Oh, well, you know, you're in the town and we're in the country. People are different in the country. Oh' – he turned his head between Grace and the young man – 'I forgot. You have met my wife, haven't you? Yes, of course you have. What I mean is, you've seen each other today?'

The young man shook his head in denial and smiled, but Grace remained still. Somehow she was waiting for Donald to go on and he did. As she poured the tea out he sat down on the left of her and, stretching out his legs, carried on the conversation, addressing her through the guest this time. 'I thought of asking Andrew MacIntyre again,' he said.

That was all.

The cup Grace had in her hand clattered to the tray, bringing all eyes to her, and as Donald's hand came out to rectify the damage she smacked it aside and, getting up from the chair, rushed into the dining-room. But she hadn't reached the hall before he was behind her.

'Grace!' It was an order and not a quiet one now. She took no notice but sprang up the stairs, and when from the foot his voice cried again, 'Wait! Do you hear me? Come here this minute!' she turned. She was at the head of the stairs now, and looking down on his upturned, outraged countenance, she cried, 'You . . . ! You . . . !' The saliva was spluttering from her lips. 'You'll bring Andrew MacIntyre back as your gardener. With just a lift of your little finger you'll bring Andrew MacIntyre . . . '

'Grace!'

'To hell with you! You try to stop me talking, go on!' Her voice was rising. 'You swine! You swine of a parson! You cruel, sadistic, unnatural swine.'

She saw him bounding toward her, taking two stairs at a time, and when he gripped her by the shoulders she struggled to free herself, yelling now, screaming now, mouthfuls of abuse. The boil had burst. . . .

She was on the bed and he had one hand over her mouth while with the other he pinned her shoulder to the mattress. Her straining, staring eyes saw the amazed faces of the children in the doorway, and when Donald cried, 'Get away and close that door!' she saw Beatrice and Jane disappear, but not Stephen. Staring-eyed she watched him moving timorously towards the bed and heard Donald cry angrily, 'Get out of here at once.'

Donald did not look at the boy, and when he realised that Stephen was not obeying him he yelled, 'Get out! Do you hear? Go on, get out. . . . Ring Uncle David . . . now, at once.'

As she struggled to draw breath into her panting lungs through her nostrils she was aware that something had burst in her head. It was in a way a relief. Words were still pouring into her mouth but she couldn't get them out. Cunningly now she became calm, and when she stopped struggling Donald slowly relieved the pressure on her mouth and shoulder. She waited, watching the seconds as it were, waiting to pick the right one. When it arrived she gave a leap and was free from his hands and in a second was on the other side of the bed and the poison from the boil was once again flowing. But now it was more terrifying, for she was laughing at it, and him. . . .

'The gentle parson. Dear, dear Vicar. Dus yer mother want any coke? Dus Kate want any coke? I mustn't talk Geordie. Oh no, it isn't refined. You've shut my mouth for years, haven't you? But no longer, no longer. The children mustn't hear me. The children . . . our children. . . . Oh, that's funny. Our . . . our . . . OUR children! Stay where you are! If you come near me I'll tear you to bits, I will! I will . . . !' She was screaming now, her arms hooked, her fingers clawed. . . .

When she felt her nails tear at his flesh the laughter stopped in her and she was enveloped by fury alone.

Once again she was on the bed, glaring up now into his blood-spattered face. He was holding her from all angles. One of his knees was pinning down her legs, with one hand he was gripping her two wrists, while with the other he kept her mouth shut. He was visibly worn out and was showing it when the door burst open and David came into the room. But he did not release his hold on her, he merely turned his face silently towards the doctor.

Grace became still as, over the rim of Donald's hand, her eyes beseeched David, calling loudly to him.

'Let her go.'

'You must give her something first.' Donald's voice was thick.

'I will in a minute. Let her alone.'

'But . . . '

'Leave her alone.' The words were more like a bark, and Donald, after a moment's pause, lifted his limbs one after the other cautiously away. And when he stood at the foot of the bed wiping his face with his handkerchief, Grace hitched herself up into a sitting position and, grabbing at David's hand, started again, 'He's . . . he's a devil, David . . . a swine . . . a bloody swine. You said I should. . . .'

'Now, now, Grace.' David's voice was quiet.

'But, David, David, I can't stand any more. . . . I'm going away . . . I'm going away now, tonight. I must get away. I'll take Jane. He's got Stephen . . . I'll never have Stephen. . . . David, Stephen doesn't like me, he doesn't. My son doesn't like me. Oh, I must get away. I'm going. . . . You . . . you bloody . . . !'

'Now, now, stay where you are.' David took one hand swiftly out of his case on the side of the bed and stopped her from rising, at the same time speaking to Donald over his shoulder, saying, 'It would be better if you went.'

When Donald did not move, Grace with another spurt of energy made to rise from the bed, and David, holding her hard now, said soothingly, 'Now, Grace, be still. Lie quiet and let's talk this over . . . eh? Look, stay still just a minute. Do that for me, will you?'

After a moment he took his hands away but kept his eyes on hers as he went to his bag again, but Grace was staring past him now at Donald, and although she didn't move she began to talk once more. First in a low mixture of abusive swearing, then suddenly her voice rose almost to a scream, and David, the syringe in his hand, said, 'Quiet, quiet; they'll hear you in the village, Grace.' He smiled tenderly down on her.

'Let them, let them, David. . . . They laugh about the vicar's wife in the village, do you know that? I'm one of the war-time jokes . . . the vicar's wife locked herself in the cellar the night of the raid. Everyone else turned out to help but not her, oh no. She dropped the key and couldn't find it. That's rich, isn't it? She dropped the key and couldn't find it. And when the lights went out, there were no bloody matches either . . . for why? 'Cause the vicar had swiped them, that's how it goes, the vicar had swiped them. Serve her right. Oh!' She put her hand quickly towards David's. 'That hurt, David. What is it? What are you doing? I'm going away. . . . Kate Shawcross set that yarn around, but he told her. You told her, didn't you?' She leaned forward, glaring at Donald. 'Dear Kate. Dear, dear Kate. When I'm gone you'll have her here, won't you? She likes this house, I can't leave it a minute but she's up here. . . . Oh, I know, I know. I've got a spy, too. You'd like to know who it is, wouldn't you?' Her voice was becoming quieter. 'Oh yes, you would, so you could take it out on him an' all.' She did not mention Mr Blenkinsop, and she addressed herself now to David, but with her glassy stare still on Donald. 'D'you know what his latest is, David? You'll never guess, not in a month of Sundays, you'll never guess. The sadistic swine. He's going to ask Andrew to come and do the garden . . . just like that.' She snapped her fingers. 'As if he was a serf, so he can torment me and make me pay for my—'

Her voice was cut off on a gulp as her mouth was once again compressed but this time vertically as David gently pressed her cheeks together and said, 'There now, no more of it. . . . And why shouldn't Andrew MacIntyre do the garden, eh? Although I don't see where he'd get the time.' He shook her face gently as he stared down into her eyes, compelling her to silence. 'Andrew's a good gardener, none better, which I've often thought is an odd thing in a farmer. Now, now,' he pressed his hand tightly across her chest, 'lie still, you'll feel better in a minute. You're going to sleep now. There now, there now. Lie still, that's a good girl, that's it.'

It was some minutes later when he released his hold on her and she lay limp looking at him. Her lips moved slowly as she said, 'David . . . Jane . . . I want Jane.'

'Jane will be all right. There now, close your eyes. Jane will be all right. I'll see to Jane.'

When her eyes were closed David stood watching her, and when her hand slid off her chest he raised her eyelid and let it slowly drop back into place. Then turning towards Donald, he said briskly but without looking at him, 'I must phone for an ambulance.' He rapidly arranged the instruments in his case before closing it.

'An ambulance?' Donald was still mopping the bleeding scratch on his face.

'Yes, an ambulance.' David now looked straight at him and asked pointedly, 'You don't think she can stay here, do you?'

'No, no.' Donald's voice was flat. 'Where will you send her?'

'To Rockforts if I can get her in.'

'Rockforts?' Donald's eyebrows moved upwards.

'Yes, Rockforts, where else? I suppose you are aware that something has snapped.'

Donald said nothing, only stared at David, and as David returned his look he saw the protective skin close over the vicar's eyes. He had seen this look before and he wanted to shout at the man, 'For God's sake come clean! Come into the open. Isn't this lesson enough for you?' But he knew the futility of such an appeal. If the girl on the bed hadn't been able to get through the barrier there was little chance that he would succeed. The man's pride and ego were a protection stronger than armour plating.

'What are they likely to do with her?'

David was moving towards the door as he said, 'Put her to sleep, I should suppose, for as long as she can take.'

'And then?'

David was at the door, and he turned and confronted the minister and said flatly, and now without the semblance of any sympathetic feeling for the man, 'Try to undo twenty years of strain, I should think. . . .' The straightening of Donald's body did not check his closing remark, for as he turned from him he said, 'And I wouldn't count on her coming back here. In fact, I would go so far as to say the knowledge that she won't have to return will be about the one thing that will bring her back to normality. . . .'

But here David was wrong, for a year later Grace returned to Willow Lea.

15

Yet, as David had foretold, it was the knowledge that she was not going to return to the house that helped Grace's recovery. She always looked back on the first three months at Rockforts as her initiation into hell. For the first week there she had slept; she would wake and be given food, then go to sleep again, and this pattern seemed to go on for years in her mind. But when finally they allowed her to wake up and she realised where she was, the shock wiped out any good the long sleep had achieved. She became a bundle of visibly trembling nerves. She was in an asylum, she was going mad . . . if she wasn't already mad, she was going mad. Nothing could convince her otherwise; even the electric-shock treatment only succeeded in dulling the fear for short periods. Until she came under the youngest of the three resident doctors. She took to him because he was not unlike David, or rather as David had once been. Brown-headed, slight of stature and bouncing with energy. It was he who first took the now intensified fear of swearing away from her. What was swearing, anyway? She could swear if she wanted to, it was her only weapon, that's why she had used it. He encouraged her to talk about her childhood. He came to know Jack Cummings and the coal depot. But it wasn't until he learned about Andrew that he saw the whole pattern, and the pattern became clear-cut in outline when she hesitantly told him of her first meeting with Andrew on the night she had tried to lure her husband by standing naked before him.

Another thing the young doctor managed to reassure Grace about was that her power to love would return to her, for now all feeling had left her, all feeling of affection and love. She thought of Andrew, but not with love, only with fear because she felt she loved him no longer. She had no feeling for anyone, not even Jane. And she couldn't cry.

It was not until she had been at Rockforts for six months that the desire to regain complete normality began to stir within her. But even so she had no desire to go back into the world. She had a very nice private room; she walked for long periods alone in the grounds; and the thought that she would one day have to leave this place became as frightening in its way as when she first realised that she had come into it.

Andrew was the first person she saw from that other world, for her past life appeared now as if it had been lived in another world, and she was amazed at her reaction to him. She sat on the seat by the stream that ran through the grounds, her hand in his, but no thrill of love stirred in her. She felt dead inside. It was as if she had had an operation and the organs that registered emotion ripped out of her. Vaguely she felt comforted in Andrew's presence, yet strangely undisturbed by his nearness, or his sadness.

When some time later she asked to see the children, only Beatrice came. Stephen was at college and Jane was at boarding school. But Beatrice came and their meeting roused in Grace the first stirrings of maternal feeling again, accompanied by one of surprise, for Beatrice, never demonstrative, flung her arms around her neck, and not only kissed her again and again but hung on to her while the tears streamed down her face. Grace could not help but be touched, yet she did not cry with her.

It was during Beatrice's third visit, when once again with her arms round Grace's neck and the tears streaming down her face, that she begged her to come home. Because . . . because . . . and then it had come out in a garbled rush. She wanted to get married, she must get married . . . she must . . . she must. Grace had pressed her away and looked at her, and then she knew the reason for Beatrice's need of her.

She did not send for Andrew; it was David she sent for, David would know.

Yes, David said, Beatrice was pregnant and the shock had caused Donald to have a heart attack. He was in hospital. It was the first time anyone from outside had spoken of her husband to her for a year, and David assured her that should she come home again she would not be likely to meet Donald, for he was in a bad way and there was a possibility that he might never come out of hospital.

It was some time before the fear of returning to the house itself – even knowing that Donald was no longer there – was overcome. But as the days went on Beatrice's happiness became more and more important to her. And on the day she said to herself, 'She is Andrew's daughter, not his' – on this day she informed the doctor of her decision, then phoned David, and wrote to Andrew. . . .

Andrew received the letter when he returned home from work. Mrs MacIntyre took it from the mantelpiece and handed it to him immediately he came in the door. It was the first letter Grace had written him since her illness, and before pulling his coat off he sat down and read it. After a moment he said quietly, 'It's from Grace.'

Mrs MacIntyre was standing by the table, her almost sightless eyes bent towards him. 'I had a feeling it might be,' she said.

'She's coming home.'

'Back to the house?'

'Yes.'

'Oh, Andrew . . . why?'

When Andrew told her she sat slowly down, but did not speak, and after a time he put his hand across to her and said, 'Don't. Don't cry.'

'But . . . but she's had enough. Why has this to happen an' all? It's as if there's a sort of . . . influence there . . . in that house, holding her there, bringing her back to it. I thought now that . . . that you and she would have made a fresh start.'

'I'm thinking that the sins of the fathers are not waiting for the third and fourth generation, we are both going to pay in this by being kept apart until we die.'

'Don't talk like that.'

'Well, I can't stand the thought of her going back there. I imagined she would have gone to the cottage, for a few months anyway, with Aunt Aggie having it all fixed and waiting. . . . Funny.' He moved his head slowly from side to side. 'I don't feel any concern about Beatrice. I suppose that's unnatural.'

'No. No, not at all.' His mother wiped her eyes. 'It's just because you're so concerned about Grace. . . . I suppose it's that Spencer boy you were telling me about.'

'Yes, it'll be him all right and I can't say anything against him, for who am I to pick holes – in that direction, anyway.'

'It was different with . . . ' Mrs MacIntyre did not finish and, as her voice trailed off, Andrew's head came up and he said, 'What is it?' He got to his feet and went and stood by her and again he said, 'What is it?'

Her two hands were pressed tightly on her stomach, her head was bowed and the sweat was oozing out of the pores of her forehead. He put his arms about her, and when at last she was able to speak she pointed towards the ceiling and said, 'Tablets in the top drawer . . . in a bottle.'

Five minutes later Andrew, crouched on his hunkers before her, said in an unsteady voice, 'How long have you known this?'

She let her eyes linger on him before she answered, 'About two years.'

'Good God.'

The two words condensed the searing compassion he was feeling and he bowed his head before her.

Grace did not like Gerald Spencer, but at least she thought he had one asset – he was not impotent. The concern in her mind now was to keep any disgrace from Beatrice, and this lifted her thoughts from herself and helped her more than anything else could have done at this time towards readjustment.

Although at times she was subjected to bouts of terrifying fear of the dark, and swearing, and thought she was back to where she had been at the beginning, at others she knew, and knew with certainty, that only now was she seeing the whole situation in its right perspective, for she faced the fact that she would never be free to go to Andrew until her children were settled. Her love for Andrew was seeping back into place, but it was subject, as it had always been really, to the children's welfare.

She had decided also, and quite calmly, that if she heard that there was the remotest possibility of Donald returning to the house she would take a long holiday, and Jane would go with her. This could be accomplished without scandal, for to the village she was still ill. Those who had been in an asylum were never . . . well, the word used was . . . right. They would say, 'They're never right, you know.' To the majority, the stigma of an asylum could only be thrown off by death. Grace was painfully aware of what the villagers thought, but this same opinion, she knew, would relieve her of their condemnation should she remove herself from the needs of a sick husband.

Oddly enough, since her breakdown she had acquired a greater fear of scandal than ever before. Had the truth come out years ago she herself would have been the main sufferer. But not now. Her family were no longer children; they were a young man and two young women at vitally impressionable stages of their lives. Nothing must affect them.

If there was one thing she was grateful for now it was that she had been prevented from screaming out the truth on that dreadful night a year ago.

Yet again things did not work out as she planned. Two months after Beatrice had married, David told her that Donald was leaving the hospital and was going to a nursing home near Hove, for he was still very ill, but the very next day he walked in through the front door and in to the drawing-room.

It was one evening early in the spring of 1959. Andrew MacIntyre was doing the garden, Jane was curled up on the couch where it was placed before the window, and Grace was sitting by her side, her hands lying idle in her lap. She was watching Andrew. She always felt soothed if she could look at Andrew; she seemed to draw quietness from him and into herself. His rhythmic movements, which appeared slow, but which speedily disposed of the work, were a kind of joy to her. . . . Andrew was good. She would say to herself numerous times a day: 'Andrew is good.' It seemed to sum up his whole character . . . his faithfulness, his reasonableness, and his patience, mostly his patience.

His mother had died three months ago, and it would not have been surprising, now he was released from that shackle, and knowing that she herself could not again bear to live in the same house with Donald, had he pressed her to go away with him. At times she had a strong feeling, and not only recently, that inside, under his patience, he was straining against the unnaturalness of his life. It would become most apparent when, held tight against him, she felt the not infrequent force of his passion. But when she would say, 'Oh, Andrew, we just can't go on like this', as she had done over the years, he would reassure her, saying, 'Patience. Things will pan out.'

Meetings were no easier to arrange than they had ever been; in fact, if anything they were more difficult, for now there were often four pairs of eyes to be wary of. Only last night, when she had pointed this out to him, he had said, 'Remember years ago, when I told you I could love you without touching you? Well, that still holds good.' Then for a few moments he had loved her fiercely. Andrew, she had learned, was a strange mixture of passion and reticence. She could not fully understand him – and considering that during all the long years of their intimacy the hours they had actually spent together amounted only to a matter of weeks, this was not to be wondered at – she could only be glad in the depths of her heart that he was as he was. . . . Andrew was good. The actual words were once again crossing the surface of her mind when she heard someone enter the room.

After she had slowly turned her head, her hands jerked upwards and clutched at her throat. She could not rise, she just sat in a twisted position, staring.

Donald sat down on the first chair nearest to hand. He looked desperately ill, weird, gaunt and ungainly; there seemed nothing of the suave parson left. He sat looking at her quite impersonally, and in this panic-filled moment she knew he wanted nothing from her, nothing at all, not even pity. Neither had he any for her. She knew that for him she had died quite finally that night of revelation in the bedroom, when she became no longer any use as a face-saver.

Still sitting in the twisted position, and too stunned to move, she watched Jane, who gave an almost agonised cry, fly to him and fling her arms about his neck. The demonstration seemed too much for him, and after patting her head he pressed her from him and asked if she would get him a drink of water.

Taking a long, gasping breath, he once again looked at Grace. Then in a few terse, unemotional words, he told her why he had come back. He knew he was to die soon, and he wanted to do it in his own home.

As in years gone by, there welled up in her a flood of pity for him, but as she continued to stare at him, the man himself, the man in the soul of him, the suave, evasive dispenser of mental torture, pressed against the feeling and it subsided. But strangely, she did not doubt his word. She did not say to herself, 'He has only come back because he knows I am alone with Jane, and he is afraid he will lose his power over her.' No, she believed him.

That his attraction for Jane had lost nothing in his absence she witnessed in the next second. Returning at a run with the glass of water, Jane hovered over him like a mother over a sick child. And Grace knew as she looked at them together that if she went upstairs this minute and packed she would leave the house alone. She could no more take Jane away from him now than she could have taken Stephen years ago. The very suggestion that she should leave her sick father would, Grace knew, lose her her daughter now. No, if she went she would have to go alone. But she couldn't lose Jane, she couldn't. She had lost the others, she couldn't lose Jane. She must talk to Andrew . . . Andrew . . . Andrew. . . . She cast her eyes to where he stood rigidly stiff, his eyes riveted on the window, then she pulled herself up from the couch and made her way towards the door. And as she left the room, neither Donald nor Jane seemed to notice her going. . . .

Three weeks later, Donald, as good as his word, died, and so prevented her from having to take refuge with Aggie. He did it dramatically one evening on the steps of the altar. And who should be with him there at the end but Kate Shawcross. Grace was not sorry that this should be so, for she had loved him. But what sickened Grace was the significance the postmistress gave to it. Throwing all discretion aside, she declared openly to Grace while her face streamed with tears that God had willed that Donald should die in her arms, and that he had done so with her name on his lips. She was so distraught she made no secret in the village of what she spoke of as the Will of God.

The village buzzed as villages will. Kate Shawcross was a fool, it said, and brazen with it. Fancy saying a thing like that! Then as usual two and two were put together and conclusions jumped to. No wonder the poor vicar's wife had gone off her head. And everyone remembered how often the postmistress had gone up to Willow Lea when its mistress was absent. Well now, would you believe it? And they did believe it. Until Christmas week, 1960, when Peggy Mather opened her mouth.

PART THREE

Grace was the only one seated. She sat at the end of the couch, her head bowed, her eyes fixed on her tightly joined hands resting in her lap. At the head of the couch Andrew stood with his left hand pressed into the padded upholstery. To his right, and both standing with their backs against the end of the grand piano, were Beatrice and Jane, and on the hearthrug in front of the fire stood Stephen. Grace could see his legs and his knee-caps twitching from time to time. She could not bear to look at him and see the hate of herself pouring like steam from his bloodless face. His colour was that of rice paper, his skin had the same smooth texture. He had been talking for some time, spewing words out, words coated with venom, words that ill-became a prospective man of the Church. But at this moment Stephen was nothing but a young man fiercely defending his heritage and denying with every pore of his body the claim of this rugged Scot as his father.

' . . . If you . . . if you were to go on your knees and swear on the Cross I wouldn't believe you, do you hear? I know what I am, I know where I came from . . . inside here.' He thumped his chest, and the action, although intent, had nothing dramatic about it. 'I know I'm like my father. My father, do you hear? His thoughts are my thoughts, his ways, his principles, everything . . . everything. . . .'

Grace raised her head, and Andrew, thinking she was about to protest, placed his hand on her shoulder. But Grace had not been going to protest. She was just looking at her son to try to convince herself that he was wrong, for listening to him she was imagining that it was Donald who stood once again on the hearthrug, his back to the fire. And it wasn't Stephen's stance alone that conjured up Donald, for even without the slightest facial resemblance to Donald he was, at this moment, almost his chosen father's double. The doubt that had assailed her over the early years from time to time recurred, and if it would have been any help now she would have said, 'All right, there is a doubt, take the benefit of it.' But she knew, even if she could have made the last great effort and brought herself to say such a thing, that it wouldn't have helped in the least. She had talked for what seemed hours trying to tell them the facts while endeavouring not to blacken Donald, trying to put him over as David had always described him . . . a sick man, even knowing as she talked that this was merely white-washing. But in spite of her knowledge she had done it, and with what result? Merely to bring forth Stephen's hate. She knew that her son had never really loved her, but now his distaste of her amounted to loathing. Whatever reaction the girls would make had yet to be seen, but one thing was already certain – she had lost Stephen. Yet hadn't she lost him even as a baby? Yes, but the pain hadn't been like this.

As she unloosened her hands and pressed them to her throat Andrew spoke for the first time.

'Whatever you say, it makes no difference. I know how you feel' – his voice was low and steady and held no bitterness – 'but the fact remains, whether you like it or not, I'm your father.' Yet as Andrew stressed this statement, a point in the conversation he'd had with

Aggie after his demobilisation sprang to the forefront of his mind, 'Impotency didn't mean a man wasn't fertile.' Whenever he and Stephen had come face to face in the past few years he had denied this statement entirely, but now, as he looked at the young man he was claiming as his son, he acknowledged for the first time a grave doubt, for he could see no trace of himself or his forebears in the ascetic face that was glaring at him. No-one had spoken in the pause and he now went on: 'If your mother had done as she wished she would have taken you away when you were a baby, but she stayed here for my sake. I was tied here, as she's already told you. But these latter years she has remained here not for my sake, but for yours, all of you.' His eyes moved to the girls. 'She wanted to see you all settled before . . . before she began to live her own life.'

Grace's head drooped again. Yes, that had been her main concern, to see them settled, with no scandal emanating from her to spoil their lives. She realised now that, strangely enough, this had always been the main purpose of her life, to keep herself clear of scandal. Her attempts to leave Donald she saw now as half-hearted gestures. She had submitted herself to years of mental torture not so much to be near Andrew, but to keep herself unsullied in the eyes of her children.

Even the breakdown and the language she had frothed out at the time had left, as far as she could see, no adverse impression on them. Rather her illness had aroused their compassion. But now here, at the very last minute, she had to be exposed to them and in such a way that it would appear that either fate or God was determined to make her pay for her sins. . . . Or was it perhaps the spirit of Donald still at work, justifying himself and his principles? As ye sow, so also shall ye reap. Whatever it was it was weird . . . uncanny, that

273

the instrument chosen to expose her should be Jane's beloved George. That this man she had seen only twice, and for a matter of minutes each time, should be both accuser and deliverer was in itself, she felt, beyond the bounds of ordinary happenings.

She raised her head to look towards Jane, but was caught once again by the glare of Stephen's face, and he was speaking to her. He was answering Andrew by speaking to her. 'No matter what he says . . . what he says, I don't believe a word of it, do you hear?'

He was shouting now, and Andrew put in sharply, 'Don't speak to your mother like that. Say what you have to say to me.'

'You . . . !' Stephen moved from the rug and it seemed for a moment that he was going to strike out at the man before him. But when Andrew neither spoke nor moved he recovered himself, and after turning one last long look of loathing on Grace he rushed from the room, banging the door behind him.

Grace pressed her throat tighter. He would leave the house, he would go back to the college. Her fingers were hurting her neck as she thought, 'That is the last I will ever see of Stephen.' She turned her head quickly and looked towards the door. Stephen. Oh, Stephen. Slowly now her eyes turned on to the girls. Beatrice was staring at her, but Jane was looking at no-one, her head was sunk deep on to her chest and she was so still she might have been asleep on her feet. She looked back towards Beatrice and from the look on her face she could almost tell what she was thinking.

Beatrice's mind was moving rapidly as, fascinated, she stared at her mother. All these years she had had a lover, and he only a farm manager . . . and a mere farm-worker at one time; and now she wanted to say that this man was her father . . . and that Daddy hadn't been capable of giving a woman a child . . . it was shocking. And the things she had said were shocking, really shocking. Yet vaguely she understood the reason for her mother going off the rails, for she knew that life would be impossible without . . . it. It being the thing her mother had inferred her father had lacked. But she couldn't think of Andrew MacIntyre as her father, she never would be able to. It was awful, really awful, and the worst of it was Gerald knowing. Her mind touching on her husband, she thought bitterly, 'He started all this. He could have warned Andrew about the man, but no.' And she didn't believe he hadn't guessed her mother was the woman, he must have. He was getting his own back and all because he couldn't have the money. She had been married to Gerald less than three years, but she knew her Gerald – he was spiteful. But that had given her a shock too . . . there being no money. She couldn't take it in that her mother was broke and there was nothing to look forward to in the way of a legacy, and nothing for the child either. She looked her mother over now, at the quiet elegance of her dress, at the heavy diamond and ruby ring glinting on her finger. She looked a woman of means. Would she mind being poor? No . . . no, she knew somehow she wouldn't; she would be quite content in a cottage . . . the cottage . . . with him. She could not look at Andrew although she knew he was looking at her. Andrew, the superior spare-time gardener, whom her mother liked to refer to as a friend of the family, was one person, a likeable person, but when he turned into your father that made him into another person, a detestable person. She hated him, almost as much as Stephen did. And her mother . . . her mother had made herself cheap, horribly cheap. It was understandable for anyone falling – she had the grace to blush at the thought – but to keep it up for

275

years and years and with a working man like Andrew MacIntyre, it was beastly. She could stand no more, she must get home, even if it was to row with Gerald. She could almost hear him saying, 'That was why she took it all so calmly, us having to get married. Kind . . . huh!' He must get the car out and get them away from here before dark. What a Christmas Day! It was terrible, shocking. And not one of them had had a bite of dinner. She dropped her eyes from her mother's as she said, 'I – I – we'll be going home. I – I can't talk now.' Then, like Stephen, she hurried from the room, but without banging the door behind her. . . .

There was only Jane left. As Grace looked at her younger daughter she began to tremble. If Jane turned against her, if her reactions followed those of Stephen and Beatrice, she couldn't bear it. She forced herself to say, 'Come here, Jane.'

When Jane did not move she pulled herself up from the couch and, after a quick glance at Andrew, she went towards her.

'Jane.' She leaned forward to take one hanging hand into her own, but it was jerked upwards away from her.

'Oh, Jane, please, please look at me . . . Please.'

When Jane at last answered the desperate plea, it was as much as Grace could do to meet her eyes. Stephen had looked at her with hate, Beatrice with shocked incredulity, but the look in the young girl's eyes showed neither hate nor incredulity. Grace could see that Jane believed all she had been told and that she was hurt and bewildered, but above all else she was shamed.

'Jane . . . ' Grace forced herself to go on. 'You have always liked Andrew, now haven't you? You know you have. Why, just yesterday you defended him to Stephen.'

Jane's eyes dropped from her mother's and her young face became hard as she murmured, 'I – I wouldn't have if I'd known.'

'Don't say that.'

'It's all right.' Andrew came slowly towards them, his voice unusually humble as he said, 'I understand. And you will too, Jane, later, when you're older . . . and married.'

'Married!' Now Jane was looking at him and she repeated, 'Married! I'll never marry now, you've spoiled it all. George will . . . ' With a swift movement she turned her back on them and leant over the piano.

'George is a good man, I'm sure of that; everything will be all right.' As Andrew finished speaking he looked at Grace and nodded in the direction of the hall, and she took it to indicate that he was going to speak to George. As she watched him leave the room her thoughts, leaving Jane for a moment, went out to him. Poor Andrew, what he must be feeling to be looked down on and spurned as he had been in the past few hours and to take it all without exploding. Andrew was big; in all ways Andrew was big.

'How could you? How could you, Mammy?'

She was startled when Jane swung round to her a moment after the door closed, and she did not reply for some seconds, and then rather wearily, for of a sudden an overwhelming sense of deflation was sapping her, she said, 'I've told you all I can . . . it's as Andrew says, you won't understand until you're older.'

'I'll never understand. . . . Daddy was so—'

'Stop it, Jane.' Grace's voice had a cold ring to it now. 'Don't make me say things I'll be sorry for.'

'Oh.' Jane shook her head helplessly. The tears began to pour down her face and in a broken voice she exclaimed, 'I can't stay here . . . I can't. I'll . . . I'll go with Beatrice.'

'No, you won't go with Beatrice. You'll stay here.'

'I won't . . . I can't . . . Can't you see, it would be unbearable?'

'You were going to George's people on Tuesday, wait until then.'

'No, no, that'll be over.'

'No it won't, darling.'

'Don't touch me.'

Grace almost jumped back, so sharp was Jane's recoil. Then, after one long bewildered look at her mother, she turned from her and stumbled out of the room, her hands covering her face.

'Jane! Oh, Jane! Don't, Jane.' Grace was muttering to herself now as she stared towards the blank face of the door, then almost like someone advanced in years she moved towards the couch. She felt alone as she had never done in her life before; even the thought of Andrew could do nothing to fill this gaping void. . . . Jane, Jane. She had relied on Jane understanding . . . it didn't matter so much about the other two, not really . . . but Jane. She put her hands between her knees and pressed them tightly. If only she could cry and relieve this unbearable feeling. Almost the last words of the doctor at Rockforts came back to her: 'You'll cry, never fear, and when you do you'll know you are better.' It was a paradox. If only she could cry now; this was the time she should cry, this moment of realisation that the main efforts of her life had been wasted.

Gerald was in the dining-room. He had his back to the wine-cabinet. His chin was thrust out and nobbled with aggressiveness, and he stood tall to enable him to look down on the smaller man, as he growled, 'Who the hell do you think you're getting at? I've told you I didn't know it was her. What bloody business is it of yours, anyway?'

'I should've thought that was plain even to someone as thick-skinned as you.'

'Now look here—'

'Oh, stop your blustering. You can't get away from it, you intended to show him up. You knew when I spoke of his wife he hadn't one, but you couldn't get us face to face quick enough. You know what I think of you? I think you're a nasty swine. A word from you and I would have been on my guard and the man would have played up to it – they both would have played up to it; but no, you let me in there and break up a family. . . . You know, I could cheerfully murder you at this moment. . . .'

'You'd better be careful.' Gerald had stepped from the cabinet and, stretching still farther, he cried, 'D'you hear what I say? You'd better be careful.'

'Of what?' The cold question was as rebuffing as a blow, and Gerald felt it, but was saved by the door opening.

Beatrice immediately sensed the tension between the two men and the reason for it, also the fact that her husband was getting the worst of it. She said rapidly, 'Get the car out, we're going home.'

'Yes, and I should damn well think so.' Gerald resorted to the supporting habit of buttoning up his coat, then, turning to the man, he said, 'But let me tell you. I'm not finished with you over this. I'm going to have this out.'

'Any time you like.' The voice was restrained, and as Gerald barged from the room the man moved to the door and held it while Beatrice, with her eyes averted, passed him. He was still holding the door when he saw Andrew.

Andrew waited until Beatrice and Gerald reached the landing, then he walked slowly into the dining-room. After the man had closed the door behind him they faced each other.

'I can't think of anything to say – only I'd like you to know I'm sorry to the core.'

'That's all right.'

'I never for a moment guessed, you believe that?'

'Yes.'

'What can I say, I'm all at sea. I – I—'

'Don't worry yourself, it's one of those . . . well, coincidences they would say. I've always felt it would come out one day, but Grace . . . she felt it was all over when he went, and we were safe – she was just waiting until . . . until Jane was settled . . . will this make any difference?'

'Don't be daft, man.'

For the first time in the past three hours Andrew's face relaxed from its grey grimness. The reply, couched in such a familiar and ordinary phrase, said all he wanted to know.

'Thanks.'

'I love Jane, I mean to marry her. I did the first moment I saw her. I would have come here before, but . . . well, she was so young. She told me she was a year older than she really is, you know.' He smiled. 'But now it can be as soon as possible. The sooner the better, I would say.' He paused now before adding, 'I never, of course, met the vicar, but I'm glad that you are her father.'

He held out his hand.

From where she sat near the bed Grace heard the taxi draw up in front of the house, and she stopped herself from rising and going to the window. Jane had said she would write. Her head bowed as if the shame was hers, she had stood in front of her a few minutes ago and murmured, 'I'll write, Mammy.' That was all. 'I'll write, Mammy.' Jane, her daughter, had left her. . . . She put her forefinger between her teeth and bit hard on it.

Would that man be good to her? Yes, yes, he would. As Andrew said, he seemed a good man. He had apologised to her with such deep humility for being the instigator of the trouble that she had to reassure him that he was not to blame. And then he had said, 'Let me take Jane to my home. I can make up some excuse for bringing her . . . suspected polio . . . or something. And I can assure you she will come round. . . . I'll do my best to see that she does. Trust her with me, will you?' He had taken her hand, and then he had said, 'I liked your Andrew the first time I saw him. I like him even better today.' Yes, he was a nice man, a good man.

There came now the sound of the taxi starting up. She got to her feet and began walking about the room. This was what she had been wanting for a long time, wasn't it, for Jane to be settled and them all to be gone. But not in this way, not to scuttle from her as if from a leper. That's what she was to them . . . a leper.

The house was quiet now. There was no-one in it but herself and Peggy Mather. Her head lifted on the thought. Yesterday, even this morning, she had been afraid of Peggy Mather because of what she knew. Now she was afraid of her no more. She would be down in the kitchen now licking her lips over the day's happenings, knowing that her tongue would be free to wag. This past three weeks must have been a torment to her. Was it only three weeks since Andrew and herself had been confronted by her at the door of the cottage? They had just kissed good night, and when Andrew opened the door he still had his arm around her and instead of drawing it away he had jerked it more tightly still when they were enveloped by the light from a torch. It seemed only a split second before he was flashing his own torch on the intruder and she had gasped aloud when it revealed the purple, suffused face of Peggy Mather. Andrew acted as quickly as if his wits hadn't received a shock. In a minute he was facing and talking to the outraged cook. She could hear him now. 'One word from you about this and I go to Miss Shawcross. You're depending on getting what she's got, aren't you? Well, you won't stand a dog's chance if she knows you've done time, and you needn't bother denying it either, for I happened to be passing away an hour in court at Durham one day when I saw you being sent down . . . stealing from your employer, pilfering here and there. Six months is what you got, and it was your third offence, if I remember rightly.'

Peggy Mather had not denied this. The strange thing was she hadn't spoken at all . . . perhaps the shock had been too much for her. She had pretended for a long time now to hate Andrew MacIntyre, the reason being that Andrew from the first had shown her plainly he wanted nothing to do with her. But why had she gone up to the cottage that night? Neither Andrew nor she could see any reason for it, except a rather delicate one but they would really never know now. Certain they were that it hadn't been to spy on them, for she had been the most startled of the three.

And now she was down there in the kitchen laughing up her sleeve. Well, let her laugh. Perhaps she wouldn't laugh so much after she had heard what she had to say. For she would say to her, 'I won't be wanting you after tomorrow, Peggy. I will pay you an extra week's wages in lieu of notice.' She would pause, then add, 'That is when you return the number of things you have taken from my house over the years . . . there are two rings and the gold watch that disappeared during my illness . . . you ascribed their disappearance to a hawker who passed through the village, I remember. And then there is the set of miniature Georgian salt cellars . . . but you will know what you have taken.' She would be cool and cutting. She'd had to put up with Peggy Mather over the years because her dismissal would have offended Miss Shawcross. Well now, this is where she could hit back.

But when some time later she entered the kitchen and saw Peggy muffled up ready to go, she said none of these things, she merely looked at her straight and said, 'I won't be needing you any more after tonight, Peggy. I will send your money and cards down tomorrow. You had better take your aprons with you.' She pointed to a drawer.

After returning her look with a dark, venomous blaze for some long seconds, Peggy tore open the drawer and hauled out her aprons. Then, confronting Grace, she muttered, 'To be pushed off like this after all these years . . . by God, I'll have me own back!'

'I have no doubt of that, Peggy, but I should advise you not to start until the end of the week when I'll have left the village. It would be a pity if at this stage your aunt and you had to part company.'

The look that Peggy levelled on her reminded Grace of Stephen, and when the kitchen door banged she went to it and, after locking it, stood with her back against it, her eyes closed and her breath coming in gasps. Well, that was over. Thank God that was over. It was all over, all the secrecy, the lying, the fear. She was alone . . . alone. She opened her eyes and saw the emptiness inside of her widen until she felt she would drown in it. The next minute she was running through

283

the hall and up the stairs and into her bedroom. Pulling the curtains back from the window, she held them wide for a second, then closed them before opening them wide again. Through the gap where the beech had stood she expected to see a speck of light far up on the fells. He said he'd be waiting for her signal. There was no speck of light. Oh, Andrew, where are you? Come quickly, quickly. She turned from the window. The house was so quiet, empty, bare. She walked on to the landing . . . 'As ye sow, so shall ye reap.' 'Ask and ye shall receive.' She had asked for Andrew and she had got him . . . at a price. But where was he? He said he would wait for the signal and come down at once. Oh, Andrew. She stopped at the head of the stairs; it was as if a hand had come out from the ornate frame and halted her. Slowly she turned her head and looked up at Donald. For a moment she imagined his eyes moved. His whole face seemed to be moving, smiling, a self-satisfied proud smile . . . there was a supercilious lift to his lips. 'As ye sow, so shall ye reap.' She put up her hand and crushed the flowers entwined in the frame . . . then slowly her fingers relaxed. She had not sworn. She looked back into the eyes and whispered aloud, 'You can do no more; I will be happy in spite of you. I can even have another child . . . do you hear that . . . another child.'

But no . . . she turned from the picture and went slowly down the stairs . . . no more children, only Andrew.

Andrew! She stood in the centre of the hall; the house was so lonely. Had anything happened to Andrew? What if he had fallen out there on the fells, he could lie there all night. . . . Don't be silly, don't be silly. Andrew knew the fells like the back of his hand. She would phone Aunt Aggie and tell her what had happened. What was she talking about? Aunt Aggie was down at the cottage.

She had thought it would be a change to spend Christmas there. Hadn't Andrew gone down with her and her friend to see them settled in, and stay with them until Boxing Day? That had been the arrangement. But he hadn't been able to stay away, he had come back. If only he hadn't come back . . . Be quiet, be quiet.

She went into the drawing-room and looked about her. It looked gay . . . tree, lights and holly. This was Christmas night and the house was dead. She put her hands to her head, and as she did so the front-door bell rang. She ran like a child to it, and when she opened it and saw Andrew standing there she fell against him crying, 'Oh, Andrew! Andrew!'

'There. There.'

'I signalled and you didn't answer . . . I was frightened.'

'I've been outside for some time. I couldn't stay up there any longer. I've just seen her go.'

'Oh, my dear, let me take your coat.'

'No, Grace, I'm not staying here.'

'What!' Her mouth was agape.

'And neither are you. We couldn't start our life here. Not in this house. Go and get your coat, wrap up well. I'll put out the lights.'

'Yes, yes, Andrew.' She turned quickly from him and ran up the stairs, and in a matter of minutes she had joined him again. He looked at her for a moment, then, pulling the collar of her coat up around her neck, he led her towards the door, and when they reached it he switched out the last light. . . .

It took them nearly half an hour to get to the cottage, and as she stood taking off her outdoor things Andrew lit the lamp and in its first fluttering gleam she saw that he had prepared for her coming. For there before the fire and between the two worn armchairs was a set tea-table, warm and inviting.

'Oh, Andrew!'

'Sit yourself down and leave this to me . . . this is my show.' He was smiling at her. 'No talking now, just sit there.' He pressed her into the chair and touched her cheek once before turning away to make the tea. When he had done this he sat opposite to her, handing her food and pressing her to eat, looking at her all the while, and her heart and spirits began to lift under his look. His face appeared almost boyish again in the lamplight. After some time, during which he still continued to look at her in this odd sweet way, she said, 'What is it, Andrew?' His eyes left hers for a moment and he leant towards her across the flame of the fire and took her hands. And when he looked at her again he said softly, 'I've dreamed of this for years, ever since the day I saw you in the kitchen, and you seemed to hold those roses out to me. It's a fact, night after night I'd see you sitting just there, and I was always pouring the tea, not you. . . . Funny, and it didn't end there.'

'No?'

'No.'

'Tell me.'

'Later when I've cleared away.'

And later when he had cleared away he came to her and, pulling her up gently, placed her on his knee, and they talked, not of the happenings of the day, but of the cottage near Buckfastleigh and how he would find work on one of the farms near at hand. She knew this too was part of his dream.

Some time later still, the fire banked down, the lamp turned out, he picked her up in his arms and, walking sideways, carried her up the narrow stairs; she laughed into his neck. And when on the tiny square of landing he placed her on her feet and, chuckling himself, said, 'It was much easier in the dream,' her laughter rose,

286

filling her body, shaking her as if with ague, until with a burst her mirth exploded in a torrent of tears which seemed to spring from every outlet of her face.

'Oh, Andrew! Andrew!'

'There, my love.'

'Nothing matters, Andrew; nothing matters any more. Nothing, nothing. . . .'

Only the loss of Stephen and Beatrice . . . and Jane. . . .

Oh, Jane. Jane.

THE END

THE RAG NYMPH

by Catherine Cookson

Millie Forester was seven years old, surprisingly well-dressed, well-spoken and composed for one suddenly abandoned by a panic-stricken mother in an all-too-obvious flight from the law. She came into Aggie Winkowski's life out of the shadows of a mean street sweltering in the heat of a late June afternoon.

Aggie was well-known hereabouts. Some knew her as "Raggie Aggie," for trading in rags and old clothes was her long-established business. Yet she could remember when this was still open country, before the progression of the Industrial Revolution turned the nearby town into a voracious city, swallowing up the land and covering it with factories and a maze of slums. But Aggie had survived and adapted to this harsh new world and so had her family's old farmhouse for which she was heading when she first encountered Millie—or "the rag nymph," as she was to be called—in this midsummer of 1854.

Aggie knew well enough the dangers waiting for such a strikingly pretty girl left alone in this rough and vice-ridden quarter. She could see nothing for it than to take her home, at least for the time being. But what began as a compassionate expediency led to the establishment of a whole new relationship that would grow and deepen, moulding Millie's destiny and giving new meaning to the life of Aggie Winkowski.

Coming in May in hardcover from Bantam Press in Canada.

ISBN 0-593-021290 $26.50

There was a scream of protesting tires

And the big white car spun in a nightmarish skid and headed straight for an enormous tree. The crash that followed sounded to Antoinette like the end of the world. And then...silence.

Rushing over to the spot where the driver had been thrown from the car, she gasped as she recognized Lewis Freemont.

The famous man opened his eyes.
"I can't see you," he whispered. "I can't see anything at all!"

And a chill of horror crawled down Antoinette's spine.

The Warrender Saga

Follow the famous conductor
Oscar Warrender—and Anthea,
his lovely opera-star wife—down
the years in these delightfully
entertaining novels. Each volume
is a heartwarming romance set
against the exciting background of
opera or theater.

1. A Song Begins
2. The Broken Wing
3. When Love Is Blind
4. The Curtain Rises
5. Child of Music
6. Music of the Heart
7. Unbidden Melody
8. Song Cycle
9. Remembered Serenade

MARY BURCHELL

When Love Is Blind

Originally published as Harlequin Romance #1244

Harlequin Books

TORONTO • LONDON • NEW YORK • AMSTERDAM
SYDNEY • HAMBURG • PARIS

Original hardcover edition published in 1967
by Mills & Boon Limited

ISBN 0-373-01244-6
First Harlequin edition published October 1968

The Warrender Saga, published October 1978

Second printing February 1979
Third printing June 1979

Printed in Canada

CHAPTER ONE

"I could have borne the disappointment of failure. At least, I think I could." Antoinette stared unhappily at her friend, Rosamund Heal, who was all attention and full of sympathy. "What I simply cannot bear—and what I'll never, never forgive—is the *way* he blasted my hopes. So—so brutally, so callously."

"I always said he looked a beast. It was hard luck you had to have him for one of the examiners. If it had been nice old Sir Horace Keen or Dr. Bankes or even—"

"Well, it wasn't," cut in Antoinette sharply, her over-strained nerves rebelling at every form of comfort. "It had to be Lewis Freemont himself. And to think how unspeakably thrilled and happy I was when I first heard he was coming!"

"Naturally," said Rosamund loyally. "If one's a ser-ious artist of course one wants to be heard by someone who is the tops. At least—" she glanced doubtfully at her friend—"I suppose you still think he *is* the tops, even if he didn't appreciate you?"

"Why, of course!" Antoinette laughed shortly. "The fact that he called me a clever automaton without a glimmer of the divine spark doesn't make him any less of a genius when *he* plays. His judgment may be cruel. Even—" she hesitated as though about to utter blas-phemy "—faulty. "But of his own standing as a pianist there isn't a shadow of a doubt."

"Perhaps," suggested Rosamund tentatively, "after another six months or a year you'll be nearer the standard he sets. You can always try again and—"

"No!" Antoinette's rejection of that was almost violent. "I'll never try again. Never, after what he said."

"Oh, Toni, you'll feel better presently."

"I shan't. What he said just killed my belief in myself. I wouldn't have thought it possible. But that's what he did to me."

She rubbed her hands together as though they had suddenly grown cold and stiff, while Rosamund watched her in growing dismay.

"If he'd said my technique was faulty or my execution below standard or that my facility wasn't equal to my artistic conception—*anything* like that—I could have swallowed my disappointment and started again. Those are things that endless work can set right. And I've never minded how hard I worked, have I, Rosamund?—have I?" A rather piteous note crept into her voice, and Rosamund shook her head wordlessly.

"But what he said meant one thing only. That *it wasn't worth while my going on*, because I'd never have more than the outer shell. The real pearl of price just wasn't there."

"Even the greatest authorities can be mistaken," said Rosamund after a heavy pause.

"I shall never know," replied Antoinette tragically. "I shall never know."

"Oh, Toni, don't be so defeatist!" Rosamund, who was ebullient and optimistic and, as she often told herself thankfully, entirely free from the artistic temperament, spoke as bracingly as she could. "You can't turn it all down on the word of one man only."

"On the word of that particular man I can. His was the opinion I valued above all others. To me he's the

6

last word in pianists. If he ways I'm wasting my time—"

"He didn't say quite that," objected Rosamund in the interests of accuracy. "And anyway, I tell you—he may be wrong."

"That isn't enough." Suddenly Antoinette was sadly resigned rather than angry. "Without the absolute conviction that one day I would make the grade I couldn't go on with those hours and hours of work and practice. I didn't mind anything—not any grind or sacrifice—so long as I could see the shining goal of the concert pianist before me. But I—I can't see that light any more, Rosamund. He's put out the light for me."

And suddenly the tears were running down her cheeks and deep sobs of disappointment and disillusionment shook her. For though most people would have thought that at twenty and with all her talent Antoinette Burney had the world in front of her, *she* knew that half her heart and all her hopes had been blighted by the chill, almost casually spoken verdict of Lewis Freemont.

By him, of all people! That was what was unbearable.

Antoinette simply could not remember a time when music had not been the greater part of her life. Her mother had been an accomplished pianist and her father a good amateur organist. She herself had known her notes before her letters, and it seemed to her now that she could not have been more than six when her mother first started saying to people:

"Toni's going to be the real musician in the family. Oh, I'm quite good and her father adores it, of course. But just look how that child stretches her little hands,

7

and the accurate way she picks out her notes even now. She's going to be something, I tell you. We'll make a concert pianist of her one of these days and be proud of her."

Antoinette liked the sound of that. When she was still at an age to have a wide blue sash tied round her small middle she used to imagine herself sweeping on to a platform in a long gown while a large and admiring audience applauded her.

Day dreams of this sort faded somewhat in the realistic light of her schooldays. But deep down inside her Antoinette never relinquished that early dream. Her music lessons remained far the most important thing in her life, and no one ever had to drive her to the piano-stool to complete her daily practice. On the contrary, she was prepared to neglect most other things in favour of it.

"I never knew another child like her," declared the junior music mistress at her school. "She's the only one who positively *likes* practising. She's at it all the time."

"Yes. She hardly givers herself time to enjoy it, does she?" replied the senior music mistress, who was a singularly perceptive woman.

"At that age! Would one expect it?" The younger woman looked doubtful. "Isn't it enough that she is ambitious to perfect her technique?"

"Perhaps. I'm not criticising. But—" the senior music mistress frowned—"I could wish that she were rather more of a music-maker for the sheer joy of it and less of a determined performer."

This was not the view of Antoinette's mother, who never ceased to rejoice in the crisp accuracy of her playing, the quite remarkable technique she displayed, and the precocious standard of her performance. Everyone said it was hard indeed that she did not live to see the sucecss she so confidently expected for her child. She died when Antoinette was seventeen, from a bout of pneumonia brought on because she insisted on going out on a bitter winter's night to hear her daughter in a school concert when she should really have been at home nursing a heavy cold.

Her death was a fearful blow to Antoinette and her father, for Mrs. Burney had been the dominating one in the household. But—incredibly as it seemed to her—Antoinette's father found consolation less than a year later in marriage to someone twenty years younger than himself.

Meriel, the new Mrs. Burney, was quite pleasant to Antoinette, without going out of her way to make her welcome in her own home. But it was something of a relief to everyone when, six months later, Antoinette went to London, primarily to complete her musical training, but also because it had become urgently necessary to break up a domestic situation which had proved completely unworkable.

Her father, whose enthusiasm for her piano-playing had never been in the same obsessive class as her mother's, suggested that Antoinette should at the same time study a foregin language or take a secretarial course which would fit her for some kind of a career if her music failed her. And although at that time Antoinette could not even entertain the idea of anything but success, since her father was paying her fees and maintaining her, she felt it was only fair to devote part of her time to this idea of his.

In London she was tremendously happy, much happier than she had been since her mother died. For she found herself among other students and companions to whom music meant everything in the world. She went to concerts, happy to queue for hours for a cheap seat. She discovered opera. She discussed, argued, followed form and once more dreamed dreams.

Few of the students around her cherished ambitions as high as hers, so mostly she kept her hopes to herself. Only to Rosamund was she really frank.

This was probably because Rosamund had no connection with the musical world. Antoinette had met her at the business-training college where she spent part of each week in deference to her father's rather vaguely expressed wishes.

To Rosamund a good solid secretarial post seemed a much more sensible proposition than any musical ambitions. But she thought Antoinette clever and courageous and quite special. And she honestly thought no one else could pay the piano so well.

She seldom accompanied Antoinette to concerts, even after they decided to share a small flat together, because, as she said without offence, "enough was enough" for her so far as music was concerned. But she yielded good-humouredly to Antoinette's insistence that she should at least come and hear the famous Lewis Freemont.

"You must!" Antoinette said. "He's playing the Brahms First and Warrender is conducting, which is unusual for him as he nearly always conducts opera. I want you to hear Freemont because there is, quite simply, no one like him."

So Rosamund obligingly accompanied her friend to the Festival Hall, sat through a concert overture which she frankly found dull, and then was considerably fascinated by the piano concerto which followed. She thought Lewis Freemont not only astonishingly good-looking, in a cool, authoritative sort of way, but also about the most exciting performer she had ever heard in any medium. (Which would have caused the conductor some sardonic amusement if he had known, since he regarded himself as pretty good in *his* field too.)

Afterwards Antoinette demanded eagerly to know what she had thought of it all.

"It was very exciting," Rosamund said slowly. "*He's* exciting, in some indefinable way. Not very nice, I should say, but—" she groped for another word, but finally could only repeat—"exciting. I liked the last movement. It had a good strong tune, and he gave one a terrific sense of power."

"But the slow movement," exclaimed Antoinette dreamily. "That's where his real genius shows. Didn't you adore the slow movement?"

"No. I lost the thread," said Rosamund candidly, "and began to think about that new dress I can't quite afford."

"You're hopeless!" cried Antoinette. But she laughed a good deal, because Rosamund's down-to-earth outlook was a wonderful antidote to some of the airy-fairy nonsense which was sometimes talked in her own circle.

She made no further attempt to take Rosamund to hear Lewis Freemont. But she never missed a concert of his herself. Sometimes she would get a seat right on

11

the platform, so that she could watch those strong, clever hands at really close quarters, and study his fantastic technique. She didn't yearn over him in the tiresome way some of the more romantic students did, and nor did she ever ask him for his autograph. That was not the way it took Antoinette. But he gradually became in her mind and world the almost symbolic figure representing her art and her ambition.

She knew Rosamund was probably quite right when she said he was exciting but not very nice. There was something almost contemptuous in the set of his mouth, and his unusually light hazel-coloured eyes could look coldly right through an over-enthusiastic audience which started its applause a fraction of a second too soon. Indeed, once when she had gone to the stage door to see him come out, she saw him thrust his way through the crowd and heard him say impatiently to his companion, "I never did suffer fools gladly."

But to all these little foibles he was fully entitled in Antoinette's estimation, so long as he played like an angel. And like an angel he played. Even the crabbiest and least zestful of the music critics admitted that. Though one of them did once add that there was a touch of the avenging angel about him.

In a half romantic, half amused way Antoinette sometimes indulged in daydreams in which she met him. The fantasy took various forms. Sometimes she just ran into him at a party and he said, "Who is that interesting-looking girl with the lovely grey eyes? With those hands she simply must play the piano." And sometimes, in her more ambitious moments, she substituted for him at a concert and afterwards he said, "My God, I couldn't have done it better myself."

When, therefore, she found that he was to be one of the judges at a very important end-of-term examination at her music college she was excited and thrilled as she never had been by any challenge before. She practised with iron determination. Nothing was too much for her and inevitably her dreams took on a brighter and brighter glow.

She knew she was good. It would have been disingenuous of her to pretend anything else, and her teacher was highly complimentary in the final run-through.

Only when it came to the actual trial itself did the curious idea come to her that something almost outside herself—something other than the real Antoinette, hidden deep down in her soul—was responsible for those tripping scale passages, those faultless arpeggios. So practised was she by now that she could do it almost without thinking about it, and in some extraordinary way she could almost watch herself performing, with a cool detachment that left her free to ask herself, "What is he thinking of it?"

At the end, Lewis Freemont unexpectedly called her over to the desk where he was sitting making a few notes. And looking up at her with those extraordinarily penetrating eyes that she had never seen so close before he said,

"Miss Burney—" he glanced down at some papers to verify her name, as though it were not sufficiently interesting to remain in his mind otherwise—"what is your exact musicial ambition?"

"To be a successful concert pianist," she told him without hesitation.

"I see. Not just to—make music?"

"Well, that too, of course." She smiled at him, but received no smile in answer.

"That is the first requisite of the true musician, you know," he said drily. "That—and to serve the composer one is privileged to interpret."

She thought it affectation for such an obviously arrogant man to advocate such humility. But she said, "I understand that."

"No, I don't think you understand it at all," he replied coolly. "Nothing in your extremely facile playing suggests it for one moment. Your execution is practically impeccable you might make a good teacher, I suppose. But if you really have any idea of being the link between great music and the eager listener, dismiss it from your mind." And then he made the unforgivable, never-to-be-forgotten remark about her being a brilliant automaton without a glimmer of the divine spark.

If he had slapped her in the face she could not have been more dismayed and astounded. She flickered her long lashes in that moment of shock, and then she turned away without a word. She thought the other examiner said something in kindly protest about harsh standards. But Lewis Freemont said quite distinctly:

"No, no. She hasn't got the root of the matter in her. And batting her eyelashes at me won't make me think anything different!"

Antoinette walked home, hardly even seeing anything or anyone she passed, and failure and fury walked with her. If the one chilled her beyond belief, the other raised her temperature to fever heat.

Fortunately Rosamund had just come in so that she was able to pour out the story into the most sympathetic ears. But nothing Rosamund or anyone else could say made any difference. The ambitions and hopes of a lifetime lay in ruins.

After a while Antoinette began to ask herself why she was so willing to accept the verdict of one man, however distinguished, however much admired by herself. Others had praised her often enough—her dexterity, her application, her unceasing hard work. More than once she had carried off high honours in various examinations. She was the nearly perfect student. It was only now—*now*, when for the first time she came up against a great artist rather than an academic authority, that she had failed absolutely.

And, to her chagrin and dismay, the answer came back at her with dreadful certainty. She accepted Lewis Freemont's cruel dictum absolutely because she knew in her heart that he was right!

It was a shattering discovery, and at least half of her struggled angrily against the realization of the truth. But irresistibly it was dawning upon her that somewhere along the line from the precocious little performer to the ambitious adult she had lost the indefinable contact between her soul—the essential inner *her*—and the music.

She would always dazzle some people with her skill, but her heart would never speak to the hearts of her audience. She would never transport them; she would only surprise and intrigue them. And that, she thought contemptuously, any conjuror could do.

During the next week or two Antoinette made drastic changes in her life.

In spite of protests from Rosamund—and even more emphatic ones from her teacher—she renounced what had been virtually a full-time training, giving as her irrefutable reason that her financial position had changed and it had become necessary for her to start earning her living immediately.

She almost violenty rejected any suggestion that she should teach music (though even Lewis Freemont had said disparagingly that he *supposed* she might make a good teacher). Instead, with her unusual capacity for concentrated hard work, she launched into a crash course in secretarial training, which brought all her slightly haphazard knowledge in this line to a remarkably high pitch. Then she joined the agency for whom Rosamund worked.

She told herself that she was content to have things this way. She did, it was true, derive a certain satisfaction from finding that she could now maintain herself without any aid from her father. While he, on his side, knowing nothing of the events which had precipitated his dauhgter's decision, wrote to say he was glad she was applying herself to something practical and financially rewarding, but "hoped she was keeping up her music for her own pleasure."

At the word "pleasure" Antoinette gave a sad, rather bitter little smile. Pleasure was no longer associated with the thing which had once been her life, and she told herself that she never wanted to attend another concert so long as she lived.

This, of course, proved to be a passing phase. One cannot fix every hope and thought upon one thing— particularly one form of art—and then suddenly root it out of one's life entirely. Less than a couple of months after the disastrous scene with Lewis Freemont Antoinette found herself longing to go to a concert.

any concert, she told herself. But in actual fact this was less than the truth.

What she wanted was to go once more and hear the man who had altered her life. She wanted to hear him again, with critical rather than entranced ears, to judge in her new mood of bitter realism whether he were truly such a remarkable musician himself that she could never reject his verdict entirely.

She said nothing about her intention to Rosamund. Indeed, not until the very evening of the concert did she quite admit to herself that she was going. And then, having left it so late, she found of course that there were only a few returned tickets—all of them much more expensive than anything she had intended to pay.

She had to make her decision quickly, with an impatient queue behind her and, faintly flustered, she said she would take the least expensive ticket available. Only when she turned away with the ticket clutched in her hand did she discover that the seat was in the front row.

Ordinarily, she would have been very willing to be near enough to watch his playing close at hand, even though it meant being too near for what was largely an orchestral concert. But, in the dismayed realization that not only would she see but also that she could be seen, she nearly turned back to the box-office and returned the ticket. But by now she felt rather self-conscious. And, anyway, others were crowding in to make their own enquiries.

Besides—suddenly her spirit rose defensively—why should she care if he did see her and, by some chance, recollect her? Her life was not going to be ruled in its

17

smallest particular by the fact that Lewis Freemont had been crushingly rude to her! If he recognized her, let him reflect that she had paid to come and decide what *she* thought of *him*, and if the reflection afforded him even a second of discomfiture, she would be the last to worry.

In point of fact, when he finally came on the stage his glance passed over her as it did over everyone else in the hall. Quite obviously, if he saw the audience at all, he saw them collectively. And once he sat down at the piano, she could not imagine that he remembered anyone in the place but the conductor and the orchestral players around him.

The first concerto was a modern work and the sheer brilliance of his execution drew tremendous applause. But Antoinette was eager to tell herself that this was merely a display of the very thing he had assessed so contemptuously in herself. Well, if not *quite* like that, at least the work plumbed no searching depths of feeling.

But when it came to the Beethoven—ah, that was a different matter entirely. The brilliant technique became no more than a means to an end. The sensitive instinct, the inner knowledge of the man, shed a light that was almost divine upon the work, so that all could share fully in one of the wonders of the musical world instead of just glimpsing it dimly.

As with all great performances, it was difficult to tell where creative art ended and interpretative art began. Like everyone else, Antoinette just accepted the miracle of the experience, so that she was transported to something a little beyond herself and came back a better and a happier person because of it.

This time the applause had warmth and affection and something like gratitude in it, as he came forward to the front of the platform, smiling at last with his task well done. He saw them as people now, not just a disembodied audience, and as his cool, keen glance travelled along the front row it came to rest on Antoinette.

There was no doubt that he recognized her as someone he knew, and for a moment she received the full force of that immensely attractive smile. Instinctively she smiled back—it was impossible not to. Then the audience surged forward from further back in the hall and the moment was over. Though he returned to the platform many times he never seemed to notice Antoinette again.

She went home in a daze of mixed feelings which she could not possibly explain to herself. She hated him still for what he had done to her, and she despised him for the heartless, arrogant way in which he had chosen to do it. But he was still the person above all others who could stir her senses and excite her imagination. If only, only he had left her her dreams she could almost have loved him for the way he had played that evening. And the way he had smiled at her afterwards.

After that, she resumed her concert-going to a certain extent. At least she never missed an occasion when he played. Once or twice she thought he noticed her again and recognized her, but he never again smiled at her in that moment of almost intimate warmth. Perhaps he had now fully recalled the circumstances of their initial meeting. It was a humiliating thought. But it did not keep her away when he played.

In late September Antoinette took a week's holiday from her work, with the half-formed intention of going home to see her father and Meriel. But her tentative suggestion to this effect brought an immediate reply from Meriel, who explained regretfully that they themselves would be in Scotland. Such a pity, but she was sure Antoinette would understand.

Antoinette understood all right. But she wondered indignantly and a little sadly why there was no word from her father about her possibly joining them—or even about altering dates somewhat to make their plans and hers fit better. With no more than six month's employment behind her she had not saved enough to afford much of a holiday elsewhere. But Rosamund took some days off too and they had one or two enjoyable excursions outside London.

It was on one of these excursions, when they were in one of the loveliest parts of Surrey, that Rosamund pointed to a faded-looking signpost and remarked:

"Your friend Lewis Freemont lives somewhere around here, doesn't he?"

"Does he?" Antoinette was constantly astonished by the odd pieces of information which Rosamund gleaned from her work or from her very casual reading of journals and newspapers. "How do you know?" she enquired curiously, and then added automatically, "He's no friend of mine, as well you know."

"It was just a manner of speaking," Rosamund assured her pacifically. "I remember seeing a photograph of his house in a magazine when I was under the hairdryer. It's a converted manor house, the article said. And that was the name of the village—" once more she pointed to the signpost—"I remember it because it was such a queer name—Pallin Parva."

"That must be the house," Antoinette said slowly, and she indicated a distant moss-grown tiled roof with what looked like Tudor chimneys at either end. From one of them a trail of smoke curled up lazily into the pale sky of the autumn afternoon.

"Do you want to go and have a closer view?" asked Rosamund.

"Oh no!" Antoinette rejected the suggestion quickly. "*I* haven't any interest in him nowadays," and she walked on.

But as she did so she knew perfectly well that neither statement was the truth. She longed to go and have a closer view, for the simple reason that Lewis Freemont still interested her out of all proportion to his place in her present life.

The next day Rosamund had to go into the office on an emergency call and Antoinette was left on her own. Again it was a lovely clear autumn day. And, telling herself that she would just go wherever her fancy took her, she boarded the same Green Line bus that she and Rosamund had taken the day before and took a ticket to the end of the run.

But when the bus neared the place where they had dismounted the previous day, something stronger than herself impelled her to ring the bell. And a few moments later she found herself alone on the country road, watching the bus disappear rapidly into the distance.

Even now she would not quite admit to herself that she was going to look at Lewis Freemont's home. Nor would she examine just what her motive might be in coming here at all. She had little reason to feel any

21

friendly interest in him. She was past the stage of the star-struck teenager. She had no wish to know him or even see him. Why then was she here?

"Why *shouldn't* I be here?" she asked herself defensively. "Or anywhere else I choose to go. This happens to be a lovely part of the country. I'm at liberty to enjoy it in my own time and my own way."

But she felt faintly self-conscious all the same as she paused at the hedge-lined crossroads about a couple of hundred yards from the house. Then, still feeling something of an intruder—though a defiant intruder—she started to cross the road. As she did so a powerful white car swept round the bend in the road, the sound of its approach obscured by the droning of an aeroplane overhead.

If she had gone straight on she would have been missed by inches. But, in a split second, she recognized that distinctive car, seen so many times outside concert halls, and a ridiculous feeling of mingled guilt, embarrassment and indecision stopped her in her tracks.

There was a scream of protesting tyres and she actually heard him shout something at her as the car swerved round her. Then, as she cast a terrified glance over her shoulder, the big white car seemed to strike a patch of oil or grease in the road. With no appreciable slackening of speed it spun round in a nightmare skid and headed straight for an enormous tree at the side of the road. There was a crash which sounded to Antoinette like the end of the world. And then—silence, utter and complete, except that, on the very edge of it, she seemed to hear the distant drone of the aeroplane fading across the autumn sky.

She was ashamed to remember afterwards that in the first moment of panic she actually turned to flee. Then, realizing that there was no one but herself to do something about what had happened, she forced her trembling legs to take her to the side of the road.

The car was a horrible buckled tangle of metal, but he had been flung clear and was lying on the grass verge face downwards, his arms outspread on either side of him.

"Mr. Freemont—" the idiotic incongruity of addressing the still figure thus hardly touched her consciousness. In any case, what else was she to say? "Please—please—"

She touched him, but he did not move. And then, with a considerable effort of strength, she managed to turn him so that she could see his face. It was pale and set and his eyes were closed. But—she could not have said why—he certainly did not look dead.

"He's only stunned. I think he's only stunned," she said aloud, as though to reassure herself, and a slight sob of frightened relief escaped her. But now the most urgent thing was to get help.

She jumped to her feet and looked wildly round her, and as she did so he stirred sharply. Immediately she dropped on her knees again beside him.

"Open your eyes," she exclaimed imploringly. "Please open your eyes!" And at that he did exactly what he was told. He opened his eyes, but he looked past her and muttered,

"What's happened?—what's happened?"

"There was an accident—"

"I remember—that fool of a girl—" he was still muttering, but it was obvious that full consciousness was returning. "What happened?" he repeated, on a note of curiously bewildered impatience. "Where's the light?"

"The—the light?" stammered Antoinette. And at the sound of her voice he seemed to focus his gaze more exactly on her, though entirely without recognition.

"Who are you? *Where* are you?" was the extraordinary thing he said. And suddenly one groping hand fastened on her arm with an urgency and a strength that almost made her cry out.

"I'm here—here," she answered helplessly. "Here—just beside you. Can't you see me?"

"No, I can't see you." And then, in the tone of someone struggling not to accept a monstrous discovery——*"I can't see anything at all.* It's all dark."

At these words a chill of inexpressible horror crawled down Antoinette's spine.

"I'll get help," she gasped. "Lie where you are. You're off the road and safe here. I'll get help. A house —your house—is quite near."

"But I don't understand—" His grip was still so tight on her arm that she literally had to prise his fingers away, and she did so in panic and dismay beyond anything she had ever known before.

"Don't move," she implored him. And then again, "I'll get help."

"Who *are* you?" He sounded wild with impatience and helplessness. "You're the girl who caused the accident, aren't you? You must be. There was no one else," Then, in a horrified burst of anger and despair, he cried, "God, you little fool, you've blinded me!" And he made a strange sketchy gesture with one powerful hand, as though he literally wanted to get hold of her and shake the life out of her.

"I'll get help," she cried for the fourth time. And she turned and ran stumblingly from the scene, urged quite as much by a panic desire to flee as by her genuine wish to fetch aid of some sort.

"It wasn't my fault," she sobbed aloud as she ran. "It wasn't entirely my fault. He was driving fast. And the car caught that patch of oil in the road. I saw it there myself. It wasn't my fault—it *wasn't!*—But he'll never believe anything else."

She was at the house more quickly than she had expected and hammered on the door.

"Quick, quick!" she gasped to the startled man who snatched open the door. "There's been a car accident. Mr. Freemont is hurt. He's lying on the grass verge, down by the crossroads."

Even while she poured out her story, the man had turned from her and was calling to several men further back in the hall who seemed to be engaged on some sort of building or decorating.

"Fetch one of those boards," he called, "in case we have to carry him. There's been an accident!"

And then, as Antoinette flattened herself against the side of the porch, several men in white painter's overalls ran past her with an air of purpose and urgency which gave her her first glimmer of comfort since the awful thing had happened. At least they knew what to do and were preparing to do it with all speed.

She followed in their wake as far as the gate. They had already outdistanced her and were running towards that huddle of metal at the end of the lane. She herself was no longer needed. And even as she realized that, the instinct of flight—barely controlled in her until this moment—rose in a flood and overwhelmed every other feeling.

Guiltily, and yet with a sense of relief that hurt, she turned in the opposite direction and ran as hard as she could.

More by luck than any calculation she found a Green Line bus stop, and she had been standing there trembling and distraught for no more than three minutes before a bus came along. It happened to be going in the direction of town, but wherever it had been going Antoinette would have scrambled on to it. Anything, anything to get away from the scene of what had just happened.

By a horrid quirk of fate the bus had to pass within yards of the scene of the accident. And only a few minutes after she had got on she heard people saying, "Oh, look, there's been an accident! It's that big white car. They're picking someone up—"

She shut her eyes tightly, so that she should see nothing, and wondered for a moment if she were going to faint. She must have gone a queer colour, because after a minute or two the woman sitting beside her said:

"Makes you feel quite funny, doesn't it? Did you see—"

"No," interrupted Antoinette violently. "I didn't see anything. I shut my eyes."

"I don't blame you, dear," was the reply. And presently several people got off the bus and Antoinette was able to go and sit alone at the back and think her own thoughts uninterrupted.

But what thoughts!—what thoughts!

Was she really to blame? Could the stupidity of that momentary hesitation really be held against her? What was she doing there, anyway? What ill-fated, idiotic impulse had brought here there?

But even worse than any question of her own responsibility was the awfulness of what had happened to *him*.

Could his blindness be merely the temporary effect of shock? She prayed and prayed confusedly that this should be so, but gained no reassurance from the words that gabbled ceaselessly through her consciousness.

All the way home she tormented herself with questions. But most tormenting of all was the realization that she must keep her fears and her knowledge to herself. There was nothing useful she could do by coming forward, she assured herself, even while another part of her said that she was a coward. She was *not* responsible. Over and over again she repeated this to herself.

No one could ever assert that she had been there. Lewis Freemont himself could not identify her. She felt sick for a moment when she thought *why* he would not be able to identify her. As for the workman who had opened the door at Pallin Manor, to him she was no more than a stranger who had disappeared as swiftly as she had come.

So far as identification was concerned, she was safe. Only she knew—and would know to her dying day—that perhaps, perhaps she had been partly responsible for this dreadful thing which had happened.

Fortunately Rosamund was late home, which gave Antoinette time to steel herself to outward calm and composure. This was put to the immediate test, for Rosamund came in exclaiming,

"Have you see the evening papers? Lewis Freemont's had a car crash!"

"No, I didn't get a paper. Is he badly hurt?"

"I don't know. There were just a few lines in the Stop Press. Let's see if there's anything on the ten o'clock news. It's almost time." And, though Antoinette felt she could hardly bear it, Rosamund crossed the room and switched on the radio.

The announcer ploughed his way through the usual tally of wars and strikes and outrages in countries which had recently gained independence, and then, near the end, he said in tones of gentlemanly regret that "Lewis Freemont, the well-known pianist, was injured today in a car accident near his home in Surrey. The car apparently went out of control and crashed into a tree. It is not yet known how seriously he has been injured, but it is feared that his sight may have been affected."

"His *sight*!" Rosamund whistled, and then observed practically, "Well, that's better than having his hands injured, I suppose."

Antoinette could only say, "I suppose so." But she still seemed to hear his voice saying, on a note of incredulous horror, "I can't see anything at all. It's all dark."

During the next few days both newspapers and radio carried quite a story about Lewis Freemont's accident. It seemed that he had miraculously escaped any real bodily injury, but the optic nerve had been injured and "his sight had been seriously affected."

The term "blind" was never actually used, but rumours began to circulate, and Rosamund came in one day about a week after the accident and said:

"I ran into that chap Charles Cane who used to queque with you for concert tickets. He says the story is all about the musical world that Lewis Freemont is totally blind after that accident."

"T-totally blind?" stammered Antoinette.

Rosamund nodded.

"It's ghastly, isn't it? I mean, one didn't like him, but one wouldn't wish that to one's worst enemy."

Antoinette said nothing. She simply couldn't. And after a minute Rosamund went on thoughtfully, "I suppose one *could* play without being able to see?"

"Yes, of course." Antoinette's voice sounded slightly husky.

"But it's not only the practical difficulties," Rosamund said musingly. "There's the question of temperament too. I mean—he's such an arrogant, independent sort of creature. One couldn't exactly imagine his being *led* on to a platform to—"

"Don't say such things!" cried Antoinette almost wildly. "How can you? How can you?"

"I'm sorry." Rosamund looked astounded. "I didn't know you felt so badly about it. I thought you disliked him so much and—"

"I do dislike him. I've no reason to do anything else," Antoinette asserted feverishly. "But one doesn't cling to one's little likes and dislikes in the face of such disaster. I—I know him well as a concert personality. I respect him as one of the finest artists of the day. The very thought of his being helpless and—and finished is unbearable. I'm haunted by the thoughts—haunted by it!"

"Why, Toni—" Rosamund sounded a good deal moved. "You mustn't upset yourself so much, dear. It's almost over-generous of you in the circumstances. Considering how badly he treated you, I mean."

"No, it's not." Antoinette was calmer now. "Personal considerations have nothing to do with it. I still think he behaved abominably to me. But that's unimportant beside what's happened to him. If only one could *do* something!" And she drew such a long, quivering sigh that Rosamund was moved to offer the very general expression of comfort—

"Perhaps you'll be able to one day. You never know. Stranger things have happened."

Antoinette laughed slightly at that, but gratefully. Because, though she could not bring herself to confide even in Rosamund, it was something to have her warm though uncomprehending sympathy.

And two days later Antoinette was asking herself if Rosamund had some sort of sixth sense which told her about things in advance.

It was at the end of an exacting day, in which she had been taking the minutes of a long and excessively uninteresting board meeting; the sort of one-day assignment which none of them liked but which each of them at a freelance agency had to take on in turn. Antoinette returned to the office to enquire about the next day's assignment, and as she came into the main corridor, Rosamund was coming out of the assistant manager's office.

"Oh, there you are!" she exclaimed on a note of excited satisfaction. "I was afraid you mightn't be coming back this evening and the chance would slip. Something quite extraordinary has just turned up—something absolutely up your street. Go in and see Mr. Parnell. He's got what I imagine is *the* job in the world you would want."

"Really?" Antoinette looked both mystified and pleased. "What is it?"

"Go in and ask," Rosamund bade her. "It's a sort of answer to a prayer."

Intrigued and curious, Antoinette went along to the office of the assistant manager who welcomed her cordially, with an air of a man who saw in her the answer to a ticklish problem.

"I think I've got the perfect job for you, Miss Burney. If you don't mind an assignment of unspecified length, that is."

"If it's something special I'd regard that as an advantage." Antoinette smiled, for the constant change which her present freelance status involved was sometimes a strain.

"I understand from Miss Heal that you're quite an accomplished pianist?"

"Well—yes," she admitted as he paused.

"Know all about musical terms? Could copy musical manuscript and that sort of thing, if necessary?"

"Ye-es, I think so. Why?"

"You know who I mean by Lewis Freemont, the pianist?"

"Why, of course!" She half rose to her feet in sudden alarm. "He's one of the finest pianists today. What about him?"

"It seems he had a car accident recently—"

"I know!"

31

"Some injury to the optic nerve and he's completely blind, poor chap. Dreadful thing to happen to anyone in mid-career," observed Mr. Parnell, with the cheerful sympathy of the totally uninvolved. "Well, he needs a secretary—someone with considerable musical knowledge. With most of our girls music is a closed book except for—"

"I couldn't think of it!" cried Antoinette. "It's out of the question."

"Why?" Mr. Parnell looked a good deal surprised. "I thought you'd jump at it, with your special knowledge. He's willing to pay well for the right sort of girl, and I imagine his need is pretty desperate."

"Oh, but I couldn't!" She was not quite so emphatic that time, though her eyes were still wide with something like alarm.

"Is it the fact of his blindness that scares you?" Mr. Parnell wanted to know. "I know some people have a horror of any abnormality."

"No, no, it's not *that*. At least, not in the sense you mean," she added confusedly.

The assistant manager regarded her in some perplexity.

"Well, Miss Heal seemed to think you'd welcome the offer," he observed at last. "She said something about an answer to a prayer."

"To a—? Oh?" Suddenly Antoinette remembered herself exclaiming in anguish, "If only one could *do* something!"

It had been her ever-present sense of guilt and remorse which had forced the exclamation from her. She had not perhaps meant it in any literal sense. But now here was the opportunity to do something about the disaster which she, or a malignant fate, had brought upon him. With her special qualifications she *could* help him. Perhaps more than almost anyone else. As Rosamund had said—almost the answer to a prayer.

She was trembling slightly, but she clasped her hands together in sudden resolution.

"I'm sorry I spoke so hastily," she said quietly. "It was a silly sort of momentary panic, a—a feeling that I might not be able to cope. But I think I was wrong. I think perhaps I *could* be of help to him. I'll take on the job, Mr. Parnell. When do I start?"

"Good girl!" Mr. Parnell looked relieved. "Can you start tomorrow? Everything cleared up from today's assignment?"

"Yes, everything," said Antoinette, with the strange sensation of someone launching out upon a tightrope without much preliminary training. "Where do I go? To his Surrey home?"

"Yes. Place called Pallin Parva. You take a Green Line bus to—"

"I know. It's slightly over an hour's run."

"That's right. There'll be quite a bit of travelling, I'm afraid. But in the ordinary way he spends a lot of time at his London flat. Once he's got used to—well, when the poor fellow's worked out some new routine, you'll probably work there a good deal."

"It doesn't matter," Antoinette said. "The ride is pleasant, and I shall be going against the stream in the rush-hour. It could be much nicer than struggling up to town."

"Very true." Mr. Parnell's tone was congratulatory now that she had decided to do what he wanted. "I'll

33

phone and let Mr. Freemont know you'll be there to-morrow morning at ten."

"Thank you," said Antoinette, and went in search of Rosamund, who was waiting for her with an expectant air.

"Did you take it?" she demanded.

"Yes, I took it."

"I'm glad," said Rosamund. "I think it's the right thing for you."

"I hope I shall be thinking so by this time tomorrow," replied Antoinette with a doubtful little laugh.

She lay awake quite a long time that night, facing the fact that she was taking something of a risk in involving herself so deeply in Lewis Freemont's affairs. He might just conceivably remember her name, though she doubted if the name of one unimportant examination candidate would have lingered in his mind. After all, he had had to glance back at his papers to verify it even when he was speaking to her!

Then it was just remotely possible that, with his unusually keen ear, he might recognize the voice of the girl who had spoken to him after the accident. But this seemed rather far-fetched even to Antoinette, and even in the middle of the night. Telling herself that any risk was worthwhile if she could atone in some small way for something she would always regard as her fault, she fell asleep at last.

In the morning her mood was neither so hopeful nor so confident. As she boarded her Green Line bus she thought she must have been mad to embark on anything fraught with so much risk and so much emotional strain. But it was too late to turn back now, and she sat there watching the inner suburbs and then the outer suburbs slip past, and presently they were in the country, and in what seemed no time she was getting out of the bus at the now familiar stop.

She even had to walk past the tree, where a long scar was a terrifying reminder of what had happened there. But this time she walked up the drive to Pallin Manor instead of stumbling along it in frantic haste.

An elderly maid opened the door to her and, having shown her where to put her coat, conducted her to a long beautiful room at the back of the house, where large windows looked out upon a pleasant garden.

Antoinette took in very few details in that first moment. All she saw was the unnaturally still figure sitting in the high-backed chair by the window. As she came forward he turned his head questingly, evidently trying to judge where she was by the sound of her footsteps. But with the pathetically unpractised air of someone quite unused to being blind he looked just past her.

It shook her more than she would have believed possible, and it was only with a tremendous effort that she kept her voice steady as she said, "Good morning, Mr. Freemont. I'm your new secretary." And she came right up to him and took his hand in hers.

His long, strong fingers closed round hers tightly, and for the first time in her life Antoinette became aware that the sense of touch is the simplest and most primitive form of communication. The tightness of that clasp told her, more clearly than any words, of his misery and frustration and the agony of helplessness which had descended upon him.

As she stood there holding Lewis Freemont's hand the last drop of her bitterness and resentment drained

35

from her. Strangely enough, she felt her nervousness go also, and she could say quite naturally,

"I should like to tell you how proud and pleased I am to come and work for you. I've often heard you play and it has always been a wonderful experience."

Even then he said nothing, so that she wondered with a flutter of the old panic if he were trying to recall her voice. Then when he spoke all he said was,

"Did they tell you what has happened?"

"I know you've had a car accident."

"And I'm blind. Did they tell you that? I'm quite blind. Like Samson in the Handel opera. "Total eclipse!" I keep on thinking of him stumbling on to the stage and beginning to sing that air. I never had the slightest conception of what it really meant until now."

She moistened her dry lips and was glad he could not know that there were tears in her eyes.

"It's ridiculously inadequate to say how sorry I am"—little did he know *how* inadequate and *how* sorry!—"but does it help you to talk about it?"

"Yes." He gave a short surprised laugh. "You funny girl! It helps me to talk about it. No one else has thought of that. They're all so horrified and embarrassed that they talk of anything but the one thing that matters."

"Tell me about it, then." She reached for a chair with her free hand and pulled it up, for he seemed either unaware that he still had her hand or unable to let it go, as though it were some thread that held him to normality. "Tell me even—" she steeled herself to say it—"How the accident happened."

36

"That's the strangest and most macabre thing about it," he exclaimed. "You may think I'm mad when I've told you."

"No, I shan't think you mad." Her voice was steady. "Go on."

"It started—oh, months ago, when I adjudicated at a big music exam—What did you say?"

"Nothing."

"Among the candidates was a girl—quite a pretty, intelligent-looking girl. I can't remember her name though I've tried to several times. She was the most astonishing performer I ever heard, in the worst sense of the term. Her technique was quite outstanding, but beyond that there was nothing. Absolutely nothing. She had no real music in her, not a grain of what I can only call musical communication. I told her so frankly and advised her not to flatter herself that she would ever be a concert performer in a million years."

"Wasn't that rather hard on her?" asked Antoinette, her tone dry in spite of herself.

He looked surprised and said impatiently, "It was the truth. I think she knew it really. She gave me a rather baleful sort of look—"

"Did she really?" exclaimed Antoinette in uncontrollable surprise.

"Yes. Why not?"

"Well—I don't know. It seems an odd sort of thing for a candidate to give the examiner."

Unexpectedly he laughed a good deal at that, and she saw the taut lines of his face relax.

"Anyway, I forgot all about her after that." He said that so carelessly that for a moment Antoinette felt again a twinge of the fury he had inspired in her all those months ago. "And then one evening she turned up at a concert. I remember it quite well. I was playing Prokofiev, I think, and then the Beethoven Fourth, and she was right there in the front row. I didn't recognize her at first. I mean I couldn't think who she was. I just knew that I knew her. I think I smiled at her. Anyway, she smiled at me. Then she began to haunt me. She was at every concert at which I appeared, sometimes in the front, sometimes on the platform."

"Did you mind?" enquired Antoinette irresistibly.

"Mind? No, of course I didn't mind. Every public performer has to put up with a sort of lunatic fringe," he explained.

"I see. She was just—part of your lunatic fringe?"

"Yes, that's what I thought."

"Perhaps she genuinely liked to hear you play. That could surely be a reason for her constant attendance?"

After the way I'd brushed her off?" He sounded sceptical. "Anyway, it doesn't matter. *She* didn't matter until a week or so ago. And then I was driving home— perhaps a little too fast for country roads. There's a crossroads near here—"

"I know," she said, fascinated.

"I came round the bend full tilt and—you'll hardly believe it—she was *standing* there, bang in the middle of the road. I avoided her by a miracle, but the car went into a spin. And then I crashed into a tree, and that was it. She'd had her revenge all right!"

"But she probably didn't mean it that way at all," cried Antoinette. "You're being almost—almost superstitious about the poor girl. There could be a dozen explanations—"

"Give me one," he cut in.

"Oh, I don't know.—Well, perhaps she had a crush on you. Followed you round, poor creature, wanted to see where you lived. People do that sort of thing. She was probably sick with horror about the whole thing."

"No," he said slowly. "No, she couldn't have been. Because—and this is almost the strangest part of it all—she simply disappeared after that."

"D-disappeared?" stammered Antoinette. "What do you mean?"

"She didn't even wait to see what she had done. Or maybe she waited just long enough to find that I couldn't see her—couldn't identify her. But I'll tell you one thing—" his hand was so tight on hers now that it hurt—"if I ever get my sight back, or even part of it, I'll find that girl if it's the last thing I do."

CHAPTER TWO

SO intense was the bitterness in Lewis Freemont's voice that for a moment Antoinette was bereft of speech. Then suddenly he seemed to become aware that he was still holding tightly to her hand, and he released her and exclaimed abruptly, "I'm sorry. Was I hurting you?"

"No." She withdrew her rather numbed fingers. "Not at all."

"One forgets how strong one's hands become if one uses them constantly." He flexed his long fingers absently and, spreading them out in front of him, gazed at them with sightless eyes. "It's so strange not to be able to *see* them," he said, half to himself. "I must have looked at them a hundred thousand times in my life. You do if you're a pianist. Just by looking at them you can assess their strength and stamina—what they will do easily for you and what you will have to coax them to do. And now—"

He broke off and sighed impatiently. And, eager to keep him from lapsing into melancholy reflection, Antoinette asked quickly:

"What would you like me to do first? I expect there are quite a number of letters waiting to be answered, aren't there?"

"Hundreds of them." He laughed shortly. "Letters of condolence mostly, I suppose. From friends and fans—and people who loathe me."

"Are there many of the last group?" she asked, smiling.

But instead of answering her he exclaimed, "What an expressive voice you have! I can tell you're smiling just by the sound of your voice. You *are* smiling, aren't you?" he added anxiously, as though desperate to check the accuracy of the sense on which he must now place double reliance.

"Yes, indeed! How quick of you to notice."

"Music-makers have to have keen hearing," he replied. "There's a Viennese saying that we can hear the grass grow.—What was your question? I didn't listen to the words, only to the smile."

That touched her so much that she had to swallow quite a lump in her throat before she could reply,

"You spoke about letters from people who loathe you, and I asked if there were really many of those."

"Lots, I should imagine," he said indifferently. "If one is successful one makes enemeis, and if one doesn't suffer fools gladly one makes even more."

"I heard you say that of yourself once!" she exclaimed involuntarily.

"Heard me say *what*?" He turned to her with such an air of interest that it was difficult to believe he could not see her.

"Th-that you never suffered fools gladly. You said it-very distinctly and unkindly, to tell the truth—as you thrust your way through a crowd of admirers at the stage door one night."

"And you were there?" He gave an intrigued sort of smile. "Did you sometimes come to hear me play, then?" Evidently he had not paid much attention to her original greeting.

"Oh, yes," said Antoinette. "I told you I did."

"You're smiling again, aren't you?" He sounded curious and even a good deal amused. "Why?"

"I suppose because I was recalling with such pleasure the times I heard you play."

"How odd!" Then he frowned suddenly. "You aren't just a persistent fan pretending to be a good secretary in order to push your way into my private life and make a nuisance of yourself, are you?"

"No, I'm quite simply a good secretary who happens to be interested in music. I wouldn't describe myself as a fan of yours exactly."

"How would you describe yourself?" She had caught his attention completely now, and that air of bewildered, restless melancholy was for a moment completely gone. "Tell me what you are like," he commanded imperiously.

Panic took hold of her but she fought it down, and even managed to laugh in a perfectly natural manner.

"Well, I suppose it's never very easy to describe oneself," she said, as though she were seriously reflecting on the matter. "I'm of medium height, not specially fat or thin. I have rather coppery brown hair—"

"Straight or curly?" he enquired as though it were really important.

"Slightly wavy—and thick. I have quite a good skin, though I'm pale. And I have eyes that are grey when I'm in a good temper and green when I'm angry. I think that's all."

"No, it isn't. I can tell you a whole lot more than that already," he declared. "You must have an expressive mouth, otherwise one wouldn't *hear* your smile. You have a remarkably soothing speaking voice that falls very gratefully on the ear, and you have strong, interesting hands. In fact—" suddenly he broke off and then said, again in that peremptory tone—"give me your hand again."

She was really frightened now. But because she had no choice, she put her hand into his, and he ran his other hand over the length and the tips of her fingers.

"You're a pianist!" he exclaimed.

"Well, I—I do play a bit," she admitted.

"Oh, no, not just "a bit",' he corrected impatiently. "Not with those spatulate finger-tips. Grip my hand.— Harder! As hard as you can," he commanded as she reluctantly clasped his hand in hers.

Then he laughed on a note of triumphant interest as she exerted the full strength of her grip.

"No one who doesn't use the muscles of the hand constantly has a grip like that," he declared. "How well do you play?"

"No more than for my own amusement," she insisted hastily. "I do a lot of typing and that might account for—"

"Nonsense," he interrupted. "Typing produces an entirely different effect. You shall play for me presently and I'll tell you just how well you do play."

"One day, perhaps," replied Antoinette, praying that nothing in her tone indicated to his keen hearing the unspeakable chill which his words induced in her. "But you mustn't scare me by suggesting anything so nerve-racking on a first meeting. It would be more to the point if I said that I hoped *you* would play for *me* one day."

"Never!" He rejected the suggestion with such violence that she blinked. "I don't want to play now—for anyone but myself. Imagine being *led* to the piano, fumbling a little until one found one's bearings on the keyboard." He gave an exclamation of sheer disgust. "I'd rather never play again than make such an exhibition of myself!"

"Stop being so self-pitying and arrogant," said Antoinette, and utter silence fell in the room.

"*What* did you say?" He was quite white as he turned his sightless gaze upon her.

"Just what you thought I said," she replied resolutely. "And, as you can probably tell from my voice, I'm *not* smiling."

"No," he said slowly, "you're not smiling. One doesn't when one tells someone the disagreeable truth. But perhaps—" he smiled wryly—"your eyes are green."

"Green?" she repeated uncomprehendingly.

"You said they were green when you're angry. I thought—" his smile deepened ruefully—"you sounded as though your eyes were green."

"Oh!" Suddenly the fact that he had not only taken her impulsive rebuke but could actually joke gallantly about it almost broke her heart—"I didn't mean—I shouldn't have said—"

She stopped, because all at once the tears were running down her cheeks. Several times during the last half hour they had been very near. This time she simply could not stop them. She could only be wretchedly thankful for a moment that he could not see what was happening.

"You meant exactly what you said," he told her drily, "and you were perfectly right to say it. I am arrogant. I suppose I've always rather fancied myself that way. And unless there is someone there to check me fairly brutally at times, I suppose I might become self-pitying. Arrogant people do when the tide turns against them."

She was silent, because only by keeping quite still could she hide from him the fact that she was in tears.

"You're very quiet." He frowned impatiently. "Have you decided to be offended or something?"

"N-no."

"Then what's the matter?—Why," he exclaimed incredulously, "You're crying!"

"No, I'm not."

"I don't believe you." He put out his hand and caught her, lightly and with some accuracy, by the wrist. Then with a questing, uncertain movement he unexpectedly put his other hand against her wet cheek. "You *are* crying," he said again, and there was astonishment and amusement in his voice, and something else which curiously warmed her cold, frightened heart.

"I'm—sorry," she gasped.

"No, don't be sorry. I can't recall that anyone ever cried for me before. Perhaps arrogant people don't inspire tears." And he laughed slightly. Then he released her wrist, but only so that he could take her face between both his hands.

"You silly girl," he said, half mockingly, half tenderly. "Your cheeks are quite wet. But I think, from the feel of it, that you have a pretty shape to your face—and laughter lines here—" those sensitive fingers traced a light curve round the corners of her mouth. Then suddenly he released her and said in a matter-of-fact sort of tone,

"Well, I suppose we'd better do some of those letters, particularly the ones from the people who loathe me. After all, we don't want them to think I'm self-pitying, do we?"

"N-no," agreed Antoinette huskily. "We'll reply to them very promptly and confidently."

"That's the idea," he agreed. "You'll find everything piled on that desk over there." He made one of those curiously sketchy gestures towards one corner of the room where a desk was standing. "Half of them haven't even been opened, I imagine. You'd better open them and read them to me. Begin with the signatures and then I can probably tell you if you need bother me with the whole contents or just reply conventionally to a conventional expression of regret."

"Very well," said Antoinette, and cleared her throat.

"Feeling better?"

"Yes. Except that I feel rather an idiot. I don't often cry. I won't do it again, I promise."

"Don't promise anything. I might *want* to make you cry," he warned her calmly. "I'm often not at all a nice person. But you'll find that out for yourself. Fetch the letters."

So she brought over the pile of letters—some still sealed in their envelopes, as he had said—and began to read them aloud to him.

In the course of the next hour or so she learned quite a lot about about him, both from the way people wrote to him and his reecption of what was written. Few wrote with intimate knowledge or warmth, though many wrote with undoubted respect and regret. Inevitably, practically the same words clothed the same sad sentiments again and again, and she was thankful that he had decreed that many of these well-meant but conventional letters should not even be read out to him. They would only have re-emphasized unbearably the horror of what had happened to him.

"That will just be a routine expression of sympathy," he said to at least half of the letters when she had got no further than the signature, and almost always he was right. Sometimes, on glancing through the letter, she would give him an odd detail or two, but usually it ended with his saying impatiently,

"Thank them politely and say that, as my secretary, you will let them know how I get on. Then file the letter and forget it."

Once or twice, for some reason that she usually could not fathom, he would say, "Put that aside. I'll deal with that later." And once he laughed with malicious enjoyment over a particularly fulsome tribute from another well-known pianist and said,

"Damn him, there's relief in every line. He always did regard me as his most powerful rival."

"Do we reply?" enquired Antoinette.

"Of course. And in our gayest and most confident vein. I see no reason why he should sleep more comfortably at night for the thought that I'm blind."

Antoinette bit her lip, poised again for a dangerous moment between laughter and tears. Then she opened a very different-looking letter—so different that she was moved to describe its actual appearance.

"This is on lovely almost dove-coloured paper, and the address is "Cornerways", Pallin Parva—"

"And it's signed "Charmian"?" he finished with a touch of genuine interest.

"Yes, it's signed "Charmian"," she agreed. "Shall I read it? It looks rather—personal."

"I can't know the contents if you *don't* read it, can I?" he retorted disagreeably.

"I thought you might prefer to have this one read out by someone nearer to you—more intimate with you."

"I have no one nearer to me," he said coolly. "I have no immediate family, if that's what you mean. And you're going to have to be my second self if you remain as my very personal secretary."

The thought both warmed and scared her. But she said in as practical a tone as she could,

"Didn't you have a personal secretary before all this happened? You must have, surely?"

"No, no!" He rejected the very idea with distaste. "I just used to get someone from an agency once or twice a week. A different one each time if possible so that I never felt dependent on or attached to any specific person. I detest personal ties—almost without exception."

"How you must hate this new arrangement, then!" The exclamation was out before she could stop it.

"I don't like it," he replied bluntly. "It's one of the things which incline me to self-pity. But possibly it's good for my arrogant soul. Read the letter."

"Yes, of course!" She glanced back at the forgotten letter and, keeping her tone as impersonal as possible, she read aloud,

"My dear, I only want you to know that I am thinking of you with love and sympathy. Since someone else will have to read this to you I cannot write much of what I would say. May I come and see you,

48

Lewis? Each time I telephone they say you are not having visitors. But I'm not just a visitor, surely? Please let me come. My love to you, Charmian."

"When was that written?" he enquired.

"Exactly a week ago," said Antoinette, glancing at the date.

"Hm. She's waited rather a long time, hasn't she? Dial the number for me, give me the telephone and— No, wait a moment! First gather up all those routine replies. You'll find a typewriter and everything you require in the small room which opens out of this one. That will be your office. You can get on with those letters for the the time being. How many more have we to deal with?"

"About a dozen. And then there are eight—no, ten—that you said you would attend to later. They required something more than the conventional reply."

"All right. Take the ones we've dealt with, and then get me Mrs. St. Leger's number. It's at the head of the letter, I suppose. In any case, it's Pallin four-seven, if I remember rightly."

"It's on the letter," Antoinette said, glancing back at the expensive dove-coloured sheet in her hand. "Pallin four-seven, as you say. Then she lives in the neighbourhood?"

"She's more or less my nearest neighbour," he replied, but he offered no further information about her.

So Antoinette transferred her letters to the small inner room, where she found, as he had said, a type-writer and a well-equipped desk. Then she came back and dialled Charmian St. Leger's number.

A light, very musically pitched voice replied, "Mrs. St. Leger speaking." And Antoinette said, "Mr. Freemont would like to speak to you," handed the receiver to her employer and withdrew to her own office.

Only then did she discover, to her vexation, that she had left her shorthand notebook behind. She went back into the room, walking quietly so as not to disturb him, and was in time to hear him say in a tone of half-mocking indulgence.

"Yes, you can come if you like. So long as you promise not to cry over me. Tears bore me."

Antoinette withdrew silently again and closed her door. She wondered if *her* tears had bored him. On the whole, she thought not.

She worked steadily for some time. And since she was both quick and efficient, she gradually disposed of most of the large pile of letters by the time a maid came and told her lunch was ready.

"Mr. Freemont prefers to lunch alone," the girl volunteered.

"Yes, of course," Antoinette agreed. By which she supposed she meant that she well understood he would hate to be observed while he was getting used to the difficult task of eating without seeing what was set before him. Oh, daily, hourly, humiliation for one who had always been so arrogantly independent! Even the simplest detail of everyday life must present its special problems now. And all because she—*she*—had been fool enough to come to a guilty stop in the middle of a road where she should never have been!

Antoinette found she had little appetite for the excellent lunch served to her in the silent dining-room. When she was actually with her new employer, or working hard on his behalf, she could hold the worst of her remorse at bay. But alone now and without the compulsion of work upon her, she could only think how quiet the house seemed and how desolate it must be to him.

Presumably he had taken pride and pleasure in it once. Now it was the prison which enclosed him, the immediate limit of the dark world in which he now wandered.

She could not bear to linger over her coffee and was back again at her desk so quickly that he unexpectedly rang his bell for her and, on her entering the drawing-room, said rather disagreeably,

"You don't have to display quite such a passion for work, you know. It's hardly half an hour since that typewriter stopped tapping, surely?"

"I'm sorry. Does the sound of it irritate you?"

"No more than anything else." He gave a sigh of weary impatience. Then he laughed shortly and added, "I take that back. More self-pity, I'm afraid, wasn't it?"

"You're entitled to a little." She tried to make that sound as though she too found it wryly amusing instead of unbearably pathetic. "I've practically finished that first batch of letters. Do you want us to deal with the others now?"

"We might as well," he agreed indifferently. And then, in a rather different tone, "Do you know, I don't even know what your name is."

"You *don't?*" She felt like a nervous rider suddenly faced by some tremendous obstacle which she thought she had already surmounted. Then, calling on all her coolness and self-possession, she said, "My name is Miss Burney, and my friends call me Toni."

"Why Toni?"

"Oh, it's a nickname." She thought she had got across her surname safely, but she dared not risk the combination with her unusual Christian name. "I never liked my real name."

"Which is—?"

"Sarah," she declared desperately, offering the first name that came into her head.

"Sarah?" He repeated it reflectively. "No, that wouldn't suit the girl I'm visualizing. Toni is much better. Am I regarded as one of the friends who call you Toni?"

"If you—if you want to, of course."

"Very well then—Toni. We'll deal with the rest of the correspondence."

Surreptitiously she wiped a few beads of moisture from her forehead and picked up her pencil.

They had just dealt with the very last letter when the maid who had announced Antoinette's lunch came in and said that Mr. Everleigh was there. Antoinette guessed immediately that this was Gordon Everleigh, the highly successful manager who handled the affairs not only of Lewis Freemont but of many other distinguished artists in the musical world.

"He can come in," said her employer, and Antoinette read quite clearly on that intelligent, sensitive face first the pleasure of one about to greet a real friend and then the doubt and uncertainty of having to face someone so inextricably associated with all that had been lost.

"Would you like me to go?" she enquired.

"No, no. You'd better stay and meet him. He's my manager and you'll have quite a lot to do with him. For a time at any rate, until we know for certain—"

He broke off and was silent until the door opened again and the maid announced, "Mr. Everleigh."

Gordon Everleigh was a tall, good-looking man, perhaps a year or two older than Lewis Freemont himself, with an air of controlled energy and good-humoured authority peculiar to successful men who deal well with people.

His greeting to Lewis Freemont was warm without being gushing, sympathetic without being too emotional. And when he was introduced to Antoinette he shook hands warmly and said with every sign of real sincerity that he was glad to see her, since her presence suggested that Mr. Freemont had decided to take up some sort of active life again.

"Not to the extent of contemplating any public playing," put in Lewis Freemont shortly.

"Too early to discuss that," replied the famous manager imperturbably. "I've postponed the proposed American tour, of course. But there's no need to make speedy decisions about anything else."

"I've made my decision—a final and all-embracing one," was the cold reply. "I shall not play in public again unless I can walk unaided to the piano and do my job properly. I'm a working musician, not a circus side-show."

"Is it all right if I go and get on with my own work now?" asked Antoinette in a small voice.

"Yes, yes, of course." Lewis Freemont dismissed her impatiently, and she went thankfully to her own office, where she despised herself for the fact that she had to wipe away a tear before she could get on with her work.

To her surprise, about half an hour later, Gordon Everleigh came into her office—but by the doorway from the hall, and not directly from the drawing-room where he had been with Lewis Freemont.

"Miss Burney, I want a confidential word with you," he said, his strong, pleasant face slightly creased with worry now that he no longer needed to give an appearance of confident cheerfulness. "Freemont seems to have taken a fancy to you and to feel that you could be a real support to him. I hope you're going to stay in this job, even though it will present quite a lot of difficulties from time to time."

"Why, of course!" Antoinette assured him earnestly. "You need have no fear of that. I've always admired Mr. Freemont as an artist. I'm only too glad if I can be of any help to him now."

"Well, of course that's how we all feel—those of us who admire him and are fond of him," said Gordon Everleigh, apparently including Antoinette in this number without question. "This tragedy is about the most ghastly thing that could have happened to him. In a way it would almost have been better for him if he'd been killed. There's something proud and splendid about going out on the crest of a wave of glory, at the height of one's career. But to an independent, arrogant rather cussed creature like Freemont it must be pure hell to be so helpless."

"I—realize that," said Antoinette faintly.

"At the present time his one idea is to withdraw into himself. A simpler—I suppose one might say a humbler —man might have come to terms more easily with the

54

situation. Sight is not an absolute requisite for a pianist. And to some men, once they had regained confidence and *learned* to be blind—there is no other expression for it—it would not have been impossible to make a distinguished career again. But Freemont is a proud perfectionist in everything. You heard what he said just now about not being a circus side-show. It's a perfectly ridiculous attitude, but a tragic one if he clings to it. What I wanted to say to you was that your day-to-day attiitude could be quite a useful factor."

"In what way?" Antoinette's voice was husky but eager. "I'll do anything. *Anything*."

"Good girl!" He gave her an approving glance. "Go carefully. Don't overdo things or give the impression of trying to coerce him. But keep always in mind the idea that we—you and I and the few who really care about him—have every intention that he shall go back to the concert platform. It's his life. Without it he's lost."

"Oh, I'll try! I'll do my very best."

"Don't nag him or argue—" Antoinette wondered how he supposed she would dare!—"Just go along with his ideas for the moment. But encourage him to play for you some time, keep him in touch with the musical world whether he shows interest or not. Put the emphasis on letters that are positive in approach and play down—or if you like, shamelessly suppress— any that are negative and depressing. Do everything you can to excite his interest and participation and don't *let* him retire into a backwater."

"I'll do everything I can," Antoinette promised softly.

"Encourage him to see people as soon as he shows the slightest inclination. At present I'm afraid the only people he will allow near him are you and me. That's why we're important."

"I think," said Antoinette diffidently, "that he is going to see at least one other person today or tomorrow—a Mrs. St. Leger."

"Charmian St. Leger?" Gordon Everleigh raised his eyebrows.

"Yes. Will she be good for him, do you think?"

"Well, yes—and no." The manager's good-looking face was perplexed but slightly amused too. Finally he said—"I suppose anything and anyone who brings him out of his present mood will be good for him. But the very fact that he was always attracted by her may make him feel inadequate now in her presence. Well—see how things go. Don't campaign too obviously. He'd rumble that immediately and be furious. Play it by ear, with all the kindness and common sense you have. You're going to need both of them."

Then he patted her on the shoulder and said, "I have every confidence in you," before he went away—leaving her wondering if that assumption that one could do anything was what made him so successful with his clients. There is nothing quite so heady as having someone express unlimited faith in one.

When she bade her employer good-bye later in the afternoon, she took it on herself to say, "I hope you're going to find me satisfactory. I've liked my first day very much."

"I hope you're going to find me satisfactory too," he retorted sardonically.

"I think I shall," she told him demurely. And she was pleased that the last sound she heard from him was a genuinely amused laugh.

On the way home in the bus she found suddenly that she was utterly exhausted, and she realized that the emotional strain of the day must have been considerable.

"But I shall get used to it," she assured herself. "I've already cleared several of the worst hurdles. He has accepted me. My name, in the version I gave, roused no dangerous memories in him. He—likes me, I think. And Mr. Everleigh genuinely thinks I'm good for him."

When she reached home an intensely curious Rosamund was waiting eagerly to hear how she had got on, and she listened with flattering attention to every word that Antoinette had to say. Only when the subject of Charmian St. Leger was reached did she interrupt to ask,

"Is she in love with him, do you suppose?"

"She could be." Antoinette gave grave consideration to what she found to be an unwelcome idea, though she could not have said why. "She wrote affectionately. But then some people do—particularly if they're under the influence of a tragedy. It's their way of saying how sorry they are."

"And he?" enquired Rosamund. "Did *he* react affectionately?"

"Not really—no. But he's inclined to be mocking and a little sardonic about any display of feeling." She thought of his reaction when he found she was crying, but she did not tell Rosamund about that scene. It would have been difficult to justify her tears, for one thing.

"Is there a Mr. St. Leger?" Rosamund then wanted to know.

"No one mentioned him." Antoinette wrinkled her forehead reflectively. "Funny, I never thought of asking. I just assumed there wasn't one. She didn't sound as though there were, if you know what I mean."

"I know exactly what you mean," Rosamund assured her. "She's a designing widow or divorcée, if you ask me, and you'll have to rescue him from her clutches, though how I can't really imagine."

"Nor can I," replied Antoinette so feelingly that Rosamund laughed.

"You don't feel anything like so badly about him now, do you?" she said curiously. "I mean—about his being so beastly to you that time at the exam."

"No." Antoinette looked away. "That's all just water under the bridge. I want nothing but to help him now, if I can."

"I suppose when you've become really friendly with him you might even tell him who you are and make him feel just a bit ashamed of the way he behaved?"

"Oh, no!" There was such real alarm in Antoinette's tone that Rosamund looked surprised. "I don't want him ever to know. Not ever! It might—it might embarrass him, so that he suddenly disliked having me around."

"Is he the kind to be easily embarrassed?" Rosamund sounded sceptical.

"No," Antoinette was forced to admit. "But I don't want to take any risk. I'll *never* let him know."

"Of course," said Rosamund reflectively, "If he ever recovered his sight—which is what we must hope for him—he might quite easily recognize you, mightn't he?"

"Yes," agreed Antoinette stonily, "He would recognize me then."

"Unless he'd forgotten all about you," amended Rosamund cheerfully. "After all, he didn't recognize your name. One would have expected him to, really. It's quite an unusual one."

"I simply gave my name as Miss Burney and said my friends called me Toni, and that it was a nickname because I didn't like my own name which was—Sarah, I think I said."

"Good gracious!" Rosamund opened her eyes wide. "You did take a lot of precautions, didn't you?"

"I was determined he shouldn't know me," replied Antoinette obstinately.

"So even if he has to repeat "Miss Burney" rather often, you still hope that he—"

"He's going to call me "Toni"," said Antoinette a little reluctantly, which made Rosamund open her eyes wide again.

"Well, well, you *have* made a good beginning, haven't you?" Rosamund laughed a good deal. But after that her questions were exhausted.

The next day Antoinette set out for Pallin Parva in a very different mood from that of the day before. A certain degree of nervous anxiety still lingered. But far stronger than any anxiety was her eagerness simply to see him again and perhaps to put into practice a little of Gordon Everleigh's advice. If she could be even remotely instrumental in helping Lewis Freemont back to public life, something of the weight of guilt which still pressed on her day and night would be shifted.

Brenda, the maid who opened the door to her, greeted her already as a member of the household, and smilingly volunteered the information that Mr. Freemont seemed in much better spirits that day. Antoinette was just wondering if she might dare to attribute this partially to her own presence when Brenda went on,

"Mrs. St. Leger came to see him yesterday evening, and I expect that cheered him up. She's a lovely lady. Everyone round here likes her."

"Is there a Mr. St. Leger?" enquired Antoinette casually, as she ran a comb through her hair.

"Colonel St. Leger there was," said Brenda in a somewhat repressive tone. "But he went off with someone else—quite a nobody. To South America, they say. No one could understand it—his leaving a lovely women like Mrs. St. Leger. But never a word has anyone ever heard her utter against him," declared Brenda emotionally. "She's been a saint about it, as you might say."

"Really?" murmured Antoinette, feeling perversely that she liked Mrs. St. Leger none the better for her saintly behaviour. Then she went into the drawing-room, where she found her employer, as Brenda had said, in distinctly better spirits.

For his part, he made no reference to his attractive neighbour's visit, but plunged immediately into some intricate business details to do with the recent purchase and partial reconstruction of the house. This involved Antoinette's reading him one or two legal documents of a complicated nature. But, though she herself found some difficulty in following them, he never seemed to lose the thread. On the contrary, he appeared able to keep a clear picture of the whole transaction in his mind even though unable to refer back to the printed or written word.

When she commented on this, he gave a slightly surprised laugh and said, "It's easier than memorizing a concerto." But she thought he was not displeased to be praised, which made him suddenly seem very human and vulnerable.

Towards the end of the discussion there was suddenly the sound of a dog barking on the lawn, and a moment later the glass door into the garden opened and in came someone who could, Antoinette felt sure, be only Mrs. St. Leger.

Not only was she in Brenda's words undoubtedly "a lovely lady". She came in with the smiling air of one confident of her welcome. She must, thought Antoinette a trifle uncharitably, have worked hard the previous evening, for instead of the rebuff she would undoubtedly have received yesterday she won a look of smiling expectancy as Lewis Freemont turned and said,

"Is that you, Charmian?—Ah, I thought I heard Rufus—" as a friendly red retriever pushed gently past Mrs. St. Leger and came to put his head on Lewis Freemont's knee.

"Are we both welcome, or are we in the way?" The visitor spoke to Lewis Freemont, but her charming smile included Antoinette in the query.

"You're not in the way. This is my secretary, Miss Burney, who hopes she will give satisfaction and thinks I shall."

Still smiling, Charmian St. Leger came over and shook hands with Antoinette. She was a tall, indescribably elegant woman, beautifully though very simply dressed, with smooth fair hair and wonderful violet-blue eyes—the kind of eyes which look soft and dreamy but which curiously often belong to strong-minded people.

"Miss Burney—I'm so glad Lewis has found you. He tells me that, in addition to everything else, you have a good knowledge of music. That's going to be very helpful to him with his book."

"His book?" Antoinette looked enquiring. But her employer said a little disagreeably,

"She doesn't know about that yet."

"I'm sorry!" Her hand brushed his arm in the lightest gesture of apology. "I mustn't interfere, must I? But I'm so *eager* for you to do things. May I ask just one more question? Have you told Miss Burney about the suggested letter to Sir Horace?—You haven't?—Oh, dear, I'm too impatient, I know. But then I'm rather proud of the letter idea because it was mine, and I think it's a good one. May *I* tell Miss Burney about it?"

"If you like." He was leaning back now against the high, carved back of his chair, and although his expression was faintly mocking, Antoinette saw that it was indulgent too.

"It's about this strange business of the girl who caused the accident," explained Mrs. St. Leger, and Antoinette felt as though someone had hit her between the eyes. "Has Lewis—has Mr. Freemont told you about her? The girl who obviously hated him because he failed her rather brutally in a music exam?"

"Yes," said Antoinette, her mouth dry and her muscles tense with the effort of appearing unperturbed.

"But I think, if I may say so, that he rather exaggerates her—her role in this."

"I think so too." Mrs. St. Leger was all gracious agreement. "But that makes it all the more important to rid him of the obsession if—"

"I'm not subject to delusions as well as blind," interjected Lewis Freemont drily. "Go on with your story."

Mrs. St. Leger looked slightly shaken for a moment, but then she turned her full attention upon Antoinette, so that it was inexpressibly difficult to meet the scrutiny of those violet-blue eyes which had become shrewd suddenly instead of dreamy.

"Well, my idea was that it should be fairly easy to identify her. One only has to write to Sir Horace Keen at St. Cecilia's College—What did you say?"

"Nothing. I—I pricked myself on the pin holding these papers. You were saying—if one wrote to Sir Horace Keen—?"

"And asked for a list of the students examined on that occasion—"

"Better make it a list of those I *failed* on that occasion. There were quite a number of them," put in Antoinette's employer unkindly.

"Yes, that's even better," agreed Mrs. St. Leger cheerfully. "If Lewis actually had that list of names in front of him—"

"I shouldn't be able to see it," he reminded her harshly. "Put it a different way, would you?"

"Oh, my dear!" There was an affecting little catch in her voice. "I meant—if you were told the names, you would almost certainly remember which she was."

"I might," he agreed. "At any rate it's worth trying. You might write to Sir Horace on those lines, Miss

Burney. Make it your first letter will you? I'm curious to see his reply—I mean, to have his reply," he corrected himself deliberately.

"Very well."

With the air of a calm and competent secretary, Antoinette gathered up her papers and disappeared into the small office. Only when the door was shut behind her and she had sunk down in the chair before her desk did she dare to become the haggard, shaking, frightened girl she really was.

CHAPTER THREE

"I'LL have to leave!" Antoinette's first panic-striken reaction was such a desire for flight that she could hardly control it. "There's no way of avoiding discovery now. When that list of names comes and I read it out to him—"

In her agitation she moved some small articles to and fro on the desk in front of her.

"When I read it out to him—" Like a gramophone needle which refused to go further on a record her thoughts stuck at that one point.

In that list of unsuccessful candidates only one would stand out. Antoinette Burney.

She could almost hear him repeating the name reflectively. "Burney—Burney. That's *your* name, isn't it? Antoinette—Burney. But that was the girl! I remember now." And then the white rage and hatred with which he would turn his sightless gaze upon her and exclaim, "Toni—Toni! That's short for Antoinette, isn't it?"

Oh, she could never, never face such a moment! Much better to leave now, to trump up any excuse.

But how could she leave now? After making such high-sounding promises to Gordon Everleigh. And feeling—she twisted her fingers together until they ached—feeling as she did towards Lewis Freemont.

Not that she must exaggerage the position, even to herself. Such wording made it seem almost as though she were in love with him. Whereas what really tormented her was her desperate pity for him and her sense of guilt. All she asked was to be of use to him, to compensate in some small way for the tragedy she had forced upon him, to have some little part in rescuing a great artist from frustrating inactivity and bringing him back to the exhilarating conflict and heart-warming rewards of a public career.

But none of that would be remotely possible once he *knew*—once she had read out that list to him. And here she was back where she had started.

Inevitably it would be she who would read it out. First Sir Horace's reply, and then the list enclosed with it—name by name until she came to her own. Unless—

Suddenly Antoinette's mind moved on at last from that dreadful, inescapable moment, with what seemed to her a terrific, breathtaking leap. For who, after all, was to know is she read out *all* the names?

She winced at the thought of such a gross offence against integrity—an integrity so doubly necessary between a blind employer and a secretary on whom he must utterly depend. Could she really bring herself to trick him like that? Could any ultimate good justify anything so hateful and contemptible?

She rubbed her cramped fingers, only then realizing how long she had been gripping them together.

"It would be in his best interests," she tried to tell herself. "If I stay here I truly, truly can help him. Mr. Everleigh thought so too. He said so. He said I was to play down, or even suppress, any letters which might depress him."

He had not meant any breach of faith like this, of course—the deliberate falsification of information her employer had specifically requested.

"Oh, what shall I do?" Antoinette whispered, and as she leant her head on her hands, she realized that it was aching from sheer concentration and intensity of thought.

Well, one thing was certain. The letter to Sir Horace had to be written. Mrs. St. Leger was perfectly capable of checking up on that before she left the house, for she was very keen on the fact that this was *her* idea. And that half appealing, half playful air of hers hid a very solid determination to have things as she wanted them, Antoinette did not doubt.

Slowly she rolled a sheet of paper into her machine and began to type a polite request to Sir Horace Keen, at St. Cecilia's College, that he would, as a personal favour to Mr. Lewis Freemont, supply a list of the students Mr. Freemont had examined and felt bound to fail in the examination early in the year.

In her capacity as secretary, Antoinette had to sign the letter, which frightened her afresh. But if Sir Horace or *his* secretary found any coincidence in the double appearance of a somewhat unusual name, at least neither would go further than a mild flicker of interest. To make assurance doubly sure, however, Antoinette signed her letter "T. Burney."

It was just as well she had given the letter her early attention, for, as she had expected, Mrs. St. Leger came into the office before she left and, having warmly admired the neatness and efficiency of Antoinette's arrangements, asked, "Did you write the letter to Sir Horace Keen?"

"Oh, yes." Without even waiting to be asked, Antoinette handed her the letter with an air of candour, and Mrs. St. Ledger proceeded to read it with satisfaction.

"I'm sure that will draw the information we want!"

The suggestion of continued interest in the subject secretly chilled Antoinette. But she tried not to take the "we" too literally.

"You're going to be so good for Mr. Freemont, I know." Mrs. St. Leger's smile was open and sweet, though her violet-blue eyes remained cool and speculative. "How did he get hold of you?"

"By applying to the agency for whom I work." Antoinette's smile was also open and sweet, but the expression in her eyes was guarded. "I was offered the job because I happen to have some knowledge of music, you remember."

"Yes, of course. Do you play a great deal?"

"Not nowadays. I used to when I had more time. But earning one's living doesn't leave unlimited time for a hobby." Antoinette determinedly sounded philosophical rather than resentful.

"You know, Mr. Freemont is tremendously anxious to hear you play."

"Is he? I don't know why he should be." Antoinette smiled as she reached for an envelope and put in into her typewriter.

"Because he says you have the hands of an experienced pianist. He says he can *feel* that you have. I told him—" she gave her charming laugh— "that I was surprised to hear he had got as far as holding hands with you."

"And what," enquired Antoinette, still smiling coolly, "did he have to say to that?"

"He was rather unreasonably cross." Mrs. St. Leger gave a rueful little sigh. "I always forget that Lewis hasn't much sense of humour. I suppose if one is a serious, dedicated artist, one doesn't. And anyway, almost anything or nothing irritates him at the moment, which one *quite* understands, of course. Poor darling, he must be so utterly, utterly wretched."

"Yes," agreed Antoinette stonily, and she went on with her work, in the hope that Mrs. St. Leger would now go. But after a moment her visitor said musingly,

"I know Lewis—Mr. Freemont—has quite a *thing* about this girl he wants to trace, but it *was* extraordinary that she should be deliberately standing there in the middle of the road when he came driving home, wasn't it?"

"Perhaps," suggested Antoinette steadily, "she wasn't standing there. Perhaps she was just crossing the road."

"Oh no! He's quite positive about that. He says she just stood there, so that he had to wrench over the steering wheel in order to avoid her."

Something in the cool, clear tone and the positive words recalled that awful moment of time so resistlessly that it was all Antoinette could do not to cry out, "Be quiet, be quiet. You don't have to repeat it. It's with me day and night."

Instead, she said rather tonelessly, "It does sound queer, put like that. But my theory is that she was a fan who had come to have a look at his house, and she felt a fool at being caught there and hesitated for a moment not knowing whether to go back or forward."

"Why, how clever of you!" The lovely blue eyes opened to their fullest extent and Mrs. St. Leger gazed at Antoinette in seeming astonished admiration. "Just as though you'd thought yourself into that girl's mind! But then," she objected the next moment, "how would she have recognized him in that split second?"

"He was driving his easily identifiable white car," stated Antoinette. "Any admirer of his would have seen that outside concert halls a dozen times."

"How do you know he was driving the white car?" asked Mrs. St. Leger curiously, and for a dreadful moment Antoinette felt almost sick. Then she said coolly,

"He hadn't any other car, had he? I just assumed it was that one. I've seen it myself several times outside the Festival Hall."

"He has two cars, as a matter of fact. But it *was* the white one," observed Mrs. St. Leger. Then she said good-bye and went away, leaving Antoinette so shattered that she was tempted to say she could not eat anything when Brenda came to tell her that her lunch was ready.

"Mrs. St. Leger's gone," said Brenda, apparently under the impression that everything her idol did was interesting. "Didn't she look lovely in that blue suit with that great red dog running along beside her?"

"Lovely," agreed Antoinette. But she had a fleeting moment of sympathy with the erring Colonel St. Leger in his escape to South America with what Brenda had described as "quite a nobody." Perhaps there was something relaxing and acceptable in a nobody after the all-embracing charm and rightness of everything Charmian St. Leger seemed to do.

Before she left that evening her employer also asked after the letter to Sir Horace Keen and Antoinette was able to say that it had been written.

"Of course he might not be willing to supply the names of unsuccessful candidates at this date," Antoinette observed tentatively, in the faint hope that she might thus pave the way for the non-appearance of *any* list if this seemed desirable.

But Lewis Freemont scouted such a notion.

"Nonsense. Of course he'll supply the names," he replied, with the careless certainty of one quite unused to having his wishes disregarded. "Why not?"

Antoinette dared not continue the discussion further, so they left it at that. And the letter to Sir Horace Keen was posted along with all the others. Though the "plop" as it dropped into the post-box had a hollow, fateful sound to Antoinette.

During the next few days she alternated between a real and deep satisfaction in her work for Lewis Freemont and an uncontrollable dread of what the post might bring. Rosamund declared a little puzzledly that it was difficult to tell if Antoinette were happy or unhappy these days.

"I'm happy!" Antoinette asserted emphatically. "I feel I'm doing something really worthwhile, and I do think that I'm making things a little easier for—him."

"I like the breathless hush before the significant pronoun," said Rosamund with a laugh. "Don't lose your heart to him, Toni. I feel it in my bones—and they're reliable bones in this respect—that Mrs. St. Leger means to have him, and she sounds to me like a lady who gets what she wants with no holds barred."

"I'm sure she is," agreed Antoinette lightly. "But don't worry. I'm not putting up any competition in that line."

"Well, you look worried sometimes when you're just sitting there not doing anything special," said Rosamund affectionately. "I know you too well not to notice."

"I think I worry a little about the work still." Antoinette produced an admirably casual smile. "I'll soon be over that stage, though."

But she knew she would not be over that stage until Sir Horace's reply had been received and dealt with.

The very next morning the reply arrived. She knew at once what it was, and her heart gave an almost physical jolt of agony as she saw the address of St. Cecilia's College stamped on the flap of the envelope.

"Here is Sir Horace's reply," she was surprised to hear herself say quite coolly. "Shall I read it first?"

"Please do." He looked grimly interested, as though he already saw a hated goal in sight.

With an unsteady hand Antoinette slit open the envelope and drew out a letter and a separate sheet on which a list of names had been typed. There were eight of them and, glancing distastefully at the list, she saw that her own name was second on it.

"Read the letter!" Lewis Freemont was suddenly impatient. "Has he supplied the list?"

"Oh, yes." And as she recognized that the moment of no return had arrived Antoinette was all at once quite calm.

She read out Sir Horace's courteous note, in which he enquired solicitously after the famous pianist's progress and expressed pleasure at being able to do him

72

any small service, either now or at any future time. Then she turned to the list and slowly read it aloud, omitting the second name.

At the end he was frowning in a puzzled way, and he said curtly, "Read it again."

She did so, hoping that her voice would remain steady to the end. She paused slightly after each name, as though giving him time to reflect, but really so that she could regain control of her voice.

He stopped her once and muttered, "Anne Boderick? —No, that wasn't quite the name. But I think it was something like that. Patricia This and Jennifer That you can rule out. It wasn't a name like that. Anne— Broderick? No, I'm practically certain it wasn't that. And yet—Are those *all* the names? You're sure?"

"Those are all the names," stated Antoinette with iron calm. "I'm quite sure."

And she felt she had crossed a tremendous gulf— safely, but with no real satisfaction to herself. In fact, never in her life before had she so completely disliked herself.

"Well," he said at last, "it's maddeningly disappointing. I felt sure I should recognize the name when I heard it. Particularly in context with the others. But it's no good. Of course it wasn't the name on paper which made the real impression. It was the girl herself. Oh, if I could only see—see—see—!"

For a moment he beat a clenched hand on the arm of his chair in an agony of frustration and despair, while she gazed at him in wordless horror, sick at the deception which so cruelly emphasized his helplessness.

"I'm sorry." Suddenly he was calm again though rather despairingly sullen. "It upsets you when I talk like that, doesn't it?"

"Oh, don't *apologize*!" cried Antoinette, trying to sound warm and eager instead of wretchedly unhappy too. "If you can't have an occasional outburst in front of your other self, as you called me, with whom *can* you have it?"

He laughed slightly at that and held out his hand to her.

"Oh, Toni! You nice child. Much too nice, as a matter of fact, to be the other self of anyone like me."

"Much too ordinary, you mean," she corrected him, as she put her hand into his. "Everyone says you're a genius, while I—"

"Geniuses are notoriously horrible to live with," he reminded her.

"That hasn't been my experience to date," she replied gravely, which made him laugh again. "Would you like me to go on with the other letters now?"

"No." Unexpectedly he shook his head. "I'm not interested in the rest of the post. Only in that list—which is no help after all. Routine correspondence would be insufferably dull after that. We'll leave it for today. You can read it for me presently and tell me if there's anything urgent. Though how can there be anything urgent now?" he added half to himself.

"Very well. What would you like me to do, instead of routine correspondence?" She was anxious to direct his thoughts into something more positive than the morning's bitter disappointment.

"What would I like you to do?" He repeated that, as though he savoured the question with interest and some amusement. Then suddenly he said, "I'd like you to play for me."

"I couldn't think of it!" Her rejection of the idea was so complete that she actually snatched her hand away. "I—I—You make me nervous even by talking about it."

"But why?" He sounded genuinely surprised as well as amused.

"You *know* why! What amateur do you suppose would want to—to parade her deficiencies before a famous artist like you?"

"You flatter me," he murmured, but obstinacy began to mingle with the amusement. "I'll be the kindest and most indulgent of judges."

"No you won't! You're brutally frank and exacting. Everyone says you are. Look how you spoke to that wretched girl you're so angry with—telling her that she would never be a public performer in a million years."

She could not imagine what perverse spirit of rashness made her bring *that* into the conversation. But he only shrugged the reference off contemptuously.

"Oh, her! She was a cocky, insensitive piece who needed putting in her place. You're something quite different. You have the hands of a good executant and the simplicity and modesty that are essential if one is to learn. In fact, you're rather too diffident, if anything. I don't know if you're truly musical. I can't tell without hearing you. But I promise not to expect too much, or to be slashing in my judgment."

"I'm sorry, I can't."

He looked surprised again and rather piqued.

"Toni—please!" For the first time in all her association with him she heard something less than command in his tone. "I'm genuinely anxious to hear you. Good heavens—" for a moment the more usual Lewis Freemont flashed out—"I don't usually have to coax them! Most often people are embarrassingly anxious to inflict their mediocre performances upon me." Then his tone changed again and he said quite gently, "As a special favour, will you play for me? There are few things I really want or find interest in these days. But this would give me real pleasure."

"Oh—" it was an exclamation of something like despair—"if you put it like that, what else can I do?"

"Nothing," he told her calmly. "I've invoked the one argument you can't set aside. I told you, I'm often not at all a nice person. This is emotional blackmail if you like—but you must play for me."

"What shall I play?" She got up and went reluctantly towards the grand piano, which had stood closed ever since she had come into that house.

"Whatever you like—from "The bluebells of Scotland" to the Appassionata," he replied. "I just want to hear you play."

As she opened the piano and sat down before it she was already searching frantically in her mind for something—anything—which would not display just the qualities for which he had failed her all those months ago. It must be nothing that would pinpoint that almost slick virtuosity for which he had condemned her and by which he would inevitably identify her. It must be something which spoke in terms of music to the man of music who had lost so much.

Hardly of her own volition, she began to play the slow movement of one of the later Beethoven sonatas. In other days she would without hesitation have chosen the last movement, in order to show off her faultless technique and brilliant finger-work. But not now—not now.

In the last year she had, without even knowing it, become much less sure of herself, but she had learned and suffered a good deal in terms of human understanding. She was no longer the confident performer wanting— though perhaps in a quite innocent way—to "show off". She was the remorseful and humbled girl using the familiar musical idiom to say to this man what she could not possibly say in words.

In a curious way, after the first few minutes, she forgot about herself and any effects she was making upon Lewis Freemont. She felt like someone who had discovered a new language in which she was, by some inexplicable means, proficient. Her practised fingers obeyed her, as they had always done. But for the first time for years it was her heart rather than her head alone which told them what to do.

At the end there was such a profound silence that she thought for a moment she had completely betrayed her identity. But when she turned to look at him he was leaning forward with an expression of pleasure and interest in his face keener than any she had seen there since she came to work for him. And all he said was,

"Go on. Play the third movement now."

"No, I can't." She was much more afraid of betraying her identity with the sheer brilliance required for that. "I'm not up to it technically," she lied. And then, before he could argue further, she suddenly said, with an inspiration that was like a flash of lightning on a dark night, "I think *you* must play the third movement. I've done my part."

"*I*?" He raised his head in a movement of startled withdrawal.

"Yes, you," she said. And she came over and took him by the hand. "Please. It's only fair. I did what you wanted, even though I was scared. Now you must do what I want."

She thought he was going to refuse her with all the peremptory coldness at his command. But then she saw his expression change in the most extraordinary way. Capitulation was plain on that hard, handsome face. But mingled with it was an almost agonizing sense of relief. He *wanted* to capitulate. He wanted to be argued out of the position he had taken up.

"Come," she said, quite gently but compellingly. And without a word he got to his feet, his hand now tight on her upper arm.

With the skill of instinct rather than practice, she guided him to the piano, negotiating any obstacles in the way with the minimum of fuss. And for a moment as he sat down she stood behind him and pressed her hands lightly on his shoulders, as though to assure him that he was back where he belonged.

He ran his hands over the keyboard. And then, with that brilliance of attack for which he was famous, he launched into the third movement.

She stood quite near to him, nearer than she had ever been when she had heard him play before, and it seemed to her that she had never heard even him play like this. There was power, beauty, authority. But these there had always been. In addition there was an almost unearthy quality of understanding, as

78

though, blind though he was, he could see further than mere human range.

To Antoinette it was the most breathtaking musical experience of her life, and at the end she was wordless.

"Where are you?" he said, and turned from the piano.

"I'm here." She came close to him, and without a word he put his arms round her and hid his face against her.

For almost a minute of utter amazement and deepest emotion she was silent. Then she timidly passed her hand over his hair and said, "Thank you."

"No." There was the faintest huskiness in his voice. "Thank *you*. I thought I couldn't—wouldn't ever play again."

"That was just part of the shock and the natural revulsion of feeling from being helpless," she told him gently. "You couldn't really live without playing, could you?"

He shook his head.

"Do you want to play any more just now?"

"No. In some queer way I'm utterly exhausted. I didn't know I could be so—" he hesitated for the word and then said a little distastefully—"emotional."

"It was a rather emotional occasion," said Antoinette. And he laughed at that and leant his head against her again, with a naturalness that stirred the strangest tenderness within her.

"You play quite beautifully," he said almost dreamily.

"Do I?" She could not disguise the happiness—indeed, the triumph—in her voice. For if ever a man was having to eat his words without knowing it, Lewis

Freemont was doing that at this moment. "I'm rather out of practice."

"Well, so am I." And they both laughed at that. "You must have worked very hard," he went on. "Your technique is excellent. You phrase musically too, though you're—what shall I say?—a bit musically inhibited. There's a great deal of feeling there, but you don't quite know how to express it. There's a sort of gap between the way you feel and the way you speak with your fingers. Do you know what I mean?"

"Yes, I know what you mean." And all at once she did.

"We'll find a way round that," he said in a singularly contented tone. And she looked down at the smooth dark head that was still against her and she was defiantly glad that she had deceived him for his own good. If she had read out that full list earlier that morning none of this could have happened. As it was—

That was the moment when something indefinable stirred her senses with a flick of warning. Nothing so strong as alarm—just a sort of awareness that they were not alone. And, looking up over Lewis Freemont's head, she saw that Charmian St. Leger was standing framed in the garden doorway.

"Good morning, Mrs. St. Leger," said Antoinette calmly, and she was keenly aware of the jerk with which her employer sat up straight again.

"Charmian?" His voice struck a note of not entirely pleased enquiry. "You'll have to make more noise when you *come* in, my dear. It's a trifle disconcerting to have someone come upon one unawares."

"So I gather." She laughed, but the sweetness of her tone had an edge to it for once.

"Don't be silly." He answered the tone rather than the words. "I don't usually prop myself against my secretary. But you come at a rather emotional moment. I'm almost literally unstrung with relief at the discovery that I can play again."

"But did you ever doubt it, Lewis dear? *I* didn't. I knew you would play again and be as great as ever."

"Then you had the advantage of me," was the dry retort, "for it was more than I knew." And, getting to his feet," he indicated to Antoinette by no more than a pressure on her arm that she was to lead him back to his chair.

Immediately Mrs. St. Leger came forward and, with a sort of possessive tenderness, took over from Antoinette whether she wished it or not. As she did so, Antoinette suddenly realized that Sir Horace's letter and the accompanying list were lying open on the table for anyone to see.

With a speed sufficient to gratify even Mrs. St. Leger she abandoned her employer to that lady's care and guidance and, in one comprehensive sweep, gathered up the morning's post.

"Is it all right if I go now?" she asked a little breathlessly. "I really have quite a number of things to do." And, hardly waiting for her employer's word of permission she fled to her office. As she went she heard Mrs. St. Leger say with a gently amused little laugh,

"Poor girl, she was quite embarrassed at being caught like that! You shouldn't play on her feelings quite so much, Lewis. You'll have a tiresome case of adoration on your hands if you're not careful."

At any other time Antoinette would have stayed to hear the answer to that subtle little dig. But something even more urgent claimed her agitated attention. She had started on a deception, and, if she were to escape sudden disaster, it must be carried through to the last efficient detail. In other words, Sir Horace Keen's list must go and another be substituted.

Having found with some difficulty a few sheets of paper of a kind seldom used in her work, she hastily typed out the list, omitting her own name. Then, resolutely though again with a sickening qualm of conscience, she tore the original list into shreds and stuffed these into her handbag. Only when she had creased the substitute list in the same folds as Sir Horace's letter did she feel virtually secure.

Anything else seemed of such minor importance after this that she had to force herself to go on with her routine work. But this she did so that the sound of her typewriter should support her contention that she had a lot of work to do.

As she had expected, Mrs. St. Leger came in presently, to ask very charmingly but quite confidently to see the list of names supplied by Sir Horace. Then she stood beside Antoinette's desk studying it for so long that Antoinette's nerves were in shreds by the time she said, rather discontentedly,

"It's so odd! One would have thought he would be bound to identify one name from such a comparatively short list."

"Oh, I don't know." Somehow Antoinette contrived to look no more than reflective. "I can't imagine that Mr. Freemont attached much importance to the names of unsuccessful candidates once he had consigned them to oblivion. As a matter of fact, none of the names seemed to recall as specific personality to him."

"Was he very disappointed?"

"Yes, he was at first."

"And then he went off at a tangent and offered to play for you?"

"Not exactly. He insisted on my playing for him first. And from that I managed to lead him on to playing for me."

"How clever of you," said Mrs. St. Leger coldly. And she looked at Antoinette with such dislike that Antoinette was both shocked and amused.

But at least that ended the interview. Mrs. St. Leger went away and Antoinette was free to file the letter and list and tell herself that she was safe.

It was difficult not to feel at least a trifle self-conscious when she saw her employer again. Not only was there the memory of that moving scene earlier in the day, there was also the recollection of Mrs. St. Leger's warning about his having "a case of unwanted adoration on his hands" if he were not careful.

Antoinette hoped angrily that he had not attached the remotest importance to this ridiculous statement, or imagined that Mrs. St. Leger had been able to see something which he could not. If either was the case it seemed to cause him no embarrassment. He began to talk to her immediately about his decision to start playing again, and to recast their daily timetable to allow for practising.

Finally, she ventured to ask, "Does this mean that you are thing of taking up your professional career again?"

"Not necessarily," he said quickly. "Don't try to rush me. I still loathe the very idea of—" he hesitated.

"I know," she finished calmly. "—Of being led on to a platform. You keep on getting bogged down in that quite unimportant detail. Which is more important to you—the figure you cut or the music you produce?"

He gave a startled, annoyed little laugh.

"You do have a bracing way of putting things, don't you?" he said disagreeably. "I wish Charmian St. Leger could have heard the way you said that."

"Why?" enquired Antoinette calmly.

"Never you mind," he retorted. But she thought she had successfully counteracted any remarks about unwanted adoration, and the reflection gave her a good deal of satisfaction.

Neither made any further reference to his interrupted career. Only, when she was going, he said, "It's been quite a day, Toni, hasn't it?"

"Yes, it has," she replied more sombrely than she had intended, for the weight of her deception was still heavy upon her.

"You sound very grave about it. You don't sound as though you're smiling at all."

"Oh, but I am!" she exclaimed, and smile she did then. And she put her hand into his with that quick gesture of friendliness which expressed as much as any smile.

"Yes, I can hear it now." He smiled too, and his fingers were strong and warm round hers.

"It's a day to be grateful for all our lives," she said slowly. And then she bade him good-bye.

"You funny child," he exclaimed half mockingly as he let her go. And then, as she reached the door, "But I'm not ungrateful, Toni. I'm not ungrateful."

All the way home in the bus her heart was singing. And for minutes on end she could forget about the destruction of that list and think only of the wonderful fact that, guided by her hand, he had taken the first great step back to real recovery. For this she had made the terrifying decision to go and work for him. For this she had done something which would otherwise have been unforgivable.

As she got off her bus someone almost beside her was hailing a taxi, and at the sound of a familiar voice she turned and recognized Gordon Everleigh.

"Mr. Everleigh!" she exclaimed on impulse, and Lewis Freemont's good-looking manager turned.

"Hello, Miss Burney. How are things going?" His hand was actually on the taxi door and the query was obviously purely conventional.

But when she said, in a great breathless rush, "Wonderfully! He played for me today," Gordon Everleigh exclaimed,

"He *what*? Here—get in. Can I drive you anywhere? I'm going to Waterloo myself, but I'll willingly miss my train if your news is true."

"It's quite true, and you needn't miss your train," Antoinette told him with a smile, as she got into the taxi with him. "Waterloo will do for me too."

This was not strictly correct, but she hardy cared where they drove as long as she could tell her news to someone who could appreciate its full significance. And certainly she could have had no more entranced an audience than Gordon Everleigh as she rapidly described what had happened at Pallin Manor that morning.

"He played! He actually played for you! And *how* did he play?"

"Divinely. I've never heard him play better."

"No insecurity or—"

"Oh, no, no!" She laughed at the very idea. "The attack was superb and the—the understanding was so complete. As though physical blindness had only increased his artistic vision."

"And you just made him take over where you left off?"

"It seemed a good idea," she explained.

"A good idea! It was a stroke of genius, you wonderful girl. If kissing in taxis were not so suspect I'd kiss you. I always knew it would have to be a woman who worked the miracle with him. A man argues with logic, but a woman improvises with inspiration. It had to be a woman—and *not* Charmian St. Leger. Well, here we are at Waterloo, and I've three minutes to get my train. Here's my office number. Keep in touch and I'll be down at Pallin in the next few days. God bless you! You deserve a medal."

He patted her approvingly on the shoulder, paid the taxi-driver and was gone in a whirl of congratulation and relief.

As for Antoinette, she slowly made her way to the Underground, not minding in the least that she now had to retrace most of the way she had come. It was worth it—oh, a hundred times worth it—just to hear him say, "It had to be a woman—and *not* Charmian St. Leger."

CHAPTER FOUR

"YOU'RE LATE," observed Rosamund as Antoinette came in. Then, turning to look at her, she added, "Have you won a fortune or something? You look—oh, I don't know!—as though heaven had smiled on you today."

"Heaven *has* smiled on me today!" Antoinette slipped off her coat and flung it with uncharacteristic carelessness on to the settee. "Lewis Freemont played for me today. The first time he has touched the piano since—it happened."

"He *played* for you?"

"And I played for him, incidentally."

"Toni!" Rosamund was staggered. "What did he say?"

"He said—" Antoinette smiled as she remembered the completeness with which he had unknowingly reversed his own judgment—"he said I played quite beautifully."

"And you managed not to throw it in his teeth that he had once dismissed you as a clever automaton without a glimmer of the divine spark?" cried Rosamund incredulously. "I think you're a saint. Or else very silly," she added as an afterthought. "For even if the poor man is blind, it's good for him to be told a hard truth from time to time."

"It wasn't the right moment," replied Antoinette, with more masterly understatement than Rosamund could possibly imagine. "He made me play for him—"

"How?" asked Rosamund curiously.

"By representing it as one of the few things which would still give him pleasure and interest. Though I think that was a bit of an exaggeration, to get his own way," Antoinette explained hastily. "Anyway, I stopped playing just at the point when he was mad keen to hear the rest, and I told him he would have to do the next movement, as my technique was not up to it. And he did just that."

"Almost without realizing what he was doing?"

"Not quite like that—no. He was startled at first. Then, in some way, he was almost relieved at having his hand forced. Almost as though he longed to be convinced against his will. He thought he wouldn't—perhaps even couldn't—ever play again. All I did was to stampede him into trying, before he could build up his wall of resistance again."

"It sounds Freudian to me," said Rosamund, "but very clever. How did he play?"

"Divinely," asserted Antoinette, as she had to Gordon Everleigh. "I don't think he ever played better."

"It must have been pretty moving," observed Rosamund thoughtfully. "Didn't you both nearly burst into tears at the end?"

"Not exactly. But—" Antoinette bit her lip at the recollection—"he put his arms round me rather gropingly and—and thanked me."

"Oh, dear, how slave-making," said Rosamund, more than half seriously. "He isn't my type, but I think that would have got round my heart. Whatever did you do?"

"There wasn't time to do anything much," Antoinette confessed. "Mrs. St. Leger characteristically chose that moment to make an entry."

"Oh!" Rosamund was enjoyably scandalized. "Was she furious?"

"Yes, I think she was," said Antoinette, not without satisfaction. "She sugared over the cracks, of course, with the best fondant icing. But I heard her warn Mr. Freemont afterwards that if he wasn't careful he would have a bad case of unwanted adoration on his hands."

"The cat! Did you let that go unchallenged?"

"Of course." She thought of the speed with which she had fled to her office with the incriminating list. But in order to give a reasonable air to her attitude, she added, "What should I have said? Why give her the gratification of supposing I cared one bit about what she said or thought?"

"Most people would have wanted at least to know what he said in return," declared Rosamund. "Did you wait for that?"

"No." And at the note of indifference in her tone, Rosamund laughed, in a slightly relieved way.

"You set all my fears at rest," she said, pulling a funny little grimace. "No girl with any tender feelings towards a man could have resisted waiting to hear his reply. I'd rate you completely safe from the famous Freemont charm."

"Oh, yes, I'm completely safe," Antoinette assured her with a laugh. And picking up her coat, she went to her own room.

But when she had shut the door of her room behind her she stood for a whole minute, her coat hanging unnoticed over her arm, her thoughts following the curious path opened up by her conversation with Rosamund.

So she was completely safe, was she? Completely safe from any danger of becoming "a bad case of unwanted adoration."

The very term was ridiculous, of course. At no time had she adored Lewis Freemont. She admired him beyond measure as an artist. She would even go so far as to say that she found him thrilling, intriguing, fascinating—any of the feelings one did have towards a great personality who could so completely transport one from the everyday world.

But all that was concerned with the artist, Lewis Freemont. As a person—?

Antoinette hung her coat in the wardrobe, ran a comb absently through her hair and sat down on the side of her bed. As a person Lewis Freemont had been for long enough an odious, entirely unacceptable figure in her consciousness, nothing more nor less than the man who had temporarily spoiled her life. For months she had thought of him only with anger and resentment. She had not exactly wished him ill, because she was not that sort of girl. But she could never have imagined herself entertaining the slightest feeling of friendliness towards him.

And then, in a matter of seconds, his whole image had been changed. From an unassailable, deeply resented figure of power he had been suddenly reduced to someone for whom she felt anguished pity, someone with a greater claim on her sympathy and loving care than anyone else she had ever known. It was a change too profound and sudden to leave her emotions reasonably balanced, particularly when along with that sense of pity went an even deeper sense of personal responsibility.

Up to a point she *had* kept a reasonably well-balanced outlook. She had been a conscientious, sympathetic, efficient secretary. But, on his own reckoning, she had also on occasion been very down-to-earth and bracing—right up to the moment when he made her play for him.

That was when their relationship had subtly changed. First because she had tried to express to him in music the deeply felt sympathy and remorse which she could not express to him in words. Then came that flash of inspiration when she made him play for her. And finally—even now she shivered a little with a sort of delicious dismay and alarm at the recollection—he had put his arms round her and leant his head against her, and in that moment he had been most curiously *hers*.

There had never been any other occasion at all like that in her life. Just as he had surrendered completely to the emotional gratitude and relief in his heart, so she had made some sort of surrender too. She was not quite sure what. But the certainty that she had been his in that moment, just as he had been hers, both frightened and elated her.

Before she could force herself to analyse that further, however, Rosamund called out cheerfully that supper was ready, and she had to abandon dangerously attractive speculation for very normal conversation, in which she must play her part however confused her inmost thoughts might be.

Although it had been unbearably difficult at first, she was now fairly used to hiding her hopes and fears even from anyone as close to her as Rosamund. But it was hard not to talk frankly that evening. It would have been a wonderful relief to share those hours of panic over the list with Rosamund and then to see if her guilty solution seemed just a little less shameful to Rosamund than it did to herself. But if she told that bit, she must tell all, and that was something she could not even contemplate.

Instead, she had to listen to Rosamund's jubilant comments on Lewis Freemont's latest verdict about Antoinette's playing.

"It only shows how fallible these examiners can be," she declared.

"Perhaps," countered Antoinette, "it only shows how much even a humble performer can change."

"But why should you have changed to that degree?" objected Rosamund.

"Don't you think life changes and develops one quite startlingly at times?"

"Yes, of course," Rosamund agreed. "But only after a considerable period of time or some terrific experience, like losing someone or something very dear or falling in love. But none of that applies to you in the last year, does it?"

"Not qiute in those terms," Antoinette admitted. "It *was* a terrible shock having all my hopes and pride pushed into the dust. I think it made me take a long fresh look at myself, and it made me change my scale of values quite a lot."

"I don't think getting that brutal brush-off from Lewis Freemont would have developed your artistic perceptions," said Rosamund in her most common-sense manner. "It's possible, of course, that your concern for him in his tragedy might have given you a fresh and deeper insight into life and art. But it sounds far fetched to me."

It sounded far-fetched to Antoinette too. But she could not possibly explain to Rosamund that during the months in question she had learned a great deal about suffering and a great deal about the sort of tender compassion which perhaps comes near to loving in the widest sense of the word.

She thought a good deal about that conversation during the next few days, when far-reaching changes began to take place in the routine at Pallin Manor. The very next morning, she arrived to find her employer in a mood of eager and positive planning.

"I've had quite enough of sitting in this chair being an aloof figure of tragedy," he informed her. "I was awake a long time last night and I did some hard thinking. The first thing I've got to do is to accept the fact that I shall most probably be permanently blind— And don't catch your breath in that silly little hiss," he interjected rather savagely. "If I can take it, you can."

"Yes, of course. But I always hoped"—or did she mean feared?—"that just as a shock blinded you, so a shock might perhaps restore your sight."

"That's the story they told me in the beginning, but more, I think, as a sort of cushion between me and the first contact with the fact of utter blindness," he said, with the grim air of a man driving himself to the acceptance of hard reality. "Anyway, it isn't the proper basis for one's future planning. And now that you've shown me that I can play—" he broke off suddenly and then said, in a different tone, "Come here, my good angel. Why did I speak to you so savagely just now when I owe you everything?"

"Oh, please——" she was so overwhelmed that her voice shook. But she came to him and gave him her hand.

"Don't cry," he said, impatiently noting the quiver in her voice. "Tears bore me and make me nervous."

"I'm not crying! And the one time I did you weren't specially bored *or* nervous, if I remember rightly."

"Don't put that to the test too often," he told her with a laugh. But he carried her hand to his lips and kept it there for a moment or two.

"Tell me about your plans," she said gently at last. "What have you decided to do, now that you've accepted the fact that you may be——maybe——"

"Permanently blind. It's odd that I can say it and you can't."

No, it's not. You're brave and I'm a coward."

"Not judging by the way you stand up to me," he told her almost gaily. "I've decided that I'll get back to the concert platform somehow, Toni. And you are going to help me."

"I am? Oh, how wonderful!" And in an access of emotion and delight she put her cheek against the hand she was still holding.

He was absolutely silent for a moment. Then he stirred his fingers softly against her cheek and said a little mockingly, "What's this for?"

"Oh——I don't know." Embarrassed, she released his hand quickly. "I was just grateful and happy to think I might help."

"Don't be quite so reverential," he protested amusedly. "I'm afraid you only know me in a somewhat chastened condition. When I'm under the nervous tension of a professional career I'm quite insufferable,

94

according to many of my acquaintances. I'm afraid it's going to be a shock for anyone as good and civilized as you."

"I'm *not* good!" protested Antoinette. "I'm perfectly horrible sometimes. And—and I've done some things I'm ashamed of."

"What, for instance?" he enquired with teasing interest.

"I couldn't possibly tell you," she exclaimed agitatedly.

"As bad as that? You excite my wildest curiosity," he said, laughing. "If ever I recover my sight, the first thing I shall do is dig into your interesting past."

"Oh, no, no, don't talk like that!" Such unreasoning panic swept over her at the very thought of such a thing that she jumped up and literally fled towards her office.

"Toni!" There was command as well as astonishment in his voice. "I was only teasing you. Come back here."

"No."

"Then I shall come and fetch you."

"You—can't."

"Are you throwing that up at me?"

"No, of course not!" She came back immediately and sat down in the chair she had so suddenly vacated. And she sat very still even when he put out his hand and felt for her. But it was not her hand that he took. To her surprise, he put his arm lightly round her and said,

"Listen, you silly girl—I don't care what your faults are. To me you're one of the nicest, most worthwhile people I know—"

"I'm not," she interrupted, in a stifled voice, the enormity of her deception over that list rising before her like a cloud.

"Don't contradict." He laughed and actually drew her against him. "I simply don't believe you've ever done anything bad enough to trouble any but the most tender conscience."

"You don't—know." To her horror a dreadful impulse to make full confession was so strong upon her that she almost choked in the effort of suppressing it.

"Yes, I do. I haven't lost my natural judgment, even if I've lost my sight," he told her. "And my guess is that whatever you did was more his fault than yours."

"H-his?" stammered Antoinette, cold with fright once more.

"Well, I suppose there was a man in it somewhere, wasn't there?"

There had been, of course! And so she was fascinated into saying, "Yes."

"Forget him. He's not worth another qualm on your part. Take my word for it." And she felt him lightly kiss the side of her cheek. "Better now?"

"Much—better," she said. And on an impulse which this time she did not even try to suppress, she reached up and put her lips against the thin, hard line of his cheek.

He gave a slight, almost startled laugh. Then he deliberately turned his head until his lips found hers.

It was not a light or careless kiss. It was the sort of kiss that made her gasp slightly. Then he released her and said coolly.

"We—ell, this discussion seems to be going rather well."

"But perhaps," suggested Antoinette with quite admirable composure, we'd better get back to—to essentials, before Mrs. St. Leger pays one of her morning calls."

"Oh, Charmian—" He said the name with a casual little air of dismissal for which she could gladly have kissed him again. Instead, however, she began to question him about the exact plans for getting back into public life.

"The task will be twofold," he said practically. "I realize that. I've got to learn to have complete confidence in my playing without being able to see the keyboard. One looks at it only seldom in any case, of course. But never to be able to see it gives one a strange feeling of uncertainty. That's the first thing to conquer—the easier part, I suppose, in my case. The other thing is that I must learn to *move* with a sort of confidence and authority."

"So that you can walk on to a platform with an air, even though you'll need to have your hand on someone's arm?"

"Exactly. No—groping or stumbling. Nothing that can fix the public's attention on my blindness rather than my playing. It's a challenge, of course—"

"But a worthwhile one," interrupted Antoinette eagerly. "When do we begin?"

"Now," he said, and he laughed as though her enthusiasm had fired him. "I want you to take me round this room, telling me exactly where everything is. We'll do it over and over again, until I get the feel of everything, the timing of distances, the confidence to move at any rate in this room with something like normality. It can be done. I know it can be done!"

"Of course it can," she declared, her tone warm with encouragement.

"Then take me—now." He got to his feet and held out his hand, waiting for her to take it.

There was something terribly moving in the contrast between his bold and authoritative planning and that singularly helpless gesture. But she was not going to allow herself the luxury of any sentimental agonizing on his behalf. He had asked for hard, sensible support and this he should have. She took his arm, rather than his hand, so that the contact between them was close and reassuring, and she began to lead him round his once familiar room, detailing exactly what was there.

He obviously had an almost photographic memory, for several times he told her what should come next even before she could describe it. Then he would run his strong, sensitive fingers over the object as though literally learning the feel of it.

Once, over something no more important than a small cabinet, he said sharply. "No! That's been moved."

"Not in my time," Antoinette assured him.

But he was almost positive—even nervously irritated in case he might be wrong, she saw. So she summoned Brenda to ask if anything in the room had been moved, and she could sense his intense relief when Brenda said,

"Yes, indeed, sir. I thought it might be in the way when—I mean if—you wanted to go into the garden."

" 'When', Brenda, 'when'," he assured her a trifle impatiently. "As you see, I'm learning to move about now."

"Yes, sir," Brenda said approvingly. "Mrs. St. Leger *will* be pleased."

"Well, I suppose she will," agreed Brenda's master drily. "Though that wasn't my primary motive in making the attempt!"

"No, sir," said Brenda, and went away.

However, Brenda was more than right. When Charmian St. Leger called in the following morning and found Antoinette and her employer going through the now familiar round of the room, she uttered a little cry of tender concern and rushed to his side.

"Lewis—darling! You're *walking*!" she exclaimed.

"I have been doing so for the last thirty-six years," he replied disagreeably. "I'm merely learning to do it a slightly different way."

"Of course. Oh, let *me* help you. I'm sure Miss Burney has a dozen things she wants to do. This is something I can really do to help you." With gentle but resistless fingers, she had already detached Antoinette's hand from Lewis Freemont's arm. "I really just called in to say I was going to London today and to ask if there's anything I can get for you. But I'm driving up and half an hour one way or the other doesn't matter—It's all right, Miss Burney, I can manage splendidly. Don't bother to wait."

So Antoinette retreated to her office, half annoyed at Mrs. St. Leger's technique, but also half gratified by the complicated expression on her employer's face. She was not a conceited girl, but she felt morally certain that he would rather have relied on her guidance at this moment than on that of Charmian St. Leger.

She did not go back into the drawing-room until their visitor had gone, and then only because her employer called to her. He was sitting up very straight in his highbacked chair, flushed and smiling, and he said immediately,

"I've done it on my own! I walked round the room on my own. Not exactly rapidly, and with a few bumps. But I managed pretty well. It was quite different being guided by Charmian. Different from you—my other self—I mean. And so I thought, when she had gone—why don't I try the next stage and see if I can do it entirely on my own? And I never really lost my way once. I'm getting a sort of built-in radar here." And he tapped his forehead triumphantly.

"It's wonderful!" Antoinette stood and smiled at him. Then, realizing that of course he could not see the pleasure and congratulation on her face, she came over and patted him on the shoulder, and said again, "It's wonderful!"

"Yes, isn't it?" Immediately he put up his hand and covered hers. "Thank you. It's largely because of your certainty and encouragement, you know. You give me a sort of confidence just by being here, in the house. As though there's a line of communication between us not entirely dependent on physical touch."

"I'm glad," said Antoinette quietly. But she was really so much moved that she was relieved that they were interrupted at this point by the entry of Gordon Everleigh.

Nothing could have exceeded the congratulation and warm-hearted delight of Lewis Freemont's impresario. As an excellent businessman, he was naturally immeasurably relieved to see one of his most invaluable artists no longer determined to rule out the possibility of a comeback. But in addition, Antoinette saw, he was personally genuinely happy on behalf of a friend.

"Everything is possible, now that you've made the first step," he declared.

"More than the first step," Antoinette pointed out warmly. "He has decided to play again, and he's already learning to move about with some confidence."

"Thanks to the mingled encouragement and bullying of my admirable secretary," put in Lewis Freemont drily.

"Yes, yes, I dared to hope something like this might happen from the first moment I set eyes on Miss Burney," declared Gordon Everleigh. "Somehow, she *looks* the kind of girl who works the occasional miracle."

"Does she really?" Lewis Freemont sounded both amused and interested.

"Well, don't you agree?"

"My dear chap, I've never seen her."

"Oh, lord, no, of course you haven't! I'm sorry, I forgot you hadn't met her until this happened."

"Don't apologize. I probably know her quite as well as I should if I could have seen her from the beginning." There was no self-pity in his tone. There was even a hint of gaiety. "You concentrate more on other things if you can't see a person. Is she as pretty as her speaking voice suggests?"

"At the risk of embarrassing her, I should say—yes," replied Gordon Everleigh judicially, and Antoinette laughed.

"You shall describe her to me some time," remarked Antoinette's employer.

"Has no one done so yet?" His friend sounded amused.

"Only Toni herself—and Charmian. I have an idea that neither did her strict justice," was the dry retort. And Antoinette, curiously secure all at once, allowed herself another slight laugh.

She left the two men together then, to discuss tentative, long-term plans for Lewis Freemont's eventual return to public life. But some time later Gordon Everleigh sought her out in her office and said,

"If you can keep him more or less in this mood of positive optimism, the musical world will owe you a real debt of gratitude."

"I shall do my best," Antoinette promised. "There will be setbacks, you know. He's a mercurial sort of creature—"

"Don't tell me!" The impresario laughed and made a face. "I make my bread and butter out of the artistic temperament. There's nothing I don't know about it."

"Yes, of course! I forgot. I only meant that the impetus of this first enthusiasm will slacken, and we shall have to be ready to deal with the inevitable depression and frustration when the day-to-day difficulties emerge."

"You think of everything," was the approving reply, "and I have every confidence in your being able to deal efficiently with everything as it comes along. I only hope Freemont realizes one day how much he owes to you."

Then he went away, leaving Antoinette divided between happiness over present approval and grief at the thought of what her employer owed to her from the past.

Nothing, however, could now cloud her bright spirits for long. And she was delighted to find on the following morning that he was determined to go into the garden.

It was a lovely late autumn day, incredibly mild for that time of year. And, having walked round part of the garden with him, describing some of the flowers and plants and letting him pause to enjoy the scent of some late roses, she left him sitting in a sheltered corner, touched by the almost naïve pleasure with which he raised his face to feel the rays of the autumn sun which he could not see.

Back in her office, she worked without interruption for some time. So deeply absorbed was she that she was almost startled when the door into the drawing-room opened. For a staggered moment she wondered if her employer had somehow found his way in from the garden alone, and then she saw, with surprise and no special pleasure, that Mrs. St. Leger stood framed in the doorway.

"Mr. Freemont is in the garden, Mrs. St. Leger," Antoinette said. "It's the first time he——"

"Yes, I know. I saw him as I passed." The voice was grave, and suddenly Antoinette realized that there was a regretful, almost reproachful air about her visitor which was singularly becoming to her type of beauty. "I didn't disturb him, because it was you I wanted to speak to personally."

Suppressing a secret irritation at the impression of gentle melancholy, Antoinette pushed aside her type-writer and said, with a sort of brisk courtesy, "What can I do for you? Is it something to do with Mr. Freemont?"

"Yes, it is." The air of a minor saint contemplating the unbelievable wickedness of the world deepened slightly. "Miss Burney, this isn't going to be at all easy for me to say. But I think you will realize something of what is coming if I tell you that yesterday, when I was in town, I called to see an old acquaintance of mine—Sir Horace Keen."

Such a frightful chill gripped Antoinette's heart at these words that she experienced an almost physical pain. She literally *could* not utter a word, even if it would have been advisable to do so, and after a moment Mrs. St. Leger went on,

"Naturally my friendship with Mr. Freemont brought me in contact with many people in the musical world, and I have known Sir Horace for some years, and it occurred to me that perhaps it would help if I went to him and asked if there were anything further we could do to trace that girl who had injured Lewis so terribly."

She paused again, but still Antoinette said nothing, and, with a slight sigh for the disagreeable necessity of inflicting the blow, Mrs. St. Leger said,

"Inevitably we came to a discussion of the list of names he had supplied. He spoke of eight names, though I knew there had been only seven on the one you showed me, and at my request he produced the carbon copy of the original letter and list. There were eight names on it, Miss Burney, and I don't need to tell you whose the missing name was."

"No, you don't need to tell me." Antoinette's voice was slightly husky, perhaps from having remained silent so long. "The eighth name was mine, of course."

"Miss Burney, how *could* you? How could you deceive a blind man so ruthlessly? I'm not a censorious woman, and heaven knows, I'm not perfect—" she obviously offered this statement as polite fiction rather than hard fact—"But it's beyond my comprehension that a nice-seeming girl like you could do all this. What is this—this sort of vendetta that you have against poor Lewis?"

"There is no vendetta, or anything so ridiculous." Antoinette's tone was curt to the point of rudeness in her instinctive reaction to the sugary reproaches that were being poured over her, "The whole thing has been misunderstood and misrepresented. I didn't like being failed in my exam, of course, but at no time did I have the slightest intention of doing Mr. Freemont any harm. The idea is preposterous. It's true that I was crossing the road near his house on that unfortunate day. I recognized his car and, in a moment of idiotic self-consciousness, I stopped dead."

She closed her eyes for a moment, hearing yet again the screech of his brakes and seeing with ghastly clarity the unforgettable scene of the crash.

"It's something I shall regret all my life." She steadied her voice determinedly. "But it was a moment of supreme stupidity, not anything with the remotest degree of ill-intention in it."

"Why did you run away afterwards, then?"

"I summoned help and then I—I panicked," Antoinette admitted with grim candour.

"But, my dear, how *wrong* of you! One should always bravely face the consequences of one's actions."

"I'm aware of that." Antoinette, who resented the "my dear" even more than the rebuke, spoke coldly. "But, as you said of yourself just now, none of us is perfect."

The older woman looked surprised, having evidently forgotten that hollow stricture on herself and resenting the idea that anyone else should presume to echo it. Her tone was also cold, therefore, as she said,

"But, having done so much harm, how could you possibly come and work for him. Surely you didn't want to watch him in his tragic helplessness?"

With difficulty Antoinette stifled her fury at the implication that she might almost have gloated over the situation.

"I wanted to make some amends," she said simply. "I realized I had certain gifts that could be of use to him. I wanted, very badly, to put them at his disposal."

"But wouldn't one have to be very insensitive to be able to *bear* to see the results of one's tragic work?" Mrs. St. Leger looked all sensitive bewilderment herself.

"It wasn't easy at first," Antoinette admitted shortly. "It became easier when I found I was really of use to him. That was why I felt justified in suppressing my name on that list, even though it meant deceiving a blind man. I'm sorry you had to find all this out in circumstances that put me in a very bad light. But what I want to know now is—what do you propose to do about your discovery, bearing in mind that I've become a real support to Mr. Freemont? I say this quite impersonally, because all I want is *his* good. If you feel the same—"

"Of *course* I want nothing but his good!" Mrs. St. Leger looked deeply hurt that anyone should question the purity of her motives. "I've had only one thing in mind over this miserable and disgraceful affair, and that is—what is best for Lewis?"

"Then may I venture to suggest, Mrs. St. Leger, that your natural good heart and good sense will tell you that much the best thing for Mr. Freemont is that I should remain here until he has been helped back to his place in public life. He needs a sort of personal security during this difficult period. For some reason or other, I seem to give that to him. It would be an immeasurable shock for him to learn the truth now. And to what purpose? Once he has regained his natural position in the musical world, no doubt I—I can gradually withdraw from the scene, infinitely grateful (if you will believe me) that I've been able to compensate in some way for what I inadvertently did. Don't you agree this is best?"

It had not been Charmian St. Leger's idea that anyone else should ask the questions. But the reference to her natural good heart and good sense was something she had to live up to. In addition, she probably saw in that moment just how she could turn the situation to her advantage.

"It isn't for me to judge," she began, "and to anyone sensitive like me it's peculiarly painful to have to inflict unhappiness on anyone. I'd much *rather* say nothing—"

Incredulously, Antoinette drew a slight breath of relief.

"—But there's one thing I feel in duty bound to add, Miss Burney. I can't help noticing—oh, how shall I put this without sounding unkind?—that you overstress the *personal* side of your relationship with Mr. Freemont. That really would have to stop, you know. Even though it is probably best that you should remain as his invaluable secretary, I simply couldn't stand by and watch anyone who had injured him so cruelly worm her way into his friendship or—or affections. It wouldn't be right of me to do so. You do see what I mean, don't you?"

There was a long pause, while Antoinette digested the full implications of this gentle piece of blackmail. Then she looked straight at Mrs. St. Leger, whose beautiful violet-blue eyes gazed stonily back at her.

"Yes", said Antoinette slowly, "I see exactly what you mean."

"Then it's agreed that your relations with Mr. Freemont remain strictly business ones? And that I say nothing about your real identity?"

"It is agreed," said Antoinette with an effort.

"Good. I think I'll go and see Mr. Freemont in the garden now." And, smiling gently, Charmian St. Leger drifted away while Antoinette looked helplessly after her.

CHAPTER FIVE

WELL, that was it! Determinedly Antoinette tried to brace herself with the thought that at least she had bought Mrs. St. Leger's silence. But she knew that, with even the gentlest of blackmailers, the first trial of strength is very seldom the last.

"I'll have to risk that." She even whispered aloud to herself in her agitation. "I've *lived* on the edge of risk for the last many weeks. I have to go on doing just that. And so long as I follow out her demands exactly—"

She paused, knowing that if she were to examine in detail the real meaning of those demands she would also have to examine in detail the real state of her own feelings. She winced away from the thought. But necessity—and a sort of fascinated sense of dread—drew her back to that confrontation of herself.

As the price of Chairman St. Leger's silence she had promised to remain on strictly business terms with her employer. That was all. Was there anything so dismaying in that? On what other terms did she want to be? Wasn't she thankful enough to be just the invaluable secretary—the girl who helped him back to professional life as some slight compensation for the injury she had done him? What more could she ask?

Antoinette leant her elbows on the desk and her head on her hands. She was no longer listening to the sound of her own inner voice. What she heard was that slightly mocking, half tender voice saying, "To me you're one of the nicest, most worthwhile people

I know—" She heard him say, "Where are you?" and felt him put his arms round her and lean his head against her in mute gratitude and emotion. She felt him kiss her, as no one else had ever kissed her before. In rapid, overwhelming succession she recalled every word and incident that had drawn them inevitably nearer to each other. And in a final moment of irresistible self-knowledge she realized that she loved him.

Antoinette was so terrified and yet elated by the discovery that she could no longer sit still at her desk. Getting to her feet, she walked up and down her small office, clasping and unclasping her hands in a mixture of rapture and dismay impossible to describe. It was the most wonderful thing that had ever happened to her—and the most appalling. It comprised all her happiness—and equally it threatened its very foundations. He meant everything to her and, by the bargain she had just struck, he must mean nothing.

"I *won't* do what she wants! Why should I?"

But a more childish question no one had ever asked herself. If she did not fulfil Charmian St. Leger's demands to the full then, with gentle ruthlessness, Lewis Freemont would be told the exact truth—that the secretary on whom he was depending more and more was the girl who had ruined his life for him.

It was not as though one could appeal to the other woman's sense of mercy or fairness. She had none. All she had was a limitless capacity for believing that what she wanted was the best course to pursue—a quality far more dangerous than frank brutality. Not for the first time, Antoinette's heartfelt sympathy went out to the erring husband who had fled from Charmian St.

Leger to South America in the refreshing company of "an absolute nobody".

Irresistibly drawn there, Antoinette crossed to the window, from which she could see a large section of the garden, including the sheltered corner where she had left her employer sitting in the autumn sunshine. It did not surprise her that Charmian St. Leger was now sitting there beside him on the stone bench, her hand lightly on his arm. He, Antoinette noted with melancholy satisfaction, was not smiling and, even as she watched, he moved his arm impatiently from under the clinging fingers of his beautiful companion.

"He doesn't really care about her," she thought. "He admired her beauty and style and charm in the days when he could see those things. But he needs something more real, more—more tangible now. Being blind has changed him. Perhaps other things have changed him too. Perhaps—"

She moved away from the window and, by a supreme effort of will, went on with her morning's work. When she looked out of the window half an hour later Mrs. St. Leger had gone, and Lewis Freemont was sitting alone, with a singularly thoughtful expression on his worn face.

Antoinette went out to him and at the sound of her footstep he turned his head at once and smiled.

"Is that you, Toni?"

"Yes. Do you want to come in now? It's not far off lunchtime."

"No. Come and sit beside me. I want to talk to you."

With an illogical conviction that Mrs. St. Leger would know and disapprove Antoinette sat down beside him and absently, though with a gesture that was

111

natural and instinctive, he felt for her hand and took it lightly in his.

She trembled a little, mostly because of the wave of tenderness which immediately swept over her and the instantaneous effort with which she now felt bound to suppress it. For a moment or two he was silent, while she listened to the lazy hum of a nearby bee and what seemed to her the loud beating of her own heart. Then it was she who spoke.

"Did Mrs. St. Leger stay long?"

"Too long." He made a slight face. "Could you tactfully convey to her that daily visits are not called for?"

"No," said Antoinette quite simply, at which he laughed.

"Why not? Aren't you supposed to be in charge here?"

"I wasn't aware of it." She smiled slightly in spite of herself. "In any case, if you don't want Mrs. St. Leger around, it's for you to drop a firm hint, not me."

"She doesn't take hints."

"Then she certainly wouldn't take anything from me! She doesn't like me, for one thing," said Antoinette before she could stop herself.

"No, she doesn't, does she?" he agreed with sudden amusement. "Do you know why?"

"No!" Said Antoinette quickly.

"I do." He spoke almost casually. "It's because she knows I do like you."

"O—oh. You mean she's a little—jealous? But that's absurd."

"I don't know that it is." He spoke with deliberation and, on sudden instinct, Antoinette tried gently to pull her hand away, but he kept a firm hold on it. "Charmian is both competitive and singularly possessive. I realize it more every time I listen to her voice. I wasn't so much aware of it when I could see her. There are advantages to being blind, you see." He laughed, though she could not. "You'd be surprised how differently one observes and assesses people when one can't see them."

"Does one?" Antoinette's lips were rather dry.

"Yes. I think that if Charmian came to see me once, or at the most twice, a month that would be quite sufficient."

"Then *you* must tell her so."

"But as for you," he went on calmly—"it's a poor day when I don't have you somewhere around me. That's why I don't like the weekends much."

It was all she could do not to say that she would willingly come to Pallin on Saturdays and Sundays too. But she immediately recalled Mrs. St. Leger's hard, beautiful eyes and the way she had said, "You do see what I mean, don't you?"

So Antoinette swallowed slightly and murmured, "It would be difficult to come *every* weekend."

He laughed, obviously touched by what she knew to be the feeblest of compromises.

"Does that mean that you would be willing to give up an occasional weekend to me?"

"If—if you wanted some work done, of course."

"I shouldn't want any work done," he told her coolly. "I should just want *you*. I tell you, it's a poor day for me when you're not around."

"I'll—I'll see what I can do." Her voice was husky with the effort of keeping herself from saying that she would come any time he liked and for as long as he

113

liked. And then, terrified that the conversation might get out of hand, she rose to her feet.

But he said, "No——" and firmly drew her down again on to the bench beside him. "I haven't finished what I have to say. Charmian insisted on advising me about my future while we were sitting here."

"Your future?" Antoinette stirred uneasily. "What had she to say about your future?"

"Mostly that, without very careful planning, I should find life—particularly professional life—quite impossible."

"How dared she make such suggestions!" Antoinette was furiously indignant that anyone should undermine the self-confidence she was so carefully building up in him.

"It was for my own good, she said." He sounded bored and also faintly amused, and Antoinette guessed instinctively that he was exactly reproducing the maddening air with which he had received Mrs. St. Leger's advice.

"But she did put forward one good suggestion," he went on reflectively. "She assured me that, as time went on, I should need someone at my side who loved me, understood me (her words, not mine), and was willing to put my interests first."

There was a slight silence. Then Antoinette said, "She meant herself, of course?"

"Of course." Again that almost cruel note of boredom crept into his tone.

"You said just now that you thought it a good suggestion. You don't sound as though you think that now."

"There was nothing wrong with the suggestion, Toni. She cast the role wrongly, that's all."

"Oh!" Panic and rapture engulfed her, but she tried to force things on to a lighter level with a scared little laugh. "Then you must find the right person. If that's another job for your secretary—"

"Dont' be so damned coy!" he exclaimed roughly and pulled her suddenly close against him. "That's not for *you*. Don't you understand? I love you—" he kissed her hard on the mouth—"I need you. And not only because I'm blind. Stop struggling. Don't you want me to kiss you?"

"No!" she gasped.

"Liar," he said coolly, and kissed her again, so that she forgot all about Charmian St. Leger and the danger that hung just over her head, and she clung to the man she loved and kissed him over and over again.

He released her at last, with an incredulous, breathless little laugh, and said with teasing tenderness, "So *that's* what my cool, self-contained little secretary is really like!"

"No, it isn't! I didn't realize—I'm not like that at all—I'm not that kind of girl—"

"What kind of girl, for God's sake?" He sounded both angry and amused. "What sort of advances do you suppose I'm making to you? I'm asking you to marry me."

"I can't!" The image of Charmian St. Leger and the enormity of her own guilt rose like a cloud before her.

"Why not?"

"I can't tell you."

"Of course you can tell me. Do you suppose I can't stand the truth, after all that's happened? Do you hate the fact that I'm blind?"

"No, no, no" she cried, and in her eagerness to reassure him she put her hands round his face and kissed him between his sightless eyes.

"Then—" his voice was suddenly not quite steady— "what is it? Don't you love me?"

"N-no," she said uncertainly.

"That isn't true! Kiss me again—and then try to tell me that"

"No. I just can't marry you. That's all there is to it."

"But why, why, why? Oh, God, this is when it's such hell to be blind" Wild rebellion and frustation made him suddenly savage, and he caught hold of her and jerked her against him. "If I could see you—if I could *see* you—I'd know the answer."

Antoinette went cold all over at the terrible, unknowing truth of that, but she managed to say calmly, "Please just accept the fact. I can't marry you."

"All right—I accept it. But tell me why."

"Because I'm married already."

She simply could not imagine from where that answer came to her, in its completeness and irrefutable strength. It was as though someone put a weapon of defence into her hand when she was almost done.

"You're—*what*?" He released her so abruptly that she almost fell away from him and she watched in fascinated despair as he passed his hands over a face that had suddenly grown bleak and older. "You're married! Why did you never tell me?"

"There was no need to. It was my affair. Until— until you spoke to me as you did just now."

"Do you live with him?" he asked harshly.

"No."

"Do you love him?"

"I can't talk to you about that. Will you please, please let me keep my private affairs to myself? I love working here. I admire you as an artist, I—like you as a person, and ask nothing more than to help you find your way back to professional life again. Can't that be enough?"

"It—has to be, doesn't it?" he said heavily. And then, after quite a long silence, "I'll go back to the house now. The sun has gone in, hasn't it?"

She bit her lip. The sun was shining still. But not, she saw, for him. There was not much brilliance about the day for her either as she gently guided him back into the house.

Nothing but the most impersonal things were said between them for the rest of that day, or the next, or the next, or the next. She was the conscientious, efficient, even devoted secretary, and he was the not too difficult, fairly reasonable employer, with the occasional mood to which an employer is entitled, particularly if he is blind and pays well.

But the golden thread of intimacy and loving understanding which had spun itself between them had snapped. Charmian St. Leger herself could have found nothing unacceptable in their behaviour to each other.

Indeed, when she made her next appearance, she must have become immediately aware of the subtle change in the atmosphere, for she was sweetly gracious to Antoinette—as to a child who was not now so naughty as she once had been.

To Lewis Freemont she was gay and tender and affectionate, though he was not encouraging, and when she explained she had been in London most of the week and asked smilingly, "Did you wonder where I was?" he replied without elaboration, "No."

The visit was not a long one, though whether from her choice or his Antoinette could not tell from the backwater of her office. All she knew was that less than half an hour later she heard her employer practising, and she knew he would not do that if Charmian St. Leger were there.

Increasingly music was becoming once more the principal thing in his life. She told herself she was thankful this should be so, that this was the way in which he would find he could live very well without her. But sometimes, as she sat in her office spinning out the diminishing amount of office work, she felt forlorn, unneeded and utterly wretched.

Then one day he said to her abruptly, "Do you practise regularly?"

"To a certain extent—yes."

"What do you mean?—'to a certain extent'?" he retorted impatiently. "You either practise regularly or you don't."

"I mean that I keep up a certain degree of facility. I don't practise as I did—would, I mean—if I were a professional."

"You never intended to be a professional, did you?" He sounded curious suddenly and she had a moment of panic.

"Of course not." She brushed that off quickly. "But why did you ask about my practising?"

"I want to see how I can tackle a concerto in the changed circumstances. It's an entirely different proposition from a solo recital. And I need someone to play the orchestral part on a second piano."

"I—don't know that I could do that." She was immediately nervous and uneasy at the thought of bringing her playing under his notice again. But he simply said rather disagreeably,

"Of course you can. I shouldn't have asked you if I hadn't known you could."

"But surely there must have been someone, much better qualified than I am, who used to work with you like that in the old days?"

"Don't be so obstructive," he countered impatiently. "If I'm going to make a hash of it I'd rather do so with you than anyone else."

"Oh—I see." The tone might be harsh, but the implication was rather touching, and she found herself agreeing to what he had suggested and even encouraging him in the idea that he might perhaps play with an orchestra again one day.

"It wasn't entirely my own inspiration," he admitted. "Oscar Warrender came to see me yesterday evening, after you had gone, and almost sold me the idea."

"Oscar Warrender did?" She could not hide her interest. "You're great friends, aren't you?"

"As far as anyone is a friend of Warrender. He's a tremendously self-sufficient creature, you know. His two real loves are his work and his wife—in that order, I believe. Well, I suppose that's all right if you're lucky enough to have both," he added, with a touch of restlessness.

"I suppose so," agreed Antoinette hastily. "You'll have to let me practise on my own first. I've never tackled a piano version of an orchestral score before."

"I'll teach you," he said. And from his tone that could have been either a promise or a threat.

From that day a new régime started. For Antoinette it was made up of artistic excitement beyond anything she had ever imagined, a great deal of personal strain, and a terrifying alternation between glowing achievement and sickening failure. For Lewis Freemont at the piano was a very different person from the man who had made love to her in the garden—or even the half mocking, half indulgent employer. He set almost impossible standards for others as well as himself.

For a solid week he took her through her part of the first movement alone, before there was any question of their working together on the two pianos. He sat beside her advising, instructing, correcting—almost willing her to do what he wanted. And, in the sheer interest of battering her into playing as he thought she could, he often lost sight of the fact that her part would merely be to supply the groundwork on which he could build his own practising.

"Play!" he shouted at her once. *"Play!* You've got it in you to make music, haven't you? And all you do is push down the keys. You drive me crazy"

"You drive me crazy too!" She was surprised to find that she too was almost shouting. *"I'm* not the soloist. I'm just the useful hack pretending to be an orchestra. And stop shouting at me anyway!"

"I'm sorry," he said stiffly.

"No—I'm sorry too!" And then suddenly she laughed at the sheer absurdity of the scene and, as the tension relaxed, she impulsively put her hand over his.

He slowly turned his hand and clasped hers, and he said, "That's the first time you've touched me since—that day."

"Oh, no! Surely not?" There was a note of shocked protest in her voice.

"Oh, yes," he assured her wryly. "And I haven't heard you smile—until you laughed just now."

"I smiled quite often," she insisted.

"Not so that I could hear you," he said simply, and she bit her lip.

"I'm sorry—I'm sorry—" She stroked the hand she was holding, and the warm, firm pressure of her fingers said more than she could say in words. "If only—"

"I know—I know," he interrupted her with a quick sigh. "I'm not trying to force your hand in any way, but—do things have to be so horribly different from what they were, Toni?"

"I didn't mean them to be. It was only that—that—"

"Is this a music lesson that I'm interrupting?" enquired a bright, sweet voice from the doorway. And as Lewis Freemont said, "Damn," quite audibly and Antoinette snatched her hand away, Charmian St. Leger came in from the garden, a smile on her lips and her violet-blue eyes like stones.

"Charmian, I've asked you before not to come in unannounced! I'm past the days of easy convalescence now, and I can't have work interrupted at any—"

"But, darling Lewis, it didn't look at all like that." There was amused protest and a touch of real concern

121

in her voice. "You know I wouldn't take liberties for the world. Any more than Miss Burney would, I'm sure," she added, and she gave Antoinette a spine-chilling glance of dislike and warning.

"I don't know what you're talking about." Lewis Freemont sounded irritated.

"But she does," retorted Mrs. St. Leger softly. "She knows exactly what I'm talking about, don't you, Miss Burney?—And you mustn't be so cross, Lewis, just because you don't quite follow. All women have their little secrets, don't they, Miss Burney?"

"What *is* this, for heaven's sake?" He turned his head restlessly so that his sightless glance moved from his unwelcome visitor to where he knew his secretary was sitting. "What's this nonsense about a secret?"

"Nothing," said Antoinette between dry lips. At which the other woman laughed and said almost gaily,

"It's just something we nearly told you some time ago, Lewis. And then we thought perhaps it wasn't the right time—that things might sort themselves out without our worrying you. But perhaps—I don't know—"

She paused provocatively and those hard, beautiful eyes gazed speculatively at Antoinette. And not all her pride or resolution could keep Antoinette from giving an imploring glance in return.

"Well, we'll see—" The other woman turned away, warning in every line of her. "I'm sorry I came at the wrong moment, Lewis dear. And if I'm really in the way, I'll go?"

The note of query in her voice invited him to protest, but he remained brutally silent. And after a moment she sighed slightly, touched him gently on the arm and said, "Good-bye, my dear. I'm afraid I'm in disgrace."

"No, of course not."

"Then may I phone this evening and find out when I *can* come without being a nuisance?"

"Yes, certainly." His tone was not gracious, and Antoinette kept her eyes down lest Mrs. St. Leger should imagine that she detected some glance of triumph or satisfaction and allow her chagrin and spite to get the better of her.

She went then, but at a slow, graceful pace suggesting the temporary retreat of someone who knew the strength of her position too well to doubt her triumphant comeback. And in silence Antoinette watched her go. For a whole long minute the two left behind said nothing. Then when he finally spoke his voice was abrupt and uneasy.

"What was she talking about, Toni? What did she mean by all that stuff about not telling me something because it might worry me?"

"I have no idea," said Antoinette coolly, and she was herself astonished at her own composure.

"*Truly* no idea?" He gazed at her with those blank, yet strangely attractive eyes, as though by sheer willpower he would somehow pierce the terrible barrier between him and her. "You wouldn't actually lie to me, would you?—not even if you thought it was for my own good."

"No," said Antoinette, and wondered a little why no affronted Power struck her down. But what could she do, once she had committed herself to this devious path? "I think," she went on, and this time she spoke the exact truth, "that Mrs. St. Leger wanted to make some sort of trouble between us."

"Yes, of course." He brushed that off as absurdly self-evident. Then after a moment he added, "To-morrow I shall start making arrangements to move back to my London flat."

"Because of Mrs. St. Leger?" Antoinette enquired incredulously.

"No, of course not." He contemptuously dismissed the idea of being forced into any course of action he had not chosen himself. "She's only one of the minor considerations." Antoinette was human enough to wish Charmian St. Leger could have heard that. "It's a decision I've been coming to for a variety of reasons, most of them concerned with the sheer convenience of being in the centre of the musical world again if I am to contemplate a real comeback. One can't expect people like Everleigh—or, indeed, Warrender—to come down here every time we want to discuss anything. In any case, it will be easier for you to work in London, won't it?"

"I suppose so." But there was affectionate regret in her tone and before she could stop herself she added, "Though I love Pallin."

"But not the master of Pallin?"

The question was so unexpected that she caught her breath. But the terror of Charmian St. Leger's warning was raw and recent, and her voice was almost cold as she said,

"I'm afraid not. And please, please don't ask me that question again."

"I won't," he promised grimly, "ever."

The move to London was effected much more speed-ily and easily than Antoinette had expected. Lewis Freemont's handsome studio flat, overlooking St. James's Park, was in the same block as those of Oscar Warrender and one or two other distinguished musi-cians, and it was obvious that here he would have no lack of congenial company. Now that he had emerged from the phase in which he thought he wanted to cut himself off from his old life, nothing could have been better for him, Antoinette saw, than this move to town.

His admirable housekeeper and a couple of the staff from Pallin Manor came too, including Brenda, who confided to Antoinette with regret that "she expected poor Mrs. St. Leger would be very sad at the change."

"I daresay she will," agreed Antoinette, unable to infuse any excessive regret into *her* tone. "But I suppose she comes to town fairly often."

"Oh, yes! Yes, indeed," Brenda asserted happily. "And she'll come even more often now, I expect," she added naïvely.

Antoinette expected so too, with a chill sense of resignation. But there was a wonderful sense of freedom, an indefinable lifting of her spirits, now that at least she was not in almost daily contact with her enemy.

She was not so simple as to suppose that a matter of a few miles would put Charmian St. Leger off her course, or that she was any less menacing because she was no longer more or less on the doorstep. But it is humanly impossible to be as frightened by a distant danger as by an ever-present one, and during those first few weeks in London Antoinette was almost happy.

The flood of letters about her employer's accident and withdrawal from the musical world had now dropped to a trickle, and there was nothing like enough secretarial work to keep her occupied. Consequently, she found herself more and more concerned with the professional side of his life. Not only was she invaluable to him for a great deal of his daily practising. She quite naturally became involved in the discussions with Gordon Everleigh about future plans. She also for the first time met Oscar Warrender.

The famous conductor was then at the height of his career. Autocratic, dynamic, loathed by some, adored by others and almost equally indifferent to both, he was probably the strongest single force in the musical field. He had even successfully challenged the engineering gods of the recording world.

"I am a music-maker, not a computer," he was reported to have said, "and I will not have knobs turned, tapes spliced, or orchestras juggled with in the cause of mechanical perfection and artistic death. Take it or leave it."

They took it, of course. No one could afford to leave Oscar Warrender. And the first time Antoinette saw him at close quarters she knew why.

There is a quality about some people—a very few—which is unique and inexplicable. They are the natural centre of the stage, the born leaders, the people for whom the world stands aside because they know where they are going. Such was Oscar Warrender, and Antoinette recognized the quality immediately when he came into her employer's flat one dull winter's afternoon.

There was nothing formal about his arrival. He merely came down from his own flat on the next floor, in a smoking jacket and very much off duty. He hardly noticed Antoinette's presence, it was true, but then one doesn't expect Olympus to take note of one on a first occasion. And he immediately started to outline exactly what he wanted.

It seemed that an important foreign soloist engaged for a concert in three months' time would not, after all, be available.

"He wouldn't have been my own first choice in any case," Warrender remarked, "so it doesn't matter. There are three other possibilities, and we have time to consider any or all of them. But my own inclination is to make this the opportunity for you to come before the full London public again."

"My dear fellow, I couldn't possibly make my comeback in an orchestral concert" Lewis Freemont exclaimed quickly. "I must try first in the much easier medium of a recital, so that I can assess the strain of actually getting on to a platform, dealing with a real but unseen audience, finding—"

"Yes, yes, I realize all that." Objections were summarily dismissed. "I spoke to Everleigh this morning. He can arrange a recital—two if you like—at the Corinthian in January. Less overwhelming, more intimate than the Festival Hall. I said I felt sure you would jump at the chance."

"What made you sure of that?" enquired Lewis Freemont disagreeably.

"My own good judgment of your good sense," was the unmoved reply. "It's the best possible way of doing things, and you know it. Trembling on the brink will only make the initial effort harder."

"I'm not trembling on the brink—or anywhere else, come to that," said Antoinette's employer drily. "On the whole, I accept your assessment of the position, but—"

"Excellent." The conductor was evidently used to having his assessments accepted. "And how about the orchestral concert in late February? I leave the choice of concerto to you. I'll build the rest of the programme round it if necessary."

"You don't even know how well—or ill—I can handle that much more complicated medium. To play with an orchestra, without even being able to see the conductor—"

"*I* shall be the conductor, don't forget." There was nothing specially arrogant about that, only a statement of fact. "There is a sort of musical radar between us, I think. But we should have to try it out, of course. I'll get Farrell down here some time during the next few days. He can play the orchestral part on a second piano and—"

"You don't have to do that," said Lewis Freemont slowly. "Toni—Miss Burney—will do that. Now."

"Miss Burney?" Oscar Warrender looked round, took in the fact that Miss Burney was not just part of the furniture and said, "Good afternoon."

"Good afternoon," said Antoinette demurely.

"Can you play the piano transcription of the orchestral score?"

"Yes, I think so, Mr. Warrender. I've been doing so for quite a while when Mr. Freemont wants to practise."

"You don't say?" The conductor looked suddenly amused. "Then we'll try it now. What are you playing, by the way?"

"The Beethoven Third," said Lewis Freemont, and held out his hand to Antoinette, who immediately came forward and led him to one of the pianos at the end of the long studio. Then, trembling a little, with mingled excitement and nervousness, she went to the other piano herself.

Oscar Warrender leaned over and picked up a ruler that was lying on the writing desk nearby and took up his stand where she could see him and he could watch Lewis Freemont's every movement and expression.

"All right," he said, and they started.

It was both exhilarating and terrifying. Antoinette, of course, had never before played under the guidance of someone who could convey by a single movement of an eloquent left hand the exact quality of tone and expression he required, and she felt a little like someone who started out on a walk and then found herself flying.

On his side, Warrender naturally concentrated on Lewis Freemont, once he had found that Antoinette was reliable and intelligent. Inevitably, the usual roles of conductor and soloist were to a certain extent reversed. Since the pianist could not visually follow the lead of his conductor, the conductor had for once to do a certain amount of following himself. Which must, Antoinette thought passingly, be a novelty for Oscar Warrender!

But there was indeed some sort of subtle line of communication between the two men, a oneness of purpose, not dependent on sight and visual direction. And except for one moment of slight confusion, almost instantaneously righted, they went through the whole of the first movement triumphantly.

"Are you going to tell me *now* that you're in doubt about tackling an orchestral concert?" enquired Oscar Warrender on a note of exultant satisfaction.

"No, I think you're right. It could be done." There was a streak of excited colour in Lewis Freemont's cheeks, and the very slightest tremor in his voice. Possibly that was not lost on the conductor. At any rate, as though giving the other man time to recover, he turned to Antoinette and said good-humouredly,

"You're extremely good. Why haven't I heard of you before? That particular gift of representing orchestral tone on a piano is very rare."

"Oh, I don't really belong to the musical world!" Antoinette assured him hastily. But the once-ambitious pianist within her rose joyously to the surface for the first time in a year. "I'm really Mr. Freemont's secretary. I happen to play the piano as well."

"Nonsense," said the conductor. "Where were you trained?"

It was indescribably pleasant to be asked—and asked by such an authority as Oscar Warrender—about one's musical background, and Antoinette smiled as she said, "I was trained at St. Cecilia's."

"Were you indeed? I must ask my friend Sir Horace Keen about you," remarked the conductor graciously.

"Oh—no" Suddenly Antoinette saw the gulf open in front of her. And at the same moment her employer said curiously,

"You never told *me* you trained at St. Cecilia's."

CHAPTER SIX

TO Antoinette it seemed that the whole tottering edifice of her deception was about to collapse around her. She gave a quick, desperate glance from her sightless employer to the all-too-well sighted Oscar Warrender. And then, with an effort she would not have believed within her powers, she replied with the boldness of sheer simplicity,

"Surely I mentioned St. Cecilia's when you were corresponding with Sir Horace about—" her voice shook for a moment—"about that girl? I'm sure I did. You were too much occupied with the—the other matter to take much notice of what I said, I expect."

"I should have noticed *that*," retorted Lewis Freemont with a touch of irritation. "I never thought of your being at St. Cecilia's. Otherwise I should have asked for your co-operation in tracing the girl."

"What girl?" put in Oscar Warrender curiously.

"The girl who blinded me," replied Lewis Freemont almost brutally, and Antoinette winced perceptibly.

"The girl who—? What are you talking about?" exclaimed the conductor. "It was a car accident"

"Not quite simply a car accident. There was more to it than that." Lewis Freemont stirred impatiently and, by accident or intention, his hand struck a jangling discord on the piano.

The other man started to say something, but he interrupted almost harshly, "It's a long story. It doesn't matter now. But it starts with someone I very much wanted to trace. She was a student at St. Cecilia's. I should have thought Toni would have been only too eager to use her knowledge of the place to help me."

He turned his sightless eyes on Antoinette and there were little lines of tension at their corners, as though, useless though it might be, he still could not help straining to *see* her in that moment.

"I'm sorry." To her own astonishment her voice was still miraculously calm. "The girl must have been long after my time. I just never thought of myself as having any special knowledge that might help."

"Anyway, it doesn't matter." That was Oscar Warrender, with the almost naïve arrogance of the single-minded artist. "What does matter is that you have proved conclusively that you can tackle not only a recital but an orchestral concert too, within the measurable future."

"Yes, that's true." The strain left Lewis Freemont's face and he smiled slightly. But Antoinette noticed with anxious tenderness that he looked suddenly tired, and she went and took him by the arm and led him back to his chair.

The conductor watched with close attention and a touch of approval. And it was obvious that he too was aware that a certain amount of reaction had set in.

"Rest completely now," he said, with an air of friendly authority. "We can discuss everything tomorrow." And then to Antoinette, who had made an eager movement—"No, it's all right. I'll see myself out."

Ordinarily people obeyed Oscar Warrender's slightest order or suggestion, and he went without even looking behind him. But Antoinette followed him into the hall, closed the door behind her and, as he reached the front door said, in a low but almost peremptory voice, "Mr. Warrender—"

The conductor turned in surprise, perhaps at her tone, perhaps at merely finding her there.

"Please—" she came quite close to him—"don't discuss me with Sir Horace. I'd—much rather that you didn't."

"Why?"

"Isn't it enough that I ask you not to discuss me with someone?"

"No," said Oscar Warrender, who seldom wasted words.

"But this is something which concerns *me*. I can't be of the slightest interest to you and—"

"On the contrary," the conductor interrupted her, "you interest me profoundly. You have a rare gift which most people would be only too eager to thrust under my notice, and yet you try to play it down. You have an air of disarming candour, and yet you apparently concealed from Lewis Freemont something he thinks singularly important. And now you invest a simple query with an air of mystery, and try to do what few people would be bold enough to contemplate—to divert me from a personal course of action. You have left out nothing that was needed to excite my curosity."

Antoinette stared at him in such blank dismay that, after a moment, he laughed not unkindly and said,

"Come, you'd better tell me what the mystery is."

"I—can't." Then she added mechanically, "There is no mystery."

He did not bother even to accord that an answer, evidently finding it absurd. Instead he enquired,

"Who is this girl Freemont spoke of in such odd terms? *Was* there a girl who had something to do with his accident?"

"He—believes so," said Antoinette with an effort. "He failed her in an examination at St. Cecilia's, and he has some fixed idea that she followed him around, wishing him ill, and that she—she made him crash his car."

"Made him crash his car?" Oscar Warrender repeated the words incredulously. "Do you mean—you *can't* mean—that he has some superstitious feeling about her? Freemont just isn't that kind."

"Not exactly—no. He says she was—there when the accident occurred. That she stood in the road and that in order to avoid her he had to crash the car."

"And *was* she there?" Those cold, penetrating eyes were suddenly full upon her.

"How should I know?"

"I—wondered," said the conductor. "Couldn't he remember the name of the girl he failed? It should be easy enough for the staff at St. Cecilia's to supply a list of the unsuccessful candidates on that occasion."

"They did," replied Antoinette stonily. "He couldn't recognize any of the names when the list was read out to him."

"Who read the list?" was the odd thing Oscar Warrender asked.

"I did," said Antoinette. And after a long moment, the conductor said, "I see."

Like many people before her, Antoinette suddenly had the curious impression that it was virtually impossible to pull the wool over Oscar Warrender's eyes.

She didn't even try any more. She simply looked straight at him and said,

"Are you going to speak to Sir Horace about me?"

"No," said the conductor, and turned away. But she caught him by the arm in her eagerness and exclaimed,

"Are you really not going to say anything about— this?"

Oscar Warrender looked down at her and for a moment she wondered why she had thought his glance was cold.

"I'm a conductor, my dear," he said drily, "Not a self-appointed judge."

Then he went out of the flat, closing the door behind him, and she was left staring at the door until her employer called,

"Toni, where are you?"

"I'm coming." A sudden overwhelming wave of relief engulfed her, so that she felt incredibly light-hearted—almost light-headed. That Oscar Warrender should have guessed the truth and found it unnecessary to do a thing about it was in such intoxicating contrast to the emotional blackmail of Chairmian St. Leger or, indeed, her employer's bitter intensity of feeling, that for the first time in months Antoinette dared to draw a slight breath of hope, and to question her own sense of proportion about the whole situation.

The respite was only momentary, of course, and was succeeded by the familiar sensation of remorse and anxiety. But that one moment of truth was indescribably strengthening and comforting. It even made her able to go in to her employer and say lightly,

"I'm really terribly sorry if I seemed in any way secretive about my musical training. It never occurred to me that I hadn't mentioned St. Cecilia's in connection with myself. I suppose it was partly that I couldn't imagine *my* musical training could be in any way interesting to anyone so professional and distinguished as yourself."

"Don't fish for compliments," he said, but he smiled. "If Oscar Warrender thought your gifts merited enquiry you needn't underrate yourself ever again. He's brutal to any amateur who masquerades as the real thing. But he was genuinely impressed by you."

"Yes, he was, wasn't he?" She managed to make that sound gay and gratified. "But most of all he was impressed by the way you proved able to play a concerto without actually seeing him conduct."

"It was largely his skill too," Lewis Freemont said quickly.

"Yes, of course. It was miraculous teamwork. But you showed between you that *it can be done*. Even now I think none of us quite realizes what that means. You're on the way back—*really* on the way back to full professional life again Oh, I'm so glad, so—so thankful"

He laughed and held out his hand to her, as though both charmed and moved by her complete identification of herself with his interests.

"Dear Toni" he said. And then more lightly, "To whom are you thankful? To Warrender for stampeding me into doing this?"

"A little to Mr. Warrender—yes, of course. But mostly to God, I think," said Antoinette seriously. "It's so wonderful to have—a second chance," she added half to herself.

"A second chance?" He sounded half puzzled, half amused. "You mean this is my second chance to create a career?"

"Why, yes," she said quickly. "Yes, of course that's what I meant."

She knew she sounded confused and she saw he was not entirely satisfied. But after a moment he laughed and remarked affectionately,

"You're an odd child! Just as Charmian said last night."

"Ch-Charmian?" stammered Antoinette, feeling the short hairs lift at the nape of her neck. "Did Mrs. St. Leger come to see you here last night, then?"

"No, she telephoned—to know if she might come to see me this afternoon."

"And—and did you say she could?" It was hard even to formulate the words.

"No," was the cool reply. "I've had enough of Charmian for the time being. She bores me. I told her that I have to give all my time and energy to my work until I've made a comeback—which is ture—and that I shall be having virtually no visitors for the time being."

"Did she accept that?" enquired Antoinette tremulously.

"She had to,". he said carelessly.

"But then," Antoinette prompted him, "she—she spoke about me?"

"Yes. For some reason best known to herself"—he smiled scornfully—"she seemed to think it was necessary for her to explain you to me in some way. She started to say that I didn't really know you; that you were—as I quoted just now—an odd girl. But I stopped her there, being unwilling to hear her views, and told her that if she really had anything to tell me about you she had better send it to me in writing."

"In *writing*?" Antoinette gave a scared little laugh. "But she would know that I should have to read it to you."

"Of course. That's why I said it. I thought it was a rather neat way of rebuking her," he added, with such satisfaction that Antoinette had the greatest difficulty in keeping herself from embracing him.

"Then you mean we shan't be seeing much of her for quite a while?"

"We shan't be seeing *anything* of her for quite a while," he corrected drily. "Nor, I think, will she be troubling us with letters."

For the second time that afternoon Antoinette drew a cautious, trembling breath of relief. It was the most extraordinary, unhoped-for cloak of protection. And it was he who had almost carelessly flung it round her. She could hardly believe it even now. But she blinked her lashes and swallowed a lump in her throat and tried not to let her voice sound too liltingly happy as she said sedately,

"I'm glad. I don't think she's very good for you."

He seemed to find that inordinately funny. Certainly he laughed more heartily than was usual with him and replied, "I don't know that she's all that good for you either. You sound curiously contented, and as though you're smiling in a rather relieved sort of way. Are you?"

"Yes," said Antoinette. And then, before he could comment further on that, she added quickly, "Goodness, how late it is. I must go, or Rosamund will be wondering where on earth I am."

"My apologies to her," he retorted amusedly. "And tell her I realize that I have far more than my fair share of your time and attention."

"She wouldn't mind that," Antoinette assured him with a smile. And—perhaps because Charmian St. Leger no longer presented an immediate danger—she touched his hand lightly but affectionately in a gesture of leavetaking before she went.

It was true enough that Rosamund would not think of querying her comings and goings these days. She had become used to the fasc that Antoinette's working hours were extraordinarily elastic, and if she sometimes thought her friend was imposed upon, she was not prepared to argue over an arrangement which obviously gave Antoinette herself such satisfaction.

That evening, however, there was something so radiant about Antoinette that Rosamund exclaimed,

"Anyone can tell when it's been a good day for you! You have the most expressive face and I don't believe you can hide anything you're thinking."

"Oh, I don't know—" murmured Antoinette, secretly staggered that anyone who knew her so well as Rosamund could feel like that. "It *was* a rather special day, to tell the truth." And she proceeded to give a full account of the scene with Oscar Warrender, omitting only the reference to Sir Horace Keen and St. Cecilia's.

"Then Warrender was really impressed with you? That means quite something in the musical world, doesn't it?"

"I should say so! His approval is about the handsomest accolade one can receive." Antoinette's professional pride and joy were uppermost for the moment. "He almost made me wonder—"

She stopped, and Rosamund finished the sentence for her.

"You wondered if you might, after all, make a musical career for yourself?" she suggested.

"Well—" Antoinette laughed, but her eyes were sparkling with excitement and an inner fire which had not been there since Lewis Freemont uttered his first devastating verdict on her. "It's too early to say yet," she added quickly. "The important thing at the moment is to get Lewis Freemont back before the public."

"And he's starting with a recital at the Corinthian in January?"

"Almost certainly. Perhaps two. There'll be weeks of concentrated work and preparation first."

"Which will require everything you've got, I suppose," retorted Rosamund a trifle protestingly.

"I shan't have any part in recital preparations It's only when he requires me for orchestral practice that I—"

"I wasn't thinking of the actual playing," interrupted Rosamund thoughtfully. "It's in the personal way that you mean so much, isn't it? You're more or less his support and inspiration in all this effort, aren't you?"

"Oh, Rosamund, don't exaggerate!" The idea was half shocking, half entrancing. "I only do what I can to encourage him, bolster his courage, counteract the occassional mood of depression—that sort of thing."

"That's what I meant. The simple fact is that he would never have got as far as this without you, would he?"

140

"Someone else might just as easily have supplied the right impetus," Antoinette asserted.

"No, I don't think so." Rosamund shook her head. "It had to be *you*. There's a curious, subtle mixture of elements in a situation of this sort, and you supplied just what was needed. You had the musical skill and understanding required, but you had the right human approach too. The fact that you'd both adored him and nearly hated him made you peculiarly aware of his reactions. You were tuned in to him emotionally, if you see what I mean."

"What makes you think I adored him?" was all Antoinette said.

"Oh, my dear! Of course you adored him before that unfortunate business of the exam. You didn't yearn over him and write him fan letters, because it doesn't take you that way. But you used to talk as though he was God's gift to every piano student and enthusiast."

Antoinette laughed rather crossly.

"It all seems so long ago," she said musingly.

"It *is* quite long ago—even in time," Rosamund replied. "It's probably even longer ago in personal development. I'm not suggesting you adore him now, of course."

"No," said Antoinette, and changed the subject.

But she thought a great deal about Rosamund's remarks in the following weeks. She tried not to exaggerate the degree of her importance to the man she loved. It was all of no use anyway. But she could not help knowing that in every way he drew strength and support from her.

He talked over every item of his programme with her, practised uninhibitedly in front of her, asked for

141

her comments, argued with her over her opinions, and whenever it came to a purely physical difficulty, like the sheer problem of getting on and off the platform with the least element of fuss, he discussed every detail with her.

At first he tried to insist that she should be the one to lead him on to the platform, but she rejected that idea out of hand.

"First, I should be nervous and might communicate my nervousness to you," she told him. "And secondly it should be another man who does it, someone unconnected with you—impersonal, tactful and self-effacing. Anything else would distract the attention of the audience from the real business of the occasion."

He considered that for a moment in silence. Then he said,

"You mean that if a lovely girl brings me on to the platform it will inevitably start some sort of romantic speculation?"

"Something like that. Though I'm not specially lovely," she added, in the interests of strict accuracy. "I'm reasonably personable, that's all. But a woman helping a man in *any* kind of difficulty always tends to start speculation of a kind."

"You don't say?" He seemed amused by this theory. But he added, "Perhaps you're right. You're right about so many things, Toni. How did you manage to make a mess of your own life?"

"Wh-what do you mean?" She was so shaken that she could not keep her voice entirely steady.

"Well, I can't help knowing that everything must have gone wrong for you at some point or another. Otherwise, why are you and your husband apart?"

"My husband?" She had almost forgotten the mythical creature she had invented as a barrier between them in her moment of most acute danger. But she recovered herself sufficiently to say, "We did agree not to discuss that subject, didn't we?"

"Oh, very well." He gave a discontented little shrug. "Though why it should all be so sacrosanct I don't know. Sometimes I don't altogether believe in him."

She nearly said she didn't either. But instead she changed the subject to something purely musical, and the moment of danger passed.

On the whole, there were fewer occasions for agitation nowadays. The menace of Charmian St. Leger was at least temporarily removed. Her employer himself seemed satisfied to accept the unsentimental though warm relationship she had established between them. And in any case, the primary interest of both of them was the tremendous challenge presented by his return to the concert platform.

"Remember," Gordon Everleigh said to her once, "that a comeback is twice as nerve-racking as a debut. You aren't borne up by the wild elation of having your chance at last; you know all the dozens of pitfalls that experience has shown you; and you are aware that there are plenty of sensation-mongering vultures ready to insist that you aren't so good as you once were."

Antoinette thought it sounded pretty grim. She wondered if her employer sometimes woke in the night in a cold sweat of apprehension. She did if he didn't. And when the evening of the first recital finally came, she could not have been more nervous if she had been making her own debut.

With every grain of self-discipline she had, however, she concealed the fact, for only one person was entitled to be nervous that evening—and he seemed singularly calm.

"Do you want me backstage or in the audience?" she asked him.

"Backstage, of course. How do you suppose I can go on if you're not there with me?" was the simple retort. And in that moment she reproached herself for refusing to go on to the platform with him.

At least she sat beside him in the car on the way to the hall, and held his arm as he went in at the stage door. They had already practised the business of entering the hall, and she was glad of it now, for a sympathetic little crowd of admirers were there to clap and call good wishes, and she knew he would have hated to seem less than self-possessed and in command of the situation.

"That went well," she assured him as they reached the dressing-room, which was level with the platform at the Corinthian and singularly easy of access. The man who was to lead him on-stage was already there— an immensely experienced and unshakably confident assistant who had turned the pages for countless performers in his time and had a positive genius for effacing himself when necessary.

"A full house, needless to say, Mr. Freemont," he observed. "Quite a lot of your old friends there, I should say."

"And an almost equal number of old enemies, I expect," replied Lewis Freemont, but with what Antoinette secretly called his fighting smile.

"Well, one wouldn't want to be without them," was the very knowledgeable reply. "They sometimes spur us to greater efforts than our friends, don't they?"

"Undoubtedly," was the dry retort. "Just one thing, though. I prefer not to have anyone round here afterwards, except the few on the list Miss Burney will give you. I still find it confusing to deal with a number of people I can't see."

"Of course, sir. Don't worry."

The man took the list—which did not include the name of Mrs. St. Leger—and went away to make the necessary arrangements. Then Gordon Everleigh came in briefly to wish Lewis Freemont luck. And when he had gone Antoinette and her employer were alone.

During the last few minutes before he went on, he sat fingering his "blind" watch, from which he could tell the time by touch. She said nothing to him. Only, just before the man came back to lead him on to the platform, she kissed his cheek and said,

"That's for luck—and with the certainty that it's going to be all right."

"Thank you," he replied, but almost absently. And she saw suddenly that even she had almost dropped from his consciousness. He was no longer the easily accessible person. He was the dedicated professional going out to face one of the biggest challenges of his life.

As she watched him go there were tears in her eyes. Not because she meant little to him at that moment, but tears of thankfulness for the discovery that as an artist he was wholly himself again.

She stood near the door leading to the platform so that—curiously like him—she could hear though not see what was happening. She heard the warmth, the almost emotional quality, of the applause which greeted his appearance, and she knew by the sudden cessation of the clapping the exact moment when he sat down at the piano. She could also judge from the tense quality of the silence that she was not the only one strung up to a high pitch of anxious excitement.

And then he began to play. He started with something of deceptive simplicity and shimmering beauty, one of the deadly pitfalls for the slick performer with shallow understanding. And, as she stood there, her hands pressed to her cheeks in the intensity of her feeling, Antoinette felt a glorious, almost loving calm steal over her. This was beauty and truth as conceived by the mind and heart of a genius, and Lewis Freemont could still convey it to those who were listening with a power of interpretation that very few could rival.

Possibly over the months Antoinette had gained a deeper, clearer understanding of his particular power of expression. Possibly the fires through which he had passed had given a new dimension to his work. At any rate, one thing was certain—the Lewis Freemont who had emerged from months of ordeal was, if anything, an even finer artist than before.

The applause which greeted each work, and culminated in a tremendous ovation at the end of the evening, was of a quality there was no doubting. Sentiment and sympathy for his misfortune would have assured him a friendly reaction without question. But the acclaim he received at the end was for his playing and his playing alone.

And he carried off the whole occasion with a coolness —even a sort of dash—that half amused and half charmed Antoinette. Once he had got over the first slight hesitancy about coming on to or off the platform, there was no sign of any difficulty. It was hard to believe that he could not see the audience for whom he bowed, with that characteristic, faintly mocking little smile.

When he came off for the last time, however, and Antoinette took his hand, she saw that he was completely exhausted.

"You shouldn't have given them that last encore," she protested gently. "You've tired yourself."

"I would have given it to them in other days," was his simple reply. "I wanted them to have no less to-night. But—yes, I'm rather done now. We'll go home as soon as possible. Cut things short, Toni."

So with all the tact she possessed—and with the able assistance of Gordon Everleigh—she cut the congratulatory visits and speeches short, and got him away from the hall by a side-exit and home to the flat.

But nothing—no exhaustion or nervous reaction— could dim the lustre of that triumphant evening. And the next morning's papers confirmed in every detail the verdict of the audience on the previous evening.

Like most successful artists, Lewis Freemont was essentially tough and immensely resilient. He recovered rapidly, went on to repeat the triumph at his second recital, and then settled down to prepare for the final and much stiffer challenge of the orchestral concert under Oscar Warrender.

From a working point of view Antoinette was essential to him in this. But from a personal standpoint he was less and less dependent upon her. She no longer needed to bolster his confidence nor insist that he would surely return to a full career. He knew that now. The lost, bitter, desperate man who had once glimpsed hope only through her eyes was indefinably changing back to the authoritative, secure artist he had been at the height of his career.

She would not have had it otherwise. All she had ever asked was that she should be allowed to help him back to his professional career and then, her debt paid as far as was humanly possible, fade into the background of his life. But she would have been less than human if she had not sometimes thought longingly of the days when she had been his essential support and comfort—when he had looked to her for almost everything and owned to missing her desperately when she was not there.

But at least she was still an essential part of his hours of practising. And when at last the day of the final rehearsal, with the actual orchestra, came she accompanied him to the hall satisfied in the knowledge that she was largely responsible for the security on which everything rested.

At the end of the rehearsal, when even the members of the orchestra had laid down their instruments and applauded, Oscar Warrender unexpectedly called Antoinette on to the platform and said,

"Gentlemen, here is someone I think we might also applaud. Without her admirable preliminary work I hardly think this performance would have been possible. Am I right, Freemont?"

"Entirely right!" He turned and held out his hand not quite in the direction where Antoinette was standing. And she came quickly and took the outstretched hand, aware that the clasp of those thin, strong fingers expressed more gratitude than any words.

Colouring a little, she bowed shyly as the orchestra accorded her amused but sincere applause. And then Oscar Warrender came down from the podium and said,

"Now go home, both of you, and take things quietly. Tomorrow morning, if you like, have a final run-through of the Haydn, but leave the Beethoven alone. There is absolutely nothing to add to it. Then leave the rest to me."

It was impossible not to accept the reassurance of such calm confidence, and Antoinette was aware of a relaxing of tension in her employer as well as herself.

On the way home in the car she did not bother him with casual conversation. It was he who finally said, "It went better than I dared to hope."

"It was practically perfect," she replied. "But I expected it after the standard of those two recitals."

"Co-ordinating with other performers is an entirely different matter," he returned, with a touch of irritation which told her his nerves were not entirely under control. "It means calling on the very last ounce of concentration—and then even something beyond that—a sort of sixth sense which one's never exercised before. Terrifying, and yet incredibly exhilarating if one can bring it off."

"You'll bring it off," she assured him calmly.

"We'll see," he retorted disagreeably. But she thought he was glad of her confident reassurance.

Nothing, of course, could make the next day anything but difficult and he was in quite a shocking temper during most of the morning. She told herself this was the prerogative of anyone under great nerve-strain and remained unshakably calm and good-tempered, which earned her no more, however, than an irritable, "Do you have to be so insufferably sweet and spineless?"

"No, not really. Were you spoiling for a fight?"

There was a moment of astonished silence. Then he laughed suddenly and asked, "Is that a smile that I hear in your voice?"

"Yes, of course. You're being rather funny, you know."

He drew a long, rather odd sigh of something like relief at that and simply said, "I'm glad you're here. You'll be backstage all the time tonight, won't you?"

"Of course," she assured him. And that was all that was said.

During the afternoon she went home, leaving him to rest completely. She too tried to rest. But after she had lain on her bed for ten minutes she could lie there no longer, and she got up and went out and walked about the streets until it was time to come home and change.

Her dress was a new one of a specially becoming sea green, and as she looked at herself in the mirror it occurred to her for the first time that she wished he could see her. Not so that he would recognize her, of course, as the girl who had spoiled his life, but just so that he could know that she really looked rather nice sometimes.

When she arrived at his flat he was ready and amazingly calm, and on the way to the hall he actually talked quite cheerfully. It was she who found the greatest difficulty in making coherent conversation, and she was thankful when they arrived and the reassuring presence of Oscar Warrender made any further efforts of hers superfluous.

The programme opened with one of the Beethoven Overtures, and even in the dressing-room Antoinette could hear something of the characteristic sweep and drive of Warrender's direction. But she was in no mood for assessing any finer points at the moment, and it seemed to her that all too soon the applause for the first item had ended and Oscar Warrender came back into the dressing-room and said pleasantly and in an unhurried way, "Whenever you are ready—?"

"I'm ready."

This time there was no question of kissing her employer or even wishing him luck. Neither of the men seemed even aware that she was there. She could only watch them go, Lewis Freemont with his hand lightly on the conductor's arm, and then stand there praying confusedly that everything would be all right.

Her degree of anxiety was so much more intense than at either of the recitals that she did not dare even to go near the stage. She had the curious impression that she might bring disaster to him again by the sheer force of her nervousness. Instead, she walked quietly up and down the dressing-room, while the familiar strains of the Haydn Concerto reached her faintly. But how it was going or if she had reason to fear or exult she simply did not know—until a great roar of sound greeted the triumphant finale.

She opened the door then and the waves of clapping and cheering seemed to sweep in like a living force. She wanted to go to him, but even then she could not. She just stood there until, through the open doorway, she saw him coming down the passage, his hand again on the arm of the conductor.

"Toni," he exclaimed eagerly, "where are you?"

"I'm here." She started forward at last and, incredibly, he left hold of Warrender and stepped forward alone in his eagerness.

"Be careful," she cried, but a second too late. For, misjudging the direction of her voice by a fraction, he collided with the side of the door, striking his head so violently that he gasped, staggered back and would have fallen if Oscar Warrender's powerful hand had not upheld him.

Characteristically, the conductor showed nothing of the dismay he must have felt, and without so much as an exclamation, he guided his half stunned friend to the nearest chair and said, almost conversationally,

"Lie back and keep quite quiet. And don't worry about anything. We have the whole interval for your recovery—or to make new plans if necessary." And then to the silent, appalled Antoinette—"Stay near him, Miss Burney. I'll get a doctor."

She nodded wordlessly and moved to her employer's side as the conductor went quickly out of the room.

Lewis Freemont had closed his eyes by now and his face looked very pale, except for a mark that was slowly darkening on the side of his forehead.

"Toni—" he said uncertainly once, and she took his hand and held it firmly, as though by the strength of her grip she would force him to retain consciousness.

"All right, I'm here."

He moved his head impatiently and opened his eyes then. But then he frowned as though in sudden pain

and, to her dismay, he cried her name aloud again—
"Toni!"

"Darling—" The loving term escaped her before
she could control her agitation. And then she stopped
as he made a strange groping movement of his hand
and gathered a fold of her dress in his fingers.

"What is it?" she exclaimed, half frightened. "What
is it?"

"You're wearing a light dress," he cried in a hoarse,
almost unrecognizable voice. "A blue dress—no, a
green one."

"Why—why, yes. How do you know?" Then her
voice died in her throat.

"Because I can see it. God in heaven! I can see it.
Not very clearly—but *I can see it*."

CHAPTER SEVEN

TO Antoinette the next ten minutes were never entirely clear in her recollection.

She remembered Lewis Freemont holding tightly to the fold of her dress and repeating over and over again, "I can see it!" and she remembered Oscar Warrender coming back into the room accompanied by a distinguished-looking man with grey hair.

She knew that someone tried to put her aside, but that her employer still held her by her dress until she herself gently prised his fingers away. And Oscar Warrender, an unusual streak of excited colour in his cheeks, drew her to one side, leaving the doctor with Lewis Freemont.

"What happened?" the conductor asked her quietly. "What in God's name happened?"

"He was lying back with his eyes closed and—" she swallowed and made an effort to steady her voice—"then he opened them and called my name. At first I thought he was in pain. Then he grabbed hold of a fold of my dress as though—as though it were a sort of lifeline. And he said—" again she had to swallow—"he said, "You're wearing a light dress", and—and then that he could see it."

"Distinctly?"

"No. But he could see it."

"It was that sudden blow, of course. One hears of such things. One never expects them to happen to the right person," observed Warrender cynically. But there was no cynicism in the glance he directed at his friend and the doctor. "You must take him home, Miss Burney, as soon as the doctor says he can move."

"But the concert?—the rest of the concert?" Even to Antoinette, with all her deepest feelings involved, the compulsive conviction that the show must go on was uppermost.

Oddly enough it was Warrender, the ruthless professional, who said coolly, "The concert can take care of itself. Or rather, I will take care of it. We'll put in something with only the slightest delay. There are certain things that this orchestra and I can do without rehearsal and—"

"You'll do nothing of the sort!" Lewis Freemont spoke suddenly, with such authority and energy that everyone stood and looked at him in surprise, including the doctor.

"I'm all right." He ran a perfectly steady hand over his hair. "Only a slight headache physically. And emotionally I won't let myself think of what's happened until afterwards. I can see a little—just a little. The difference between light and utter darkness—" for a moment his iron self-control faltered, but he recovered again and ended, "I'm playing that concerto tonight and no one is going to stop me."

"It might be wiser—" began the doctor, but he was brushed aside.

"I'm playing tonight. Has the first bell gone?"

"Half a minute ago. I heard it," Antoinette said, in a fascinated tone.

"Then we still have a few minutes left. I'm all right, I tell you! Get me a drink, Toni. No more than a dash of whisky and some water."

155

She went over obediently and mixed the drink and brought it to him. He groped slightly for the glass, and she saw that whatever vision he had was anything but clear.

"It will be difficult," Warrender warned him. "You've learned an entirely different technique of following. You're sure—"

"Yes, I'm sure. I shall play it as a blind man. Conduct for me as though I were. I can't see any of you clearly anyway. Just that you're—there." His hand closed on Antoinette's as he spoke and she gripped his fingers warmly in return.

"There goes the second bell!" They all spoke in unison. And Lewis Freemont got to his feet.

"Give me your arm, Warrender. The full hall lighting will dazzle me, I expect."

"I still think—" began the doctor.

But no one took any notice of him. The two men went out of the room together, and Antoinette—strangely cool and calm now—followed them as far as she could without being seen from the hall.

She stood just inside the door at the side of the stage, watching with her heart in her eyes as Warrender led her employer on to the platform, the first violins making way for them as they came.

With an air of quiet assurance Lewis Freemont sat down at the piano, and even glanced round, as though testing the faint degree of vision he had regained. Oscar Warrender went to the conductor's desk and picked up his baton. There was that moment of expectant silence which precedes any eagerly awaited performance. And then the opening notes of the concerto fell on Antoinette's ears like the answer to her most ardent prayers.

She stood there throughout the three movements, hardly shifting her position once, not actually tense, but so utterly absorbed and enthralled that physical movement never occurred to her.

As a pianist herself, however unpretentious, she could not help knowing what tremendous concentration and, indeed, sheer physical strength were required for a work of this sort. And once, halfway through the exacting final movement, she wondered if he could possibly stay the course after the shock and emotional crisis of the evening. Then she glanced at the conductor and knew from his slight, watchful smile that he was certain all was well. And if Oscar Warrender was satisfied, who was she to doubt?

The ovation at the end surprised even Antoinette. Perhaps it surprised and overwhelmed him too. At any rate, he went on sitting at the piano, not even attempting to stand and acknowledge the applause, the darkening mark on his forehead very noticeable now that he was pale with exhaustion.

Then the conductor came down from his desk and went to him, and Antoinette saw her employer raise his head quickly and speak a few urgent words. Immediately, with that air of authority and almost nonchalant grace peculiar to him, Warrender turned to the audience and said,

"Mr. Freemont wants me to explain to you that there was a slight accident this evening, as you can possibly see for yourselves. But this was not entirely a disaster. So many of you showed great sympathy and support when his sight was destroyed by a blow, and he would like you—his audience—to be the first to know that the accident this evening seems to have restored some measure of sight. In these circumstances you will understand—"

But whatever it was they were to understand was drowned in a fresh outburst of clapping and cheering. It was Lewis Freemont himself who silenced them by striking a chord on the piano. And then, to the stupefaction of everyone who had ever thought him a self-sufficient, cold-hearted creature, he began to play the strong, simple familiar tune of 'Now thank we all our God'.

There are some moments so fraught with emotion that they tremble perilously on the thin line which divides sheer sentimentality from pure gold, and only the smallest detail is necessary to push them one way or the other. On this occasion it was supplied by an insignificant-looking little man who was sitting in the third row near the gangway. As though compelled by something outside himself he got to his feet. In fascinated concert one group after another followed suit until, in less than a minute, everyone in that vast audience was standing.

At the end, Lewis Freemont got up, bowed to the audience and then, taking Oscar Warrender's arm, he left the platform in absolute silence—the most deeply felt tribute that had ever been paid to him.

Almost in tears, Antoinette took him by both hands as he came up to her. Quite unselfconsciously he raised her hands to his lips and kissed them and said, "I wish I could see you properly. But that will come, I know—that will come!"

"Home now. And at once." Oscar Warrender's brisk, authoritative words broke in on this emotional moment. And it was he personally who bundled Lewis Freemont into his coat. Then, with Antoinette in close attendance, he shepherded him through the excited crowd at the stage door and drove them both home himself.

A telephone message from the Hall had already ensured that Lewis Freemont's own doctor was waiting for him, and once he had been handed over to such expert care there was really no need for either Antoinette or Oscar Warrender to remain.

"Shall I drop you anywhere?" the conductor enquired, as they stood in the hallway of the block of flats together. "I am collecting my wife from Covent Garden, but if you don't mind our stopping there first"—he glanced at his watch—"I'll drive you home afterwards."

Antoinette started to say it was not at all necessary but he interrupted her.

"Of course it isn't necessary. I know you can get a taxi just as well. But do you suppose either of us can go home in cold blood without discussing this incredible evening first?"

She laughed a little at that, rather incredulously, for she had never even suspected this almost boyish side of the formidable conductor—the side which his young wife, Anthea, always declared had finally won her.

"I'd like to come if I may," she said shyly. "I forgot —of course your wife was singing tonight, wasn't she?"

"Yes. That's why she wasn't at the concert. We usually arrange things better, but we just couldn't avoid dates clashing tonight. I don't want to keep her waiting.

She'll be nervous anyway, as someone else was conducting for her."

Even as he was explaining, he was leading Antoinette out to the waiting car. And before she could wonder if she might have learned just a little more about her employer by remaining at the flat, he was driving away. As though reading her thoughts, he observed, not without sympathy,

"You've had enough for tonight. We all have." And then, with a short laugh, "I think I was more scared when I heard him saying he could see than I was when the accident happened."

"Scared?" Antoinette was both amused and incredulous. "I don't think you are ever scared, are you?"

"No more than I can conceal," he replied goodhumouredly. "But while I thought he might just be able to recover from the effects of a physical accident, I was certain no artist could take the impact of a near-miracle and have the self-discipline to go on and do a performance just the same."

"Yes!" Antoinette's voice was warm with affection and pride. "He *has* self-discipline—more than I've ever seen in anyone else. Wasn't it terribly moving, that last scene?"

"Very," agreed the conductor briefly. "It was a risk, though. The sort that even a great artist should hesitate to take. With the reaction just a shade the other way we might have had the hysteria of a revivalist meeting on our hands."

"I don't think he thought about that," Antoinette said simply. "I think it was just that he was so immeasurably thankful for what had happened and had to say so in his own terms."

"Perhaps," replied the conductor. "Perhaps." Then, as they turned into Floral Street, he added, "Do you mind waiting here in the car for a few minutes while I go up and fetch my wife?"

"No, of course not."

So Antoinette sat alone in the darkness of Oscar Warrender's car, her glance idly on the distant group of fans round yet another stage door, her thoughts still milling round the fantastic events of the evening, from the moment when he had clutched at her dress until he came off the platform and kissed her hands and said, "I wish I could see you properly. But that will come—that will come."

All her hopes, all her fears, were implicit in those short sentences. She must wish too that full sight would be restored to him. But if it were—he would know the truth.

At that moment she saw the crowd round the stage door part respectfully, and Oscar Warrender came back towards the car, accompanied now by a smiling, fair-haired girl in a magnificent mink coat. They were talking together with the eager intimacy of people who share most things with zest and pleasure. And, concerned though she was with her own affairs, Antoinette looked with interest at the girl who was said to be not only Oscar Warrender's greatest operatic discovery but the love of his life.

There was an indescribably winning air of vitality and warmth about her and, even as she got into the car, she greeted Antoinette with the frank eagerness of an old friend.

"You're Lewis Freemont's secretary, aren't you? And you're the one who's most responsible for getting him back to his career again."

"Oh, I wouldn't say that," disclaimed Antoinette quickly.

"Oscar says so. And he never throws idle compliments around. Do you, darling?" she added as her husband came round and got into the driving seat beside her.

"Do I what?"

"Throw idle compliments around."

"Certainly not. They're the curse of the profession. But what are we talking about? Your singing?"

"Oh, no! There's only one possible topic tonight—the wonderful news about Lewis. I'm so happy for him. Tell me all about it, Miss—Burney, isn't it?" She turned to Antoinette in the back seat. "*All* about it. Oscar gave me only the barest outlines."

"There hasn't been time to do much more," said her husband drily. "Will you join us for supper, Miss Burney?" Afraid of being an intruder, Antoinette began to make polite excuses, but Anthea Warrender interrupted her.

"Please come. I'm always excited and tremendously wide awake after a performance. And I can see Oscar is beginning to feel the strain of the evening, which means that he'll get more and more uncommunicative, and I shan't ever have a first-hand account of what must have been one of the most exciting scenes that ever happened in the musical world."

So Antoinette yielded, not at all unwillingly, and went with them to a small, exclusive Italian place where they were evidently very well known. And while Oscar

162

Warrender listened and interjected no more than an occasional comment, Antoinette gave the other girl a clear and detailed account of what had happened.

"Then even now he can see only hazily?"

"Yes. But there's all the difference between that and —total eclipse," said Antoinette.

"Total eclipse! What an odd and telling phrase," exclaimed Anthea with a slight shudder.

"He used it himself, the very first day I went to him as his secretary," Antoinette said slowly. "I never forgot it. He said it came from an opera—"

"Handel's 'Samson'," put in Oscar Warrender almost automatically.

"Yes, that was it. He said he kept on recalling Samson staggering on to the stage and beginning that air. And he said that until then he hadn't had the slightest conception of what it really meant."

For a second they were all silent, savouring again the full force of the disaster which had fallen on the man they all, in varying degrees, liked or loved. Then Anthea said,

"But now that's over—over! At least he can see something again. Will that be *all* he can see, Oscar?" she turned to her husband as though he knew the answer to everything. "Or may he get back his full sight?"

The conductor shook his head slightly,

"My dear, how can I say? Only an ophthalmic expert could venture an opinion on that. The man we called out of the audience at the Festival Hall when the accident happened seemed to think it very possible. But I don't even know how well qualified he was to pronounce. Only time will tell."

"But we'll go on hoping! I *believe* in hoping, don't you, Miss Burney? We'll hope with every bit of concentration we've got," declared Anthea passionately.

"Yes," said Antoinette slowly. "We'll go on hoping."

And long after they had taken her home and she had told the dramatic story over again to Rosamund, she lay awake in bed, staring into the darkness and thinking, "I'll go on hoping."

But for what she was to hope she hardly knew.

The next morning all the newspapers of course carried a full account of the concert and the sensational announcement which had been made.

"You'd better be along at your Lewis Freemont's place in good time," observed Rosamund over breakfast. "The reporters are probably already champing round the block, trying to get statements and fresh information. I must say I feel a bit like champing myself."

"You?" said Antoinette, laughing. "You've always disclaimed the slightest interest in him."

"Oh, well—it's the element of human drama that intrigues one, even if one doesn't know or specially like him. I suppose you yourself feel desperately involved?"

"Desperately," agreed Antoinette, but so sombrely that she gave a much deeper meaning to the word than Rosamund had intended.

"Oh, come! It's not an occasion for literal desperation. After all, this *is* a happy business, isn't it?"

"Yes, of course." But Antoinette sighed involuntarily, and Rosamund looked at her curiously as she slipped on her coat and made ready to go.

"I suppose I'm to expect you when I see you?" she said, but good-humouredly.

"I should be home reasonably early," countered Antoinette. "But I can't say for sure. I don't know quite what I'll find when I—when I get to his place." And not all her self-control was sufficient to keep a slight tremor from her voice.

Early though it was when she arrived at Lewis Freemont's flat, his manager, Gordon Everleigh, was already there, walking up and down the long studio drawing-room with an air of restless expectancy.

"Hello, Miss Burney. Freemont isn't awake yet, they tell me, which is probably just as well. Last night must have been a hell of a strain, and if he can rest well that's all to the good."

"What is the latest report?" Antoinette asked eagerly. "I came away last night before his own doctor had examined him. I thought it was best. He'd been surrounded by people all the evening, and what he needed was peace."

"Quite right. I understand Dr. Butler wasn't willing to commit himself to any firm opinion. They've got Sir Everard Blakin coming this morning. Until then no statement can be given out, of course. That's really why I'm here. I thought you might find some of this tough to handle without a man to back you."

"How kind of you! I'm so glad you're here—and so early too.

"Well, that was Warrender's idea." Gordon Everleigh grinned suddenly. "He phoned me at some unearthly hour and suggested I got along here. He seemed to think you needed some support, and he has a rehearsal this morning himself."

"He thinks of everything," exclaimed Antoinette gratefully. "He's really a wonderful man, isn't he?"

"Hm-m—" Gordon Everleigh rubbed his chin meditatively and smiled again—"That's a matter of opinion. I *have* heard him described as a monster, but that was by an angry prima donna who had failed to get her own way. I suppose it depends if you keep on the right side of him or not."

"I suppose so," Antoinette agreed. And then she realized that they were just making conversation, and she forced herself to open the post and deal with one or two routine matters.

Presently Mrs. Partridge, the housekeeper, looked in to say that her master was awake and had had breakfast, and if Mr. Everleigh liked to go in and see him he would be welcome.

"He's staying in bed for the time being," she said. "Dr. Butler wanted him to do so until Sir Everard has seen him."

"Is he—can he—" Antoinette hardly knew how to form her question. "Mrs. Partridge, can he see any better this morning?"

"He didn't say so, Miss Burney. Only that he can see."

Gordon Everleigh went away to the bedroom then, and Antoinette typed a few letters and answered, in the most diplomatic way possible, some pressing telephone calls. Then, just as she was wondering what else she could do, the telephone bell rang again, and when she picked up the receiver it was Charmian St. Leger's voice which said smoothly,

"Is that you, Miss Burney?"

"Yes, Mrs. St. Leger." Antoinette strove to make that as cooly official as possible.

"Oh, you recognized my voice?" There was a charming little laugh from the other end of the wire. But as Antoinette offered no comment on that, the well-pitched voice went on, "I've seen the news in the papers, of cours. Is it—true?" Even then she could not resist the affecting little break in her voice. "Has Lewis really recovered his sight?"

"To a small degree. How far that can be improved one doesn't yet know."

There was a pause, then Mrs. St. Leger said, "It's rather awkward for you, isn't it?"

"I haven't found it so."

"I mean, it will be if he completely regains his sight."

"That's hardly the primary consideration, Mrs. St. Leger. Was that what you rang up to say?" asked Antoinette coldly.

"Oh, no." Again that slight laugh. "Please tell him that my thoughts are very much with him and that I hope I shan't much longer have to communicate with him through a third person. Can I trust you to give him the *whole* of that message?"

"Certainly." Antoinette's tone was icy.

"Well, unhappily, one has to question the integrity of anyone who has altered information to suit herself on other occasions," Mrs. St. Leger explained plaintively. "I hope I can trust you this time, Miss Burney." And then the line went dead.

Antoinette uttered a word she seldom used and hung up the receiver. As she did so she heard the sound of a mellow, resonant voice in the hall, and gathered that the famous Sir Everard Blakin had arrived during her telephone conversation with Mrs. St. Leger.

A minute or two later Gordon Everleigh came back into the room and said, "The Great Man is here."

"How did you find Mr. Freemont? Was he cheerful?"

"Very. I wish I were half as cheerful. I thought I had no nerves left. In my profession you go mad if you allow yourself that indulgence. But today I feel as nervous as a kitten."

Antoinette felt so too. But she managed to hide the fact, and Gordon Everleigh went on moodily,

"It isn't only that he's a great artist. He's shown such guts over this. One can't bear the thought of a disappointment now. And anyway, I like him," he added after a long pause.

"So do I," said Antoinette.

"I know you do. You ought to marry him, you know," remarked Gordon Everleigh, and laughed.

"Oh, please don't say such silly things!"

"I mean it," declared the manager more seriously. "You've done more for him than anyone else over this, and he's well aware of it. He was talking just now about his accident—about that strange girl who caused it, or so he insists. And he said, 'Isn't it strange that one's life can be ruined by one girl and rebuilt by another?' That was a pretty handsome tribute to you, I thought."

"He—said that?"

"Yes."

"He does hate that—that other girl, doesn't he?"

"Well, wouldn't you?"

"I don't altogether believe in her," Antoinette managed to say. "I think he just attributed all sorts of evil intentions to some perfectly harmless creature."

"You'd never convince *him* of that." Gordon Everleigh shook his head and smiled. "I hadn't realized how constantly he still thinks of her. He says that one of the reasons he's so thankful about the return of his sight is that now he has a chance of finding her."

"It's a ridiculous obsession," cried Antoinette desperately. And when Gordon Everleigh looked at her in astonishment, she passed her hands over her cold, pale cheeks and muttered, "I'm sorry. I think I'm getting jittery too."

But after that she managed to appear calm. Until they heard Sir Everard and Dr. Butler come out of the bedroom, and then she said feverishly,

"Go and speak to them. Find out what Sir Everard has to say. As Mr. Freemont's manager you're perfectly entitled to ask."

He seemed a long while gone, and Antoinette felt strangely numb by the time she heard the front door close. Then a moment later Gordon Everleigh came back into the room, looking so relaxed and cheerful that Antoinette felt like a drab ghost beside him.

He must have felt the contrast too, for he exclaimed, "Good heavens, don't look like that! It's good news, not bad. Blakin won't commit himself absolutely, of course. They never will. But he's strongly hopeful that a very large measure of sight can be restored. He wants Freemont in his own nursing home and under his immediate care for a week or so. There may even be a minor operation—"

"Nothing that involves one's sight is minor," interrupted Antoinette almost irritably.

"Well, that's just a manner of speaking. Anyway, on balance, Blakin is very hopeful. And if that's so I don't know why we should be otherwise."

"No, indeed!" said a voice from the doorway. And, as they both uttered exclamations and turned, Lewis Freemont came slowly into the room, feeling for anything in his path, it was true, but with already a much greater degree of confidence than he had ever displayed since he became blind.

Antoinette started up and went to him quickly. But he smiled and put her aside, though gently.

"No," he said, "let me do it myself. You can't imagine the fascination of being able to see where things are even dimly when you haven't been able to see them at all for so long.—Is that you, Gordon?" He turned accurately in his manager's direction, though obviously without being able fully to identify him.

"Yes." Everleigh came forward. 'I''ve just been talking to Blakin, and I hear that you're going into his nursing home for treatment. As far as these cautious experts will ever commit themselves—"

"They can't, you know," interrupted the other man with a smile. "It's only the confident amateur who knows all the answers. In his field as well as mine."

"Well, that's true," Gordon Everleigh conceded with a laugh. "But he did seem to think there was a good chance of success."

"So he told me." By now Lewis Freemont had found his way to his usual chair, and he sank into it with a certain air of relief, Antoinette noticed, like a man who had successfully accomplished a rather daring feat.

With difficulty she resisted the desire to go to him and put a comforting and congratulatory arm round him. Instead she merely asked, "When will you be going into the nursing home?"

"This afternoon."

"So soon?"

"It can't be too soon, Toni, if it's really going to mean the restoration of my sight."

"No, of course not."

She was silent after that, and the two men discussed the reports of the previous night's concert and—on the optimistic insistence of Gordon Everleigh—the possibilities that would open out if something like full sight were restored.

Everything was on a determinedly cheerful note. But after Everleigh had taken his leave, Antoinette's employer sat silent, a very thoughtful expression on his handsome, rather worn face. Then at last he said,

"You'll stay on here while I'm away, won't you?"

"There won't be anything much for me to do," she pointed out.

She had not thought until that moment of anything but staying. But his words suggested to her that this might be her one chance of making a logical break with him. He, however, evidently had no such idea.

"I'd rather leave everything in your hands," he said almost impatiently. "What else should I do? And anyway, I couldn't imagine your not being here when I come home."

"I'll be here," she promised him. "Of course I'll be here."

"And then—" he smiled slowly—"if Blakin has done his work properly, I shall really see you at last."

"Yes," she said sadly, "you'll really see me at last."

But he was too much absorbed in his own bright hopes to notice anything odd in her tone.

CHAPTER EIGHT

DURING the week following the Festival Hall concert, Antoinette was torn by conflicting emotions. With all her heart she longed for Lewis Freemont's sight to be fully restored. Yet she dreaded inexpressibly the moment when he would look at her and know her for the girl she blamed for his blindness.

She had been shattered to learn from Gordon Everleigh that, even in the moment of his brightest hopes, he had recalled his implacable determination to track down that girl; and now that discovery was so near she was shaken with terror.

Identified as the object of his almost obsessional hatred, bereft of the very special link which his blindness and her tenderness had forged between them, she would be simply the girl who had spoiled his life and then grossly deceived him. How would the love of *any* man—much less a ruthless, arrogant man like Lewis Freemont—survive such a discovery?

With fresh anguish and remorse she recalled reading out that list of names from which she had deliberately omitted her own, and it seemed to her now that this had been the ultimate in contemptible deception. She might tell herself that desperation had driven her. She could even imagine that some people might understand and have pity for her terrible situation. But could she really suppose that *Lewis Freemont*, of all people, would look with sympathy and understanding on the fact that she had actually profited by his blindness to deceive him?

She wished now that she had not allowed herself to be stampeded into saying she would be at the flat when he returned from the nursing home. How *could* she be there? It was unthinkable that the moment of his return should also be the appalling moment of truth. But he had made a point of it and this at least she had promised him. Was she to fail him even in this?

From the regular reports which she received she knew that the day after he entered the nursing home an operation had been performed. But after that there had just been the conventional bulletins about "as well as can be expected", "in good spirits" and so on. The important fact was that he had to be kept absolutely quiet and no visitors were allowed.

Not until the end of the week did Gordon Everleigh come in—full of the vital optimism which contributed so much to his successful handling of artists—bringing the news that Sir Everard Blakin had the very highest hopes of complete success.

"The great man declares that everything has gone exactly as it should," Gordon Everleigh said. "Freemont is still in a darkened room. But, barring any dramatic change, he should be home in a matter of days."

"Of days?" Antoinette could not keep from her voice a slight quiver of mingled joy and apprehension.

Mistaking this for disappointment, Gordon Everleigh said cheeringly: "Yes. But you won't have to wait as long as that to see him. He wants you to go along there tomorrow. There's something he wants to discuss with you. He'll expect you about three."

"*What* does he want to discuss with me?" She was frightened and could not hide the fact.

"I have no idea," said the manager, looking rather surprised.

Antoinette moistened her dry lips with the tip of her tongue and said nervously, "He—he won't be able to *see* me yet, will he?"

"I'm afraid not." Again misreading the reason for the tremor in her voice, Gordon Everleigh patted her shoulder kindly. "He's still in a darkened room, as I told you. But cheer up! He'll soon be home now, practically as good as new. You go along to see him tomorrow and let him give you his own news."

So the following afternoon Antoinette went to Sir Everard Blakin's fashionable nursing home, trying, though without much success, to control the tremors of anxiety and dread which shook her from time to time.

A pleasant-faced young nurse told her she was expected and took her along a wide, elegant-looking corridor and ushered her into the darkened room where Lewis Freemont was sitting. He turned eagerly at the sound of her entrance, but it was plain that at this stage he was still relying largely on his acute hearing to tell him who was there and what was happening.

She came to him immediately and, taking his hand in the warm, firm clasp which she knew meant so much to him, she said, "It's wonderful news about the success of the operation! But I can well imagine that these last days of waiting must be the worst."

"Well—" his fingers were tight on hers—"I get a sort of panic occasionally, in case everything is going to be dark again after all. But most of the time I keep my nerve—" he laughed slightly, in a sort of self-mockery

—"and I tell myself that everything is going to be all right."

"I *know* it is."

She could sense that her quiet confidence communicated itself instantly to him. But not only that; it also suddenly settled the worst of her own inner conflicts. For all at once she knew, beyond any doubt or confusion, that whatever the outcome to herself—or indeed, to him—what really mattered was that his sight should be restored.

It was a discovery which brought a fresh wave of revulsion for the tangle of deception in which she had involved herself. In that moment she thought calmly that it would not have taken much to make her confess the whole thing.

But, as she reached for a chair with one hand—still letting him hold the other hand—her new-found calm was put to an immediate and terrifying test. For he said, almost conversationally,

"Toni, there's a question I want to ask you, and I wish you'd promise in advance that you'll answer it truthfully."

She was so petrified with shock and fear that her hand closed spasmodically on his, though she was not aware of it until he exclaimed, "What's the matter? What are you so scared about?"

"I'm not scared," she managed to insist. "It's just— just such an odd way for you to speak to me. As though—" she swallowed—"you thought I might *not* tell you the truth."

"Well," he said sombrely, "have you always told me the truth?"

"Of course! To—to the best of my ability." She hated herself for this further lie. But what else could she do, short of making a full confession? And for this she simply had not prepared herself.

There was an odd moment of silence and she felt he was looking hard at her, as though willing himself to pierce the darkness of the room and the veil which still hung between him and complete vision. Then, even as he drew breath to speak again, she rushed into the first words that came to her.

"There's something *I* want to say first!" Her tone was unnaturally bright and, with an almost symbolical gesture, she drew her hand away, as though severing the real line of communication between them. "It's about the—the different situation there will be in the future, now that you're going to recover your sight. You won't really need me any more for—"

"Of course I shall need you," he interrupted almost irritably. "What is all this nonsense? You know more about my affairs by now than I do myself. There's no question of my doing without you."

"But you didn't have a full-time secretary before you were blind," she reminded him. "You told me so yourself. You said you disliked personal ties, and that you preferred just to have someone from an agency from time to time. You could do that again, couldn't you?"

"I don't want to do that again!" He sounded angry and, in some odd way, almost scared.

"It would truly be the best way. Particularly if—you force me to say this—if you still have some sort of romantic feeling for me."

"Why cant' you say it frankly?" he demanded roughly. "You mean—if I love you still. Well, suppose I do? What about it?"

"N-nothing," she stammered. "Except that—you must see it!—it would be best for us to make a break *now*. Believe me, you have quite an idealized notion of me. You've literally never seen me. You hardly know me, in the real sense of the word. If you met me—"

"Not *know* you?" he repeated. "Not know you, Toni? Why, I know you as well as it's possible to know any woman without making love to her in the final sense of the term!"

"Don't talk like that!" she cried. "You're putting a totally false value on our relationship. The whole world is opening out for you once more. Your career has been given back to you. You will be the complete musician again. It's *music* that is your world! Not me or any other woman. The very way you talk of music is proof of that. I'll never forget some of the things you've said—"

"What, for instance?" he interrupted her suddenly.

"Oh—I don't know. A dozen things." She groped confusedly in her memory for some of the revealing, telling phrases he had used; anything that might distract him from the dangerous subject of herself. But only one thing came to her very clearly, and she could not quite recall when he said it. On his insistence, however, she spoke again, not very steadily.

"You told me once that the first requisite of the true musician is to make music. Just that—and to serve the composer one is privileged to interpret. You claimed no honour, no glory. Just the right to make music—and to serve the great."

"I said that?—to you?"

"Yes."

"When?"

"I don't exactly remember when. It's the sort of thing which just sinks down into one and becomes part of one."

"But you can't remember when I said it to you?"

She was struck by the extraordinary change that had come into his voice, but she could only say uncertainly, "N-no. Does it matter?"

"I'll say it matters!" There was a note of grim triumph in his voice that was frightening in its intensity. "I remember! I remember exactly when I said it to you. My God, what a fool I've been! That explains everything. I said it to you the day I failed you in that music exam at St. Cecilia's."

"No!" she cried in utmost terror. "No!" And she struggled to withdraw the hand which he had suddenly seized again. But he held her so that there was no possibility of escape. "That wasn't me," she lied wildly.

"Of course it was! Why did I never think of that before?" There was still that note of triumph in his tone, and his grip was so tight that it hurt. "And the name—" he obviously made a tremendous effort of memory—"the name was Antoinette. That was it! Antoinette—Toni—Antoinette. You looked at me as though you could have killed me. And then—you began to follow me round—"

"I didn't!"

"You were there at nearly every concert. You even sat in the front row and smiled at me once. And finally—" his voice dropped to a harsh half-whisper— "you were *there*, in the middle of the road that day. Toni, in God's name, why did you do that to me?"

"It's all wrong—" she began wildly, and at that moment, the pleasant young nurse opened the door and said,

"Sir Everard to see you, sir."

"He can wait," replied Lewis Freemont savagely.

"Sir Everard doesn't *wait*!" exclaimed the nurse in a scandalized tone. And, as though in proof of this, the famous surgeon came briskly into the room with an air of great authority.

"Ah, Freemont—" he began genially.

But Antoinette heard no more. This was her moment, her one chance of escape. Snatching her hand away, she fled to the door, where the nurse was waiting determinedly to escort her elsewhere. In her view, quite obviously, mere visitors dwindled to extreme unimportance once the Great Man arrived. But she said pleasantly to Antoinette:

"You can wait in the room on the right."

"No, thank you. I can't wait."

"I don't think Sir Everard will be long."

"I can't wait!" Antoinette repeated almost frantically. "I must go. Please tell Mr. Freemont—tell Mr. Freemont—"

But *what* was she to tell Mr. Freemont?

For one moment of tragic confusion she could do nothing but stare at the other girl, until she saw astonishment written so plainly on her face that sheer necessity forced a decision.

"Tell him," Antoinette said slowly, "that I'm sorry I couldn't wait. But we had already said everything there was to say."

Then she went out of the nursing home and into the sunlit street, and she walked and walked, not really knowing where she was going.

After a while, a sort of leaden order began to come into her chaotic thoughts.

It was over. *Everything* was over. The long, long months of deception. The alternation of hope and despair. His desperate need of her. The bitter-sweet knowledge that he loved her, and would do so until he knew who she really was.

There would be no need now to make excuses for not being there when he returned home. The fact would be self-explanatory. She would never have to face the moment when he looked at her and she saw appalled recognition dawn in his eyes.

In a way, she supposed, she would be thankful for that small mercy. But she felt thankful for nothing— only sick and dazed and despairing because her world had finally crashed around her.

Without knowing it, she had walked instinctively in the general direction of his flat, and now she found herself within sight of it. Perhaps subconsciously the part of her which was the conscientious secretary was still aware that there were one or two minor matters to set right. This was her best opportunity to tie up those loose ends. He was still in the nursing home and could not possibly come home and surprise her. Even tomorrow might be too late.

She went into the block and up to the well-known door which had been for her the threshold to so much happiness. Everything was very quiet when she let herself in with her own key, so Mrs. Partridge and the maids were evidently out. And in the silent flat, and alone, she began to sort out and put right the few matters still outstanding.

The shock of disclosure and the scene which had followed seemed to have left her with a strange clarity of mind. She worked without pause for perhaps an hour. Then she glanced round and knew that any competent secretary could walk in there tomorrow and take things up exactly where she herself had laid them down.

Another secretary.

She sat at her desk for the last time, trying to imagine the place without her and failing. Though that, of course, was absurd, she told herself. Life went on and the waters closed over the place one had left. New contacts were formed, new friendships made, new plans hatched, new triumphs achieved. He would manage all right without her.

That was what hurt most of all. *He would manage all right without her.* After being his support and his inspiration for so long she was suddenly entirely superfluous. And at that thought she buried her face in her hands and sat there for a long, long time, until she roused herself with a violent start to realize that the front door bell was ringing.

A sort of illogical panic held her rigid for a moment. Then common sense told her that this could be no one specially important. And getting to her feet, she went into the hall and opened the door.

"No one specially important," was not quite an accurate description. It was Oscar Warrender who stood outside.

"I looked in to hear the latest news," he said. "Everleigh told me you were going to the nursing home this afternoon."

"Oh, yes—yes—" All that beautiful clarity of thought seemed at this point to desert her, and she stood there staring at him, unable to imagine what she was going to say to this terrifyingly penetrating man.

"May I come in?" He spoke a little abruptly.

"Yes, of course." She stood aside and then, closing the door behind him, she followed him into the study.

It was ridiculous, but she could think of nothing with which to start the conversation, and after a moment he said, grimly but not unkindly,

"Well, I see it's bad news. You'd better tell me."

"It's *not* bad news. Not about him. What makes you think such a thing?" she exclaimed.

"The fact that you've obviously had some sort of shock."

"Oh—" she passed her hands absently over her cheeks which felt cold and probably looked pale, she supposed. "It's nothing to do with—him. I mean, nothing to do with his sight. He was—quite well, when I was him. Sir Everard came while I was there—"

"And what had he to say?" Oscar Warrender asked quickly.

"I don't know. I didn't—stay."

"Didn't wait to hear his report, you mean?" the conductor looked incredulous. "Why not?"

"I couldn't." She swallowed nervously.

"What do you mean—you couldn't?"

"Mr. Warrender," she said desperately, "I'm going away. I've finished here." She looked round helplessly. "It's—over."

"Oh, I see." Oscar Warrender was not one to need his facts underlined. It obviously cost him no effort of memory to recollect almost word for word the disclosure Antoinette had once made to him. It might not have been of great importance to him, but he remembered it, and he said, without hesitation, "You mean that Freemont recognized you at last?"

"Yes."

"By actually seeing you?"

"No. By something I said. But it was equally conclusive."

"Did he upbraid you?—tell you you could go?" He seemed to think he had a right to know. And without hesitation she conceded him that right. People did where Oscar Warrender was concerned.

"There wasn't time for that," she explained. "Sir Everard arrived just at that point. There was just a—a ghastly sort of moment of truth before we were interrupted. I think he could have killed me." She shivered.

"Oh, no, no, no." The conductor dismissed that idea impatiently. "People don't kill each other for reasons like that."

"You don't understand," Antoinette said painfully. "You don't understand even now. Not even you. I've lived with it all too long not to know what the real situation is. Rightly or wrongly, Mr. Warrender, he regards me as the cause of his blindness. For months and months he has nursed his hatred and the hope of one day identifying the girl who caused the accident. Well, he *has* identified her. He's found that I am the girl. And even that isn't all. He has also found that for months I've deceived him. I took advantage of the very fact that he was blind to deceive him."

"He fell in love with you, nevertheless."

The statement was so coolly positive that Antoinette derived an odd moment of comfort from it even then. But she sighed and said, "Only because he didn't know who I really was."

"So he both loves you and hates you?" The conductor gave an odd little smile and added half to himself, "And then they say that the love-hate relationships of opera aren't true to life!"

She was silent, and after a moment he asked, "What are your plans now?"

"I—have no plans." She looked slightly dazed. "It's a little early to make plans, isn't it?"

"It's never too early to make future plans when present ones have failed," was the dry retort. "And brooding over failure is the one sure bar to success."

"I'm not looking for *success*." She almost resented being forced to the painful use of her numbed thoughts and emotions.

"No, I know," replied the great conductor brusquely. "You want to creep away into a corner and nurse your grief. A dismal and excessively boring exercise when put to the test. Don't waste time and thought on it. The fact is that your musical gifts interest me, Miss Burney, particularly your unusual capacity for reproducing orchestral tone on a piano. I could use you quite a lot, and put a good deal of such work in your way. Would you be interested?"

Would she be interested? At one time she would have been transported with joy to have Oscar Warrender ask her such a question. But now only one consideration operated. She stared at him and said apprehensively, "You're a dangerously close link with—*him*."

It had evidently not occurred to the famous conductor to regard himself as a mere link with anyone. He made a slight grimace of amused protest.

"I have a certain significance apart from that," he pointed out. And at that Antoinette laughed, though shakily.

"Don't think I'm ungrateful for the compliment—the kindness—"

"No kindness is involved, Miss Burney." Oscar Warrender spoke categorically. "In professional matters I am not kind. One cannot afford to be if one wishes to maintain standards. If I offer you work, be sure it is because I know your work has value. What is your answer?"

"Do I have to give it now?"

"I will give you until eight o'clock this evening."

"So exact a deadline?" She was startled.

"Major decisions should always have strict deadlines. And in any case, I need a quick decision. I must make other arrangements if you are not willing to co-operate. Telephone me before eight."

"I will." She was surprised to hear the docile note in her voice. But she was even more surprised to find that, as she watched him go, there was already a faint stirring of interest—almost excitement—in her heart. And this served to blunt the inevitable pain of leaving the familiar flat for the last time.

She walked home, putting off the moment when she would have to give some sort of explanation to Rosamund. And she was guiltily relieved to find a note to say that Rosamund had gone out and would not be in until late.

If she had had to sit alone with nothing to think about but the afternoon's disaster she would have been wretched indeed. As it was, Oscar Warrender's sudden offer demanded immediate consideration, in a way that forced everything else out of the exact foreground of her thoughts.

It was true that, if she accepted, she would still be in contact with the world of Lewis Freemont; something she had dismissed as impossible only a few hours ago.

But was her whole life to be directed by the fear and pain connected with one man? And, if she were careful, she could surely manage to avoid him. With some sympathetic co-operation from Oscar Warrender—

She paused, recalled his irrefutable statement that in professional matters he was ruthless, and decided that she must not expect help in any emotional problem from that quarter. Why should she, come to that? Her life was her own, and she must learn to live it.

Without her knowing it, the conductor's bracing words were already beginning to take effect. There *was* no virtue in creeping into a corner to nurse one's grief. She had been made a splendid—an unprecedented—offer. The kind of challenge any real musician would embrace with pride and delight. Had she really imagined for one moment that she could reject it?

It was not even eight o'clock before Antoinette telephoned to Oscar Warrender and told him that she was ready and willing to work with him.

"Good!" She could not but be flattered by the fact that there was genuine satisfaction in the great man's voice. But she did feel something of a check when he added, "Then come along right away, will you? There's a good deal to discuss."

"To—to your apartment, do you mean?" It was only a matter of hours since she had left the building, telling herself she would never return.

"Yes, of course." There was nothing in Oscar Warrender's voice to suggest he would have any sympathy with nostalgic reflections of that sort. "I'll expect you in about twenty minutes." And he rang off.

Antoinette slowly hung up the receiver, since there seemed nothing else to do. Than she hastily threw on a coat and went out and hailed a taxi. Perhaps speed was better than reflection if one wanted to avoid nervous tension.

For all her resolution, it cost her a pang to enter the familiar building, take the familiar lift, past the floor where she could never, never go again, and on to the apartment where the famous conductor and his wife lived.

Anthea Warrender herself opened the door to her and greeted her like an old friend.

"How *nice* to see you again!" she exclaimed. "Give me your coat, dear, and go into the studio." And she gave Antoinette's arm an almost affectionate squeeze before ushering her through the doorway which had proved the threshold to her own career.

Antoinette went forward—and then stopped dead. For the man who turned from the window to face her was not Oscar Warrender. It was Lewis Freemont.

CHAPTER NINE

"WHERE did you come from?" she whispered at last, as though he were a ghost. "Where did you come from?"

"From the nursing home, of course. Warrender fetched me—with very little opposition, I might say. Blakin had completed his miracle." He spoke in short, jerky sentences. "I can see almost perfectly again. I can see —you."

She had no idea what she could answer to that. She just stood there, almost motionless, without defence against any bitter verdict he might pronounce. And what he finally said was:

"How—lovely you are. I'd forgotten how lovely."

"Oh—" she blinked her lashes against the sudden rush of tears. And then he went on, exactly as though they were taking up their conversation where it had been interrupted that afternoon, "Toni, tell me *now*. Why did you do that dreadful thing to me?"

"But I didn't," she cried. "I didn't! *Won't* you understand? There was nothing deliberate about it. I was there, crossing the road, it's true, but I didn't even hear your car coming. There was an aeroplane overhead making a tremendous noise. You were almost on top of me before I realized you were there, and then I recognized the car and was paralysed with fright and shame and a sort of guilt that I was there at all. It was all over in seconds. And after that there were just the days and weeks and months of useless remorse, while I asked myself again and again why I hadn't moved."

"But you disappeared. Once you had done it—"

"Don't use that term!" she cried in furious despair. "As though I did it on purpose. It was an accident, I tell you! An accident—an accident—an accident!" And she began to cry wildly.

"But after that—you came to me." He spoke almost as though he were reading something from an unwinding scroll, and he hardly seemed aware of her sobbing. "You came into my life with the first gleam of light and hope and reality in all that nightmare. What made you do *that*, Toni?"

"I wanted to make some sort of amends. There was suddenly this incredible chance. I knew I was mad to take it, but I had to do it. It was like—" her voice dropped to a whisper again—"like the hand of God, that second chance."

As though drawn irresistibly, she came close to him then. And, equally without the power to resist, he put out his hand and touched her cheek.

"Your cheek is wet," he said, as though even now he relied on touch rather than sight to confirm an impression. And then, almost tenderly, "Don't cry, Toni. Weren't you afraid of being found out?"

"Every day. Almost every hour. But I had to go on. And then Mrs. St. Leger had the dreadful idea of sending for the list of the students who failed that exam. I think she sensed I was deadly afraid for some reason."

"But the list came! Why wasn't your name on it?"

"It was. But—" she drew a deep breath—"don't you remember? It was I who read it out to you."

"Oh, my God, so you did!" And suddenly he dropped into a chair and buried his face in his hands.

189

"I deceived you, you see." Her usually warm and flexible voice was quite toneless. "I took advantage of the fact that you were blind, and I deceived you."

"Yes, I see."

He was silent for quite a long time after that, and at last she said:

"What was the question you wanted to ask me this afternoon? Had you already begun to—suspect?"

"The question?" He looked up haggardly at her. "What question?—Oh, it seems almost unimportant now. You're not really married, are you?"

"Married." In the midst of all the other tangle she had almost forgotten that extra piece of fabrication. She laughed a little bitterly, now that she remembered it, and said, her voice running up almost hysterically, "No, of course I'm not married. That was just part of the miserable, ever-growing deception that I practised upon you. Once I'd started to live that lie, I just had to go on lying. There were other details, other contemptible evasions. Would you like to ask about them? Are there any other questions before—" she caught her breath on a sob—"before I go?"

"Yes," he said, and he drew a long sigh, like a man who has carried a heavy burden for so long that he hardly knows if it has been lifted or not. "Yes, there is just one other thing I must ask you."

"What is it?" She stood there trembling a little and again with that curiously defenceless air about her.

"Come here," he said gently, "my good—and bad—angel." And he held out his hand to her with such a compelling gesture that she came in a sort of fascination, and actually knelt by his chair.

"This is the moment of truth between us, so look at me, Toni."

She looked at him, somehow without flinching, and he put his strong, beautiful hands lightly round her face.

"There is really only one question of importance between us." And suddenly she was aware of the tenderness of his touch. "Do you love me, my darling?"

It was not at all what she had expected, and the reply came instantaneously from her heart to his.

"Now—and for ever—whether you want me or not."

"I want you," he said, catching her close and kissing her. "I want you as I've never wanted anything else in my life. Not even my sight."

"Don't! Don't put it like that." But she was returning his kisses with almost wild eagerness. "Oh, my dear, do you mean that you've forgiven me at last?"

"No!" He brushed off the idea almost angrily. "One doesn't presume to *forgive* where one loves. There is nothing to forgive. What is it the Bible says?" He gave that half mocking, half tender smile. " 'You shall know the truth and the truth shall set you free.' I never thought until this moment what that really means. I know the truth—and I am free. It's like recovering my sight in double measure." Then, as though in contrast to the solemnity of the moment, he added lightly, "God bless Warrender for his interference."

"Why, of course!" She sat back and looked at him. "It was Mr. Warrender who engineered this scene."

"Anthea too. I heard her playing her sympathetic part as she ushered you in. It seems—" he touched her cheek again with a gesture of loving amusement—

"that you're not the only one with a taste for deception."

"Oh, don't call it that. It was so good of them, *good* of them to bother so much about us, wasn't it?"

"Well—" there was a flash of the familiar sardonic humour— "I believe every conductor has a secret longing to be a producer too. Usually with atrocious results, I might say," he added with a touch of professional realism even at that moment. "Perhaps this was just Oscar Warrender the conductor allowing himself the indulgence of producing a drama."

"But with marvellous results!" she cried warmly.

"With marvellous results," he agreed, smiling at her.

"Let me call them in, so that we can thank them!" She made as though to rise, but he drew her back into his arms again and said, "Wait!"

"What is it?" She too was smiling now.

"Just that I want to look at you again. To look at you and see you—see you—see you. Let me savour the miracle one moment longer. I can look at the woman I love—and *see* her."

"You can look at me for the rest of your life," she told him with a laugh, but her eyes were very tender.

"It will hardly be long enough," he told her as he kissed her again. "Now call them in. I can bear to share you now."

And he watched her as she went across to the door, as though every movement she made were a dear and fresh miracle in the world that had been restored to him.